Mambo Peligroso

Also by Patricia Chao

MONKEY KING

MAMBO PELIGROSO

A NOVEL

Patricia Chao

HarperCollins*Publishers*

FIRST EDITION

Designed by C. Linda Dingler

Printed on acid-free paper

Library of Congress Cataloging-in-Publication Data
Chao, Patricia
    Mambo peligroso: a novel/Patricia Chao—1st ed.
        p. cm.
    ISBN 0-06-073417-5 (alk. paper)
    1. Mambo (Dance)—Fiction. 2. Cuban American women—Fiction. 3. Japanese American women—Fiction. 4. New York (N.Y.)—Fiction. 5. Miami (Fla.)—Fiction. 6. Women dancers—Fiction. 7. Cuba—Fiction. I. Title.

PS3553.H2765M36 2005
813'.54—dc22   2004054019

05 06 07 08 09 ❖/RRD 10 9 8 7 6 5 4 3 2 1

This book is dedicated to my dance partners,
without whom I could not have taken a step.

Acknowledgments

To name all who contributed would require another volume. Below, an abbreviated list:

For their help on this journey I thank the New York Foundation for the Arts, the Robert M. MacNamara Foundation, Fundación Valparaiso, Fundaciāo Sacatar, the MacDowell Colony, the Virginia Center for the Creative Arts, the Center for Cuban Studies, Writers of the Americas, and La UNEAC in La Habana. As always, thanks to my mother and father for their steady support.

So many gave this book Cuban *sabor,* including Orlando Luis Pardo, Leonel Relova, Michaelangelo and Marisella Castro, Jane McManus, and most of all Humberto Malaqón Gonzalez. José Andres Debros Oliveros showed me where the music begins. Humberto Middleton gave me a clear picture of Palladium nights. Kent Morris provided technical assistance on munitions. Jennifer Cook fine-tuned the gymnastics. Constanza Melo and Celerina J. Garcia taught me Spanish. Tom Miller checked the facts and got me to Cuba in the first place. Henry Barrow guided me through navigational difficulties with utmost grace. Martin Isaac put a face to the South Bronx. Any errors in any of these areas are entirely mine. It should be added that I took many liberties in imagining the Cuba scenes, particularly those in Santiago.

For faith and friendship I'm forever grateful to my New York City dancing friends, most especially Jimmy Anton, Almyra Ayos,

Sandi Feinblum, Wayne Hosang, Jamal Jbara, and all the members of Casa de la Salsa.

Finally, thanks go to my best and closest readers: Mona Simpson, Mia Yun, Stephanie Grant, Allan Hoffman, Rachel Cantor, and Pearl Abraham. Thank you, Heather Schroder, who makes sure the music is playing, and Terry Karten, who shows me, even when I don't believe it, that I can dance.

Explanation of Structure

The traditional Cuban musical form, the *danzón,* typically consists of six distinct parts: theme A, theme B, theme A, theme C, theme A, theme D. Themes A through C are stately; theme D, also known as *mambo,* is much faster and became even faster as the form developed. When theme D is medium speed, it can be called *danzón-cha.*

Roughly following the styles explained above, I have divided this book into three sections. The first section, *danzón,* is slow and elegant, with a flute carrying the melody and the percussion emphasizing the first beat of each four-beat measure. The second, *danzón-cha,* is livelier, with a slow *clave* rhythm overlaying the four/four time signature. The third, *mambo,* is driven by a strong *clave* and so fast as to be undanceable by the average person.

Iré a Santiago.
Siempre he dicho que yo iría a Santiago
en un coche de agua negra.

I'm going to Santiago.
I always said that I'd go to Santiago
in a coach of black water.

—Federico García Lorca

Mambo Peligroso

Prologue

The music has to do with a port city, the squall of a steamer approaching the slip, cars honking, a husband and wife quarreling in the bodega downstairs, dogs barking. Those are the harmonics—trombone, trumpet, piano—jangled against percussion: trucks rumbling by, a metal pipe being hammered into place—tumbadoras, bongos, timbales.

Hang that chord in the morning air, over the supple waters of the Bay of Santiago. Start the journey here, or end it.

What you're listening for, what you're dancing on, is clave—that relentless one-two-three/one-two meter from Africa.

If clave is the heartbeat, tumbadora is the breath. Listen to how he plays—palm up, palm down.

You can't have a downbeat without an upbeat.

You can't breathe out without breathing in.

DANZÓN

1

Catalina

*In order to get asked to dance
you have to already be dancing.*

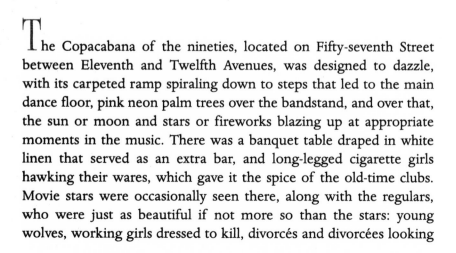

The Copacabana of the nineties, located on Fifty-seventh Street between Eleventh and Twelfth Avenues, was designed to dazzle, with its carpeted ramp spiraling down to steps that led to the main dance floor, pink neon palm trees over the bandstand, and over that, the sun or moon and stars or fireworks blazing up at appropriate moments in the music. There was a banquet table draped in white linen that served as an extra bar, and long-legged cigarette girls hawking their wares, which gave it the spice of the old-time clubs. Movie stars were occasionally seen there, along with the regulars, who were just as beautiful if not more so than the stars: young wolves, working girls dressed to kill, divorcés and divorcées looking for easy fun, and of course the die-hard *mamberos* and *mamberas*, including teachers and their followings and a sprinkling of old-timers from the Palladium.

If you walked through the swinging double doors behind the bar, you came to a more intimate room upholstered in crimson velvet. Early in the evening this was where you saw hustle at its Latin finest, in its way just as mesmerizing as mambo on the main floor. Many dancers split their time between the two rooms, the dreamy continuous pulse of disco providing the perfect counterpoint to the syncopated stop-and-start of salsa. Around midnight they dimmed the lights in the back room and put on Latin house, and became strictly a pickup joint.

Catalina's first time at the Copa was a Friday night in March of 1997. Her image of the legendary club had been ceiling fans, people sitting around in rattan armchairs sipping tropical drinks: languid tanned women in jungle-print dresses and men in white suits and panamas. But after checking her coat she looked around and saw that there was not a jungle-printed woman or Panama-hatted man to be seen. She got herself a paper plate of complimentary rice and beans from the buffet in the back room and ate by herself standing up at the bar. Afterward she went back out to the main floor and hovered by the railing on the ramp until she spotted someone she knew—her dance teacher's assistant. Among the sequined dresses and Armani pantsuits Wendy Cardoza stood out like a hip scarecrow in her black velvet T-shirt and matching leggings. She was dancing with a slender man with a mane of dark hair. Catalina watched Wendy's ponytail snapping around on the spins, the way she dropped down into a lunge and slid back up on the next beat, how purely flexible she was, as if she had no bones. Her partner had beautiful hands, a soft and precise lead. As soon as the set was over, Catalina waved, but Wendy didn't see because at the same instant another man grabbed her and began leading her into triple turns.

From where Catalina was standing the dancers looked like molecules, spinning and almost bumping and rearranging themselves into new configurations after each song. The man with whom Wendy was now dancing turned out to be Carlos from their class, whom Catalina hadn't recognized at first with his hair slicked back. Wendy

was easily fifteen years his senior but he was working her hard—
there was the lunge again, obviously a trademark.

The set finally ended, and Catalina leaned over the railing and
again waved wildly in Wendy's direction. This time both Wendy and
Carlos saw her and blew kisses. While Wendy got nabbed by another
partner, Carlos walked over to the floor underneath where Catalina
was standing and held out his arms in an extravagant gesture as if he
were about to serenade her.

"Why are you hiding up there?"

"It's my first time."

"A Copa virgin. Then you have to dance with me."

She had to start somewhere. She came around and met him on
the steps, and he took her hand and led her out to a spot on the
edge.

Nobody ever forgets their first moment on the floor of the
Copacabana.

With their first cross-body lead he carved out a niche.

*Mambo in New York is horizontal. The more crowded the floor, the
smaller and tighter the slot.*

Cross-body into a single right turn. The floor was so slippery that
most of her energy went into keeping her balance and braking coming out of the turns.

"*Me encanta tus vueltas.*"

"What?"

"Your spins are great."

How nerve-racking it was, dancing at the edge of the floor,
with all the people at the tables and lining the rail ogling them.
Carlos compensated for the encroaching crowd and the slickness
of the floor by maintaining a firm grip and keeping her close.
Because he could feel that she was nervous he didn't try anything
tricky.

The music was Cuban, a song Catalina recognized but at first
couldn't name. As she would later learn, the DJ at the Copa on Friday nights was Henry Knowles, a famously creative mixer, blending
contemporary stars like Ray Ruiz, Los Adolescentes, and Gilberto
Santa Rosa with old-timers like Celia Cruz and Cheo Feliciano so
smoothly you couldn't hear the segue unless you were listening for it.

In that set he was juxtaposing Vocal Sampling's funky a cappella cover of "La Negra Tomasa" with Rubén González's shimmery piano *descarga*. He ended with the version by Beny Moré.

> *Kikiriboom mandiga*
> *Kikiriboom mandiga.*

When the set was over, Carlos picked up Catalina's hand and kissed it.

That dance, it seemed, was the seal of approval, because from then on she had no trouble getting partners, the most memorable an older man with a diamond tiepin and a red carnation in his lapel. But she was still a beginner, after all, with only a month of classes behind her, and it seemed every guy was on a different beat. Her spins might be pretty, but what did that matter if she couldn't even do a basic? It was a relief when she felt a touch on her elbow and heard Wendy's voice.

"*Nena,* I'm so glad you came! Are you having a good time? I saw you dancing with the King of the Copa."

Wendy looked radiant—color up, eyes glittering, ponytail damp with sweat.

"This place is something else."

"Isn't it? C'mon over to the bar; there's someone I want you to meet." She took Catalina by the hand and led her through the crush along the edge of the floor. Her grip was powerful and insistent—no surprise, Catalina thought, given her athleticism on the dance floor.

"Whaddya drinking, Lina?"

"Just water."

"*Dos Perriers, por favor.*" Wendy reached to put her arm around a very dark-skinned man leaning up against the bar. He was garishly dressed in tight white jeans and a yellow button-down shirt with black polka dots. "Lina, this is Juan. Juan, *mi buen amiga Catalina.*"

"*Encantado,*" said the man, and then he and Wendy started chattering away in Spanish and Catalina stopped following. She drank her Perrier from the bottle and watched as men onstage moved the mikes around. A spotlight went on, the men exited, and the MC, a heavyset man in a gold vest and jeans, waved the crowd to quiet. Catalina turned to ask Wendy what was happening, but both she and Juan were nowhere to be seen.

The MC was making the introduction in Spanish. Catalina caught that it was someone *muy especial.*

El Ruiseñor.

The Nightingale.

More lights went up and illuminated the band. A trumpet warbled a habanera introduction, the congas pattered, and Wendy's friend in the polka-dotted shirt stepped forward, mike in hand, and began to sing in a startlingly high, pure tenor. His voice looped over the brass, jumped in and out of the percussion, and though Catalina could not follow the lyrics she was entranced. It was obviously a love song, a slow country tempo, almost bolero, but urbanized by the nerviness of the trumpets and trombones.

She was so spellbound that she almost missed the entrance of her teacher. She happened to catch the bartender looking over her head, and she turned and saw him on the stairs that led to the dance floor. El Tuerto was resplendent in a bronze satin button-down shirt and black peg-legged trousers. Beside him was a tiny blonde she had never seen before. As they descended the steps hand in hand Catalina could swear she felt an odd lifting sensation from the crowd, a collective intake of breath.

Right in front of the steps they started to dance. He bent and whispered into the girl's ear, holding her left hand pressed close to his neck. One basic and then he whirled her out into a double spin, picked her up from a one-armed cross-body lead. He had his hand right in the middle of her back, holding her so tightly that it bunched up the cloth of her dress. It made Catalina anxious just to watch, but the blonde didn't seem to mind. They did the tightest switch places Catalina had ever seen, the girl spinning twice with her arms up, he spinning once and catching her behind his back.

Catalina looked toward the bandstand and spotted Wendy and Carlos. As if in answer to El Tuerto's presence, their intensity had hiked up a notch: he was twisting her, spinning her, and she leaned into everything, extending her arms, and although they were beautiful, Carlos's lead did not have the tightness of El Tuerto's and his choreography lacked that sexy ebb and flow.

For all that she was a slip of a thing, El Tuerto's partner was following everything he led her through without the slightest appearance of effort. He wound her up in front of him so their arms were like pretzels, and then unwound her and let her go, and they spun separately. The pink sheath and kitten-heeled beige sandals she was wearing reflected her dance style, elegant and slightly reserved. Catalina remembered what Katharine Hepburn had said about Ginger and Fred: "She gave him sex and he gave her class." The opposite was true here: El Tuerto was hot and the blonde was cool.

When El Ruiseñor and his band finally bowed off, Henry put on merengue, and this got all the older, short men excited. Catalina, still at the bar, watched them scuffling for partners. She'd always considered merengue a boring dance since it was basically just two steps, back and forth. The way El Tuerto was doing it, though, was spectacularly erotic, and not just in a rubbing-up-against-your-girlfriend kind of way. She couldn't take her eyes off his hips. Up down, up down, up down. Just when it became almost unbearable to watch, he unlatched his partner and led her into a turn.

"Whatchoo lookin' at?" Carlos had come up right beside her.

"Tuerto."

"He'd be touched, I'm sure." Carlos's shirt was now unbuttoned so that she could see his chest hairs. He pulled a pack of Marlboro Reds out of his pants pocket and offered her one.

"I shouldn't."

He lit it for her and said: "It's that ex-con thing. You *chicas* can't resist it."

"What are you talking about?"

"How do you think he lost his eye?"

"I thought he was born like that."

"Bar fight." Carlos dragged, paused for effect, and added, "The woman died."

"*Woman?*" Catalina, who rarely smoked, was getting a rush. She shook her head to clear it.

"He got off on self-defense."

"When did this happen?"

Carlos shrugged, cooler than the Puerto Domingo boys, cooler than El Tuerto himself. "A long time ago. In the seventies maybe."

Catalina imagined El Tuerto at Carlos's age, two-eyed with dark hair, even leaner than he was today, provoked to a white-hot rage.

The rage part was not difficult since he was always yelling at them in class. Anger alternated with praise, that was how he kept them hooked, it didn't take a genius to figure that out. Catalina pictured him slapping a woman on the side of her face with one of those preternaturally large hands of his, leaving a mark that might turn into a bruise. A woman so hot-blooded she would go for him with a switchblade? stiletto? gun?—Catalina knew nothing of these things.

Another set of merengue came on. El Tuerto was back out on the floor with a new partner, a busty redhead who seemed more his style than the blonde. The redhead was wearing a white lace T-shirt, skin-tight black bootleg pants, and sky-high red platforms that looked impossible to dance in. El Tuerto ran appreciative fingertips down the girl's sides as she did a slow close turn in front of him. All the men around them were watching her butt.

Carlos offered Catalina another cigarette, which she declined. He was definitely flirting, but she had no intention of risking the wrath of his girlfriend, Angie, whom she'd watched stalk out of class with Carlos behind her pleading: *"Mami, por favor, no te preoccupes."*

Finally Henry changed the music back to salsa. It was *her* song, "Catalina la O" sung by Pete "El Conde" Rodriguez.

Catalina la O, Catalina la O.
Eso es un dia muy especiale
Y todo el mundo sale a bailar.

Catalina la O, Catalina la O.
Today's a very special day
And everyone's going out dancing.

Carlos had disappeared, probably to go look for Angie—their jealousy was a two-way street. Out on the floor, a pair of women had walked right up to El Tuerto. One was in her twenties, pretty, with long wavy hair down her back, and the other, older, was even more arresting, elegant in a black lace cocktail dress. El Tuerto kissed them enthusiastically and then took the left hand of each and started dancing with both at the same time. He let the younger one go and began to alternate: a few measures with one, a few measures with the other. Whichever woman was out, mother or daughter—Catalina had figured out their relationship by this time—would do the basic in place while she waited.

The next set started with an oldie, Alfredo Valdez Jr.'s "Almendra," a danzón that morphed prettily, as danzóns do, into a cha-cha-chá. El Tuerto kissed his two partners good-bye and looked up, scanning the crowd. For one panicky instant, Catalina thought: *He's looking for me,* and then she saw Wendy across the floor, tightening her ponytail. He waited, waving several other women off—Christ, the *arrogance* of him—until his partner reached him. Wendy had changed from the black tee into a silver satin halter top. She crossed herself and kissed her fingertips before settling into ballroom position. Catalina admired her pristine posture, the grace of her muscular arms even at rest.

The danzón was a kind of Cuban fox-trot: but on the *clave.* It was easy to see their footwork since the floor had emptied. They stepped with absolute clarity, her right knee grafted to his. Catalina was almost disappointed when the rhythm changed.

One-two, *cha-cha-chá.* El Tuerto flashed his movie-star smile, and Wendy smiled back. Every week they demonstrated for the class but this was different. They were showing off; they were *on.* As El Tuerto had been the alpha male the minute he had stepped onto the floor of the Copacabana, Wendy was now the alpha female. She was not wearing a bra under the flimsy satin top, and El Tuerto, along with all the other men watching, was appreciating this. As she passed him on the cross-body she gave him her bare shoulder, the very edge of her hip, her ponytail, the arc of her jaw, her arms flung up in a flamenco pose. Catalina looked at their feet and saw that they were no longer doing the simple one, two, cha-cha-chá basic; they were syncopating, using every beat of the measure, even using half beats.

He pulled her into a simple hand-behind-the-back spin, the one he had taught in Catalina's first class, and Wendy turned it into a triple, finishing it with a flick kick. Someone whistled. El Tuerto answered with one of his own flamboyant triple spins before the next pattern, which was a cross-body into a Copa turn. *Bring her in, push her out.* As Wendy whirled out of the Copa she lifted the back of her hand to her forehead as if it were too much, *he* were too much.

Ay, papi!

Although the floor had filled again with the change of rhythm, many people had stopped dancing to watch. Catalina could not have described exactly what made Wendy and El Tuerto so charismatic, only that each gesture seemed part of a long calculated tease. El Tuerto took Wendy into a series of double dips, her ponytail switching madly in time. How would that feel, Catalina wondered, to be held with your crotch pressed against his thigh in those tight black pants, balancing on your right leg, your left looped high around his hip, not a split second to think as you were flung backward over and over? He held her wrists over her head and dropped her down into a perfect split and when she slid up, led her into tight tucked spins, stop and reverse, stop and reverse. He checked her everywhere: on the shoulder, elbow, waist, hip, and finally, leaning down, on her ankle.

As the floor cleared around them their dancing took up more and more room. He flicked her away and then, as the song segued seamlessly into a mambo—this one by Cachao—they began a shine war, improvising off each other, crossing and kicking and twisting in impossible combinations, spinning to mark off each set. El Tuerto was dancing more aggressively than Catalina had ever seen him, his shoulders punctuating every step, every kick. Wendy not only kept up, but double-timed him, added her own arm and hand flourishes, snapped back her head, sank down on the last revolution of a triple spin.

People were clapping the *clave* and cheering, *Juepa! Juepa!*

He turned his back to her, and she danced right up behind him and put her hands on his shoulders. The crowd screamed as she began to do showgirl kicks, first to the left, then to the right. El Tuerto was ready—his back still turned, he caught her instep with his right hand at the peak of one of the kicks and drew her leg around his torso so that she faced him again. Then he locked his hands around the small of her back and pulled her up into a shoulder lift.

The crowd was beside itself. A measure later, he set her down again and, using what looked like the nape of her neck for leverage, spun her violently. Her head was down, she was spotting the floor, her ponytail whipping around until from where Catalina was standing it became a circular blur. The way Wendy's neck was angled against the heel of El Tuerto's hand made it look as if he were about to strangle her. He brought her out of the spin into a cross-body and a deep dip with a head swirl on the floor—perfectly timed to the closing chord of the song.

Catalina wanted to scream with the crowd, but for some reason nothing would come out of her throat.

"How the hell is anyone supposed to follow that?"

It was Hank, from their class. Good old Hank, dressed in a blue blazer, khakis, rep tie. Gringo, and proud of it. His bald head gleamed with sweat. It was a mystery to Catalina why he and El Tuerto were such good buddies.

"What's up?" she asked.

"Nuthin' much. I never seen *you* here before. You look good enough to eat."

"Thank you."

"Can I buy you a drink?"

"Okay."

"What's your poison?"

"Rum and coke."

He said appreciatively: "Cuba Libre."

When the drink came in its little plastic cup, she slugged it down like a shot. "You don't kid around," Hank said. He set his own glass of whiskey on the bar and held out his hand. "Dance?"

"Okay," she said, regretting the drink. She let him lead her out to a spot at the edge of the floor over by the steps, as it happened right beside El Tuerto, who was dancing again with the blonde.

"Do we have to be right next to *them*?"

"It's crowded. There's not a lot of choice. Relax. He's not watching."

But he was. Catalina knew it. Just as she knew that Hank had purposely picked this spot.

She missed his first turn cue.

"Are you all right?" he asked.

"Yeah."

"Are you sure you're all right?"

"Yeah. Sorry."

The crowd had swelled; the people at the railing were now three deep. She was off balance and the back of her neck felt clammy. She managed to get through the song by counting: *One-two-three, five-six-seven.* Fortunately Hank was both predictable and easy to read. Cross-body, one spin, cuddle turn, basic, back break, Copa turn. When the song ended, she thanked him and started maneuvering her way across the floor to where she'd seen the sign for the ladies' room.

She ran smack into El Tuerto.

"Well, hello there," he said, reaching out to steady her. In his other hand he held an opened bottle of mineral water.

"Hi," she said, swallowing hard. She could just imagine it—puking on the floor of the Copacabana all over El Tuerto's shiny black custom-made boots. She'd never live it down.

His hand still on her shoulder, he bent to kiss her cheek, his lips cool from the water. She got a whiff of sandalwood, which made her even queasier.

"Looking good, Lina."

"See you in class," she said, not quite shaking him off, and kept going, not turning around to see how he was reacting to her rudeness.

In the ladies' room she hid inside a stall and sat on the closed seat with her head down. She shut her eyes, took deep breaths, cast her mind back to a certain scene from a long ago summer, that always calmed her.

When it finally felt safe, she got carefully to her feet and left the stall and went over to the sinks and splashed her face with cold water. She could hear the music—something romantic by Mickey Taveras. The door burst open, and a group of girls streamed in. One of them was Angie, Carlos's girlfriend. She was wearing a shirt made of white strips of material crisscrossed in artful ways. The gang headed straight for the mirrors, where they started reapplying lipstick and eyeliner.

"*Mami*, you're falling out of your top. Let me fix it."

"*He* ask you to dance yet?"

"No, he's busy with Soni Bologna." Angie threw a sharp glance in Catalina's direction, her light eyes spooky in the fluorescent light, and Catalina realized they were talking about El Tuerto.

The girls peed and left. Alone except for the attendant, Catalina regarded her reflection. Her face was not easily identifiable. People took her for Japanese, Chinese, Korean, Filipina, Mexican. She was sick of explaining, sick of their incredulous expressions when she

told them she'd been born in Cuba, had grown up in the Boston suburbs, and was more American than any of them.

Here, at the Copa, that kind of thing didn't matter. The only
thing that counted was whether you could dance or not.

Catalina took a deep breath, smoothed her braid, gave one last
check to her dress straps, and went back out onto the floor.

2

Catalina

Half of dancing is listening.

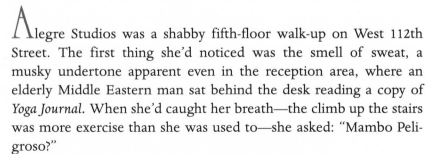

Alegre Studios was a shabby fifth-floor walk-up on West 112th Street. The first thing she'd noticed was the smell of sweat, a musky undertone apparent even in the reception area, where an elderly Middle Eastern man sat behind the desk reading a copy of *Yoga Journal*. When she'd caught her breath—the climb up the stairs was more exercise than she was used to—she asked: "Mambo Peligroso?"

The man looked up and jerked his thumb toward a half-open door behind him. "Studio 5B. Pay after the class."

On the studio door were tacked various flyers, including the one she'd spotted on the bulletin board of the bagel shop in her neighborhood.

YOU THINK YOU'VE SEEN LATIN DANCE?
DONE LATIN DANCE? YOU'VE NEVER EXPERIENCED
MAMBO PELIGROSO.
BEGINNERS WELCOME.
TUESDAYS, 6 PM

The address was a fifteen-minute walk from her apartment.

Catalina Ortiz Midori would never be able to say afterward exactly what had drawn her uptown that snowy February evening. She wasn't a party girl, and although her background was Cuban she hadn't danced or really listened to Latin music since she was a teenager in Calle Ocho with her relatives. Growing up in a white suburb, attending a Seven Sisters college, spending those years with her ex-boyfriend Richard the *über*-WASP—all that had bleached her to the point where she could hardly call herself Latina at all.

I am an American.

Catalina was an old soul. She believed that simply surviving New York City was a triumph. Alone since her breakup with Richard, she'd been subsisting on the pay of an English as a Second Language teacher. Manhattan, it seemed to her, was a brilliant party at three A.M.—you were exhausted and knew you should go home, but you had been there so long it was impossible to pull yourself away. At thirty-one she felt too old for it, but there was no place else she could imagine living. Perhaps that was why she'd answered the challenge in the flyer—she was looking for a reason to stay.

Despite the snow, which had tapered to flurries but was still slowing traffic, the room was crowded with about twenty-five people who spanned adolescence to middle age. As she would later learn, it would take much more than bad weather to keep them away. Some were in warm-up or dance gear, but most were wearing street clothes. Skin color ran the gamut. There were even a couple of Japanese girls giggling in the corner.

There was no sign of anyone who looked like a teacher.

She lingered in the doorway, hoping no one was taking notice of her. A teacher herself, she was surprised by how shy the idea of a new class made her. There was no music, but a fiftyish couple was practicing a dance pattern, as smooth as if they had little synchronized engines inside their torsos. He looped his arms around her shoulders and she spun out and away from him, and then he picked her up and brought her across. Away from them, in front of the mirrors, a boy in T-shirt and sweatpants and sneakers was showing off: a moonwalk, then a wave, then a short tap routine, ending with his right arm in the air just like John Travolta in *Saturday Night Fever.*

"*Juepa, Carlos!*" someone yelled.

I hope this class isn't going to be in Spanish, was what she was thinking when she felt a pair of hands close down on her shoulders. She waited, expecting them to move her aside, but they stayed, and suddenly every eye in the house was on Catalina, or more specifically, on the person standing behind her. She did not turn but registered that it was a man, from the size of the hands, the height, and his cologne, something heavy on sandalwood.

What she would remember most clearly afterward was that when he finally did firmly guide her to one side—in the manner of someone used to handling women, as if, in fact, the gesture were part of some elaborate choreography—and brushed by her to enter the room, she felt a distinct tingle at the back of her neck.

He entered the studio in long, feral strides and once inside stopped and turned to speak to one of the women. His was the kind of face once seen you would never forget: skin slightly darker than hers—maybe Puerto Rican—thick salt-and-pepper hair cut close, high cheekbones, a nose almost feminine in its daintiness, thin lips, the kind of defined jawline you saw on movie stars. Most distinctively, he only had one sighted eye, the right one. It was dark, glittering, almond-shaped. The blind eye was a milky twin and focused straight ahead.

The class had gotten subdued, watching as the one-eyed man finished his conversation and walked over to the sound system. This seemed to be the signal for everyone to arrange themselves into two semi-orderly rows in front of the wall of mirrors.

Somehow Catalina found the courage to enter the room and walk over to an empty folding chair against the wall, where she changed from hiking boots into high-heeled Mary Janes, the closest thing to dance shoes she owned. The teacher, who'd shed his coat, was wearing black jeans and a white T-shirt, both skin tight, and boots.

She made herself a space in the back row, scooting around a little until she could see her reflection.

Body-wise, she was no competition for the twenty-somethings in the front row in their midriff tops and low-cut dance pants, hair wild and loose or piled into elaborate styles. Catalina had on baggy jeans and an old Newport Jazz Festival T-shirt. Her hair was in a single braid down her back, the way she'd worn it all her life. She tried not to stare at the other girls, wishing she were taller, her shoulders broader, her breasts smaller, her thighs not quite so thick.

Just one class, she told herself. *I'll stay for one class and then I can leave.*

In front, with his back to them, the one-eyed man raised his arm and cued the CD player. Immediately he began to dance, starting with what looked like a basic step repeated over and over. Forward on the left, step in place with the right, back on the left, hold for a beat. Repeat it backward starting with the right foot—a mirror image of the first part of the step.

The class followed, and Catalina did, too, cautiously, taking tiny steps so as not to call attention to herself.

The music was medium tempo, jazzy, no vocals, heavy on the hand drums. The first thing she noticed was that the rhythm of the dance was syncopated; that is, they were taking their first step not on the first beat of the measure but on the second. Dancing not on the four/four, but on the *clave* beat.

Bam-bam-bam, bam-bam.

Dancing on the *clave* did not mean following it beat for beat. In one measure you were against it, two on three, and in the next exactly on it, two on two.

"One-two-three, five-six-seven," the teacher was barking, in English, thank God, his baritone a raspy edge over the tumbadoras. Where, wondered Catalina, were four and eight? She could follow the step, but the counting confused her. Finally she figured out that four and eight were the pauses. It was like doing an equation with your feet.

When the teacher was certain they were all in sync, he began footwork patterns, which she'd later learn were called shines.

Walk to the left, then to the right, add a kick, add a skip. Again. Basic. Back to the pattern.

She struggled to follow, cheating when she had to. In black ankle boots strapped around the tops, the teacher was slamming his foot into each basic, delicate as a young girl on the skips. Moving his shoulders in contramotion to his hips. Exaggerating for them, his students. In the mirror, she caught a glimpse of his face. All angles and edges—so different from the men in her family, from her father for instance, with his sweet mouth and soulful eyes, or from her cousin Guillermo, who resembled him.

Three steps to the right, tap, three to the left, tap. Then a turn pattern: half turn back, half turn forward, full turn to the right.

Finally she gave up and just stood there and watched. For some reason she couldn't keep her eyes off one particular dancer. Not the prettiest nor the youngest, this woman was nevertheless a tidy package: small and slender and dark-skinned. In a black sports bra and leggings, her arms and calves were pure lean muscle, and she wore her hair in a high ponytail, which she used to punctuate her dancing.

The next round, Catalina imitated as best as she could, forgetting about the swing of the shoulders, the hands up, concentrating only on the steps.

"Grapevine!"

This she recognized from aerobics class, although in mambo it looked completely different because of the rhythm, because you added a sharp kick to the end of it. To the right: step in back, side step, step in front, side step, step in back, *stop with a kick*. Same thing to the left.

She kept her eye on the small dark woman and managed to copy her, just about a half beat behind.

"Right-hand spiral!"

"Left-hand spiral!"

Beginners welcome, indeed.

Giving up for good, Catalina stepped out of the line.

The teacher went into high gear, playing with the beat on the increasingly complicated kick and twist patterns. This was nothing like the dancing she remembered from Calle Ocho. This looked *professional*. One by one the rest of the class dropped out as she had, and stood back and watched. After a few minutes there were only three left: the moonwalking boy and two women, including the one who had caught her attention. Cross, cross, kick, hop, bend, spin, flick, flick. They were mesmerizing, the three of them following their leader, each with his or her distinctive style, all dead on the beat. This was as good as any dancing she'd ever seen, in the movies, on Broadway, anywhere.

The teacher was no longer bothering to call out the patterns.

The younger woman was a beauty—light eyes and long wavy auburn hair, white tank with no bra and low-cut jeans. But it was the other woman who again stood out in Catalina's eyes. She was dancing without effort, it seemed, as if her limbs were plugged directly into the percussion, not looking at the teacher but following without a single mistake. Her feet barely left the floor and yet she gave the impression of skimming it. Up, down, went the ponytail, the arms up on the spins, the shoulders circling, everything small, neat, precise, and inexplicably seductive.

The younger woman was the first to quit, wiping the sweat off her upper lip with a grimace. A minute later the older woman followed suit, although as she left the floor she made a little flicking motion with the fingers of her left hand as if to say: I could do this, I've just had enough.

Now only the teacher and the boy—Carlos was his name, she remembered—remained, the two of them clearly involved in some macho contest. The teacher's footwork was so honed, if he'd put ink on his soles his footprints would have made a perfect pattern on the floor, like the ballroom-dance diagrams Catalina had once seen in a book. He was an efficient dancer, taking small steps in those heavy black boots, hips insinuating just enough now, hands up in front of him as if to beckon. The boy was showy, athletic, wasting energy but equally fun to watch, dancing right into the floor, kicking high, snapping his head back so that droplets of sweat flicked into the air.

The song ended suddenly on a dissonant chord, and the boy collapsed forward, palms on his knees. The teacher spun around to face the class, smiling, a smile that transformed his face from predatory into playful. With elaborate casualness he extracted an olive bandanna from his breast pocket and patted his temples.

"Wassamatta with you guys? I thought you were champs. Okay, I'm gonna break down the flare for you. Slow, first. Remember: feet to knees to hips, that's how the energy flows."

They formed rows again and watched him as if he were a god, Catalina included, because she was paying twenty bucks she couldn't afford to learn this. Left toe over the right, point the right to the side, bring the right toe back behind the left heel, left toe out to the side, then behind the right.

Broken down, Catalina recognized the shine pattern for what it was—an exploded star. You simply slid alternating feet out to each of its four points, one after the other.

The teacher performed it several times for them in slow motion, and Catalina, studying him in the mirror, mimicked exactly, using the inside of her big toe as if it were the blade of a knife and she were etching the star into the floor.

In the mirror, the teacher caught her eye.

"Good," he said. "Remember, ladies, keep your wrists up."

She tried to place his accent but couldn't. Queens maybe, but smoothed over, as if some time in his life he had taken elocution lessons. To the jazzy song they repeated the flare over and over until the back of her T-shirt was plastered to her skin, and when she reached behind to unstick it, she felt the sweat running down in a sheet. But she kept on, along with the rest of them. The other dancers were giving her energy she didn't know she had.

The song ended. "Get a partner," said the teacher.

Carlos immediately paired up with the auburn-haired Latina in the white tank top. A burly bald-headed man approached Catalina, and despite his menacing appearance she turned to him gratefully— at least *somebody* wanted to dance with her. But as the man put his hand on her shoulder he turned her so she was facing the front of the room. The teacher was pointing his finger.

"You," he said. "Come up here."

She walked up, conscious of the eyes. Before she had time to think, he had settled her into ballroom position, stiffer than what she was used to. Their forearms were aligned, hers over his, like some complex geometric figure. Under the cotton of his T-shirt, his biceps were hard, flexed. Catalina's heart was racing, and she was sure that he could feel it. She smelled sandalwood, studied his jawline, tried not to look at the milky eye.

"Relax," he said.

"This is my first time."

"That's not a problem. The rule is, don't anticipate. We'll go over the basics some other time." He angled his head toward the class. "An experienced dancer can lead anyone, even a beginner."

She felt herself flush.

"This is the combination. *Mira.* She turns, he turns, she turns, she steps left-right, then left behind him, he slides his hand down his back and gives it to her, *gives it to her,* that's right, he turns her double spin to the left, shoulder check, then around again so she faces him— like this—and then back into closed position."

The pressure of the teacher's hands made it impossible to step any way but where he was leading her. She was not sure whether she liked this or not.

He looked at her, raising the eyebrow over his good eye. "Your steps are too big." Addressing the class: "Leads, rotate!"

He handed Catalina to the man of the couple who had been practicing together before the class. His name was Tino, and he led so politely she wasn't sure if they had done it right. Her next partner was the large bald guy who had originally approached her. He introduced himself as Hank. The teacher talked them through the figure again, this time in Spanish. Catalina, who did not understand a word, concentrated only on Hank's hands and her own feet.

"Looking good," Hank said.

"It's my first time."

"You got *sabor.*"

"What?" Even though she had lost her Spanish it was plain to Catalina that he had the worst accent she had ever heard.

"Flavor, girl."

They did the move again, and this time she overrotated on the last turn and knocked into Hank's chest.

"Easy," he said, steadying her. "So, whaddya do?"

"What do you mean?"

"How do you pay your rent?"

"I teach ESL."

"Yeah? You live in Jackson Heights?"

He thought she was Chinese. She shook her head. "Manhattan."

"I'm a security guard at the Museum of Modern Art."

"Really?"

"Yeah. Just call ahead, I can get you in for free."

"*Ay ay ay!*" the teacher was yelling. Catalina jumped, although no one else in the room looked the least bit surprised. "You're awful, all of you," he scolded. "If you're gonna spin that way, don't tell anyone you're students of mine. Keep the weight on the foot you're pivoting on. This is *beginner* shit. I can't believe I have to remind you."

The next round there was no partner for her, so she did the combination by herself, pretending she was being led. Again she lost her balance on the double turn.

"Take your shoulders with you when you spin, ladies."

Catalina's next partner was Carlos. He smiled impishly, showing large white teeth, and fingered the tiny gold crucifix at his neck as they waited further instruction.

"I suck," she found herself saying to him.

"Don't worry about it."

"*You* don't have to worry."

"Neither do you. El Tuerto likes you."

"Torto?"

"Tuerto. One-Eye. *No hablas español?*"

She shook her head.

El Tuerto was clapping his hands to get their attention. He added one more phrase to the combination, a complicated under-the-arms turn for the guys involving something called the cut illusion while the girls danced in place. With Carlos the figure was easy. His hands were deep, giving her leverage on the turns. The trick, she was finding, was not to try so hard to follow. There was a certain push and pull if you let yourself feel it.

Finally they had all nailed the combination, with El Tuerto calling out: "One-two-three, five-six-seven." He had been using the women's count for the shines, she realized, because the leads stepped back on *two*. There was no repeat of his temper tantrum, but he observed them sharply, coming over to correct minute body positioning. "You're sticking your elbows out like a chicken," he told

Catalina, adjusting her wrists up as if she were a marionette. "Keep your back straight on the spins, and remember, take your shoulders with you. *Mira,*" he called, waving his arm behind him, and the small dark woman appeared by his side. The teacher lifted her arm and she spun—single, double—as if he were merely willing her to do so. In the second of the two spins, Catalina noticed, although the woman's footwork remained on the beat, her shoulders slowed down, catching up at the last split second. Long after the demonstration was over, Catalina kept replaying it in her head.

I will never look like that.

El Tuerto put on music again, a cut Catalina would hear many times in the months to come—"Vivir Lo Nuestro," the Marc Anthony/La India torch duet that was number one on the Latin charts that year. The class continued to repeat the figure over and over, switching partners at the teacher's command, so that Catalina began to feel as if she were dancing *casino rueda,* that Cuban circle dance where the women were passed from man to man. She was sorry now she had not paid more attention to it when she was a child.

"Okay, kids, see you next week."

It did not seem that two hours had passed. Taking her cue from the others, she went up and handed the teacher twenty dollars in cash. He tried to catch her eye, but she looked away. *I know your type.* As she was changing back into her boots she felt someone touch her shoulder and hesitated before turning around.

It was the small dark woman. She was not pretty—her eyes were set too close together—but there was something striking about her face, which was fine boned and sharp chinned.

"Hi there. I'm Wendy. Welcome to the class."

"Funny, you don't look like a Wendy."

The woman's husky laugh surprised Catalina; it seemed too big for her body. "My dad had this fantasy I'd turn out to be an all-American teenager or something." *Her* accent was not hard to figure out—pure Bronx. Like Carlos, she was wearing a crucifix on a chain—hers had a reddish stone embedded in the center.

"I'm Catalina."

"Catalina la O."

"That's it, just like the song."

"I hope he didn't scare you off."

"I was thinking maybe this class is too hard for me. That footwork at the beginning—forget it."

"Don't worry, you'll master the shines. You just have to get them into muscle memory. Ever done ballroom? Jazz? Ballet?"

"Never. None of them."

"You been to any other mambo classes?"

"No, this is my first. What's the difference between mambo and salsa?"

"Salsa's the whole mixed bag, Latin dance. Mambo is what we do here in New York, breaking on two. Stepping on the second beat. I was watching you. You were keeping up. You got the rhythm."

"I was *barely* keeping up."

"Everyone feels like that at the beginning. Wait a moment, I'll walk you out."

Catalina watched as Wendy made her way to the CD player where El Tuerto was still collecting money. The two spoke, and then he leaned down to kiss her on the mouth, tugging playfully on her ponytail as he did so.

Out in the reception area, Wendy gave the man behind the desk a high five.

"Wassup, Basil?"

"Not much, hon."

"When you gonna learn how to mambo?"

"I'm too old for that."

"I'd be happy to give you a private," said Wendy, and Basil showed his teeth in a grin.

"You just name the time, hon."

"*You* are a wonderful dancer," Catalina said when they were on the stairs. *Wonderful* didn't quite describe it, but she couldn't think of anything else.

Wendy gave the briefest of smiles. Her face, for all its animation, was not inherently a happy one. "Thanks for saying so, *nena*."

"How long have you been doing it?"

"Since before you were born, probably."

"I seriously doubt that."

"About fifteen years. God, has it really been that long? Yeah, fifteen, give or take."

"All the time with him?"

"Tuerto was my first teacher. Now I'm like his assistant. When he's not being a dick."

"He's difficult?"

"They all are."

"Who? Teachers or guys?"

Catalina was flattered that she had been able to make Wendy laugh yet again.

"Both."

"So like is he the best?"

"*He* thinks he is. You want ballroom, you go to one of the big studios like Fred Astaire or Sandra Cameron. You want smooth styling, you go to Jimmy Anton. Carlos König will help you with spins. Eddie Torres is good for the really flashy stuff. So is Puerto Domingo. What Tuerto does is street. Like him, I guess."

"You're an expert."

"No way. Just your average *mambera*."

It was already clear to Catalina that there was nothing average about Wendy.

Wendy took out a pack of Newports and offered them.

"No, thanks."

They had reached street level, and Wendy pushed open the steel door, pausing for a second to strike a match. Strains of some old Tito Puente song—offhand Catalina couldn't tell which, but it sounded familiar—had been following them down the stairs, and she wondered if the teacher was dancing, and if so, with whom? One of the twenty-somethings? By himself, in front of the mirror?

Why did she care?

As if it were the most natural thing in the world, Wendy linked her arm with Catalina's as they walked. "So, you with us now?"

"I don't know."

Wendy tossed her cigarette and reached behind her head to tighten the elastic of her ponytail. "You should. You want to keep up, you should come."

"What's the story with attitude girl?"

"Attitude girl?"

"You know, white tank."

"Angelina?" Wendy made the flicking motion with her fingers, wagged her head. *"What the fuck you lookin' at?"*

"That's her."

"Don't mess with Angie; she'll eat you for breakfast."

It had finally stopped snowing, and a chill wind was blowing over from the Hudson, but Catalina could still feel a steamy layer emanating from the pores of her skin. At the entrance to the Number 1 train Wendy said, "This is me." She let go of Catalina's arm, gave her a light kiss on the cheek—*"Hasta la próxima,* mami"—and skipped down the stairs, knapsack and ponytail bobbing in time to an imaginary *clave.*

3

Catalina

Know at all times where your partner
is in relation to you.

By the age of twenty-three she'd been an orphan, and this was why she decided on a practical career. Advertising would be a good way to use the writing skills she'd picked up getting her degree in English lit. It was at Young & Rubicam that she'd met Richard. What had intrigued her from the start was his extreme Americanness: sunburn-prone skin, sandy hair and freckles, nasal Massachusetts accent, the family who lived in a town with a street named for his great-grandfather. Every holiday they'd drive up to that WASP stronghold thirty miles north of Boston; every August was spent at the cottage in Wellfleet. Richard's family was always excruciatingly polite to her, and perhaps that was the problem. Catalina couldn't stand his mother, who insisted on practicing her high school Spanish on her and at the same time kept hinting that it would be a good idea if her future daughter-in-law joined the Junior League.

After six years, Richard announced one day out of the blue that he had fallen back in love with his girlfriend from prep school. Catalina would have left New York then if she'd had somewhere to go. What saved her was quitting her job—she couldn't have borne running into Richard at the office—and subbing as a teacher of English as a Second Language for a friend who was quitting to go to law school. To her surprise she loved teaching ESL, had a flair for it, and within a year she was on the faculty full time, going to school nights to get her master's in theoretical linguistics.

"How many of you are planning to become American citizens?" was always her first question to a new class. They all would raise their hands, even if they were lying, because they thought it was a test. Citizen-bound or not, Catalina was aware of how crucial this class was to each and every one of them. In addition to the normal syllabus she taught them how to shop at a grocery store and at a pharmacy, how to order at a restaurant, how to speak to a bullying landlord. She introduced them to American humor by bringing in comics from the *Daily News,* or for a more sophisticated group, the Top Ten List from the David Letterman show. She took them to movies, everything from *Aladdin* to *Robocop II* to *American Beauty.*

Sometimes Catalina believed that she was teaching in memory of her mother, who had never learned English well enough to get a job worthy of her talents and education in the United States. She herself felt a kinship with her students, who no matter how long they lived here, would probably never feel at home. She knew what it was like to lose a language; for the three years following her father's death she had not uttered a single word. The school counselor in Miami, where they lived when they first came to the States, had wanted to enroll her in a program for slow children, but her mother had pleaded to let her stay in the same class as her cousin Guillermo, pointing out that Catalina was as smart, even smarter, than most of the other kids.

Then they'd moved north, and during her first week of sixth grade the math teacher put an algebra equation on the board and asked if anyone could solve it. Catalina raised her hand, and the teacher, forgetting that she was the girl who couldn't talk, called on her. Catalina provided the correct answer, her voice lower-pitched than one would have expected given the sweet oval of her face, her accent standard American TV English.

"*Milágro,*" Tía Ana said when Jun called to tell her, and Tío 'Nesto paid for a mass at the Iglesia de la Virgen de la Caridad. Soon, however, it became evident that there was a twist to this miracle. Lina spoke fluent English, but not a word of Spanish. Tía Ana said there was no use questioning the workings of *Dios Todopoderoso.*

After Richard, Catalina had lived like a nun, going out only for the occasional dinner with her girlfriends, watching them get married and pregnant, biding her time for she didn't know what. She went back down to Miami for vacations, helping her aunt and uncle, who were now in their sixties, in the *botánica* they owned on Calle Ocho.

And suddenly here she was embroiled in the world of New York mambo, the hottest boy-girl game in town. Too much information, maybe, that first class, but she had gone back to Alegre Studios every week since that February evening. During the shines she'd make sure to get behind Wendy, whose size-five feet in their pointy-toed lace-up practice shoes clearly described every pattern.

"Not bad, *nena,*" Wendy would say, and this, plus El Tuerto's occasional grudging nod, was enough to have her walking on air.

Why did mambo enthrall her so? Was it the music? She'd never especially loved it; it was her cousin Guillermo who was obsessed with his father's old 78s and would play them over and over until everyone groaned. But now she had started listening to Radio Caliente and checking out the CD stores on Eighth Avenue.

Was it because, like teaching ESL, she had a knack for it? She could always picture shines three-dimensionally, like time-lapse photography. And she was an exceptionally light follow, all the guys said. *I was born for this.* She'd do little hand accents by instinct and catch girls at clubs studying her with expressions that asked: *Where did she learn that?*

Lina, the dance people called her, the Spanish diminutive of her name, instead of the formal "Catalina" or "Katie," which had been Richard's nickname for her. She didn't feel Latina exactly, but she didn't feel like she stood out either, as she had for most of her life.

Breaking into the social scene was another story. The tough girls, like Angie, were a closed circle. During the break they'd practice shines and gossip about their club nights out.

"José dissed me for that fucking Eddie Torres chick; you know the short one with the fat ass."

"My L.A. friend Elena got the Groper; I tried to warn her."

"Nestor hit on me. I said I'll dance with you, but I won't fuck you."

They chewed gum and acted as if they were doing their partners a huge favor. But the nonchalance was just an act. They were good. They were great. They had *attitude.*

The Japanese girls were aloof in a different way, keeping notebooks with intricate diagrams of the turn patterns. They spoke little English but fluent Spanish, which they used to communicate with Wendy and El Tuerto.

Thank God for Wendy. If not for her patronage, Catalina would have stayed on the fringe for weeks, months, even years. She had to laugh when she remembered how anxious she'd been that first Copa Friday, trying on everything in her closet and finally going out to buy her first new dress in years, a blue-and-white-flowered slip with spaghetti straps.

"High heels," said the salesgirl, who was Puerto Rican. "Put your hair up. Red lipstick."

She hadn't taken the advice except for the lipstick, but everything had turned out just fine.

Easter morning she spent as she always did—practicing. She'd danced in leggings and a tank top and her brand-new suede-bottomed three-inch stilettos from World Tone Music on Twenty-third Street until her downstairs neighbor, a retired gay architect, had complained. After that she practiced in socks, which gave her a nice slip on the oak parquet, although her footwork wasn't nearly as precise.

Her CD collection had bloomed: El Ruiseñor, Jimmy Bosch, Wayne Gorbea, Oscar D'Leon, Gilberto Santa Rosa, Frankie Ruiz, Eddie Palmieri. "Cogelo" by Wayne Gorbea was her favorite practice tune—medium tempo, more than nine minutes long, and she loved the jazzy piano and the strident blare of the trombones.

She practiced in her foyer where there was a mirror, picturing Wendy in front of her, feet striking the floor exactly on the beat, or in syncopation between the beats, shoulders angled, hands keeping time. No margin for error, because no matter how intricate, how it played around the *clave*, every pattern had to come out landing with a forward step on the two.

"Make every kick *count*," El Tuerto would bark over the music. "Cross cross cross, kick, pivot, cross, left toe out, drag it in, step step step, basic, that's it, pivot again."

He'd teach them one or two or sometimes even three new shines and then string them together into a routine. On Wednesday mornings Catalina wouldn't rest until she'd nailed the combination from the night before, and then she'd keep going for a song or two, to seal it into muscle memory, as Wendy would say.

After shines came spins. Right, left, half, swivel, traveling, spot. The trick to all of them was to find the center, the plumb line from the tip of your head down through your spine to the balls of your feet, that axis that remained still no matter how fast you whirled, or how many times, or what was happening with your hands or your shoulders or your hair.

If you did it right, it felt like flying.

It was only when her thigh muscles began to cramp that she'd quit, staggering to the kitchen to pour herself a mug of coffee.

As the music continued, though, she couldn't help it, she'd get to her feet and in the kitchen with mug in hand go through the routine again—one right spin, one basic, one left, one basic, one double right, one basic, one double left, one basic—sipping her coffee on the basic.

If she could do a double one-footed spin in her socks holding a cup of scalding coffee, there was no telling how she could shine in her stilettos on the slick floor of the Copa, where she had become a Friday-night regular.

Her calves were now so muscular that she had to buy socks in the boys' department. The balls of her feet were thick with calluses, which she scraped off with a razor even though they would reappear immediately.

"Looking buff," one of her boy students had remarked.

After she was done practicing she took a long steamy shower, braided her wet hair and tucked it into a cap, and went out for the *Times* and takeout yellow rice and black beans from Rosa's.

She had just sat down to eat when the phone rang.

Tía Ana, she thought, guilting her for not going to church.

"Happy Easter, Catty."

It was her cousin Guillermo. "What's up?"

"*Nada.* I just wanted to hear your voice."

"In the morning?"

"Mami says at night you're always out."

"Salsa dancing."

"*De veras?*"

"Yeah, well, maybe I'm getting back to my roots. What's going on?"

"The natives are restless."

"What do you mean?"

"Papi wants to go back to Cuba."

"To live?"

"Just for a visit."

"What about those planes that got shot down?"

"Brothers to the Rescue? Isolated incident. Ever since he got diagnosed with angina he thinks he's on his deathbed."

"How do you get to Cuba?"

"Apply through Cuban Interests. You should come with us. Visit your *papi.*" It was a curious custom in her family to refer to the dearly departed as if they were still alive.

To Catalina, Cuba was a dream, a history to which her mother had referred occasionally and vaguely. Somewhere in this dream was her father, whom she rarely thought about. She'd never considered going back. "Maybe."

He changed the subject without skipping a beat. "So with all this dancing, what's going on?" Have you met anyone, he meant.

"Nothing special."

All the way from Coral Gables Catalina heard her cousin sigh, as he had when they were teenagers on the phone, she north and he south, the two of them so close Tío 'Nesto said they were more like *gemelos* than *primos.*

"You okay?" she asked.

"When you coming down?"

"Christmas."

"Not before?"

"I got my classes to teach. You sure you're okay?"

"Of course. Bye, Catty."

"Bye," she said, and they hung up.

This was the way it always was. Whenever they made contact, no matter how many months had passed, it was as casual as if one of them had gone into another room and come back a few minutes later.

Maybe it was because they shared a secret.

To Catalina the best part of landing in Miami so many years ago had been Guillermo, two months older and completely American. The first time they'd laid eyes on each other all he said was "Hey" but that was enough. She was in love. Maybe it was because he resembled the men on her father's side of the family—lanky and laconic and infinitely kind. When the neighborhood kids called her *muda estupida,* he beat them up and the two of them built a fort out of old lumber in the live oak in the front yard and dropped clods of dirt and water balloons on passing enemies. In the fort he taught her to play checkers and dominos and poker for pennies. Summers they'd lie for hours on their backs listening to old Cuban tunes and baseball games on the radio. Guillermo did not find it odd that she didn't talk in those years. They developed a sign language in which their names for each other were Catty and Doggy. Later, when she started speaking, they continued the names. Like everything else about their relationship it seemed natural.

When she moved to Massachusetts, they wrote each other every week, one-page letters as regular as diary entries. She lived for the summers when as soon as school let out she'd take the Greyhound down and move into her old room at her *tíos'* on Calle Ocho.

The secret happened the summer before college. It was one Sunday afternoon when they were home alone on the back veranda drinking beer and smoking some extra primo Hawaiian from the stash Guillermo's brother Rafael kept in his sock drawer. Her cousin had put on one of Tío 'Nesto's scratchy 78s, and they started to dance. Nothing fancy, just what everyone did at parties. The pot was starting to hit her, and she had to concentrate on moving her feet.

Left. Right. Stop. Her cousin said, "I have an idea," and let her go, and she fell languidly onto the porch swing while he disappeared inside the house. He came out hauling his father's beat-up tumbadora—fire-engine red, with the finish peeling off. He set the drum up in front of them and tuned it and started playing along to Arsenio Rodriguez.

"Now it's your turn," he said.

"Gimme a break."

"I'm serious."

He showed her how to hold it between her thighs, thud with the ball of her hand for the upbeat, then slap with the fingers for the downbeat. After a few false starts she got it.

"Good, good. Now listen." As she played Guillermo rapped his knuckles against the glass of the patio table so that she could hear the relationship between the *clave* and the tumbadora.

Pah-pah-pah, pah-pah.

"This song is too fast," she complained.

"All right, all right." He went into the living room and changed the record to Beny Moré. Catalina lasted about half the new song and then had to quit, slipping blood-heavy fingers into her mouth. Her cousin took her fingers and put them into his own mouth. This was new. Recently they'd been experimenting, tongue-kissing for instance, in Tío 'Nesto's Plymouth on the beach at night. What he was doing now, however, felt not playful but aggressive. Guillermo let go of her fingers and kissed her hard on the mouth, and she felt his hand slip under her T-shirt and, his fingers slide under the wire of her bra, heard his indrawn breath as he found her nipple.

She didn't try to stop him. The next thing she remembered was lying flat on her back on the floorboards, shorts and underwear shimmied down to her ankles. He was fast and clumsy, but she was ready. From a million miles away she heard those curious raspy cries that no one but her cousin would ever induce.

Pah-pah-pah, pah-pah.

When it was over, Beny was wailing: *"A mi me gusta el son mon-tuno."*

Once they started they couldn't stop. All that summer—nights on the beach, afternoons in each other's bedrooms when no one was home. Only Tía Ana seemed to have an inkling. After dinner, when the grown-ups would be sitting around with their *cafecitos* spiked with rum, doing their usual moaning about how El Lider had squeezed the life out of Cuba like the juice out of a pineapple, the streets were like tombs, the buildings crumbling like chalk, Guillermo would announce casually, "Me and Catty are goin' out." Tía Ana would give them a long look but say nothing.

In late August Catalina found herself shivering over the toilet and didn't have to buy the test to figure it out. She never told Guillermo but back north went to a clinic one of her girlfriends had told her about. Two days later, on the train up to Northampton for her first semester at Smith, she sat with her hands folded over the place in her body that was empty now except for the cramps that were so excruciating it took all her will not to double over. To calm herself, she imagined she was back on the veranda on Calle Ocho playing the tumbadora, playing like an angel, until her cousin pushed the drum away and started to kiss her.

A mi me gusta el son montuno.

It was hard to see him at Christmas, but she steeled herself and made it through that holiday and subsequent ones. He seemed more serious but somehow not as intense, his energies dispersed into the business of being a grown-up. Once in a while, always in the presence of others, they'd dance like they used to—they were first cousins, after all—and she would feel the way their bones still rhymed, he taller and broader now, with cologne over the sharper scent of his skin.

Although she was resigned to their new distance—*there was no way we could have kept doing that*—she was unprepared for the stab she felt when she learned he was dating Lilly Cruz. *You learned on me,* she'd think, watching them together. She knew that Lilly, a blond version of Gloria Estefan, could not love him as well as she did. But Catalina was sure that her cousin hadn't forgotten her. Once in a while she'd catch him studying her with an absorbed, distant expression, as if she were a movie or TV. Trying to figure her out, what she'd become.

On her desk she kept a photo of the two of them, aged ten and eleven—it must have been taken during that two-month window when they weren't the same age—leaning against the side of the house in Little Havana. They were both barefoot. She was wearing a yellow dress printed with tiny red flowers, squinting into the sun. He, in T-shirt and shorts, was looking away from her, off to the side. Their hands were close together but not touching.

He was married now with three sons, living in a house so fancy it had a name, the Casa Rosada. He'd call her out of the blue, as he had today, and from time to time sent her postcards, the cheapest kind with garish colors, of sunsets and bikinied women frolicking on the beach, with messages that were short and to the point. "Thanks for the trumpet you sent Santito. When are you coming back down?" His printing, slender and slanted, was exactly the same as it had been when he was a child. The postcards reminded her of the valentines he used to give her, homemade with the glue dried all over the doily cutouts he'd pasted on red construction paper. *To Catty with love from Doggy.*

4

Catalina

Partner dancing is like a conversation.

———— ✺ ————

On income tax day there was a new guy in class. He didn't seem familiar with the shines, but El Tuerto welcomed him with a hug and a slap on the shoulder. After class, as Catalina was changing out of her dance shoes, Wendy came over with the young man in tow.

"You're coming out with us tonight."

"I'm not dressed for Copa."

"No, this is downtown, this kind of hole-in-the-wall I like. This is my son, Luis. Luis, Lina."

Luis was built like a linebacker, a good foot taller than his mother. His head was shaved, and she guessed he was about twenty.

Who could say no to Wendy?

The weather that week had been sloppy: sleet and rain, and then the temperatures dove at night so everything froze over. Catalina

found herself entertaining strange fantasies: What if she were crossing the street and slipped and broke her leg? What if a taxi skidded
and ran her over, paralyzing her from the waist down? Now it was
sleeting, but on Broadway they managed to catch a cab heading to
the West Side Highway.

"What is this place?" she asked when they were on their way.

"You'll like Baracoa," said Wendy. "It's a little Chino-Latino joint.
Chino-Latino like you, honey."

"I'm half Japanese."

"What, *nena?*" Wendy asked.

It always made Catalina uncomfortable when people asked about
her background. People in the salsa world, however, seemed exces-
sively interested, would nod sagely when they found out she was
Cuban. *That's why you dance like that.* She told Wendy and Luis about
her Japanese grandparents who had farmed pineapples on the Isla de
Pinos, now Isla de la Juventud, and how her parents had met at the
University of Havana. That her father had suffered greatly when his
tobacco factory was nationalized, and had died shortly afterward.
She did not mention that he had committed suicide, nor that it had
been she who had found him hanging from a beam in his office.

"You have family there?" Wendy asked.

"Some of my dad's people live around Pinar, but we haven't
heard from them in years."

"Japan?"

"There, too, but I don't know them."

Luis said, "Japan would be cool. We should go, Mami."

"DR first, honey. You never met your *ti-ti* in Puerto Plata."

This exchange had the feeling of an ongoing discussion.

Baracoa was on Broadway, just north of Houston. The three of
them were waved in for free and all the way to the dance floor it was
kiss kiss kiss; Let me introduce you to *mi buen amiga.* "*Feliz
cumpleaños,*" people were saying to Wendy.

"You didn't tell me it was your birthday."

"Yeah, *nena*, double fours."

"You don't look it."

"Mambo keeps me young. That, plus a lot of you-know-what."
Wendy winked at her.

When they got a table at the edge of the dance floor, Catalina immediately felt at home, although this was about as far away from the Copa as you could get. The floor was splintery and sodden with spilled beer, the ambience just this side of sleazy, the band heavy on off-key trombones.

"Honey, get us some mineral water," Wendy said to her son. She, too, seemed more relaxed here than at the Copa. For Catalina's benefit she pointed out who was who. Some of the faces Catalina recognized, but here the groups were clearly segregated. You could practically draw a floor plan. There were the dazzling show-offs from Puerto Domingo—the Spanish Harlem enclave that was Mambo Peligroso's main rival, and Jimmy Anton's intermediate class held nearby on Fourteenth Street, plus a sprinkling of Arthur Murray devotees, as well as the ubiquitous Eddie Torres crowd. Always in evidence at Baracoa, Wendy said, was Big 'Berto, black and heavy-lidded with his red silk fan inlaid with silver, holding court at the corner table near the band and chatting up every pretty new thing.

And then there were the imports—wild men from Cuba, gentle two-steppers from Colombia, exhibitionists from Argentina—as well as the usual mix of Village locals who'd never taken a class in their lives but came for the music.

Catalina watched, studying. The Eddie Torres boys had their hands all over their partners, with lots of checks and contratwists, and the women tended to have the most isolation in their body movements, resulting in that disjointed effect she coveted so much. Jimmy's students were jazzy and loose, flexible-armed, soft-toed, a swingy style. But most impressive to her eyes was the Puerto Domingo crew. They were as syncopated as the Eddie Torres people, but their footwork was even more intricate and creative; they did multiple dips, low spins, footwork so complicated she lost track of the beat as she watched. The women were uniformly young and curvaceous in tight T-shirts and jeans and blood-red lipstick, and they never smiled, as if following took every ounce of their concentration, which it probably did. Knees high, arms sharp, shoulders back in a street stance, they were ready for anything.

All these dancers, according to Wendy, owed a debt to the great Eddie Torres, who had revolutionized mambo by categorizing shine steps and naming them. Besides the breaking-on-two rhythm, shines were what made Bronx-style mambo unique.

The man with the dark full hair and angelic hands, with whom Wendy had been dancing when Catalina first saw her on the floor of the Copa, sat at the bar surrounded by a gaggle of girls. Catalina pointed him out to Wendy.

"That's Jimmy Anton."

"You guys look good together."

"He's been trying to pirate me away from Tuerto for years. He and Effy from PD."

"PD?"

"Puerto Domingo."

As Luis came back with their waters Wendy was pulled out onto the dance floor. She was looking especially feline that night in a low-cut V-neck tee, tight spandex pants, and high-heeled boots, all black. Luis held his hand out to Catalina. "Just a minute," she said, and changed into her dance shoes while he waited.

She still had trouble following new partners. In class El Tuerto would correct her specifically and relentlessly: *Right arm relaxed, let your elbow bend, feel the push and pull.* She would try to make her mind blank, her arms like spaghetti. For a while it would work and then he'd start picking on her again. "You're anticipating. Keep your hands close together on the double spin, otherwise you'll make it hard for him." She'd discovered this trick: closing her eyes. It heightened all other senses: hearing the music, feeling the lead—and also created the kind of trust needed for a perfect follow.

Why do I love this so much? Why do I feel so at home on the dance floor?

Luis was a good lead, stable, with large soft hands and perfect timing. He was gentle, single turns only, waiting for her to finish a move before he started another. Now Catalina could see the resemblance to his mother, something around the nose and eyes. Mischievous and sad at the same time.

The band had a distinctive raunchy sound, and as Catalina would come to know, varied from week to week, depending on who was sitting in, but the repertoire was always the same: old Tito Puente standards like "Babarabatiri" and "Guaguancó Margarita," as well as the house favorite, the cha-cha-chá "Sopa de Langosta." They were dancing now to "Cuando Te Veo," and when it was over, they went back to their table and watched Wendy, who was on the floor with a black man in a pink polo shirt. He was putting her through her paces, whipping her into free spins, swinging her into hesitations with his legs open so she could do her lunges, her left toe sliding between his feet like an arrow.

Puerto Domingo, Catalina guessed, and it turned out she was right.

"Mami's showing off," Luis said.

"Isn't that what this dance is about? Showing off?"

"Sometimes."

Someone yelled, "Happy Birthday, Monita!" as Wendy walked back to the table.

"Monita?" Catalina asked.

Wendy didn't answer but said: "Don't look now, but here's Big 'Berto."

The grandiose man came up to their table and made a deep bow, snapping open his fan with a flourish like Three Little Maids from School. He kissed Wendy.

"*Feliz cumpleaños, mi amor.* May I steal your friend?"

'Berto danced on the three, which was on the bass instead of the *clave.* He started her out slow, giving her a basic and then a cross-body into a single right spin, the classic sequence El Tuerto claimed would tell you all you needed to know about any partner.

'Berto, maybe because of his size, did not move a lot, barely shifting his weight. His hooded eyes were sly.

"You like this? You like dancing with your teddy bear?"

Catalina laughed and nodded.

'Berto hooked her into him, close, pressing his right hand into her lower back, a two-second grind, until she started to resist. He immediately let her go.

"*No te preocupes,*" he said. "It's just for show."

Show, my ass, she thought, but for the rest of the dance he was a gentleman.

There was a flurry at the edge of the floor, and she saw that El Tuerto had arrived and was doing the kiss and greet. Some of the girls were defecting from Jimmy to go over. These teachers were like royalty.

The next song, Puente's "Ran Kan Kan," turned out to be

Wendy's birthday dance. The guys formed a circle and took turns with her. *Gang bang,* Wendy would later describe it, laughing. With each pass they upped the ante—a double spin, a triple, a quad, this kind of dip, that kind of dip. With Wendy you could not see the cue, she responded so instantaneously—*How does she do it?* Catalina wondered for the thousandth time. Luis started with a cross-body, a couple of turns. Big Hank from their class did the exact figure they had learned that evening. Carlos spun her ten times in a row. Jimmy took her into a series of switch places in double time. With the guy in the pink shirt she did her trademark crossovers ending in a split. Her last partner was El Tuerto, who gave her a couple of triple pretzels before leading her into a series of traveling spins and a spectacular dip that involved her falling straight back to the floor while he cradled her neck.

Of course everyone went nuts, whistling and clapping and shouting. There was no way Wendy was going to sit down after that. Luis went off to talk with friends, and Catalina ordered a glass of the house red and sat by herself at the table watching the endless show mambo dancers put on. High-energy and free-wheeling, everyone was looser here than they were at the Copa. El Tuerto did a two on one with Wendy and a Puerto Domingo girl, and afterward she watched him whisper something to Wendy, who gave him an answer that made him laugh uproariously. He slapped her on the ass and must have left right after that because Catalina didn't see him again. Toward midnight the lights came up, revealing everyone sweaty, drunk, disoriented, but determined to dance out every last note. The band dragged the song on and on, the tumbadora player in an impromptu solo, then the bongos, the lead guitar. A clean-cut white guy in dress shirt and jeans asked Catalina to dance. He stepped on the first beat and reminded her of Richard, the kind of liberal preppy who liked to backpack through third-world countries, the kind who always hit on her.

"You're fabulous," he shouted through the music. "Who do you study with?"

"Oswaldo Melendez."

"Who?"

"Tuerto."

"You're kidding."

"Why should I be kidding?"

"I hear nobody lasts in his class."

"So far so good."

He tried another tack. *"De donde eres?"*

"New York," she said in her best Smith accent.

"I mean really."

She raised her eyebrows at him, and he shut up.

Maybe she did have some Latina attitude after all.

The band ended on a long sloppy chord and the vocalist shouted: *"Esta canción es para tí, Monita,"* and Wendy blew him a kiss. When she came back to the table, wiping the sweat from under her eyes with her forefingers, Catalina asked her; "So did you have a good birthday?"

"It's not over yet. Luis, honey, come here." Wendy's son was wearing a blue-jean jacket, a fact that his mother only just seemed to notice. "That all you have on?"

"I'll be okay, Mami. I'm just walking to the train." He kissed her. "See you at home."

"He's not coming with us?"

"He has to get up early for class. You ever hear of Belmont Lounge?"

It turned out that half the people at Baracoa were headed to just that spot, within walking distance north of Union Square. It had stopped sleeting, and now the streets were icy. Wendy took Catalina's arm as they walked. Belmont Lounge was choking with smoke, and the dance floor was industrial carpeting, but the salsa—old records from the sixties—was faster than fast and hotter than hot. It was so crowded and the floor was so slow you couldn't really do anything, but Catalina got up with man after man, not remembering their names or even what they looked like, and let herself be led without thinking. The preppy guy, she was relieved to see, was not in evidence. She escaped to the back garden to get some air, which is where Wendy found her.

"There you are, *nena*."

"I was getting hot."

"Yeah, you *are* pretty hot."

Was Wendy flirting?

"We got one more stop, *mami*."

"It's almost two."

"It's my *birthday*. Please?"

Out on the street again Catalina said, "I better go home. I have a bunch of papers to grade."

"Half an hour, I promise. Look, I'll catch us a cab."

Wendy waved randomly, and as if by magic a cab careened around the corner and stopped in front of them. They headed southeast to a dive between First and Avenue A where transvestites worked the bar and trust-fund cokeheads drowned in red banquettes while a half a dozen die-hards danced close and wild in the candle-punctuated darkness. The music was Latin LPs again, but slower. A woman wailed over the tumbadoras, and Wendy said, "Remember this name: La Lupe."

Catalina was so tired she felt as though she were in a trance. She ordered a glass of Merlot. Wendy wanted club soda.

"Don't you drink?" Catalina asked her.

"Not my poison. It's a long story. I'll tell you someday."

"Bum a cigarette?"

"Be my guest," said Wendy, and pushed the pack across the table.

"I really like Luis."

"Yeah, he's a good boy."

"Tell me something."

"Anything, *nena*."

"Are you and Tuerto, you know, involved?"

"We're dance partners."

"And?"

"Sex is the best way to ruin a partnership."

"But it happens."

"Of course it happens."

"So are you?"

"My, you're curious tonight." Wendy reached up and, in a now-familar gesture, tightened the elastic around her ponytail. "Are you interested in him?"

"Tuerto? Are you kidding?"

Wendy exhaled a stream of smoke and said casually: "He thinks you have gorgeous tits."

Catalina concentrated on not coughing out her own cigarette smoke. "How do you know that?"

"He told me. Better than Angie's, is what he said."

"Jesus. You *gossip* about us?"

Wendy put out her cigarette, got up, and extended her hand to Catalina.

"Oh God, I can't."

"Sweetheart, you do it with men all the time."

"I'm drunk," she lied.

"So much the better."

It was strange to dance with someone smaller than herself. In that narrow aisle between the tables, where it was so dark she might as well have been dancing blind, Catalina closed her eyes again. It was delicate, she realized, this fine art of following, of surrender to a partner no matter who he or she might be, of softening your hands, the small of your back, so that you were ready for anything. Wendy, unlike the boys, did not lead by force, but with subtle changes of pressure so that you were already in the middle of a move without realizing you were doing it. She lifted both of Catalina's hands and guided her into a double spin—*one-two-three*—with her wrists so close together they might have been bound. El Tuerto would have approved.

The singer was La Lupe and the song was "Fiebre."

They were the only ones left on the floor. The other couples had either left or were languishing at various tables. A businessman had picked up one of the transvestites, and they were huddled together at the far corner of the bar. Catalina spotted the bartender, a sinuous black woman with a crew cut and flimsy white undershirt that clearly displayed her small round breasts, observing them dance as she leaned against the cash register. She was smoking, using an ornate ivory cigarette holder.

"That woman is watching us."

"Who? Oh, don't worry. That's just Omara."

"She looks jealous."

"Does she? Let's give her something to look at."

Wendy pulled Catalina closer as 'Berto had done, but this time she did not resist. The trance feeling was stronger than ever. Wendy did not grind. Her hair smelled like cinnamon and sweat. When a woman seduced you, it was so different. It was delicate, almost ambiguous, with lots of ways out in case you changed your mind.

When the song ended, Wendy led her over to the bar and introduced her to the bartender, who folded her arms over her little breasts and examined Catalina impassively.

"Pretty," she said.

Wendy bent over and whispered, "I'm sorry, *nena,* but I have some business. You don't mind taking the train home alone, do you?"

You're the one who usually takes the train home alone, Catalina had to keep herself from snapping. She shook her head. "I'll be fine." The trance had lifted and now she had a foul taste in her mouth.

She couldn't find a cab, so had to take the subway, which took almost half an hour to arrive, and then walk five freezing blocks to her apartment. Once in bed, she couldn't sleep. Even after she brushed her teeth her mouth was sour from wine and cigarettes. Finally she got up and drank two glasses of water standing at the kitchen sink. She decided she was hungry and made popcorn with butter and devoured it standing by the stove.

She was wide awake now, craving a cigarette. It was clear Wendy had brought her along to that last dive specifically to make Omara jealous. And she had lied about El Tuerto. *Sex is the best way to ruin a partnership.* What kind of bullshit was that?

Drinking her third glass of water, she decided that all of them—Wendy and Tuerto and Carlos and Angie—were a narcissistic and promiscuous bunch, wrapped up in convoluted sex and mind games. She'd be better off keeping her distance. Better off emulating the Japanese girls, who, as far as she could tell, stuck to dancing only. She would attend class and go to clubs and leave early. If anyone flirted, she would be *Muda,* as the kids in Havana used to call her.

They could gossip about her all they wanted.

She would keep to herself and stay safe.

Like many before her, Catalina had underestimated the seductive power of mambo. That Friday night she attended a baby shower and found it torture spending an entire evening with a bunch of decorous thirty-something women in an Upper East Side townhouse, oohing and aahing over receiving blankets and crib mobiles.

She couldn't wait to get out of there.

Maybe if it's over early enough I can run home and get my dance shoes and cab down to the Copa.

The party dragged on and on, starting with catered hors d'oeuvres and ending with cheesecake and coffee served by the maid. Catalina ate more than anyone else.

"You're looking good these days," someone said.

"I'm dancing salsa."

"Oooh, salsa," they said, with faces that looked as if they wanted to be invited.

They didn't get that this wasn't a hobby, something she did on the side.

It was her life.

The following Tuesday night the first person she saw in class happened to be Wendy, who merely waved hi and then turned back to the mirror where she was teaching Angie how to style a pivot. It seemed to Catalina that Wendy was standing extra close and doing a little too much touching as she showed Angie how to cross her arms over her chest before lifting them up.

Remember, Muda.

She took her time about changing her shoes and was relieved when El Tuerto entered, ten minutes late as usual, and began the shines. After the break he waved the class to attention.

"*¡Oigame!* Today we're gonna do hesitations!"

There was a unanimous groan from the men. Hesitations were for girls. The lead stopped his partner, either in front of him, or off to the side, supporting her palm on palm so she could show off the best of her fancy footwork.

Despite herself Catalina was excited. Now she'd finally learn some of the tricks that made Wendy such a coveted partner.

"We'll do something *fácil.* The crossover. The paintbrush. The Tropicana kick."

Wendy demonstrated. Her crossovers were tiny, flickering, pristine. Cross cross cross pause. Cross cross cross pause. The paintbrush was pretty: you brushed your foot in, pigeon-toed, and then flicked it outward, then the same thing with the other foot. The Tropicana kick was Radio City–showgirl style, but you did it contained, at an angle to your partner.

No lunge. No split. Catalina was disappointed, not that she could have done a split to save her life.

El Tuerto announced that first the boys would partner the girls doing hesitations, and then the girls would partner the boys. This, he said, would teach the follows not to depend too heavily on their partners, and the leads not to be too controlling.

The idea, Catalina had to admit, was genius.

There weren't enough leads, so Wendy and El Tuerto both played boys. The crossovers Catalina got first try, although El Tuerto told her she was bouncing. In the floor, *this dance is in the floor.* Bouncing was the sure sign of a novice. The preppy guy at Baracoa had been bouncy. Her Tropicana kick was okay, although she foresaw hours of refining it in front of the mirror to get the angle of the knee just right, the toe hot and quick. It was the paintbrush that did her in. She could manage it with her right foot, but not the left. She tried not to look at Angie on the other side of the room, flicking away, tossing her mane of hair in time.

El Tuerto said nothing, just shook his head. Which was actually worse than if he *had* said something.

When he had them switch, the guys were loose and jokey, making fun of each other in Spanish. "Am I leaning too hard?" they kept asking. Hank was afraid to give her any pressure at all, no matter how much she reassured him that she was strong enough to support him. Carlos not only went through the whole routine—four crossovers, four paintbrushes, four Tropicana kicks—without a hitch, but then repeated the whole thing double time.

"Why are you even in this class?"

"It's my warm-up for Thursdays."

"What happens on Thursdays?"

"The *real* Mambo Peligroso."

"Excuse me."

"Don't worry, you'll get there someday."

"Gee, thanks."

With El Tuerto she was nervous. His large palms and fingers

were callused and felt alive to her, even in the passive position of being led.

"I can't feel what you're doing with your feet," she said.

"You're not supposed to."

Wendy looked alert and happy, as if she had a secret.

"Hey, *nena*. You're supposed to watch my feet and admire me."

Muda.

"How will I know when you're done?"

"I'll let you know." And Wendy did, sliding down into a split and back.

Catalina almost dropped her.

"Loosen up, will you? Don't be such a white girl."

"Fuck you," said Catalina. It just came out; she couldn't help it.

The corners of Wendy's mouth twitched, but she didn't say anything.

You can't out-Latina a Latina. And whether Catalina liked it or not, Wendy was La Reina Mambera. Mambo Queen. That's what she'd heard some of the Puerto Domingo guys calling her at Baracoa.

El Tuerto put on "Perdoname" by Gilberto Santa Rosa, a song that usually sent Catalina into ecstasies. It was the live version, where the crowd starts clapping the *clave* and Gilberto is improvising: "I get down on my knees and beg you, beg you, Forgive me, Forgive me, tonight at Carnegie Hall."

One-two-three, five-six-seven.

For the first time ever mambo was not making Catalina happy.

After class Wendy disappeared into the ladies' room and reemerged in her silver halter and tightest black pants. "See you next week," she said to the room at large, put on her coat, and left.

By now Catalina had other buddies in the class besides Wendy: Hank and Carlos and the sweet middle-aged couple, Mindy and Tino. But things were different now. As Muda, she was on her own. Who needed Wendy, or that sadist El Tuerto? She'd start going to Eddie Torres, or maybe even Puerto Domingo. In a couple of months people would be asking: Who is that girl? Where did she come from?

Changing into her boots, she watched the activity around her, thinking how superficial everyone was. As usual the Japanese girls were conferring with one another as they recorded the hesitation sequence in their notebooks. Carlos was showing Hank the gold dance sneakers he'd just bought. Angie practiced her pivot in front of the mirrors with her arms up, making sure everyone got a good view of her belly-button ring. All they cared about were their bodies and how they looked on the floor. All they talked about was music and who had done what last night at this club or that.

She was no better, but that didn't mean she had to socialize with them.

She was about to hand El Tuerto her twenty dollars when he put his arm around her shoulders.

"Don't worry, Lina," he said.

"Worry about what?"

"The paintbrush. It'll come." He smiled that glamorous smile, and she felt herself blushing. *He thinks you have gorgeous tits.* Then one of the other girls walked up behind him and tapped his shoulder and he turned around, his attention switched, just like that, as easy as shifting weight.

The *real* Mambo Peligroso, what did that mean?

5

Catalina

You do not find the rhythm. The rhythm finds you.

———∞———

At a minute before noon on an unseasonably hot day in the beginning of May, she climbed the last of the five flights of stairs for her
first private. By now she was in good enough shape so that her
breathing was still regular when she reached the studio. The door
was open, and he was over by the windows gazing out over Broadway as he talked to someone on his cell. *Tuerto,* as she thought of
him now, dropping the formal "El." "Yeah. Yeah. Okay. Mmm-
hmmm. All right." Somehow she knew it was a woman. He was
wearing faded blue jeans molded to his body, a pale aqua T-shirt, and
his summer dance shoes, black with soft uppers and hard soles that
sounded like taps on the worn floorboards as he paced. In sunlight
the studio looked shabbier than it did at night—you could see the
streaks on the mirrors, the slight unevenness of the floor, the spackle

showing through the ochre paint on the walls. For the first time she could actually read the gold lettering on the middle window, which said, in a backward arch, ALEGRE DANCE.

He hung up and came over to kiss her. "How are you, Lina?" There was not a hint of flirtation in his voice. Catalina recognized the tone from her own teaching, the barrier she had to keep up in order to discourage lascivious male students, needy female students, and at the same time allow enough warmth so that they would trust her.

Still, his manner made her feel like a teenager. "I'm okay; how are you," she said, plunking herself down on a folding chair, letting her bag crash gracelessly to the floor. She bent over to change into socks and dance shoes, and when she looked up he was across the room going through his CD book.

He moves like a ghost.

There was no air-conditioning and only one medium-size fan going—like many dancers Tuerto believed that sweating was good for you—but he looked cool and composed as he gestured for her to take her place beside him in front of the mirrors. Even in the middle of the day there was a whiff of sandalwood about his person, although he was sporting an uncharacteristic five o'clock shadow.

"Let's get started. I want you to turn for me. Simple turns. First a right one."

Head up, hands up, forward on the left foot, pivot, feet together, left again, pivot, feet together.

"Now a left."

Theoretically left turns were harder for a right-handed person like Catalina. For some reason, however, lefts had come easier to her from the start. You had to rotate a little more, but you got good leverage on that first forward step.

"Mmmm-hmmm." If she had been expecting praise, she wasn't going to get any. In the mirror Tuerto was stroking his stubbly chin as he considered something. "Okay," he finally said. "Your footwork is passable, but we're going to have to fine-tune the weight shift. Also, your styling leaves something to be desired. There are some very basic elements you haven't gotten yet. First, spotting. You're spotting your right turn but not your left. You've got a good center of gravity, and you can get away with not spotting now, with these simple turns, but it's bad form and will prevent you from going on to anything more advanced. I also want to see you have more control when you change your weight. Think about it while you're doing it. Count, if you have to. And watch your arms, honey. Flailing never looks good, in a man or a woman. Keep it tight. Like this."

He demonstrated a left turn, shifting his weight precisely over each hip, his center of gravity low, his hands following his feet with a motion like playing the tumbadoras.

"Okay. Now give me a right."

She gritted her teeth and spun slowly, trying with all her might to control her arms.

"Better. Again. Relax your shoulders."

She did as she was told.

"*Está bien.* Now give me five in a row, traveling. Like this."

Turning away from the mirror, Tuerto did a series of right turns in a line diagonally across the studio, spotting ostentatiously, giving the effect that his head was turning his body. In effect, pirouettes. Then he spun five times back to the mirror. After the last turn, he drew his right arm up and then over his head, front to back.

"*Como así.*"

Catalina took a deep breath, pointed her right toe.

I am light, I am very, very light.

And went.

Trying to keep it tight, aerodynamic, but it was so much work to contain, to control her arms—trying to concentrate on the *center of the spin,* that ephemeral point around which she turned. She felt it at the Copa with Carlos and Wendy, felt it when she was practicing alone in her apartment, but it eluded her now in this sunny studio, in front of this man.

Me encanta tus vueltas.

She remembered to keep her back straight, her head absolutely level. Counting: *one-two-three-four-five,* and coming out of the fifth turn, she tried to imitate Tuerto's combing motion with her arm.

He was shaking his head. "Your spotting was good, your arms were okay, but I don't know what the hell you're doing with your right foot. Some kind of weird squiggle. Who taught you that?"

Now, finally, she flushed.

"Again. Without the squiggle."

This time she had to spin directly toward him, and it was his face she had to spot, with both his eyes, the good one and the blind one, watching her. The sun was behind him so she couldn't see his expression. She put all her concentration into her wayward right foot, willing it to be precise and steady, a perfect pivot.

He counted for her: *"Un-dos-tres-cuatro-cinco. Otra vez."*

She spun away from him.

Un-dos-tres-cuatro-cinco.

Finally she was starting to feel it, although not as true as when she was on the dance floor or by herself at home wearing socks.

"This is what I want," Tuerto said. "I want you to look like a puppet. *Ven acá.*"

Catalina went to stand in front of him, trying her best not to seem sulky. He said, "Don't take this the wrong way; I'm not being fresh," and put one hand on her shoulder, the other lightly on the opposite pelvic bone. "Right turn. *Despacio.* Head last. Watch yourself in the mirror like you're so beautiful you can't bear to look away."

First her hips went, then her shoulders one after the other, and finally her head, his hands restraining each body part until the last moment. She felt like a deck of cards being shuffled. Like an old-fashioned black and white newsreel where the frames follow one another jerkily. She felt as if she were flickering.

She could hear Tuerto punching out the *clave* under his breath. *Pah-pah-pah, pah-PAH.*

"How did that feel?"

"Good," she admitted.

"Now let's talk about phrasing. Do you play a musical instrument?"

"Piano in high school. A little flute."

"Too bad no percussion." She thought of the summer she'd played the tumbadora with Guillermo but said nothing. "Okay. A single spin is three beats. You know you can make all three beats even. PAH-PAH-PAH. Or emphasize the first, or the last. Or stop—PAH-PAAAAH-PAH—just a hair longer on the second. If you are a beginner, I will lead you the way I want to, to how *I* hear the music. But most men will just raise their arm—so—and the phrasing and footwork are up to you."

Tuerto took the remote out of his back jeans pocket and pointed it at the CD player. The song was "Conciencia," off the *Gilberto Santa Rosa Live at Carnegie Hall* CD. He demonstrated the phrasing on the turns: first even and legato, then emphasizing the first beat, and finally her favorite—drawing out the second beat. There was something else he was doing besides slowing down in the middle of the turn, and for the life of her Catalina could not figure it out. Then, all of a sudden, she did.

With the song still playing, Tuerto came over and got her into ballroom position. "Now you're gonna show me what you've learned today."

He gave her a cross-body into a single right turn, then a left, then a double right and a double left, and finally a triple right. Coming out of the triple right he checked her and let her go into a triple the other way. On the single turns he allowed her to phrase; on the others he timed it for her. For some reason Catalina felt herself stepping higher, lifting her arches more than she usually did. The song ended, Gilberto chatted with the audience, and then "Perdoname" came on.

He let her go. "Ah. You know what's special about this song?"

"I love it."

"The *rhythm*, Lina, the rhythm."

"It's got a reverse *clave*."

"Very good. And how do you dance a reverse *clave*?"

"The same way you do a normal one."

"Which is how?"

"Listen for the first beat of the first measure."

"*Si, señorita. Por favor, escucha.*" He extracted the remote and another CD spun into place. "Pedro Navaja," that great Rubén Blades classic that begins with police sirens and then goes into Rubén singing over pattering congas. Tuerto began to dance by himself—a basic, a grapevine, a couple of spins, and then, at the place when the orchestra comes in, syncopations and flick kicks and little skips. Rubén's voice was cut off by another man singing drunkenly, then came the orchestra, then the chorus, then Rubén, then the orchestra and police sirens, then Rubén, then the chorus. To Catalina it sounded like a traffic jam.

But she was listening.

Tuerto stopped dancing and turned around to face her. "Did you hear what happened?"

"The *clave* switched in the music. And then switched back. And so forth."

He smiled. "No, honey, the *clave* did not switch. The arrangement switched in relation to the *clave*."

"Whatever."

"This is important. Now what do you do when the arrangement switches like that?"

"You dance in place. To make up the measure."

"That's an option. But in this song, it switches too much. So you just dance on the other side of it, wait till it comes out right again. I'll count it; you dance it with me. Just a simple shine routine. Two basics, four Suzy-Q's, left turn, semi-right, semi-left, double right."

Suzy-Q's were the first shine any *mambero* learned. You crossed one foot over the other and twisted. It was a simple step, but there was something so Bronx about it. Tuerto cued the music back to the beginning of the song, and they danced, side by side, he slightly in front of her so she could watch his footwork. He kept it simple, adding only crossovers and a double spin to the end of the turn pattern.

She listened for the *clave* as if it were going to save her life.

One-two-three, five-six-seven. One-two-three, five-six-seven.

I'm not so terrible. I don't look like Wendy or Angie, but I'm not so terrible.

When the song was over, they stopped. She was sweating; he was not. "Okay," he said. "That was very good. Do you have the notebook and pen I asked you to bring?"

"I'm listening."

"What I am about to say is of tantamount importance."

"I'll remember."

"This week I want you to practice turns. By yourself. In front of the mirror. Singles only for the first two days, then you can graduate to doubles. No triples. I'm serious. We're working on technique here, not speed. When you have it down, we can start to style. Are you listening?"

"Yes."

"And also this. I notice you smoke. Try to quit."

"Wendy smokes."

"And she shouldn't. Quit. Otherwise, it's not worth my while to teach you. *Hola, nena.*"

He was no longer talking to her but to someone who had just entered—a girl in a sleeveless white dance tunic and leggings. It took Catalina a moment to recognize her as the blonde from the Copa, the one the other girls had called Soni Bologna. She walked straight up to Tuerto, and he kissed her on the mouth. The diamond studs in her ears caught the sunlight. Catalina could understand why Angie hated her.

Catalina turned away and sat down to change her shoes. By the time she had finished and dug into her bag for three twenties, he was talking on his cell again and the blonde was on the floor in front of the mirrors, stretching.

Tuerto hung up. "All right, Lina, I'll see you in class then. And next Wednesday, same time."

"See you," she said. And then, reluctantly, "Thank you."

Outside, she reached into her bag and took out her notebook and pen and wrote: *Body wave on beat 2 of pivot turn.*

The first couple of days after her private she did exactly as she'd been instructed, simple spins, two hours every morning in her foyer, as if she were a beginner, which she reminded herself, she still was. No coffee mug—she had to concentrate on her arms. She started without music: first right spins, then lefts, as slowly and with so much control she felt as if she were doing t'ai-chi. Then she added the arms, the delicate wind and then unwinding into that pretty hustle reach coming out of the right spins, an angled reach out of the lefts.

By Saturday she was bored. She started to dance to Juan Luis Guerra's "Lagrimosa," based on the "Lacrimosa" section from Mozart's Requiem. It was actually a bachata, not a mambo; and as well as having the wrong rhythm, it was way too fast. Tuerto would have not approved, but spinning to "Lagrimosa" made her high, especially when she was doing the five pirouettes in a row.

Un-dos-tres-cuatro-cinco.

Spot. Spot. Spot. Spot. Spot.

In her heart of hearts Catalina knew that learning mambo was not as critical as, say, mastering the language of a new country. But what a pure rush it was to feel her memory working at maximum capacity, to ingrain exactly what she saw and heard into her muscles, her bones, her very blood—she could not express, even to herself. Never had she paid so much attention to anything, never had she *wanted* to pay so much attention to anything.

That said, she wouldn't have given Tuerto high marks as a teacher. He was manipulative and impatient, a classic narcissist. Tyrannical and a pushover at the same time, the kind of bully that could be stopped in his tracks by a woman's tears. Catalina had seen this more than once in class during a particularly grueling turn pattern.

What Tuerto did have was an exceptionally extroverted dance style which made him easy to watch and imitate. His eye was brilliant—sometimes she wished not so brilliant—and when he felt like it, he was good at explaining, breaking things down. Compliments were rare and doled out strategically. When she was just about to give up on a shoulder isolation, for instance, he would tell her casually: "Your center of gravity is great. That's one thing you'll never have to fix."

Otherwise both in privates and class he continued to be relentlessly critical. "This dance isn't only about feet," he snapped after correcting her wrist position for the hundredth time.

"What's so fucking important about hands?" The teenager again. She couldn't help it.

"If you'd bothered to do any research, you'd know that in mambo the hands and arms are based on flamenco. Tap feet, West Coast–swing slot, hustle turns, flamenco arms and hands."

He taught her the Bronx setup, twisting the left foot to get torque for a right turn, and then something called the articulated triple right spin—first two turns on the right foot, then tuck it under and weight on the left. He drilled her on other fundamentals: crossovers, lunges, spot turns, wraps, dips. With his coaching she was finally able to master the paintbrush. He noted that her left knee was weaker than the right, and told her that she might have a meniscus tear. "Wrap it," he said. "No surgery?" she asked. He gave her an ironic smile. "You want to be out of commission? Wrap it and take Aleve."

After some cajoling, he even showed her that heart-stopping move he did with Wendy, the one in which it looked as if he were about to choke her. It was actually a shoulder spin, the woman's head was bent down to maneuver under the palm of her partner's hand, which brushed her neck.

This move was called, appropriately, the guillotine.

At the end of each lesson he tested her. He led her by the hands, wrists, elbow, shoulder, the wings of a long chiffon scarf she happened to be wearing one day.

Once he remarked out of the blue: "I'm thinking you could make your spins cleaner."

"What?"

"Don't get bent out of shape. Your spins are okay. What I'm saying is, you could make them perfect. They could become your trademark."

This was worth listening to, so she did.

He made an "X" on the studio floor with masking tape. "I'm going to lead you right onto that spot, take you into a triple, and you are not going to deviate one millimeter. Got it?"

For that entire hour she practiced spinning on the spot. After the lesson, on the way home, she stopped at a hardware store and bought a roll of masking tape.

June began with the Puerto Rican Day Parade. Catalina stood on the steps of Saint Patrick's along with Hank and Mindy and Tino and others from the beginners' class and watched Las Chicas de la Calle dance by, all in white, led by Tuerto and Wendy. He looked strangely small, wearing white jeans and a tank, and she realized for the first time how fine-boned he was, almost as delicate as Wendy. The girls had on white halters and shorts. From somewhere in the crowd Catalina heard a woman's shrill voice: *"Juepa, 'Dita!"* When she looked around it seemed to be coming from a heavyset middle-aged woman brandishing the Boricua flag.

As if they had strategized to contrast with Mambo Peligroso, Puerto Domingo marched in black leather outfits reminiscent of S and M gear. You could pick out the red of the girls' lipstick fifty yards away. There were the Eddie Torres dancers, in sequins, and bringing up the rear, Jimmy Anton with his current partner, a lithe black woman with the lines of a champion figure skater, not unlike Wendy.

Catalina's six-week summer break came just in time for her to show off her new Tuerto-honed prowess. She went into full throttle, going out every night: SOB's on Monday, the Copa or Baracoa on Tuesday, Nell's or Spice on Wednesday, Latin Quarter or Belle Epoque on Thursday, the Copa or Wild Palm in the Bronx on Friday. It didn't matter if she went alone because she would invariably run into dancers she knew. It was Salsa Nation, and she was part of it. She danced with doormen, taxi drivers, contractors, exterminators, investment bankers, lawyers, surgeons, poets, filmmakers, computer geeks. Every skin tone you could imagine was represented, as well as every language, although Spanish predominated. At Nell's especially, the rapid-fire singsong of Cuban would turn her head. She didn't understand exactly, but it made her feel something, like someone familiar you see in the periphery of your vision walking down the street.

After her first experience at the Copa Catalina avoided drinking. It was well known that clubs had mixed feelings about serious *mamberos;* they livened up the atmosphere but did not spend at the bar. At Nell's and the Copa they'd search your bag and confiscate bottled water so when you were thirsty you'd have to buy it at five dollars a pop or go to the ladies' room and drink from the tap, which was what Catalina, on her limited budget, ended up doing, unless some man friend was buying her drinks—Hank usually, or occasionally Carlos, if Angie wasn't around.

Saturdays were for hobby dancers and the club DJs would play mostly merengue and house. Catalina stayed home and returned the phone messages her nondance friends had left during the week: "I know you're out dancing, but . . ." A couple of these friends hinted they'd like to join her on her nights out, but she discouraged them, saying clubs were noisy and stressful and overwhelming. These friends happened to be white, and when she thought about it later she realized she didn't want to be a tour guide. This was prejudiced thinking, racist even, but she couldn't help it.

As she had built up her CD collection, Catalina constructed a dance wardrobe. She'd noticed that the high-profile *mamberos* sported a trademark look: Wendy's black Spandex and boots, Angie's formfitting white, Sonia's pastel sheaths and kitten-heeled sandals, Tuerto's silk and satin shirts and peg-legged trousers. Catalina decided to make her own uniform flowered slip dresses, for which she combed the outdoor markets, and stilettos, an extra python pair in the same style as her regular brown.

Following instructions from Wendy, who had become friendly again although never as flirtatious as she'd been the night of her birthday, Catalina started powdering her face and wearing eyeliner and mascara and dark lipstick that matched the polish on her toenails. Made up, her reflection in the mirror surprised her. She looked old-fashioned, like Tía Ana in those photos of her sweet fifteen in Pinar del Río. But there was something else. For the first time, apart from the Asian cast of her eyes, she could see her mother in her face—Jun, with her high samurai cheekbones, her look of being half in the other world.

The more she dressed up, the more attention she got. Night after night she made her entrances, strutting down the steps of the Copa for instance, high-heeled, bold-mouthed, showing just enough cleavage, and every guy on the floor would turn to check her out. *Muda,* she'd say to herself, keeping her composure.

There was nothing like it. It made her understand why men dressed in drag.

At clubs Tuerto was always cordial but not once did he ask her to dance. It bothered her enough to ask Wendy why.

"Don't worry, *nena,* it's no reflection on your ability. The man just has issues."

"What kind of issues?"

"He's got a jones for you. He's keeping it on simmer until he gets some kind of response."

"What are you talking about?"

"You playin' with me, *mami*? He *wants* you."

It was Wendy who was playing with her. How could Catalina make a move? She'd never risk her alliance with Wendy, Wendy who was so much fun, who knew *everyone:* most of the dancers and many of the musicians—not only El Ruinseñor but Jimmy Bosch and Wayne Gorbea and all the members of the house band at Baracoa. Wendy would ask Wayne to play an extra-long *descarga* of "Cogelo," and she and Catalina would dance together until some guy would finally break in.

One Friday night—actually Saturday morning—after Wild Palm, they took the train to Washington Heights and over coffee and onion omelets and black beans and rice and a pack of cigarettes Catalina learned about Wendy's aborted gymnastics career, her days on the street, her girlfriend Isabella, and finally how Tuerto had taken her under his wing and given her a reason to live again. In turn Catalina told Wendy about arriving from Cuba at the age of eight, the muteness that was chalked up to trauma, how alienated she'd felt growing up in Massachusetts, her twenties with Richard, teaching ESL.

"Well you're in the right place now, honey," said Wendy, much as she had after Catalina's first Mambo Peligroso class. She leaned over the table and laid her bare forearm alongside Catalina's. "Seems to me you're getting darker."

Catalina laughed. There was no one like Wendy, nothing like mambo in New York City. On good nights, like tonight, she felt as if she'd been reborn. On the not-so-good nights—and they did happen, the ones when she didn't feel in the music or when she got a string of bad partners or when walking down the steps of the Copa made her seasick—she felt as if it were the first day of school in Miami, with all the kids staring at her and her foreign-looking mother.

But for better or worse she was in it now. Mambo had laid its claim on her.

She didn't broadcast her birthday, but somehow word leaked out, probably through Wendy, and that week after class there was a birthday dance. Tuerto, either out of mischievousness or in memory of their first private, put on "Pedro Navaja." The shifting *clave* separated the men from the boys—the only ones who finessed it were Carlos, Wendy, and, of course, Tuerto, who double dipped her so violently that one of her earrings fell off.

On the day of her birthday some nondance friends took her out to the East Village for tapas, in honor of what they still called her new hobby. When she got home there was a message on her machine: Guillermo singing "Cumpleaños Feliz."

She would never remember exactly why she didn't call him back. Had she been too tired? Had she sensed a tension in his voice that she didn't want to deal with, the same tension she'd heard when he'd called her Easter Sunday? Or had she just blown him off, taking it for granted that it was only Guillermo, who would always love her?

That night, though, she dreamed of a man—not dancing, not making love, but walking hand in hand with him through an empty brown and gray house with tunnel corridors. At first she thought it was Guillermo, as it always was in her dreams, but no, it was Tuerto. They wandered from room to room. In the last room he took out a machete and hacked at her feet, methodically, until she could no longer stand up. How could she bear this, the pain, all that blood, but she did, and when she bolted awake her heart was pounding hard enough to choke her.

Finally Catalina had gotten her wish: she was the new mystery girl, and everyone wanted a piece of her. At clubs she never sat down, dancing with dozens of different men as well as the usual suspects: gentlemanly Tino; Hank, whose bulk made her feel fragile; and Carlos, whose antics left her breathless and who flirted relentlessly—for him it was part of the dance. She could now usually follow whatever beat a partner pulled out of his hat; she even, one night at the Copa, got a lesson on something called Old Palladium Style. This syncopation made her high, especially during long, fast Tito Puente numbers. The man who taught her this esoteric rhythm had once been, he told her, King of the Palladium, as he was now King of the Copacabana.

But even he, she thought, had never had the charisma of her teacher, his arrogance, the thrilling cruelty of the lead when he thought she was not up to par. During privates, when the music was cranked up, instead of talking he had taken to giving her hand signals: *smaller steps, work from the diaphragm, loosen your right arm, loosen your left arm, faster, slower, you're off the beat, don't back lead, wait for me.* Because sign language had once been her only way of communicating Catalina was ultrasensitive to these signals. When it was obvious she had completely lost the beat—she could always hear the *clave*, but it occasionally would refuse to translate to her feet—he'd pull her close and dance her in place, their knees flexing, feet barely lifting off the floor.

This was what made her know she was doomed, because she so willingly let him have that kind of control.

She knew his body now, the smell of sandalwood hot off his skin getting stronger as the lesson progressed, the texture of the Egyptian cotton T-shirts he favored, his large palms and the long fingers that gave just the right amount of flex to signal a semi, single, double turn. His good eye, his blind eye, which seemed to be looking at her all the time, the effeminate nose, the pure cut of his mouth and jawline. His large feet in their hard-soled shoes, percussive, dead-on, relentless. And there was something else about him that was not exactly sex. Something that she could not name but that was irresistible.

She had no private the first week in August because of the Congreso de Salsa in Puerto Rico, where Wendy and Tuerto were performing. It was the longest week of Catalina's life. She imagined them on that final night bringing the house down and carrying home the crystal trophy and was surprised at her jealousy.

When she showed up for her next private, Tuerto said, without greeting her: "You should wear your hair loose."

"Why?"

"You could use it when you dance."

"It's too thick, that's why I braid it."

"Just take it down, will you? I'd like to see something."

She'd wanted to congratulate him about the trophy but as usual he'd thrown her off balance.

Slowly, she reached behind her and pulled off the elastic and fluffed her braid out. Standing behind her, he picked her hair, rippled and thick from being plaited, up off her shoulders with two hands.

She saw him in the mirror, considering its heft and texture, as if he were examining a bolt of cloth.

"*Que linda.*"

And then, instead of stroking it, or turning her around so he could kiss her as she half expected he might do, Tuerto actually did show her how she could play with it coming out of a turn, wrap it around her throat, then let it unravel—"This will drive the men crazy." Also how to toss it during a hesitation, as Angie did, or whip it around coming out of a cross-body. He demonstrated the gestures on himself, his long fingers flicking back a head of imaginary wavy hair, insinuating his shoulder as he let it fall across his face coming out of a spin. Catalina did not know why it was so erotic to watch a man being a girl. It would not have looked good on Richard, for instance, but on a Latin man it only accentuated his masculinity. He had her imitate him while he watched, standing in front of her, arms crossed over his chest.

"*Guapisima,*" he said.

Did he want her? She still couldn't be sure.

One-footed, Catalina spun three times in place, and after the flick of her fingers through her hair coming out of the last turn, without knowing she was going to do it, continued the gesture to reach down and draw her T-shirt over her head, almost playfully. Underneath she had on a flesh-colored sports bra, lacy, which she sometimes wore with nothing else on top while practicing at home. It was high noon, there were picture windows overlooking Broadway, and Soni Bologna was due in fifteen.

Catalina had never done anything so bold in her life. For a moment she thought he was going to tell her to put her shirt back on.

"*Ay.*" That was all he said before he leaned forward and took her by the wrist and led her away from the windows, toward the door of the studio, which he shut with the hand that wasn't gripping her. With surprising delicacy, he drew his fingertips over the sides of her breasts, and then bent down to lick them through the lace, dip the tip of his tongue into her cleavage. She didn't care that he was crude, that he went for what he wanted without kissing her on the lips first. Wendy had told her what he liked, and she let him have it.

His mouth on her neck, in her hair, his beard stubble scraping her cheek, one long forefinger sliding into her, what she had wanted for weeks and weeks.

They fucked standing up, his back against the door, her leggings pulled down and wrapped around one ankle, her inner thighs pressing against his ribs. He bit her left breast, right under the nipple, so hard she had to bite her own lip to keep from screaming.

"Ven," he said. *"Chinita linda, ven."*

And then she finally got it, about the Spanish. How all these years, without knowing, she had remembered, and now she was ready to speak again.

6

Oswaldo

*Anything, absolutely anything,
can happen on the dance floor.*

———∞∞∞———

The year was 1960, and I was a junior in high school. Over the years I've seen it all: the ballroom boys, the street kids, all the old hustlers claiming *they* were there, they know the style. But for my money there's nothing to beat the mambo as it was done at the Palladium Ballroom in my day by black and Spanish kids from Harlem and Brooklyn and the Bronx.

Ma wanted me to go to college, but I was never interested in anything school could give me. My father, who I never met, was a hotshot in the Peruvian delegation to the United Nations. They met, believe it or not, at the Palladium in 1944. He knocked Ma up, and shortly thereafter went back to his wife and four children in Lima, and we never saw or heard from him again.

Still, Ma wanted me to have his name, and so I was Oswaldo Niles Melendez until 1980, when I lost my eye. Then I dropped the Niles in case it was that that was bringing me bad luck.

When I was seven, Ma married this guy from our neighborhood in East New York, Pepi Delgado, who owned an exterminating business. My stepfather and I had little to say to each other. Once in a while I'd hear him complain to Ma that I was *flojo,* a lazy bum. Pepi gave my mother three daughters, one after another, which was fine with me you know because girls always have friends. The thing about Pepi, he was this kick-ass conga player. Around the house he always had on those old scratchy 78s that have kind of a round rhythm—the trumpets and flute and *tres* and piano bouncing around each other and the percussion like a merry-go-round. Very Cuban, which is what he was, from the city of Trinidad, to be exact, not to be confused with the Caribbean island of the same name. According to Pepi, Trinidad was very black, unlike Havana and the western part of the island, and bred the best musicians and dancers outside of Santiago de Cuba. On holidays Pepi and his buddies would go down to Mas Preciosa Sangre and jam all night. It was here, in a church basement, that I saw mambo dancing for the first time. I could not believe my eyes, how hot those boys and girls looked.

"Where do you learn that?" I asked some guy.

He said: the Palladium.

Next Saturday night I told my parents I was hanging out with some friends and took the train alone to Manhattan. I didn't get past the door. The bouncer said, "Listen, kid, come back tomorrow. That's when your friends will be here."

The Palladium started letting teenagers in as a way of making extra money because they were always losing their liquor license due to drugs and mob activity. On Sunday nights they'd make a show of carding you, but there was no problem if you were dressed sharp— that is, in suit and tie and good, shined shoes.

Needless to say, I passed the test.

My first night at the Palladium I was bowled over, stunned. I'd heard the music all my life, seen Ma and Pepi doing a little one-two-three at a party once in a while, and then those kids at Mas Preciosa, but this was something else, this was like *Hollywood,* with that endless slick floor, the band in white dinner jackets and all the brass shining so bright it hurt your eyes, sequined cigarette girls strutting around in stockings with seams. But the most spectacular thing, without question, was the dancing. The floor had a kind of fence around it— you'd lean up and watch the women's heels flickering so fast it looked like they were under a strobe, watch the spins, the dips, the figure eights, the moves you couldn't describe, moves that wouldn't have names until years later when you became a teacher of mambo and called them what you thought they should be.

When I got home that night, I didn't sleep a wink, I was so fired up. The next Sunday I went back just to study; for six weeks I watched. The more I watched, the more I could see the difference in the dancers. There were only a handful you could call really great, with true originality.

You know you've found your calling when you see something and think, *I can do that*. I memorized everything I saw, and then at home I practiced with the open bathroom door, pretending the door-knob was my partner's hand. I practiced before school, after school, on the weekends; I spent more time thinking, dreaming, doing mambo than I did on homework, or on my very favorite thing, which was chatting up the freshman and sophomore *muchachas* who hung out in front of the candy store near our high school.

You could say I was falling in love.

The next time Pepi and his pals went down to Mas Preciosa I was ready. I danced with girls I knew from school. A live girl gave you back something, a live girl did things you didn't expect. One even corrected the way I turned her. "Keep your wrists up," she said. It turned out she was on the pep squad at my high school. I got this girl's phone number, and we met a couple of times at her house to practice—just practice, since she already had a boyfriend. She said I had promise.

Finally one Sunday at the Palladium I got up the nerve to ask someone to dance. I'd had my eye on this girl, Lorraine, her name was, a plain jane, and she wasn't the star of the place or anything, but I had noticed she was popular because she could follow anybody. I led her onto the floor, in the middle so we wouldn't attract too much attention. The song was Tito Puente's "Mambo Diablo," which has the clearest *clave* in the world, and so many years later I can still remember that exact feeling, as terrified as I've ever been, my shirt soaked through already, and then I heard *pah-pah-pah,pah-pah,* and I took her around the waist and my feet began and her feet began.

I tell you, that Lorraine was a sweet follow. At first I stuck to the routines I'd practiced with the cheerleader. Lorraine looked so good doing a single spin that I started giving her a double here and there. Brought her across me, once, twice, half turn into a shoulder check, then a full turn the other way. She didn't bat an eye; it was like we'd been dancing forever. After two songs, I knew I had it.

And no one, except for maybe Lorraine, knew that it was my first time on the floor of the Palladium.

Of course I was doing everything wrong: holding my hands too high, not emphasizing my forward step, leaving way too much space between us in the cross-body. But I had the rhythm down, and any dancer will tell you if you have the rhythm down, the sky's the limit.

I should explain here about the kind of mambo we were dancing. It had a history. As far as I could tell, these high school kids had been watching the older folks with their danzóns and pachangas and cha-cha-chás and then reinterpreted what they were doing to Tito Puente and Tito Rodriguez and the great Machito until it became their very own dance. Not only were the moves showy and often athletic, but we danced on the offbeat. The adults were dancing on the first beat—*One*-two-three-four—but we'd take our first step on the second beat—one-*Two*-three-four, which is on the *clave*. Flicker step, syncopation, dancing on *clave*, breaking on two—whatever you call it, you're right on the congas and once you feel it, you never go back.

Not to say that it was easy. It was ages before the best girls would even consider dancing with me. But I showed up every Sunday, kept watching, kept dancing with whoever would dance with me, and inside of six months I was giving the hotshots a run for their money.

How good was I? Let me put it this way: I had only one serious rival. His name was Manny Carleton, a tall skinny black kid with glasses from the Bronx. Manny and I were always stealing each other's moves—I made up the slam-against-the-pillar; he made up the dip where you swirl your partner's hair on the floor before snapping her back up. Now they call it the Brazilian or some such thing, but let me tell you, it was born on the floor of the Palladium Ballroom. Manny was big on dips in general—many years later I heard that he became a teacher of Argentine tango. I always preferred lifts. We were always at it, Manny and I. If he saw me do three double turns in a row, he'd do three triples and have his partner screaming. Manny maybe had a larger repertoire of shines—he'd throw in tap moves he'd seen Gene Kelly do in the movies. I think he went to see *Singin' in the Rain* fifty times. We used to call him "Rubberlegs." *My* specialty was not two partners—as you'll often see me do today—but three, four, even five. The most I ever did was seven, and you won't believe it but they were sisters from Canarsie. And I'll tell you a secret—if you know how to do two you can do seven. The trick is to play fair, give each girl the same amount of time, the same quality in your moves.

On an average Sunday at the Palladium we danced six hours straight, from eight o'clock to two in the morning. I would bring an extra shirt or two, maybe another pair of shoes. Manny would show up with a garment bag and about midnight disappear into the men's and reemerge with an entire new outfit, including spats over two-tones. One of his nicknames was "Cinderfella." At closing we'd limp to the subway, some of us carrying our shoes, and sleep all the way home.

Monday in the lunchroom kids would be talking about how they passed the weekend, and finally someone would ask—"So, Oz, what'd *you* do?"

"I went to the P, man."

"Your parents let you go to the P?"

"Yeah," I'd say, and that would be it; there'd be this respectful silence, and then some girl would offer me her potato chips, or the rest of her soda.

After I graduated I got a job working a forklift and, out of respect for Ma, tried night school for a while. Accounting, business-management techniques, that sort of thing, but I started falling asleep in class, so after a few months I quit. This left my nights free. I never did drugs and I didn't drink, but I sure did girls. In those days I had long kinky hair, which I wore loose, and I'd strip to the waist when it started getting suffocatingly hot, as it always did in those clubs. I must have looked like some fucking crazy Tarzan, but the *chicas* loved it. The ones who came in from Scarsdale or Connecticut or whatnot were the worst. I'd take them home—by this time I had my own place—one, two, three, however many would fit into a cab. *Coño*, I was in heaven.

That was my real education. But exactly where I went, what I did, and who I did it with doesn't matter. What's important to this part of the story is that I was out on the floor, at least three nights a week and more if I could swing it. The Palladium closed in 1969. Sunday nights it was the Casa Amarilla on the Upper East Side, which is where a certain Tomás DeSelva, who owned a dance studio, found me. He invited me over to his table, a prime spot on the edge of the floor, for a drink. I sat down and let him buy me a Coke. He was wearing a sky blue sports jacket with wide lapels and had a faint mustache, in the style of a forties *suavecito*, like what I used to imagine my father had been. He had no expression and his cologne was overpowering.

"Would you consider teaching a class in Latin?"

"You mean as supposed to Greek," I said.

He didn't say what he was obviously thinking: *Jesus Christ, a smart-ass.*

"I'm not a teacher," I said.

He took out a pack of Kents and offered me one, which I declined. After he lit one for himself he said, "But you can dance."

"What are you offering?"

"Forty bucks a week. That includes two one-hour classes, plus we expect all our teachers to oversee a practice session once a month."

"I need an assistant."

"We have many advanced students who would be glad to help you out."

"Your students only know ballroom shit. Look." I directed DeSelva's attention to Anna María Piliaz Rodriguez, who happened to be out on the floor with Big 'Berto, who wasn't so big in those days. Anna María was six feet tall, busty but slender everywhere else. She had almond eyes, a luscious mouth, wavy hair down to her butt—a big Colombian beauty. I had fucked Anna María a couple of times, but that wasn't the point of our relationship. We were dance partners. That night she was wearing a cheap white knit top and lemon yellow bell-bottoms and totally outshone all the other *chicas* in their color-coordinated Mary Quant and Peter Max dress-to-impress outfits. At that moment Anna María happened to be doing a little shuffle back step on her platforms. She wiggled her butt at 'Berto when he pulled her around in front of him, and the whole time she had her free palm up as if to say: No, no, *papi*, don't touch me. It made me hard just to watch her.

From the look on his face I guessed it put DeSelva in the same condition.

"All right," he said.

"Twenty bucks a week for her."

"Fifteen."

We shook on it. Anna María threw a little fake hissy fit when I told her, claiming she couldn't get a babysitter for her kids, but then she said she could use the money and would figure something out. I actually thought about ditching Anna María and asking Lorraine, my old partner from the Palladium days. We were still on good terms, but she was married to a white tax lawyer who didn't dance and didn't approve of dancing. So the following Tuesday at six P.M. it was me and Anna María who showed up at DeSelva Studios on Amsterdam and Seventy-eighth. Anna María was wearing a white halter top, matching hot pants, and strappy stiletto sandals. No one would have ever guessed she had three kids. She'd had her finger- and toenails done in scarlet. "This ain't no show," I told her, and she gave me a dirty look and snapped her gum.

The first thought that came into my head when I got a look at the class was: *What a bunch of losers.* Most of the men had their eyes glued to Anna María, and most of women were trying not to look at her. This gave me an idea. I told Anna María to put on something slow, maybe even a cha-cha-chá, and get the women going on the basic. I herded the men out into the hallway and shut the door behind me.

"Listen up," I said. "Do any of you guys know the true purpose of dance?"

They all stared at me like idiots.

One of them muttered: "To have a good time."

"More specific. Why do we dance?"

They shrugged, looked down, or just continued to stare at me as if I were from Mars.

"The purpose of dance," I said, "is *foreplay*. That's what it is, and that's what it's always been. Yeah, yeah, I know what you're going to say. But if you're good enough, I'm telling you, *you can get away with it.*" I pantomimed the shape of Anna María in the air in front of me. Then I pretended I was holding her in ballroom position. "Her right hand in your left, clasped. Your hand position will change, depending on what you're leading, but we'll get into that later. Right hand in the middle of her back. You know where that is?"

"The waist," someone volunteered.

"Wrong. It's right over her bra strap. And do you know why your hand is there?"

Snickers.

"It's her center of gravity. With your hand there, you can guide her anywhere, make her do anything." I paused to let the words sink in and then said, "So what other way is there to lead a woman?"

"Her hand," some genius yelled out.

"Yeah, if you're a fag," I said, and there was uneasy laughter. This wasn't fair, really, because there were and are some great *mamberos* who were homosexual, the fabulous Manny, for instance, although they didn't exactly advertise the fact, and you certainly couldn't tell by watching them on the floor. But I was trying to make a point.

"You lead her by the shoulder," I said. "Her waist, of course. Her elbow. The back of her knee. And if you want to get the most leverage—here. Her hip." I pointed to my own hip bone, thrust out for emphasis. They gawked, but I could tell they were beginning to get my drift. "Look," I said, "you're in a bar and see this very hot *mami* and you sit down next to her, chat her up. But if you even touch her on the shoulder, she pulls away, starts talking to her girl-friend, all that bullshit, you know what I mean?" Some of them were nodding. "Whereas on the dance floor," I continued, "you can do this"—I pantomimed an even closer ballroom hold than before—"practically even before you introduce yourself. Practically second base. *Capisce?*"

A little heavy-handed, I admit, but I had nailed them. They were looking at each other and laughing.

"Okay, let's practice the basic. I want you to make this your fuck-ing mantra. ONE-two-three."

No syncopation for these guys. Breaking on two would come later, in my intermediate class.

When I thought they had the basic down, I cracked the door to the studio and called to Anna María that me and the boys were coming back in. It turned out she had gotten the women completely confused. Sometimes a natural dancer is not the best teacher. A couple of them had managed to pick up the basic anyway just by imitating her, and I could see that these were going to be my best pupils. For the rest of the hour I made everyone couple up and do the basic, over and over, get comfortable in ballroom, and then a simple two-hand hold. At the end I put on "Oriente" by Joe Cuba, and Anna María and I did a little exhibition. She showed off her very best, shaking her *tetas* and *nalgas* and tossing her head so her hair made a big gorgeous fan. We got a huge round of applause. When I looked up, DeSelva was leaning against the doorjamb watching and I knew I'd made the grade.

"You dance different from the other teachers," one of the guys said to me on the way out.

"Yeah, why is that?" someone else chimed in.

"No es un baile lindo," I said. *"Esto es peligroso."*

It's not a pretty dance. It's a dangerous one.

By 1970 I was making enough to afford to rent a studio of my own in Spanish Harlem. Besides classes at DeSelva's I was taking on private students at twenty bucks a pop—mostly women, the occasional man if he was promising enough, sometimes couples for thirty-five. It doesn't seem like a lot today, but back then it was a fortune. Anna María was still my assistant, although her attitude was always a problem. She did manage to become a passable teacher, but her heart wasn't in it. She didn't want the competition. But she knew she had to toe the line because there was always a student or two who would have been glad to take her place.

Which leads me to the main point. Over the years I've had maybe half a dozen assistants, but the best, without question, was Wendy Cardoza. She came to me back in the early eighties, when I was starting up the dance business again after a break. By then I had lost my eye and needed a partner I could lead by feel, someone whose reflexes were even better than mine. Cardoza was a skinny little thing, former user, but *coño,* could she dance. If you did one thing she'd turn it into something bigger and throw it back at you and so on and so forth. Mambo with Cardoza was an example of how dance can be like great sex. Right off I recognized her as a master technician—dead-on rhythm, never a shine I pulled out that she couldn't make at first or at most second try. She wasn't as responsive a lead as Lorraine, or as sexy as Anna María, but she was perfect for my purposes. Once she lost her rough edges, she was good enough to become my assistant, and eventually my performance partner, an honor few have had.

Before we became official partners Cardoza was my spy in the world of mambo. She took classes with the other popular teachers of the day: Eddie Torres, of course; Freddy Rios; Mambo Pete. She sponged up their moves and brought them back to me. It took them a while to figure it out, and by then it was too late.

Another big advantage of Cardoza is that opposed to, say, Anna María, she liked women. Not necessarily to hit on, although she always had her favorites. And women liked her. After Cardoza joined me, my classes doubled in size.

That's why I didn't think twice about it, this friendship between her and Lina. Hot, hot little Lina shows up all by herself one winter day—most of them come in with a girlfriend or two. She had that sexy *china* face and a body to stop traffic and her rhythm wasn't bad, but when she opened her mouth she sounded so white it made you cringe.

Ma would have called her Miss La-di-da.

"The Jews of the Caribbean, Cubans. *Cubanas* are princesses. You want a princess? She's gonna put on weight as she gets older."

Ma herself was on the skinny side. People used to say she resembled a young Rita Hayworth—high cheekbones; aristocratic nose; dark, deep-set eyes. Blanquita, her girlfriends called her, because of her complexion, so pale she could pass for white, in contrast to her hair, which she kept as dark as the black cats she had as pets. Classy, which was why she'd caught the eye of my father, who must have been pretty jaded by the time he met her.

She died in the mid-seventies of liver cancer. I rarely visit her grave because cemeteries give me the fucking heebie-jeebies, just as they did her. What she wanted was to be cremated and her ashes thrown into the Caribbean off the island of Culebra, where she was born, but Pepi sent her off in an open mahogany coffin with brass handles, her face covered with a double layer of black veiling because it was still puffed up from the steroids. When I lifted the veils to kiss her good-bye, she smelled like disinfectant, and I saw they'd put the wrong color lipstick on her, plum. She always wore red.

But I am getting way off track here. What I was trying to say was that even though Ma would have bitched, Lina is the type who would have met her standards.

That first class she flirted like a *puta* with my buddy Hank. Then she got all quiet and shit, like the class had intimidated her. When I saw her standing in the corner getting ready to go, wrapping twenty scarves around and around that long skinny neck of hers, I doubted she would ever come back. Maybe the boyfriend was out of town and the class had been a distraction. Cardoza went over and started chatting her up like she did with all the new girls, and it was then that I saw the *chinita* had a fabulous smile.

I decided to give her a signal, a kind of test. Right after her and Cardoza walked out the door, I went over and put on "Hong Kong Mambo," Tito Puente at his classic best. I knew she couldn't miss it, blasting down the stairwell. Did she know it was for her? She never mentioned it later, and I never asked.

God, those marimbas! It took me back to the Palladium, the Casa Amarilla, the Corso, Colgate Gardens, all those venues of the golden age of mambo. I can see it now—Tito and his orchestra sweating their heads off in a long, long *descarga,* all of us on the floor sweating equally, giving it everything we had, though we didn't know it then, in a way we'd never do again for anybody or anything for all the rest of our lives.

And that was it. After the song was over I have to say I basically forgot about her until she showed up for class the following week. Once or twice I remembered the look she'd given me when I was using her to demo. Like she wanted to chew me up and spit me out. It still makes me laugh to remember, even with everything that happened in the year that followed.

7

Oswaldo

You're either a follow or a lead.
Nobody is equally good at both.

———⊶⊷———

Cardoza asked me once how many women I'd had.

"Not enough," I told her.

A thousand. Two thousand. How many pairs of dance shoes, how many silk shirts have I gone through in a lifetime? Not the kind of thing you keep track of. Of course there were the special ones. Milly from South Beach, who had lips *como una angel*. Letitia, who introduced me to leather. Isabella, who could come if I licked the butterfly tattoo over her left nipple. Amanda the Wellesley girl, who recited gibberish while I was eating her out; later she told me it was Walt Whitman. Whatever. Redheaded Betsy from Sheepshead Bay, who ended up going to Hollywood and didn't get famous, but if I told you who she married you'd know who she was. María Elena, my first dyke. Models, Playboy Bunnies, college professors, lawyers, doctors, beauticians, waitresses, girls from the hood.

And of course *la reina bitch* of them all, *mi Carmencita*.

Picture this: 1979 and I, Oswaldo Niles Melendez, am thirty-five years old, the most high-profile *mambero* in New York City, Sunday nights DJing at the Casa Amarilla on upper Broadway, performing all over the city, teaching twice a week at DeSelva's and also with my own exclusive list of privates. I had a dance outfit for every day of the week and a loft down near Chinatown with a water bed and a mirrored party ball over it.

I met Carmen at the Egyptian Club, which is where I went on Thursdays. Basically it was a dyke disco lounge—think Studio 54 with estrogen—and I was there to score.

Every heterosexual man in the United Fucking States fantasizes about doing two, and what happens when they actually try?

They freak, that's what.

Not me.

They knew me at the door. I was friends with the owner and the bouncer and quite a few of the regulars, many of whom were hookers or ex-hookers.

Carmen was alone the night I met her—I could have sworn jailbait, but she told me she was nineteen—in a red bandanna halter and tight pink Sassoon jeans, so Queens you blushed for her. Later I dragged her to Macy's and bought her an orange Spandex jumpsuit with a zipper down the middle. Gold chains at the throat, bronze lipstick to complement her *trigueña* complexion. I taught her to wear her hair up instead of hanging all over her face home-girl style.

Carmen wasn't pretty, in fact you could say her face was a little repulsive, skinny with a too-large nose and small eyes and too-full lips. I could see right from the start that she wasn't no dancer; she couldn't even stay on the one-two one-two Donna Summer and *Saturday Night Fever* hustle beat, which was the main music at the Egyptian, but I liked how she teetered on her platform sandals, red to match that chintzy halter top, how she sneered with those Mick Jagger lips, how she kept working that room. Girls followed her with their eyes. Next time she passed by me I pulled her onto the floor, and this is what that crazy *chica* did; right in the middle of

"Try me try me try me, just one time," she reaches up behind her neck and undoes the red bandanna and stuffs it into the back pocket of her Sassoons. Bare-breasted in the middle of the Egyptian, and the floor's so packed it takes a while for the bouncer to make her way over to inform Carmen, politely, that she needs to put her shirt back on.

I took her home that night. Only Carmen, because that's the way she wanted it that first time. Ninety pounds sopping wet, and she devoured me. Took me into her mouth—did I mention that mouth of hers?—and she wasn't as fast as Milly but a champion tease, and generous, and as much as I grew to distrust her, I could never accuse her of holding back, in bed or anywhere else.

When she spread her legs I was a goner. Her clit, the color of a pomegranate seed, exactly resembled the tip of her tongue.

Nineteen, did I tell you?

Carmen fucked with the intensity of a teenage boy who had just discovered pussy. No surprise, she was happiest on top, and all these years later I still remember the way her biceps strained, sweat dripping onto my chest, all the humid heat of her, how hoarse she screamed. Carmen smelled funky, a mixture of dirt and rotting things, a jungle smell. She was long-waisted and had no hips, almost flat-chested but with long mahogany-colored nipples.

The first night, or morning I should say—it was dawn already—we fell asleep in my king-size water bed wrapped around each other. I woke with the sun in my eyes and a piss hard-on. I tried to disentangle her arms from around me, and what she did was hang on even tighter in her sleep—clutching my back, cheek pressed to my chest, jaw clenching as if she were about to bite. I couldn't remember her name. *"Nena,"* I said. She didn't budge. "Hey," I said louder.

Her thighs came up around my hips, and before I knew what was happening, I was sliding inside her even though I had no intention. Still wet from the night before, she was fucking me in her sleep. *"No,"* I said, reaching up and taking her by the shoulders to push her away. Then she did bite me, drawing blood on the side of my neck.

Fucking vampire, but I let her have her way.

Wouldn't you have?

That girl could pick up trade. She'd stick out that little bud tongue of hers and lipstick lesbians would fall all over themselves. We'd go cruising together, those nights at the Egyptian and at other places, too. Sometimes our trick would get cold feet when she found out I was included in the package, but Carmen was very persuasive. She courted them like a man, pouring sweet nothings into their ears if that's what they wanted, boldly feeling them up on the dance floor if that's what they wanted.

Carmen with her head between a woman's legs—if I am lucky that will be the image imprinted on my brain in the last seconds of my life.

Or Carmen shiny with sweat, lying back on the pillows after fucking, going for a shot of rum straight from the bottle, tipping it back like a wino.

The truth was she was usually drunk or on the way to getting drunk. I know she was using, too, blow mostly, and I suspected occasionally H, though I think she just did that recreational. I could be wrong. There were lots of things I didn't know about Carmen—for instance, how she made her living. I was pretty sure she wasn't a hooker, even though I *had* met her at the Egyptian, and if anyone had the soul of a prostitute it was Carmen. Sometimes she claimed she was a waitress—which was hard to believe because of that foul mouth of hers—sometimes a manicurist, which was more likely because she'd do anything to get her hands on a woman. And certainly I was not the only one she was fucking. Often an entire week would go by and I would not see her until Thursday, when she would show up at the Egyptian. There was no way I could reach her even if I had wanted to because she claimed to have no phone. We made our appointments in person.

It was August when I met her. Around October was when it became clear that things were going very wrong.

Carmen had a temper. More specifically, she was crazy jealous. We would bring a girl home and first Carmen would do her and then I would do her and then it would be kind of a free-for-all. The problem arose when Carmen would get it into her head that the girl we had both agreed on might prefer me to her.

Without warning she'd leap up on top of us like a monkey and start clawing at the girl's face, the girl she had just been soul kissing between the legs, the girl whose stomach she had just held pressed flat under her palm as she quivered in a long, long orgasm.

You'll understand when I tell you I started to lose patience. When Carmen pitched these fits, I'd throw her out of my loft, even if it was in the middle of the night, even if she had no cabfare.

The last straw came in the middle of November. The girl and I had fallen asleep, and Carmen doused our sheets with what was left of a bottle of rum and struck a match to it. The couple on the ground floor heard her running down the stairs screaming: "Fuck you, you big black dick," and tripping over her platforms just as the smoke alarm in my loft went off. The damage was not extensive, and I managed to put the flames out with the kitchen fire extinguisher before the fire department arrived. What the couple in my building heard came in handy months later at the inquiry, as evidence that she was totally *loca.*

The Thursday after the fire, when I saw her at the Egyptian, Carmen acted as if nothing had happened, winking at me over the shoulder of a bull dyke she was dancing with. This was our signal, her way of asking: Do you like this one? I took her to the side and told her, "Look, it's over; it was fun while it lasted, but obviously you can't handle ménages."

She took it so quiet, I should have known. All she said was: "Well, Oz, from now on you'll have to do your own pitiful scoring."

I still saw her at the Egyptian, to kiss hello and good-bye and exchange pleasantries with, but that was all. She went her way, and I went mine. What with the holiday season and all, I got very busy, Christmas parties to DJ and extra privates, and I ended up missing a couple of Egyptian Thursdays. New Year's Eve, though, I was determined to party. I had a date, Ms. Lynn Shapiro from Little Neck, Long Island. The thirty-first fell on a Monday, and I'd made reservations for a table at the Casa Amarilla, on the house, of course. I was not on that night, they were having a live broadcast and some hotshot from Radio Caliente was in the DJ booth.

All the regulars showed up. Anna María Piliaz Rodriguez, looking juicy as always, with her stiff of a husband in tow. Big 'Berto and three giggling girls from Tokyo, who were excellent dancers. Eddie Torres and his new wife, María. Freddy Rios, one of the three

Mambo Aces from the Palladium, came with *his* wife, Mimi. Even the fabulous Manny Carleton made a cameo appearance, causing the girls who were watching as well as the ones he danced with to swoon.

The Casa Amarilla in those days was not the type of place you would expect to see a girl like Carmen. Certainly she had never come around on my watch. But there she was, cleaned up, in an ultra-femme outfit I had never seen: red-sequined tube and black miniskirt, little glittery disco bag around her wrist, lipstick and eye makeup, hair in a French twist like I'd taught her. She came in on the arm of a Mafioso type I assumed was her sugar daddy because when I approached them to say hi she gave me a look that said STAY THE FUCK AWAY. Her pupils were so dilated her eyes looked black.

So I did not acknowledge her, but went on with my own evening, mamboing into a new decade with Lynn Shapiro in her silver stilettos and crimson velvet toreador pants. It was past midnight: the horns had gone off, and we'd all kissed and shaken hands and were now onto a new, even more frenetic level of partying. I was coming out of the men's into the little hallway they had there when Carmen jumped me.

"*Feliz año nuevo, Oz.*" Never one to be subtle, she pulled down her top so I could catch a good glimpse of those long nipples.

"*Cuídate,*" I said. "Guido is watching."

She laughed and then grabbed my face and whispered: "Fuck me, Oz. Fuck me right here."

As she said this she was pulling me down the hallway, not back toward the dance floor, which was to the right, but to the left, where there was a little nook under the stairs. How she knew about this nook I have no idea, but I knew enough about Carmen never to be surprised.

Her eyes were still black and she was as high as a kite and I knew even as it was happening that it was a stupid idea, but to tell the truth I already had a hard-on. Carmen always did that to me. She hiked up the hem of that tiny skirt which barely covered her crotch to show me she wasn't wearing hose or underwear. Then she stuck the tip of her tongue in my mouth—as usual it tasted like rum—and I could feel her tugging at my zipper. I helped her.

I told you how that girl fucked. She was already wet for me, and when I felt that there was no turning back. I rammed her up against the wall under the stairs and she threw back her head and *te juro*, I wanted to kill her and make her come at the same time.

I missed you, papi. Ven, papi, she hissed in my ear.

I was so close.

I told you how that girl scratched and bit. I thought at first it was her nails and I turned my head, but in the next instant it registered, what she was doing.

The bitch was trying to blind me.

I had no leverage, us being pressed up so tight against each other, so the first thing I did was let go of her, but still she hung on, with the hand that wasn't holding the knife, with her thighs, with that devil pussy of hers. It was just like that first morning when she practically raped me. She had already gotten the blade exactly where she wanted. How I did what I did next I have no idea. I jerked my head back hard to dislodge the knife and then I grabbed her hair with one hand and with the thumb and forefinger of the other pressed against the twin carotid arteries in her neck, the ones that feed oxygen to the brain. I knew if I pressed long enough her circulation would be cut off and she'd pass out. I thought I was going to pass out myself, from the pain, which was so bad the only way I can describe it is to say that it felt like forked lightning. I couldn't see a thing out of either eye by then, so I did what I did by feel. Her arteries under my thumb and forefinger, pulsing, her pussy around my cock, pulsing.

"Aiiiiiiii," she said, just like a sigh.

How was I to know that she was dying? She did not feel like someone who was dying. I do remember that when I finally let her go, her skin was burning hot to the touch. By some miracle my right eye had cleared up and I could see that her eyes were wide open and rolled back, like maybe she was having an orgasm. I laid her back on the floor under the stairs. All that blood was mine, but she was the one who wasn't moving. I took out my bandanna and pressed it as hard I could over my left eye.

A woman screamed. Thank God it wasn't Anna María, or Lynn, or anyone else I knew, just some random tipsy *chica* who, looking for the ladies' room, took a wrong turn and stumbled onto what was a very gory scene, even for New York. Not to mention that my dick was still hanging out of my pants. With one hand I zipped up and then took this woman by the wrist, tightly, the way I do rebellious partners or those who can't keep the beat, and said: "Look, *nena*, tell the bouncer to call nine one one. Also, have them ask on the P.A. system if there's a doctor around. Go. I have to stay here with my friend."

The next thing I remember is sitting on the floor and someone telling me the ambulance was on its way. Some guy was down on his knees giving Carmen mouth-to-mouth. By this time there was a little crowd, mostly men, watching, and other men trying to hold the women away. The mafioso was nowhere to be seen, although months later at the inquiry I spotted him in the back of the courtroom wearing mirrored shades.

Like in a nightmare I watched that guy hold up the back of Carmen's head—her hair by that time had fallen out of its French twist—as he exhaled hard into her mouth. He tried and tried, but he just couldn't fill up those lungs. I wondered if she still tasted like rum.

All I could think of was that two minutes earlier she'd been whispering, *"Ven, papi,"* into my ear. I don't remember anything more because it was just about at that moment that I passed out again.

My lawyer told me later that, according to the autopsy report, Carmen had an aneurysm brewing in the middle of her brain stem. That girl was ready to blow; she might have drunk and/or coked herself into a stupor that night and died in bed with her mafioso, or on the dance floor, or simply stepping outside for some fresh air—the change in temperature would have done it.

I saw a photo of the little folding knife, the kind you keep on a key chain. But this one was execution quality, maybe a Christmas present from her sugar daddy. She must have had it tucked into that tiny disco bag. Back then clubs didn't have metal detectors.

After the surgery they told me there was no way to save my sight, something about the angle of the blade. Although the wound wasn't deep, the optic nerve had been permanently damaged.

In the hospital I did not lack for visitors. Ma was gone by then, but Pepi showed up a couple of times and we watched basketball on

TV. Lynn Shapiro—who should have been pissed because I'd ruined her New Year's Eve 1980—came to see me every morning before work, bringing homemade rugelach and rice pudding. In the afternoons it was Anna María, pretending to be my wife, smuggling in her youngest daughter, who was seven then and the most beautiful child you ever saw. I memorized that *niña's* face, and twenty years later when she came up to me at the Copa all grown up, it was all I could do not to start bawling like a baby.

During the six months before the inquiry I dropped out of circulation. My schedule was simple: eye therapy twice a week, TV, food delivered, the occasional girl up to my loft. I made projects for myself to pass the time. One of them was to clean up the way I talked because I had always thought about becoming an actor. Since I was a teenager people had commented on my looks, my stage presence. Now I had only one eye, but you never knew. I sent away for this self-help program: "Speech Makes the Man." Some of those exercises were pretty silly, but I still do them, especially when I can't sleep.

Away she flies, over the mooooon.

At the inquiry I found out that Carmen was a runaway from Lynchburg, Virginia, of all places. Her mother was Filipina and her father Lebanese, and they hadn't seen her for over four years. They sat in the front row and would not meet my eye because I was the villain who had led their innocent baby down the path of corruption. Never mind that they didn't give enough of a shit to try to look for her all those years she was gone, never mind that that monster they'd produced had taken out my left eye. Who was going to give that back to me?

First thing I did after the inquiry was to buy a plane ticket to South Beach, where I spent a month at Milly's condo, lying out by the pool and getting my color back. I also taught myself to dance with one eye. It was hard in ways I don't even want to talk about now. What I will tell you is that I danced blind; that is, I tied a bandanna around my eyes so I couldn't see at all and did shines until I could feel I had got them down again. I videotaped myself, watched, corrected; and when I had the footwork, I practiced leading with the blindfold on. It wasn't so bad, in fact it kind of turned Milly and me on, and our sessions usually ended up in bed.

After two months of this I hitched my way back north and pulled my mambo practice together again. DeSelva had hired this rinky-dink couple from L.A. to replace me. I convinced him how truly Mickey Mouse they were—the guy would not have graduated my Mambo I class; the gal was okay but her style suffered from a lousy lead. DeSelva was a little skittish to take me on again what with all the publicity the incident at the Casa Amarilla had gotten but I was straight with him, told him the story pretty much as I've told it here, and he ended up keeping the couple for Mambo I and letting me handle the intermediate and advanced classes.

OSWALDO MELENDEZ, STAR OF THE PALLADIUM it said under my new, improved photograph in the lobby of DeSelva Studios. In the hospital my hair had been cut short for the surgery, and when I got out, I had kept it that way. And of course there was my eye, which I never tried to hide. Girls were always giving me fancy patches for presents, but I never wore them; they made me feel claustrophobic. Besides, who wants to look like a fucking pirate? Strangely, over the years, I've gotten fond of my blind eye. It's not ugly or anything. And if nothing else, it's a reminder to me that in this world you can trust no one but yourself. The only thing that throws me is that sometimes when I'm looking in the mirror, shaving for instance, I stare right into that dead eye, and it can't see me back.

The Egyptian had closed by then, and you can guess I did not exactly run back to the Casa Amarilla, which was on its last legs by the early eighties anyway. The Copacabana was always reliable on weekends, but what was making big news in those days was the Village Gate on Wednesdays and all the smaller clubs that kept on popping up all over town, like that little Chino-Latino place on lower Broadway. Under no circumstances could you have termed Baracoa a dyke bar, but they had a liberal ambience, and if a girl came in with a girl, it was no big deal. I liked that, although the prime of my ménage days were over. Isadore "Mofongo" Ayela, the lead vocalist of the house band, was a buddy of mine from the Palladium, and they always comped me in. And another funny thing—I'd become friendly with one of the witnesses from the Casa Amarilla New Year's Eve incident, Hank Pursner, a beefy blond narc from Miami whose testimony had been my main defense at the inquiry. He was the one who had given Carmen mouth-to-mouth. Wouldn't you know it but he'd moved up north and started hanging out at Baracoa—he said it was to make sure I was behaving myself (it was true there was a little trafficking going on in the bathrooms, but I was not involved)—and then I noticed he had this regular table and was trying to pick up girls, without much luck. For fuck's sake, the guy was trying to *emulate* me. I felt it was my duty to take him aside and persuade him that he needed mambo lessons if he was ever going to get anywhere.

At Baracoa I had a table in front where I could chat with the band and girl watch—it wasn't as scenic as, say, the Copa, but it had its nights, and some nice rough trade, if you were looking. Like that *chica* from the Bronx, Isabella Sanchez, with the butterfly tattoo, who introduced me to Wendy Cardoza.

My first impression of Cardoza was that she looked like Carmen with a ponytail, enough like her to give me the fucking chills. Her features were finer, like Carmen had been the rough cut and Wendy was the finished product. Wendy also had more of a bust, and she was older, of course. But the main difference between them was that, unlike Carmen, Wendy Cardoza could dance.

She knew my predilection for threesomes, and although, unlike Carmen, she didn't share it, there were times when I suspected she might have humored me. But it just never came up. The chemistry between us both in bed and out was way too good, and we didn't want to fuck with it.

But once in a while, although they were nothing alike in personality, I have to admit that when Cardoza would take her hair down, or turn a certain way, I'd have this crazy fantasy that she was Carmen reincarnated, and that this time things were going to turn out different.

8

Wendy

Never depend on your partner.
Every dancer must pull her own weight.

At the 1997 annual International Congreso de Salsa in Puerto Rico Wendy and El Tuerto performed a free-style interpretation of Chucho Valdés's "El Manisero." For years afterward people would recount how he took her into traveling spins the length of the auditorium and then bent so she could roll over his back and land on her feet, still spinning. This move came to be known as *la trompita por la espalda,* and, as much as it was copied, no one ever pulled it off with as much pizzazz as Wendy and El Tuerto did that night in San Juan.

The spring she turned fourteen, Wendy María Teresa Cardoza was the sweetheart of the South Bronx, her elfin figure and question-mark ponytail vying for space with the Mets and Yankees in the sports pages of every New York City paper. There was a paragraph from the *New York Times,* which her *papi* kept in a gilt frame on the mantelpiece.

> This tomboy from Hunts Point is famous for two things: her razor pirouettes on the balance beam and her unflappable poise. When asked how she keeps her cool, she replies without self-consciousness: "La Virgen María."

Young Wendy, the third of four daughters, prayed constantly, not only during Sunday mass at Saint Augustine, but in bed before she fell asleep, in school when the teacher's voice started jumping around in her head like a *cucaracha,* on the subway when she was alone and some guy across the aisle started looking at her weird. She prayed to la Santisima Virgen as she pictured her in the chapel at Saint Augustine—a life-size statue of painted mahogany with a creamy oval face and deep-set tragic eyes and a voluptuous body swathed in blue and gold drapery. The Virgin was holding Jesús balanced on the palm of one hand as if He were a grapefruit, was Wendy's sacrilegious observation. The fingers of the other hand were raised gracefully in benediction.

Wendy prayed especially hard before performing her specialty, the balance beam. *Por favor, Madre de Dios, let me whip their skinny white asses.* You could count on her to double her two-footed turns, hold her one-arm split handstand a full second longer than required, and execute four aerials instead of three.

The crowd would go wild.

"Your timing was off coming out from the split," her coach would scold, but Wendy didn't care.

Mil gracias, Virgencita.

In elementary school her nickname had been Monita—"Monkey Girl"—because she could slither up and down a rope twice as fast as any of the boys. A gymnastics scout had come to P.S. 98 and picked her out for a special federally funded gymnastics-training program geared toward kids from the inner city. By the time she was thirteen everyone said that she was going to go all the way. Her *papi,* who'd been a featherweight boxer in the Dominican Republic, was Wendy's biggest fan and came to all her meets. Her *mami,* although she claimed to be proud, did not exempt Wendy from certain household chores—such as going to the Laundromat—which is where she met her real fate.

If the elevator was broken, as it frequently was, Wendy would make her younger sister Lourdes go with her to help balance the overladen cart down six flights of stairs and two blocks down Jackson Avenue and then the whole process in reverse. If she went alone while she was waiting Wendy would practice pirouettes and splits or just stretch to the salsa Mrs. Vaquiz always had going on the radio. When someone new came in, Mrs. Vaquiz would point to Wendy: "Monita. You haven't heard a her? She's gonna go to the 'Lympics."

The only one who was not impressed was Miguel, Mrs. Vaquiz's teenage son. Wendy didn't think he knew she was alive until one Saturday afternoon when he was filling in for his mother he leaned over the counter and said loudly, over the radio: "Hey *nena*, you dance real pretty but you're not doing it to *el ritmo*."

Lourdes wasn't there that day. Miguel had been drinking beer; Wendy could smell his sour breath from all the way across the room where she was doing her pliés. Her best friend Luisa Fuentes claimed he was a dealer, and Wendy *had* noticed him hanging out in front of their school. Now he slid himself over the counter instead of going through the little door like you were supposed to and held out his hand. *"Ven acá."*

She tried to mirror what he was doing. "No, no, you're takin' too many steps," he said. "It ain't no fuckin' speed dance." He let go of her hand and made her stand beside him and copy the way his feet moved. "Step forward on the left foot, step in place with the right, back to the beginning with the left, step back with the right. *Bueno, niña, pero* you gotta listen to *la música*. Feel that bass. Ba-BAM. Ya hear it? Take a step when it goes ba-BAM. That's it. Now, when I raise my hand, you're gonna turn. Not so fast. Again. That's it." He gave her a big crooked grin and a high five, just like her *papi* when she'd go running into his arms at the end of a meet.

Wendy had a classic gymnast's build, so lean she rarely got her period, but there were times, like now, when she would have rather looked like Luisa, wearing lacy bras and having guys scope out her *nalgas* as she strutted down the street. But—could it be?—it seemed as if Miguel was looking at her the way guys looked at Luisa. Part of his hair had flopped onto his face, so it was hard to see his expression exactly. Embarrassed, she did a double pirouette into a side lunge, just to get away from him.

"Good move," he said. "You do that at the Corso, you'll bring down *la casa.*"

She had no idea what he was talking about. Flustered, she checked to see if the sheets were through the spin cycle; they weren't, but she opened the washer anyway and started loading one of the wheeling carts for transfer to the dryer. He climbed back over the counter to watch a ball game on the miniature TV, but as she left he called out: "Next week, I'll give you another lesson, eh *nena?*"

He doesn't even know my name, she thought.

Nonetheless, she stopped complaining when it was laundry day and even when the elevator was broken, never again asked Lourdes to go with her. Miguel was there maybe one time in three. Then he wasn't there at all. On the street they said he was in juvie.

The 1967 Olympic Elimination Trials for the state of New York were held in Huntington, Long Island, that October. Looking back, Wendy could think of several factors that contributed to her failure: the tendon in her calf she'd sprained on a dismount in May that had never completely healed; the pot she'd smoked with Luisa the night before; the fact that she and her *papi* got lost on the Long Island Expressway and arrived forty minutes late with no time for her to warm up.

What she would never forget was emerging from the tunnel into the bright fluorescents as she heard her name being announced for the floor exercises. She stroked the gold crucifix around her neck, a confirmation present from her *papi;* she believed that, along with *la Virgen,* it was responsible for her good luck. The blue mat in front of her extended like an ocean. Over the crackly loudspeaker came the opening bars of "Twist and Shout" by the Beatles, chosen to accentuate the playfulness of her style. She went into the run before her first tumbling routine, which was a roundoff two back handsprings into a double tuck, then a slide into a back lunge. She loved this opening because it felt like flying, her palms and soles bouncing off the plastic. *Dulce Virgencita, make me strong, make me good.* But as she went into the first handspring, instead of the Virgin's serene face under its blue wimple, she got a flash instead of Miguel, that dumb cowlick over his eye. She overrotated the landing, barely recovered to do the next handspring, and on the lunge overreached with her right foot and fell backward.

Although she had never in all her years of competition made such mistakes, she knew to pick herself up, find her place in the music, and continue the routine as if nothing had happened. The audience was dead quiet. Here and there a flash went off halfheartedly. Afterward she limped off the mat, looking neither right nor left, ignoring her coach, who put his arm around her; ignoring most of all her *papi* standing there with his camera limp on a cord around his neck, knowing she had messed up but not how badly. She went through the uneven parallels routine, but there was no strength in her arms, and she could feel that she wasn't quite hitting the top and bottom of each arc. Worst of all, on the beam it was as if she were a beginner and her feet could not find the center of gravity. Barely keeping her balance, she did the minimum, no extras, and stumbled on the dismount.

Back on the bench she used a towel to wipe the clammy sweat off her forehead and neck. A television lady came over with a microphone. "Are you hurt, dear?"

Wendy said: "I want to go home now."

Madre de Dios, why did you desert me in my hour of need?

There was no answer. Maybe there had never been any answer.

After school she started to hang out at the Laundromat with no loads to do, flirting with Miguel who was back out. He had just turned eighteen and was no longer eligible for juvie; the next time he got into trouble it was Riker's. When Wendy's calf bothered her, Miguel would score pills from the street, not as good as codeine or Fiornal, but they did the trick. Having stopped training, Wendy gained weight and curves and, though it was fall, took to wearing a tank top with no bra and the tightest jeans she owned. "You ever try smack, honey?" he'd ask, running his fingertips over her bare shoulder. "Nah, I don't do the *hard* stuff," she'd reply, switching her ponytail, and they'd both laugh at her double entendre.

Around Christmas Miguel told her his *papi* was making him go to the Dominican Republic for four months, to get to know his relatives, supposedly, but Wendy guessed it was a way to keep him off the streets. He said when he got back he'd take her out for her fifteenth birthday. All winter she moped, and then at the end of March there he was, three shades darker but with the same smile, hanging out with his homies in front of the Tingo Deli Grocery.

In the DR a sweet fifteen was special, but Wendy didn't want a party. On the day of her birthday she skipped school—she'd been flunking worse than usual, so it didn't matter—and waited in front of Tingo's, floating a little from the 'lude she'd popped with breakfast. Miguel drove up in a borrowed, jacked-up Chevy and leaned to open the passenger door. *"Feliz cumpleaños,"* he said, handing her a bunchy bundle wrapped in teddy bear paper. She thought it was pot but inside found a Ray Barretto eight-track and a Baggie containing what looked like dirty sugar.

"Where you wanna go, honey?" he asked her. "Anywhere you want, I'll take you."

"The ocean," she said, thinking of the blue plastic mat the day of the Olympic trials.

They drove to Orchard Beach with the tape player turned up full blast. Wendy liked the music right away; the conga player sounded as if he was on acid or something, crazy, the way she herself often felt even without drugs. At the beach they parked as close to the water as they could get. Since it was off season they had no company.

"Now your other present," Miguel said.

She had never seen smack being cooked before. "It looks like chocolate," she said, as he used a lighter to heat it up in the bowl of a spoon.

"And it'll make you feel just as sweet. Hold it for a second." She held the spoon while he took out a Q-tip and plucked out a speck of cotton, which he dropped into the liquefied dope. "Now make a fist, honey." As professional as a doctor, he tied her off with a length of rubber tubing he got from the glove compartment.

Wendy gazed dreamily out the windshield. The gray waves looked rough, but she imagined they might be as warm as bathwater.

Can you drown in bathwater?

Miguel seemed to be having trouble finding her vein.

"You sure you know what you're doing?"

"Don't worry," he said. "I won't mess up this pretty skin of yours." His breath was on her neck, and she shivered.

She felt the sting before it slid in.

"Happy Birthday sweet fifteen."

Madre de Dios. ¿Por qué me abadonaste en ese momento? *What were you telling me? Are you here now? Is that you I feel?*

"I can't hear the music," she said.

"It's cranked way up, honey. If I turn it up any louder, the cops'll come."

"You gonna do some, too?"

"Not this time, sweetheart. It's *your* birthday." He was putting everything away: tubing, spoon, syringe, lighter. Then his face came toward her and his tongue was in her mouth, an eel-shaped bitter-tasting tongue. Her body was on the car seat, pressed back into it, but she was somewhere else, outside, flying over the ocean with the screeching seagulls.

"Ay, you're so wet. You know that, honey, you're so wet."

"Say my name."

"Monita."

"Jesúcristo, no one calls me that anymore."

"Wendy," he said. "It doesn't suit you."

She made a noise like a laugh. "It's 'cause I'm like a boy."

"You got muscles, but you ain't no boy."

She didn't know how much time had passed when he pulled her shirt up and put his mouth on one nipple, sucked, and then bit.

She felt it coming up and gulped. Without missing a beat he reached over her head and opened her door and then turned her over and slid her halfway out. She heard herself retching violently onto the asphalt, but it wasn't much, coffee and what was left over of the 'lude.

"You done?" he asked, his hand on the back of her neck. "Don't worry, that's normal, no big deal."

"I'm okay," she said, and he pulled her back in and closed the door. He wiped off her face, and, after a few minutes, they picked up where they'd left off.

"Ay mami," he whispered. "I knew it. I knew it when you were a little girl."

She was still queasy, but he was so comforting, his skin so hot. And then his dick, the skin so unbelievably soft. It was something secure to latch onto, and it didn't even hurt that much. She knew what to do. Luisa had coached her. Wendy María Teresa Cardoza tightened her killer gymnast's thighs around Miguel's skinny ribs and fucked him back as hard as she could while the seagulls screamed outside.

It was only a matter of time before she quit going home. It was more than she could stand, her *papi* in his armchair with *El Diario,* those stupid trophies gathering dust on the mantelpiece behind him. Sometimes she slept over at Luisa's, climbing in by the fire escape into her bed and in the morning out the same way so no one would know she'd been there. "Take a bath, 'Dita," Luisa would snipe, so Wendy began spending more and more nights with Miguel, huddled on the floor of some abandoned apartment or another, or sometimes in the back room of the Laundromat, where there was a toilet and sink. Sex was still fun, but for some reason she'd lie there afterward shaking like a crazy person. *"Nerviosa?"* Miguel would murmur into her ear, wrapping his arms around her from behind. "Please," she'd say, until he'd get up and cook her some smack, like her *papi* used to make her hot chocolate at bedtime. At first she couldn't watch, but then it became part of the ritual, seeing the blood go up into the rig as he hit the vein. She learned to do it herself, but it was never quite as magic.

School was ancient history. Days she subbed for Miguel at the Laundromat so he could take care of business, or sometimes she'd just hang out in front of Tingo's with the guys, smoking and talking shit. For drugs she depended on Miguel, for money the occasional handout from her *papi* or Luisa.

One day Miguel sat her down and gave her a lecture. "Look, *niña,* I love you and all that shit, but you're going down fast, and I can't support that. I can't support *you* neither. No more free drugs. I gotta living to make, and my *mami*'s getting pissed about us messing up the back room so much."

"You kickin' me outta your life, *nene?*" Wendy might have been on a nod thirty percent of the time, but she wasn't blind. She'd seen the way Miguel had been eying Connie Rodriguez, who wore hot pants to accentuate her long skinny legs. Connie had light skin and black hair in a Farrah Fawcett style. She had pointy tits, too. Wendy couldn't blame Miguel. If she'd been a guy she would have wanted to do Connie too—in fact lately she'd been looking at girls more and more that way, as if spending so much time with the guys were turning her into one of them, with only pussy and maybe sports on their minds.

Miguel told her: "*Niña,* you gotta get a job."

"I could hook." It would be easy; Hunts Point Market was walking distance.

"*Estúpida.* Ask around the neighborhood. Somebody must need a cashier." He picked under his nails and then added, as if he'd just thought of it: "And you should go back to school, too."

"*¿Qué pasa?* Ain't I smart enough for you?"

"You're too smart, that's the problem."

Wendy tried. Luisa gave her a haircut and enough money for a skirt and a boy's button-down shirt that covered her tracks. But even cleaned up Wendy still looked like a junkie, and no one would hire her.

It was either quit or die in Crotona Park, where she'd sometimes taken to sleeping when the weather was mild.

She never knew what gave her the strength to go cold turkey, but she finally did, suffering through the shakes and shits and puking in the unused back room of the office of a super Miguel knew on Timpson Boulevard. Some time during the fourth day she came to, staring at the grungy water-stained ceiling and its bare bulb with a string hanging down.

She felt drained and weak and absolutely pure, as if she had just confessed every sin of her life and the priest had absolved her with only one hundred novenas.

She fell into a career as a freelance bartender, and it turned out she was fast, with a perfect memory for orders, and the customers liked her attitude. Her longest gig was at El Campesino Lounge off

Bruckner Boulevard, where she made enough to afford her own apartment. She got pregnant by accident. The father was not Miguel, who had long ago ditched her for Connie Rodriguez, and had then moved on to Connie's little sister, but Bobby Casanova, a football player who used to hang around Wendy and Luisa in high school. It was a one-night stand and Wendy never told Bobby, who'd been in town on a week's leave from the Marines, but she went ahead and had the baby. She named him after Luisa, who was his godmother.

One night when Luis was six, out playing with the cook's kids in the alley behind El Campesino while Wendy tended a busy bar, Isabella O'Connell strolled in. It was the height of the disco era, and this sultry *mami* was wearing a tight fuchsia slip dress and black stiletto heels and pretty much nothing else. Half Irish, half Puerto Rican, she had a white cameo face with full stained lips and dark wavy bedroom hair. For all her overt sexiness she seemed untried and tentative—something about the way she looked down instead of meeting your eye—so that you wanted to be the one to corrupt her.

Isabella la Virgen.

"Vodka tonic," she said, leaning over the bar so Wendy got a good view of the butterfly tattooed over her left nipple. "Hold the ice."

All Wendy could think about was running her fingers around that tattoo and then licking it.

Isabella was a nurse at Mount Sinai, pushing forty although she looked a decade less, married with no kids. Her hobby was girls. For the next two years she and Wendy were best friends as well as lovers. They even moved into a two-bedroom in Washington Heights, just down the block from Luisa and her family. In response to Isabella's encouragement, Wendy joined NA and got her high school equivalency. She had just started a full-time job manning the admissions desk at a methadone clinic in Jamaica when Isabella suddenly moved out, leaving a note saying she was going back to her husband. When Wendy finally reached her, Isabella told her she had decided to turn over a new leaf, start going to church again.

During Isabella withdrawal, Wendy was as edgy as any of her clients, chain-smoking and gnawing at her cuticles so hard she left blood smudges all over the folders she was supposed to be filing.

After work she'd pick Luis up from school and the two of them would lie in bed watching TV and eating Mickey D's until they conked out. After six months, when Wendy finally started to feel better, Isabella called out of the blue.

"I miss you, honey."

"What do you want?"

"Just to see you."

"What happened to turning over a new leaf?"

"Oh." Isabella laughed, then said: "You know me."

"I don't know if that's such a good idea."

"Please, honey. I promise I'll behave."

Before Wendy realized what she was doing she had agreed to meet her ex that very evening for a drink in the Village. She popped a TV dinner into the microwave for Luis and when he was done eating, took him over to Luisa's, who now had two daughters of her own. "I'm going to be late," Wendy told her friend, who just shrugged and said, "I'll make sure he gets to school."

Tuesday nights, Isabella had told her, Baracoa had a live salsa band. Sure enough, half a block away, Wendy could hear the trombones. She couldn't remember the last time she'd gone out; even in the best of times she was more of a suck-down-a-few-beers-and-watch-the-game kind of a girl than a club bunny. Besides, after her years of bartending, she'd had more than enough of smoky rooms and watching people pick each other up. She pulled open the heavy door and paid the six-dollar cover, blinking at the bubblegum pink walls, the papier-mâché woman being plucked into the ceiling by a monster pair of chopsticks, the dragon canoe filled with maniacally grinning Chinamen. The dance floor was all the way in the back past the bar, and as she made her way through the crowd she felt herself being checked out. She was wearing new black jeans and a white tank top, a little lipstick borrowed from Luisa—and she knew she looked good, although she would never be anybody's idea of a beauty. Finally she spotted Isabella dancing with some hotshot in tight silver pants. When Isabella saw Wendy, she stopped dancing, waved her over, and greeted her with a big hug and a sloppy kiss on the mouth.

"This is my friend. . . ."

Wendy couldn't make out the name over the din. Isabella's hair, dyed blond, looked terrible, and she had put on weight. Still, Wendy could see that all the guys were ogling her ex's cleavage in her black velvet tank top. The song had ended, and the band was warming up to another. The man dropped Isabella's hand and gestured to Wendy.

"*No sé bailar,*" she said. Whatever Miguel had managed to teach her at the Laundromat, she'd forgotten long ago.

He pulled her onto the floor anyway. At first his looks made no impression. She was preoccupied wondering where Isabella had gotten to. The milky eye she did notice; it was impossible not to. He was a strong and confident lead, even for a Latino. She gave up and followed.

"Step on the second beat, honey," he said. "*Segundo tiempo del compas. Uno-DOS-tres.*"

She did her best. He was arrogant, he was relentless, but he was good, she had to give him that. When the song ended, he held her by the wrists as she tried to look over the crowd, an odd mixture of Latinos and West Village ex-hippie types.

"*Una más,*" he said.

"All right."

It was a cha-cha-chá. Wendy had to get used to a new basic step. He twisted her waist as they traveled across the floor, a move that she barely managed to follow. She knew people were watching them. He was the kind of dancer everyone watched. He lifted her arm and spun her, in what started out to be a single turn, and turned into a double.

"Gymnast," he said.

"How did you know?"

"The way you hold your arms."

He just wouldn't let her go. Finally she escaped to the bar and found Isabella well on her way to getting smashed on margaritas. Wendy took the glass out of her ex's hand and set it down on the bar.

"Who is that creep? Your new boyfriend?"

"He likes you," said Isabella.

"I don't think so."

"He's into ménages."

"You're fucking him."

"I'd rather fuck you."

"Rot in hell, Isabella."

Wendy slid off her stool and headed for the door. A hand grabbed her elbow. There was no mistaking that touch.

"I don't do two," she said, shaking him off.

"All right, all right, I get the message." Away from the music, his voice was arresting, husky like a singer's. Wendy could see that he had once been almost too pretty. Even the blind eye had long curly lashes. Cheekbones to cut yourself on. Too bad he wasn't a girl.

"I want you to come to my class," he said.

"What?"

"My mambo dance class. Look, I don't do this. I come here to meet girls, not to drum up business. Your friend's a nice woman, but she can't dance. You can."

Mostly so he would stop bothering her, Wendy took his card.

"Mambo Peligroso?"

"*Si. No te vas arrepentir.*"

"You're pretty sure of yourself, aren't you?"

For the first time he smiled, and then she saw exactly how he got his women.

To the world they were dance partners, but the truth was Wendy was more like a long-suffering wife, putting up with Tuerto's infidelities, waiting for him to tire of this girl or that. It was worth it because they were the team of teams. She knew his body, his reflexes, his predilections, his timing better than anyone in the world. Dancing, she compensated for his blindness. When she had to pass him on the left she danced as close as possible so he'd feel her exact location and tempo. On spins she'd brush his chest with her shoulder or flick his calf with the instep of an upraised foot. *Here I am.* During a fast song she'd drag her fingertips along his shoulder blade or, if she were mad at him, if he were spinning her too many times in the same direction for instance, she'd make sure her ponytail caught him square in the face. *I'm a woman, not a fucking mannequin.*

Much of what they did was by feel, not visual cues, and this gave their dance a peculiar intimacy that everyone wanted to emulate but couldn't. For Tuerto Wendy made sure that each step she took was articulated, so that he could feel it in her hands, feel exactly when she was syncopating or otherwise playing with the beat. In the past couple of years his reflexes had slowed discernibly, so she'd hold her back break a fraction of a second longer than she was supposed to, giving him time to prepare his next move.

But they'd always had it and always would, that perfect centrifugal force. Two bodies in space, forming the most complex of patterns, keeping as close to each other as the laws of physics would allow. She'd watched them obsessively on video and knew that their best sequences were unchoreographed. More often than not she was the extrovert, the dominant one, all skinny arms and ponytail and showing her teeth when she laughed, stepping into the cross-body with the confidence you can learn only on the streets of the South Bronx. Sometimes, though, it wasn't so clear—he could be the most demanding of leads, his hands on her just enough and no more but absolutely compelling, working her into a knot, unraveling her so that she had to concentrate with all her might.

The question that always kept the audience on edge was: *Who is in charge here?*

It was only afterward when they stopped, that she'd feel it, her bum calf, the opposite knee that had gotten tricky, the twinge in her recently fractured instep, or worst, the stab in the middle of her chest that meant she'd been smoking too much.

"I'm gettin' old," she'd say.

Any other man would have contradicted her, but not Tuerto. He'd smile and reach over and wipe the sweat off her upper lip with a corner of his bandanna. "Yeah, Cardoza, so you are."

He needed her as much as she needed him. If it weren't for her to come home to, he'd never have been able to keep up his womanizing. Despite appearances, the man was a homebody. He'd wine and dine his flings at fancy restaurants, but for Wendy he would cook. When he'd phone her out of the blue: "Come over for dinner," Wendy would get a manicure and pedicure, dig out her fanciest underwear, her reddest lipstick. Although she was by no stretch of the imagination a girly girl, she had finally learned to do herself up. On their reunion nights he'd make her all her favorites: *arroz con pollo, bacalao* in tomato sauce, octopus salad, and, if he were feeling particularly magnanimous, shrimp tempura. *If only his girls could see him now,* she'd think as he prowled around the kitchen in a canvas apron, the sash double-wrapped around the thirty-inch waist about which he was so vain, lifting pot lids and tasting every two minutes as Tito Rodriguez or Joe Arroyo blared from the speakers. In cooking, as in dance, Tuerto was a perfectionist.

After dinner they'd roll up the rugs and practice: an ice-dance lift he'd seen on TV, a hip-hop shine the Puerto Domingo kids had made all the rage, or they'd just improvise to the latest Grupo Gale or Gran Combo single. Then they'd sprawl on his black satin sheets swigging passion fruit juice mixed with seltzer and watch old dance videos— everything from Fred and Ginger to bootleg tapes of Eddie Torres in his heyday—commenting and analyzing and comparing.

Sooner or later he'd reach for her. Lemme give you a massage, he'd say, and that was how it would start, his fingertips and tongue cold from the fruit drink. She'd go along, although she had been doing her own moonlighting—with Omara, or young Justico from Puerto Domingo, for instance—in the weeks he'd been otherwise occupied.

She'd think of two cougars, lean and muscular and savage; she'd never been with anyone, man or woman, who was her match that way. He fucked like he danced—no, *better* than he danced, as if he hadn't had it in months, although of course this was never the case. His favorite way to do it was from behind, either when she was lying on her stomach or when they were standing up pressed against the wall, or sometimes when she was kneeling over the edge of the bed. Did he just prefer this position or was it because he couldn't see her face? Maybe he was imagining she was somebody else. *She* never pretended he was anyone else, how could she, with him whispering shit in her ear the whole time.

"Sexy bitch," he'd hiss, grabbing her nipples and twisting them just before he, and often she as well, came.

And then there was his outsize cock, famous in the mambo world. Who could get enough of that? Once in a while he'd give it to her in the ass, and although it had hurt at first, over the years she'd developed a taste for it. He'd yank her ponytail until she wept: *"Ay, papi, no más, por favor, no más."*

"*Sí, más,*" he'd say, and bite her ear till she screamed.

He loved to mess with her head, choosing some sweet thing in the beginner class with whom to torment her at moments of high passion. "How would you feel if Marisol stuck her tongue up your pussy? And how about that luscious ass of hers?"

As the crowning touch, in real life Tuerto would usually end up scoring with the girl himself. Not surprising, given how she'd met him in the first place.

After they'd fucked a couple of times he'd run a bath. Since he loved it scalding hot—he joked that in a past life he'd been a samurai—Wendy would position herself by the faucet so she could sneak in some cold. This was when she felt most wifelike—massaging his feet and then scraping the soles with pumice, trimming his toenails. Tuerto was self-conscious about his feet—flat with bunions on both sides. She, Wendy, was the only one allowed to give him pedicures.

"Lucky me," she said, when he'd point this out.

The honeymoon never lasted long. There was always some aspiring dancer in the wings, someone who wanted to learn to mambo so badly she'd sell her soul for it. No matter how cool the girl seemed, Wendy could always tell by the tension in her jawline as she tried to nail a shine, her eyes dreamy in a kind of Zen concentration as she watched a turn pattern for the first time.

Tuerto would single this woman out for a few weeks, praising her natural ability, then turn just cool enough so she'd get worried and come to him for privates at sixty dollars a shot. Wendy would always know when they had started fucking because the girl would arrive in class looking sheepish, sometimes as if she had just gotten out of bed, which might have been the case. The water bed Tuerto had favored when Wendy had first met him had been replaced by a king-size platform. Those black satin sheets complemented a range of skin tones: coal, burnt umber, light olive, dark gold, light gold, and all shades of white from milk to parchment. Tuerto was an equal opportunity employer.

In class he'd treat the girl exactly as usual, but it was as if the guys could smell him on her and they'd keep their distance.

The quality of the girl's dancing would jump one, two, three notches, and at the Copa the Eddie Torres and Puerto Domingo boys would put her through their paces—high-energy spins, shoulder-wrenching turn patterns, syncopated shine steps—all of which she'd follow with ease because after Tuerto they were easy leads, predictable even. The girl's appearance would change in some dramatic way—she'd dye her hair, or cut it, or if she had been a modest type, start wearing short skirts or tighter tops with cleavage. She would develop an edge to her walk and lose weight because she was dancing so much.

This would last one, maybe two months. Then one day the girl would not show up for class. The next week she'd come in wearing either sloppy sweats and no make-up or so overdressed and made up it was alarming. She'd be fidgety, not paying attention, and at the end, when people were paying, she'd sidle up to the CD player and wait, arms folded over her chest, while Tuerto ignored her and took his time about chatting with everyone else. At this point Wendy would usually leave because it was obvious what was about to happen. Sometimes as she was starting down the stairs she'd hear the girl's voice, shrill. English or Spanish, it was always the same. *Why are you doing this to me. . . ?*

You wouldn't see her for weeks. She'd move to Miami, or join another class, or quit dancing. Once, a mere two days after a breakup, Wendy spotted Tuerto's latest at the Copa with Effy Duarte, the director of Puerto Domingo. Now *there* was an ambitious *mambera*.

Occasionally a girl would show character and take it in stride. She'd return to class, expecting no favors, ready to go. She might have been wooed and then dumped, but she was confident that whatever happened she would never again be one of the crowd. She'd keep the weight off, continue dressing well, and most important, dance her ass off at every opportunity. Eventually she would get her reward: Tuerto would ask her to join Las Chicas de la Calle.

Over the years Wendy had learned to cope, to take care of herself during the lean times and, most of all, to pretend she didn't care. Soni Bologna had been particularly bad news. Ballet lessons since she could walk, and an amazingly quick study, according to Tuerto who raved about her posture, how she could spot the *ceiling*. She was a buyer for Saks, which explained the clothes. Despite the pastel colors and fancy education, Wendy could see that Sonia was as hard as nails. And *pale.* The hairs that grew down her temples were so white as to be invisible. Like a ghost. How could Tuerto stand dancing with her, much less fucking her?

But Sonia was his type dance-wise—small and athletic with quick reflexes, like Wendy herself, although Sonia was more ballroom than street. Wendy could see them shifting to accommodate each other, she sharpening her phrasing, adding some vogue styling, he making the transitions more fluid and paying close attention to her body language.

If only she'd wipe that snotty expression off her face.

"So, is Sonia *the one?*" Wendy asked Tuerto once, half in jest.

"Wassamatta, you don't think I'm classy enough for her?"

"You said it, not me."

"I fucked a Harvard Law student once. She wasn't so special."

And now here was Lina.

Wendy had never been a fan of white Cubans—they had too much attitude; and what was their problem anyway, bitching about a country they had chosen to desert when the going got rough? Meanwhile, they had turned South Florida into North Cuba. Wendy's boss at the clinic, who was Chinese, hadn't been able to go back to China for *twenty-seven years* after it went Communist. You never heard *her* complaining. What made Cubans feel so entitled?

Unlike every other Cuban Wendy had ever met, however, Catalina had no politics, no opinion; in all their conversations she had never once mentioned Fidel Castro. She rarely talked about her family. If Sonia looked like a ghost, Catalina behaved like one, floating, not tied to this world or that. That blank-slate quality, however, was what made her such a dream follow. What the two of them could do to the boys at the Copa and Wild Palm! There were nights when Wendy could actually see the erections growing.

But that Tuesday evening in August when Catalina walked into class with her hair down and so much black liner on that it had smudged under each eye, Wendy was taken off guard. "Wassamatta, your man treating you bad?" she asked as the two women kissed hello, and reached up to erase the smudges with a fingertip.

Catalina flinched. "Thanks." She turned away toward the mirrors, where Carlos, as usual, was showing off. But it wasn't Carlos who was distracting her.

You, too, Wendy thought, surprised at how quickly it was registering. At least Catalina wasn't acting smug, the way some of the others did.

The music for the shines was Jimmy Bosch's *descarga* "Un Poquito Más." Basic. Corner to corner. Add a kick, add a skip. Swing step, back to front. Corner to corner. She could have done it in her sleep. In the mirror she saw that directly behind her Catalina was styling, holding her wrists up, doing a little body roll on the corner to corner. Already there was sweat streaking down her temples. It was especially stifling in the studio that day; Wendy could feel her own tank sticking to her skin. There was Tuerto studying Catalina in the mirror. When he caught her eye, he winked and licked his lips.

Wendy missed a step.

Come on, she told herself, *Get a grip. Your arms. Your hands.*

The song was all horns and drums. Grapevine. Grapevine with a lunge. Grapevine with a turn and a lunge. Suzy-Q's. Lazy Suzy-Q's. Flare. Flare into a syncopated flare. Double crossovers. Double crossovers into a slide back and mambo jazz.

"Un Poquito Más" ended and a *guajira* came on. It sounded slow but wasn't. Willy Chirino and Celia Cruz were going back and forth about how beautiful Cuba was. He called her Negra, Hermana.

Where had Catalina said her family was from?

Hot toe, cross cross cross, hot toe, hook flick three times. Turn combination: one left turn, semi turn, semi turn, one right turn, double right turn.

Pinar del Río, that's right.

Catalina was in a trance. All she cared about was getting those steps perfect, the styling just right. Now her face was shiny with sweat and her mouth set into a line as she danced so hard Wendy could hear the tap-tap-tapping of her stilettos as they struck the floor. *Very polished,* Wendy thought, *but you can see her trying.* Lina aimed for the ceiling with the middle fingers of both hands as she raised up for a spin, combed her hands over the crown of her head as she came out of it, stopped herself as neatly as a Rollerblader before she rocked into the back step. Her head toss was precisely on the beat, maybe too precisely.

At the end of the next turn combination, knowing she had to somehow assert her dominance, Wendy did a triple right spin instead of a double. Catalina managed to follow but stumbled on the back step.

Welcome to the club, Cinderella.

Danzón-Cha

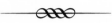

9

Catalina

Dancing is a form of walking.

Un día regresaremos.
Some day we'll go back.

Ten years to the day after the assassination of JFK, two weeks after Javier Ortiz hanged himself from a beam in the tobacco factory that had been in his family for six generations, his widow and eight-year-old daughter boarded a milk truck bound east at two o'clock on a chilly November morning. The plan was to stay with Javier's cousins in La Habana until they could eventually all emigrate to Miami, where Javier's older sister had settled in the sixties. Javier, the dutiful heir, had stayed behind to make sure Tabaco Ortiz maintained its reputation as the "smoke that was worth its weight in gold." But now he was dead, and Jun couldn't wait to leave the town where everything reminded her of what she had lost.

In the cab of the truck, squeezed in tight between her *mami* and the driver, Catalina could not stop shivering. She had not spoken a word since she had discovered her *papi*'s body.

As they wound down from the squat green mountains (*"elefantas,"* she and her *papi* had called them) where she'd spent all her short life, and onto the *autopista,* where palm grove after palm grove stood black and ghastly and sad against the gray sky, Catalina's shivering got worse. She clenched her jaw to keep her teeth from chattering. It helped a little that her mother hugged her tightly all the way to Artemisa—hometown of the great trumpeter Arturo Sandoval—where they stopped and went off into the cane fields to do their business. Then the driver took out a couple of quart bottles from the back of the truck, one of which Jun made Catalina drink. Used to the warm richness of the milk of their nanny goat, Catalina found cow milk cold and chalky. She had to shut her eyes and breathe slowly through her mouth to get it all down. Back on the road, while her mother and the truck driver shared the last Populare in his pack, Catalina fell asleep, awakening only when they reached the outskirts of La Habana, clattering mule carts and bicycles and other trucks rumbling by them. Her *papi* had bought her a bicycle made in China, which he'd been teaching her to ride but Jun had sold it along with everything else they owned, except for what they were carrying in the two suitcases stowed in back with the wooden crates of milk.

The sun was rising. Catalina had finally stopped shivering, but now she felt strange in a different way. It was hot now, so hot that the driver rolled down both windows and, while Jun held the wheel steady, wriggled out of his T-shirt. He had a muscular pale chest decorated with sparse curly hairs, contrasting with his forearms and hands, which were the color of caramel. Around his head was knotted a navy blue bandanna.

"Did you know I went to school here," Jun said to no one in particular, the first words she had spoken since Artemisa when she had told Catalina to finish her milk.

"No me digas," the truck driver said. He unwrapped the bandanna and used it to blot his temples. Where the cloth had been was a pale stripe on his forehead. Catalina could smell his sweat now, strong and a little sour but not unpleasant, like the wood sorrel in their backyard

in Pinar. For the first time she noticed his eyes, which were large and green, the color of swamps, as they regarded her mother.

"Si," said Jun. *"Catachan"*—addressing her daughter now—"it was here that your father and I met and fell in love."

Catalina couldn't imagine. A country girl by birth and by nature, she hated La Habana on sight. In the fourteenth year of the rule of Castro everything was going to ruin. The pale buildings inlaid with blue and gold tiles, the peeling walls and crumbling columns, reminded her of the tombs in the graveyard where her *papi* had been laid to rest. When they drove onto the Malecón, however, she was impressed by the bay as it crashed in swoops against the sea wall. *"No has visto nada,"* said the driver, when he saw her expression. "Just wait till the tide comes in, or better yet, when there's a hurricane out to sea. Then you'll see waves. Sometimes this road is so flooded I have to cut around and use the Prado."

He drove them to the apartment bloc of Javier's cousin in Centro Habana. When they finally found the building and had climbed four flights of scooped out cracked marble stairs with their suitcases, the door was closed and padlocked and no one answered when they banged. Right beside them another door flew open and a man in an undershirt and army pants leaned out. *"¡Coño, compañero, la gente están durmiendo!"*

The man calmed down when the truck driver explained whom they were looking for. *"Se fueran,"* said the man, and made the motion of snapping something around his wrists that Catalina didn't understand but the truck driver and her mother apparently did.

"¿Cuándo?" the truck driver asked, and the man said, *"La semana pasada."*

Catalina's mother, whom she'd never seen cry, not even at her *papi's* funeral, put her head down. The truck driver wrapped his arm around her, and the man in the undershirt just stood there shaking his head. A few minutes later they were all sitting in this man's living room, and his wife in a pink-and-white flowered housedress and her hair in curlers was serving them coffee. *"Hermana, hermana,"* they kept on calling her mother, who was wiping her eyes on the sleeve of her cardigan. The wife knelt down in front of Catalina and asked if she wanted some bread with *guayaba* paste.

Catalina shook her head as black splotches appeared before her eyes, and the next thing she knew she was lying in a big bed in a dark room that smelled of talcum powder.

"*Te desmayaste,* Catachan," her *mami* said when she came in and pressed a cool wet cloth to her daughter's forehead. Catalina's hair was in one long plait, as she would wear it for most of her life, and her mother undid this and spread the waves out on the pillow and stroked them and told her that she was a princess trapped in a tower but did not have to worry, the prince would soon come to rescue her.

In the dark bedroom they slept until the truck driver, who had gone to make his delivery, came back and took them to a place called Playa, where he lived with his parents.

There they stayed for two months with the bald old man who sat and snored in the corner of the living room and the skinny dark brown woman with a sharp nose and big watery green eyes just like her son's. Jun and Catalina slept on a cot in the front room under a big painting of a naked lady lying down. During the days Jun helped the truck driver's mother cook and clean while Catalina sat on the stoop and watched the neighborhood kids playing games that were not that different from what they played in Pinar. But she was too shy to join in, so the kids, after some initial sniffing around, left her alone. *Muda,* they called her, because she still hadn't said a word since the sunny morning she'd raced back across the street from the factory and tugged on her *mami*'s skirt. At ten o'clock the truck driver would come beeping his horn down the street, scattering the children, who would yell and hoot. He'd park in front of the door and rub the top of Catalina's head and then go in and stay until four o'clock. Sometimes when she went in for lunch, he and her *mami* were nowhere to be seen, but she knew they were together in the bedroom behind the curtain.

One afternoon the three of them went to Coppelia Park in Vedado, and the truck driver bought Catalina and her mother metal dishes of strawberry ice cream, three scoops each with chocolate sprinkles, which they ate in the round building overlooking the trees. That night, as Jun was tucking her daughter into bed, she said, "He's good to us, isn't he, Catachan?"

Yes the truck driver was good, but her father was dead and her mother never smiled and they were living in a place she hated, and why couldn't she go to school with the other kids?

Right after New Year's they packed their suitcases again and left, this time for Los Estados Unidos. In a small cove at twilight her *mami* and the truck driver hugged for a long time. *"Tu me salvaste,"* Jun kept whispering, while Catalina, who liked the truck driver well enough, although unlike other grown-ups he was oddly shy with her, never inviting her to sit on his lap for instance, gazed fascinated at the ancient blue and gray trawler that was to ferry them across the Florida Straits. They were embarking from the tiny port of Rosa Marina, tucked between the towns of Mosquito and Playa Baracoa just north of La Habana. As Catalina would later learn, their journey was highly unusual, taking place between the Freedom Flights of the late sixties and the Mariel Boatlift of 1980, a period when there was little immigration, legal or otherwise, from Cuba to the United States. Their skipper was the truck driver's second cousin's best friend, a commercial fisherman out of Miami, one of those *cubanos* known as sea wolves, who would brave the journey to Cuba and back for five hundred dollars a head. The man was a pioneer; in the nineties he would be the head of a huge human-smuggling empire, using a fleet of speedboats to outrun the Cuban and American coast guards. In all his years of ferrying human cargo the fisherman himself would never be caught, although some of his subcontractors were not so lucky. It was said that he had a pact with Yemayá, Goddess of the Sea. Before and after each journey he'd open a bottle of Mulata rum, spill half of it into the ocean as an offering, and drink the rest.

In 1973, the sea wolf would take ten passengers. The fact that he was risking his life for only the two of them spoke of the truck driver's devotion—he'd used his entire life savings to pay the voyage minimum of twenty-five hundred U.S. dollars.

On the way to Florida they caught the tail end of a squall off the coast of Andros Island, and despite the danger of helicopters with their sweeping floodlights, Jun spent the first three hours dry-heaving over the starboard rail as the fisherman nursed the wheel against the swells and sang under his breath. Catalina huddled down in the fish-slimed hold and dreamed of strolling down the main street of Pinar del Río with her *papi* on a Saturday afternoon after the factory had closed for the day, stopping as he chatted with his friends on the sidewalk while a *charanga* band played in the park. She breathed through her mouth so as not to inhale the stink of years of dead fish, tried not to listen to the sloshing of the bilge water, which made her feel like heaving as her *mami* was doing. She relived spring mornings when her father would wake her up with a plate of fresh mango slices. He'd sing a song he'd made up just for her:

Pa' ti, pa' ti
Quien eres como una manga amarilla
Espero toda mi vida.

Me encanta tu piel tan suave
Tu aroma de angelitos.
Soy hijo de Pinar del Rio
Y me conozco las frutas.

For you, for you
Who are like a yellow mango
I will wait all of my life.

I adore your soft skin
Your aroma of angels.
For I'm a son of Pinar del Rio
And I know my fruits very well.

As the seas finally calmed around 24 degrees latitude, Jun crept down into the hold to join her daughter lying against the suitcases, tucking her salt-soaked cardigan behind their heads to make a pillow. "*Nete iruno?*" Jun murmured, but Catalina, who was not asleep, pretended to be. Her mother began to talk in the dark to herself, declaring in her low-pitched voice that this trip was heaven compared to some others she'd heard about, trips on rafts and inner tubes, with sharks and dehydration and accidents, which ended more often than not in drowning. Soon they'd be in Miami, at the *casa* of Ana, Javier's older sister, *muy simpática.* Catachan would have new dresses, and hamburgers any time she wanted, and when she was fifteen, a fancy

quinceñera with a hired band. They would book a professional photographer and send pictures back home to Pinar.

The fisherman chose to land on tiny Knight's Key, just below
Marathon. Key West was impenetrable, patrolled heavily by the U.S.
Coast Guard since the Bay of Pigs and not worth the risk. He called for
them to come up on deck, and after the staleness of the hold Catalina
could not get enough air; her lungs felt taut from breathing in so hard.
The fisherman was humming "La Negra Tomasa" as they approached
harbor, but Catalina was not listening because she was still hearing the
mango song in her head. In the hint of dawn she could see the carpet
of palmettos and sea grapes stretching down to the water's edge.
Venus was paling in the western sky, and phosphorus flicked the lap-
ping black waves like stars that had rained from heaven and were now
dissolving. What the fisherman had accomplished that night was
almost too extraordinary to be believed: weaseling them out of Rosa
Marina, past the infamous Cuban PT boats, whose habits he knew
inside out from his days on his father's fishing boat, through gaps in
the radar he'd mapped out after conferences with other fishermen,
yawing expertly over choppy seas in the dead of night, navigating only
by the stars, and then putting past Key West, under the very noses of
the American Coast Guard, who after midnight tended to concentrate
farther out to sea watching for cocaine runners. All in all the journey
had taken slightly less than ten hours.

Now the fisherman throttled back his engine, and they drifted
silently ashore as the sky lightened. The hull bumped, and the fisherman made fast at a cluster of pilings and put his forefinger to his lips
before lifting them and then their suitcases onto a rickety dock.
Catalina stumbled; her *mami* caught her. This was it. They were in
Los Estados Unidos. In Catalina's imagination Los Estados Unidos
was an island just like Cuba, maybe a little smaller, where some of
her relatives had gone to live.

But then she spied the building beyond, larger than any house
she'd ever seen, covered with weather-beaten shingles. It looked
closed up and deserted. There was a smaller building beside it, which
Catalina took to be a second house, but her *mami* told her it was a
garage, a *casita* for *automoviles*.

The fisherman pointed out the road that would take them to the bus that left once a day to downtown Miami. He opened his bottle of rum and drank, then offered Jun a swig, which she accepted. When she and Catalina had watched him drift out to sea again, they walked on wobbly legs the length of the dock and down onto the beach, where Jun scrubbed Catalina's face with a handkerchief and smoothed down the wisps that were sticking out of her braid. They shared some bread and ham washed down with the few sips of water left in their bottle. When it was light enough to see, they set off through the mangroves, Jun carrying both suitcases, damp and thus heavier than when they had started out. Catalina held on to her mother's skirts, sucking her thumb, which she had not done since she was two.

They had been journeying for fourteen hours, but the time felt as long as her whole life before that.

The truck driver had given Jun fifty American cash, most of which they used to pay their bus fare. Before they fell asleep on the long ride up U.S. 1 Jun whispered: *"Un día regresaremos."*

Later when Catalina recalled the night before as they'd stood on the shore at Rosa Marina and the truck driver's watery green eyes, how he'd murmured, *"Juanita, amor de mi vida"* and the way Jun had kissed him for the last time but not looked back, she knew that her mother was lying.

Their first days in Miami, while her *mami* was busy doing paper-work that would make them legal, Catalina sat in the back room of her *tíos' botánica* watching cartoons. *Bugs Bunny* was her favorite. Customers would peek their heads in and exclaim: *"¡Ay qúe preciosa chinita!"* Tía Ana would relate to them, in a low voice, the tragedy of her brother, another victim of El Diablo, who had promised to democratize Cuba but instead had taken it over with the ruthlessness of dictators before him. Not to mention Tía Ana's cousin the economics professor and his wife who had been hauled off to jail and now, it was rumored, were sequestered on the Isla de la Juventud. And this *pobrecita,* Tía Ana would say, pointing to her niece, was trau-matized for life, for it was she who had found her dead father, with his face all purple and the piss running down his leg. No wonder she had lost her tongue.

When they were alone, Tía Ana would pump Catalina about the

time she and Jun had spent in La Habana: where was the house, who lived in it, were they nice to her and her *mami*. Perhaps her aunt hoped that Catalina would betray something by her face. If she'd been able to speak, she would have replied thus: *It was the family of the milk-truck driver; the kids on the street didn't like me; La Habana was awful, hot and crowded, and there wasn't enough to eat. The bread, when we got it, tasted funny, and the vegetables were too salty.*

Tía Ana seemed to intuit the food part, maybe because Catalina was always hungry.

"*Sí,* it must have been terrible, no fresh fruit or vegetables. He's starving our whole country, *diablo loco.*"

What Catalina would not have mentioned, had she been able to speak, was that there had always been fresh milk, so much that they not only drank it at every meal, but the green-eyed woman had often made flan and rice pudding, and on one memorable occasion, hot chocolate.

They spent three years in Miami, crowded but not uncomfortable in the house in Little Havana, and then they moved again. Jun was having trouble finding work. A friend of Tía Ana's was a live-in maid in a town near Boston, Massachusetts, and when this friend quit her job to get married, Tía Ana finagled things so Jun could inherit the position. The move, which took place during a particularly cold January, was a terrible shock for Catalina, almost worse than her *papi*'s death. It did goad her into speaking again, and she stopped hearing the mango song in her head as she had for years every night before falling asleep.

She missed Miami. The house in Calle Ocho felt like home to her in a way her mother's apartment never did. Her *tíos'* house was jammed with family history, including numerous photos of her *papi*. Tía Ana would explain: "Here's Javier when he was eight, *mira,* look how happy he is. Here we all are at my *quinceñera*. Our *abuela* worked on that dress for three months. And look, here's you right after you were born, Lina. You have your *papi*'s smile."

Her mother had only one picture from Cuba, her wedding portrait, which she kept on her bedside table. Javier was wearing a white suit and panama hat and didn't have his glasses on, but you could see where they had been from the marks on his nose. Jun was unrecognizable, her hair covered with Spanish lace, dark lips. She didn't look the least bit Japanese.

In America, Catalina thought, Jun seemed to be asleep. She was not a mother who fussed or scolded, like Tía Ana, but one who went through the basic gestures of cooking, cleaning, and shopping in a daze, so that some of Catalina's friends said she was crazy. In America she began to speak Japanese more. Because Catalina could no longer speak Spanish, the language between her and her mother was an odd mixture of Japanese and broken English. *"Tadaimah,"* Catalina would say, entering the house, and her mother would answer, *"Okaerinasai."* Jun never remarked on what Catalina wore or how late she came home, not that Catalina was the kind of daughter who would give cause for worry. Except for that last summer in Miami, and there was no way she would have told her mother about that, much less what she had been up to the day before she left for college when she said she was going to the dentist.

Although Jun never directly discussed her dead husband, he was a constant ghost. "Your *papi* should be here," was her mother's reaction when Catalina brought home all A's, or broke her ankle playing soccer, or got into Smith. Jun was a dutiful parent, attending Catalina's assemblies and parent-teacher meetings, although she was shy because of her lack of English. Catalina spent her fifteenth without her mother, down in Calle Ocho, and it was just a regular birthday party, although Tía Ana did send an announcement to one of the neighborhood papers. Her mother's gift was Catalina's great-grandmother's sandalwood and ivory fan, wrapped in a silk *furoshki* patterned with white cranes on a gray-green background.

It was Catalina's junior year of college when Jun got sick. No more vacations in Florida; she spent them instead tending to her mother. In the decade during which Catalina had grown from chubby girl to lissome adolescent, her mother's face had turned into an old woman's with hooded eyelids and deeply carved parentheses around her mouth, her salt-and-pepper hair worn in a sloppy bun or half pulled back with plastic child's barrettes. She was up to two and a half packs a day. In Cuba Jun had smoked exactly once a day, at ten o'clock in the morning when she took a *cafecito* across the street to Javier and, sitting on the front steps of the factory holding hands, they would listen to their favorite *radionovela* broadcast from La Habana.

In middle age Jun Midori Ortiz still had the figure of a woman in her twenties, although you would have never known it from the baggy blouses and skirts that had become her uniform. Old face and young body, was how Catalina remembered her mother. Thank God the couple she had worked for let her stay on in the garage apartment and had provided enough insurance to cover most of the medical costs. Their own children were grown up and out of the house by then, and they let Catalina use their car to take her mother into Boston for medical appointments.

Jun continued to smoke even after she was diagnosed with the throat cancer that would end her life. She spent days with her feet up in her lace-choked parlor watching Mexican *telenovelas* while she sipped *yerbabuena* tea with jasmine honey in an effort to soothe the dry cough that made Catalina queasy; it reminded her of her mother's retching on their sea voyage from Cuba.

In Cuba Jun had had the distinction of being one of the last of the pure-blooded Japanese, but she was not special in America where everyone and their best friend were immigrants. Besides family and the couple she'd worked for, there was hardly anybody at the funeral. Teresa Martinez, who was from Honduras and ran a beauty salon across the street from Catalina's high school, flew down to Miami with Catalina and the casket. Teresa, her mother's only northern friend, said: *"Que tragedia.* Your *mami* could have had a new life here, found a man, she was so pretty and sweet-spirited, I was always encouraging her, but it was like she had given up."

For years Catalina had harbored the childish notion that the reason Jun was so unhappy was not because of Javier's suicide, nor because she missed Cuba, but because God was punishing her for taking up with the milk-truck driver so soon after her husband's death. Was she sorry to die in a strange land? Catalina never asked but suspected that to Jun it didn't matter. As she watched her mother's coffin being lowered into the ground she finally realized: after Javier Ortiz left this world there was nowhere Jun would have felt at home.

10

Guillermo

Following takes strength, attention,
and a certain mind-set.

———— ⧓ ————

How at age thirty-two Guillermo Javier De Leon Ortiz found himself at the heart of a Miami *exilio* plot to overthrow Castro was a mystery he was never quite able to solve.

Like the rest of his generation Guillermo had inherited the idea of Cuba from his parents, a romantic image of their hometown of Pinar del Río—long sleepy days, tobacco plantations, beautiful girls with sprigs of jasmine in their hair. Although he hadn't even been born when the Bay of Pigs happened he was aware, along with everyone else in Little Havana, of the complex relationship between this group of privileged white émigrés and the government in Washington. His parents liked to tell the story of how they had taken their two older sons to the Orange Bowl for JFK's speech about bringing the flag back to a free Havana. Rafael had been drinking Pepsi, and a bee had flown into the paper cup and stung him on his eyelid, which had swelled so badly he had to be rushed to the emergency room. It was an omen, his mother said, of the president's assassination just days later.

Guillermo the boy was a loner, not inclined to hang out with the neighborhood kids or his older brothers. He spent weekends watching old movies on TV—his favorites were sea adventures—or listening to his dad's old 78s. Skinny, with deep-set eyes and theatrically high cheekbones, he was extremely nearsighted, and the only sport he liked was sailing which he started as soon as he was old enough to take lessons. His family took his oddness lightly, his father telling people he had been born in "island head," that is, with the capacity to let life flow on and around him without getting too involved in it.

The year he turned eight his mother's younger brother killed himself, causing his mother to become a nervous wreck and to curse Castro even more hysterically than she had previously. The following spring Tía Juanita and cousin Catalina appeared, literally on their doorstep. His cousin was chubby and silent and smelled like fish. It was clear to Guillermo that she needed taking care of and that he was the one to do it.

Catty was the one pure thing in his life. That was his thought as a child, and even after what happened the summer they turned eighteen, what he did not confess to the priest (*Bless me father for I have sinned; I fucked my* prima). He'd never forget that night on the beach when they were sitting in his dad's car working on a six-pack and he kissed her for the first time. It was something about the way she was sitting—knees drawn up, the little hairs sticking out of her braid, her mouth half open—that made him do it.

She didn't respond, but she didn't push him away either, so he did it again.

"That was practice for my girlfriend," he explained.

"You don't have a girlfriend."

It was true. He was retarded that way; all his buddies said it.

It became a habit. After dinner they'd pick up some beers and head to the beach and make out. Practice, they called it. They never went below the neck; it was an unwritten rule, although it was an understatement to say that he was tempted. It was not lost on Guillermo that his cousin had advanced from an A cup to C over the past school year. What finally happened was inevitable. One Sunday afternoon in July when no one else was home and they were hanging out on the back veranda, they ended up going all the way, zero to a hundred as he thought of it later. Afterward she got dressed without saying anything and went inside to her room and shut the door. When he walked past to take a shower, he could hear the radio going.

He knew she wasn't mad, just freaked out, like he was. The next night when he got home from work, she was waiting for him on the front porch.

She asked: "Wanna go to the beach?"

They still called it practice, joking that if this was practice, they couldn't wait for the real thing. He thought maybe his mother suspected because she was always suggesting that he and Catty invite this or that friend along on their nights out. He started making up names of people they were going to meet.

That was the summer Guillermo woke up to girls in general, especially the ones in the sailing classes he was teaching at the Deering Yacht and Country Club. During the past year he'd shot up six inches and gotten contact lenses, and now they were looking. The most desirable without question was Lillian Cruz. She was a favorite topic among the guys on staff, who all claimed to have done her, but one look and you knew they were lying. She was royalty, and they were serfs. Her father owned the largest chain of Mercedes dealerships in southern Florida as well as interest in several downtown Miami banks. You could follow her social life in the society pages. Neither Guillermo nor anyone he knew had been invited to her *quinceñera* at the Surf Club, where it was said a helicopter had showered the guests with white gardenias as they were getting into their cars.

Guillermo enrolled at Florida State with a major in business and no particular plans about what he was going to do with it. One Friday night his freshman year when he was out with his buddies at a little dive in South Beach, there was Lilly, slumming in bicycle shorts and a cropped top with no bra. He was entranced by the glamour of her hazel green eyes and her streaked hair, up in a chignon, a lock of which had come undone and brushed her bare shoulders. In all his life he had never seen such beautiful shoulders. Perhaps because of the way she was dressed, he not only had the courage to pull her out on the dance floor but to ask her out as well.

Before he knew it he was being invited to the house in Palm Beach for Sunday dinner. Lilly's father, a self-made *campesino* from Camagüey, took a shine to him right away. Guillermo for his part admired the plain-speaking Humberto Cruz, who was said to be tight with Marco de Las Villas, founder of the Cubans for Free Americas Alliance lobby group. Throughout their courtship Lilly's mother and sisters remained icy, but Humberto Cruz made it plain that he was fond of Guillermo, and this was enough for Lilly, who was Daddy's girl. She didn't mind that Guillermo wasn't from a Havana dynasty; in fact, as far as she was concerned, his rough edges were a plus. He invested in a tuxedo and now it was he who appeared alongside her in the society-page photographs so that his chums at the Deering Yacht and Country Club whistled their envy. Their first son was conceived in her bedroom at the Palm Beach mansion. It was after New Year's Day dinner; Humberto Cruz had fallen asleep by the pool, and everyone else was watching football in the game room. Lilly had forgotten her diaphragm, she claimed, on Calle Ocho. When she revealed her pregnancy, she added in the same breath: "We should start planning the wedding right away, don't you think?"

Why did he acquiesce? Why didn't he at least discuss the possibility of an abortion? Catholic or not, it was the eighties after all. Why did he let himself get swept up into a situation for which he was completely unprepared? There was no good answer to any of these questions, except that he was under the spell of Lilly's beauty, her wealth, her father's connections. He was the frog who had been kissed and turned into a prince.

At their wedding reception Marco de Las Villas—also known as *Oso*, or Bear—gave the first toast, to Cuba *divina*, Lillian *divina* his godchild, who looked sublimely regal in a half-sleeved custom-made Carolina Herrera satin dress with a thirty-foot train of antique Bruges lace and matching mantilla. The gown's dropped waist barely concealed the bride's four-month pregnancy, which was common knowledge anyway. What Guillermo would remember later was that

Oso pressed his hand especially hard when he introduced himself in the receiving line, raising those famous caterpillar eyebrows that had earned him his nickname. Was this some kind of a signal? Guillermo had wondered, or simply an aggressive idiosyncrasy Las Villas displayed upon meeting another man? Was it meant to intimidate? Did he apply that much pressure when shaking the hand of Ronald Reagan, for example, as it was said he frequently did?

Is this really happening to me? he kept asking himself. His father told him: "Junior, you did good." His mother had tears in her eyes as she had not for his brother Ernesto's nuptials. Catalina sent a set of eight crystal champagne flutes from Tiffany and a handwritten note expressing her regrets, although she did not explain why she was unable to attend.

The couple moved into a two-bedroom condo in South Beach, and when the baby came, they named him Guillermo Ernesto Humberto, Guillé for short, after the father and two grandfathers. Under Humberto Cruz's guidance Guillermo set out to learn the dealership business from top to bottom. The salary he drew was so obscenely high that when his mother asked, he hinted at a quarter of the real amount. On the face of things he was a grown-up. He read the papers, watched the news on TV, dandled his son on his knee. At his father-in-law's insistence but not without qualms he signed on to the board of various Cuban American organizations, including Cubans for Free Americas, or CFA, as it was commonly known, and attended their luncheons and banquets with Lilly on his arm. He made a down payment on a secondhand seventy-five-foot Rhodes ketch named the *Catalina la O* after the salsa tune the Fania All-Stars had made famous.

The real Catalina he saw all too rarely. It was only after her mother died that she started coming down for holidays again. If he had seen his cousin more often, he would have confided in her that the spell was broken, that his marriage was beginning to pall, that his father-in-law had been setting him up, all those Sunday afternoons after dinner when he took Guillermo into the study and over cognac and Esplendidos they talked. What did Junior think about the ongoing trade embargo with Cuba, this little leftist newsletter that had sprung up on Calle Ocho, or the mayor's latest proposition concern-

ing zoning in downtown Miami? Guillermo puffed the earthy sweetness from the leaves grown and aged in the valleys of Viñales, his
ancestors' homeland, and humored his father-in-law: it was a pity
about the trade embargo, Castro and Raúl were decimating the spirits of the Cuban population on both sides of the Straits. The newsletter should be shut down. As for the zoning—Guillermo didn't care
one way or another, so long as decent, family-run businesses had the
freedom to prosper.

He knew the right things to say, but he didn't really believe them.
If truth be told, he had always found the *exilios* to be overzealous. It
was only a matter of time before Castro died and the United States
would work out a normalization deal with whomever succeeded
him. Fidel's brother, Raúl, was next in line, but he was no spring
chicken and did not have the charisma of El Maximo Lider. He,
Guillermo, was neutral, a position he'd taken as a teenager and never
found reason from which to deviate. He and Catty had often discussed the dramas of their parents and had sworn to each other that
they'd never get involved.

Reenter Marco de Las Villas, not in the flesh, but in the form of a
representative. Oso's messenger was a laconic bonds trader named
Jorge Crespo, whom Guillermo had met socially a couple of times.
The first contact occurred the day after his father-in-law underwent
his first quadruple-bypass surgery. While Lilly was holding vigil at
the hospital, Crespo phoned the house and invited Guillermo for a
game of tennis at the Grove Isle Club. After Guillermo had won, or
Crespo had let him win—6–4, 6–3, 7–5—and they'd shaken hands
over the net, Crespo said in his affected tenor: "You're a good man.
There's something I want to talk over with you." Over beers in the
clubhouse Crespo told Guillermo he needed help on an arms deal.
Guillermo felt his stomach turn over but couldn't say he was surprised. The deal involved Polish guns and matériel sold through a
Swiss middleman, eventually destined for Cubans for Free Americas.
They needed a front buyer in Miami, a high-profile business, to laun-
der the money. Bridge financing, was how Crespo put it. The Mercedes dealership in Hollywood would be ideal. Crespo hinted that
the chief accountant at Mercedes-Benz Unlimited, Israel Gomez,
would be more than familiar with the bookkeeping required. For the

record they would be investing in "specialized automotive parts." Everything of course would be handled in cash.

Guillermo said: "I'll have to talk this over with my father-in-law when he gets out of the hospital."

"Humberto Cruz," said Crespo, combing back his wet curls with his fingers, "is one of us."

One of us? "You mean CFA?"

"That and more. I'll call you at home in a couple of days, and we can work out the details."

It was so much like a bad spy movie that Guillermo was reluctant to discuss it with Lilly. He finally tried one night when they were having a nightcap after the opera before heading home to their new Spanish revival mansion in Coral Gables. He went straight to the point and asked his wife if her father was involved in any political and/or paramilitary dealings.

In the dim light sparkling off the mirror over the bar, Lilly looked back at him not exactly blankly, but not giving much either.

"Pipo loves Cuba," is what she said.

"And?"

"He'd do anything for Cuba."

"Which Cuba? This one or that one?"

His wife's slender fingers slid up the stem of her Art Deco martini glass as she raised it to her lips and sipped without answering. She was as beautiful as ever, he thought, although now he found her brittle.

I'll do it just this once, he decided. *A gift for the old man; he's practically on his deathbed.* When Crespo called, Guillermo said the deal was on but he needed guidance. Crespo assured him that it was a lot easier than selling cars. All Guillermo had to do was alert Gomez and note down certain numbers and dates. Everything went smoothly. The cash was dropped off and handled by Gomez—Guillermo himself had only to sign a few receipts—and a week later a shipment at Miami International was loaded onto a small truck and delivered to an apartment in South Kendall. Ten days later the same truck transported the goods to Fort Lauderdale.

In by air, out by sea.

It wasn't until months later that Crespo called the house again. "Check out the papers; I think you'll be pleased."

The front page of the *Miami Herald* showed photographs of four hotel lobbies in Havana decimated by pipe bombs. Fortunately there were only a few minor injuries.

CASTRO BLAMES TERRORISM ON WASHINGTON was the headline. There was a quote from Marco de Las Villas, which said essentially that Castro was crazy and paranoid.

That same morning a messenger dropped off an envelope at the Casa Rosada with two box tickets to the premier of *La Traviata*, featuring the great Spanish tenor Cesár Solaris at the Metropolitan Opera in New York City the following Saturday night. Saturday afternoon a car arrived at the Casa Rosada to bring Lilly and Guillermo to Miami International, where there was a private Learjet waiting. The pilot had on a pin depicting a bear's head with two wings attached.

La Traviata happened to be Lilly's favorite opera and Cesár Solaris her favorite tenor. After the performance she awakened Guillermo, who had fallen asleep during the last act, and insisted that they go backstage. Solaris, who was even more imposing in person than onstage, kissed Lilly's hand and said that he had heard so much about her from their mutual friend. Along with Solaris and his entourage they were chauffeured to a famous Japanese restaurant in Tribeca and fawned over by the staff. After that it was the Plaza, and back to Miami the next morning.

Guillermo called Crespo in order to set his mind at ease about something that had been bothering him. *"Gracias por todo, compadre,* but I have one question."

"Go ahead."

"What happened to the guns?"

"They're safe, don't worry."

Something about Crespo's tone discouraged Guillermo from pressing the subject.

About a year later the call came again. This shipment was warehoused at a different address, in Hialeah. To Guillermo's knowledge, there was no pickup scheduled. A couple of weeks later he and Lilly and the boys, now two in number, traveled to Spain on vacation. "Everything okay?" he asked Gomez over the phone, and his accountant answered, *"Tranquilo, jefe, todo bien."*

This call took place on April 17, the anniversary of the Bay of

Pigs landing. That afternoon the headquarters of a major Spanish-language radio station in Miami was decimated by three pipe bombs. *Happy Thirtieth Anniversary to Traitors* was scrawled in red paint on the sidewalk across the street from the demolished building. In these blasts five people were killed, including the Cuban owner of the station as he was walking out to his car to drive home. The owner was notorious for his outspoken political editorials, the last of which had been a castigation of the Miami *exilios* for not being more open to a dialogue with Havana.

The De Leons watched the coverage on CNN in the bar of their hotel in Barcelona. A right-wing splinter organization in Miami was claiming responsibility. The group was called La Última Lucha, but according to the reporter no one knew who its leader or members were.

At first Guillermo did not make the connection. It was only when he happened to catch Lilly's face as they watched the broadcast, that Mona Lisa smile on her lips, the smile that had driven all the guys at the Deering Yacht and Country Club crazy, that he figured it out.

"*Que buen trabajo,*" she said. "That pig deserved to die."

Again it was clear where some of the matériel had gone, but what about the bulk of the shipment—the firearms?

The day they arrived home a '93 cream-colored Mercedes SE400 sedan—Guillermo's favorite—in mint condition was delivered to the Casa Rosada. Later that week, Guillermo suffered wracking pains in his abdomen and was diagnosed with bleeding ulcers. At the next Palm Beach dinner party Humberto Cruz raised his glass in a toast to his son-in-law, who was *one of us in La Lucha.* Guillermo felt a wave of nausea and had to force himself to throw back his shot of Matusalem. As soon as he could, he excused himself and left the room to retch blood in the toilet.

Still, he thought he was holding it together until he saw his mother's eyes. And his wife made no secret that she scorned his weak stomach. Lilly, shortly after giving birth to their third son, had begun spending more and more time out of the house, ostensibly at activities involving her guild friends, leaving the care of her children to a team of nannies. Guillermo saw her only if he made it home for dinner, which was rare, although they still shared the same bed. Once she said to him, with a coldness of which he hadn't thought her capable: "Buck up. You are only a small cog in a giant machine."

It was shortly after that conversation that he moved into the guest room.

He was terrified. Terrified to beg for an out, terrified of what La Última Lucha would do to him if he acted in any way that could be construed as a betrayal. At best he'd be disgraced forever; at worst he would have a convenient accident and his parents and brothers would be ostracized and be forced to move to another state.

Most days he was able to bury himself in work, in inventory lists and accounts and meetings with his managers, but then the call from Crespo would come, and he would be jolted back into the nightmare. It was at these times that he most missed his childhood, those long slow days on Calle Ocho when his world consisted of his family and his beloved cousin Catty. Crespo, a practiced seducer, kept him supplied with high-grade snow. And two or three nights a week Guillermo would go out alone to this or that new South Beach Club and sit at the bar and drink—only Stoli, because rum reminded him of his father-in-law, and only straight—and wonder how the hell he had gotten where he was. The only thing that brought him any joy those days was the face of his youngest, Santito.

In due course he learned the fate of the guns. After one of their monthly tennis games Crespo told him: "The final show will be on the *isla*. Our contacts there are in place. A dozen or so more shipments and we're ready to rumble." At Guillermo's disbelieving expression Crespo added, "De Leon, this is when I need your word of honor that you're with us all the way."

"Of course you have my word."

At the beginning of 1996 the shipments became markedly larger—besides assault rifles and ammunition they included equipment such as portable radios, satellite phones, and night-vision goggles. There was even a shipment marked USED CLOTHING, which Gomez let slip were military fatigues from Afghanistan. Guillermo was now directly responsible for the warehousing. He decided to use an industrial garage in Boca Raton, which he could lease in the name of the dealership. His father-in-law paid for the installation of a state-of-the-art security system at the Casa Rosada—all the windows of which, Guillermo discovered, had been already fitted with bullet-proof glass. Cruz also donated burly Seraphim, the Venezualan butler, who lived in the carriage house out back and never called in sick. The dealerships were officially handed over to Guillermo in a ceremony followed by dinner with the mayor of Coral Gables and a few close family friends. Marco de Las Villas was out of the country, it was rumored in Colombia, and thus unable to attend.

To keep himself sane, Guillermo turned to the *Catalina la O.* Every Saturday morning, rain or shine, he made the drive up to Fort Lauderdale to spend time on his ketch, cleaning and polishing the boards and brass fittings, the radio tuned to those old Cuban songs he'd loved since he was a boy. Afterward he would hang a hammock on the aft deck and drink beer and read the poets Lorca and Neruda, whose books his cousin had sent him during their college days. On the *Catalina* Guillermo felt suspended in time. No drugs, no vodka. The boat was enough. Once in a while, under the pretext of doing a little fishing, he'd call a couple of his old yacht club buddies for a day sail to one of the smaller Keys. There was no craft more striking than the *Catalina,* with her crimson trim and tan bark sails, and out on the open sea Guillermo would feel himself a free man.

In early 1997, Marco de Las Villas died at age sixty-eight of a massive coronary at home in bed. The Bear was gone. There was no direct heir to his throne, and the CFA was in chaos. Guillermo spent more time on the boat and listened to his father Ernesto talk about going back to Cuba. Easter morning, while Lilly and the boys were at church, he called his cousin on a whim. For some reason the sound of her voice made him want to cry. She had no idea what he'd turned into; she thought he was the same old Doggy who had loved and protected her all those years ago.

And I am, he thought, but he knew he was lying to himself.

That summer Crespo stopped by the office after hours with a bottle of brandy and two snifters and said to Guillermo, "You know, *hermano,* that all these deliveries have a sea leg."

"To Cuba, of course."

"We need your special help with the next one. With Oso gone

security got a little sloppy and the vessels that we usually use are no longer available to us."

"How does this involve me?"

"We need the *Catalina la O*. If you could skipper her to Kingston, we'll take over from there."

"That route is a pain in the ass. Why not sail direct to Havana?"

"They're on the lookout for us, *hermano*. A high-profile yacht like yours on a little cruise through the Bahamas is the perfect cover."

Guillermo was silent.

"This is the last shipment. Do you understand what that means?" When Guillermo still didn't answer, he continued: "Pretend you're on a family vacation. We can even give you a send-off bash and get it in the papers."

"I will not place my family in danger."

"There's no other way."

"Why can't you use another vessel?"

"The *Catalina* is the most appropriate for our needs."

Feeling as if he'd been punched in the stomach, Guillermo remembered how he had acquired the *Catalina*. Someone claiming to be a buddy of his father-in-law had phoned saying he'd suffered a stock market hit and would be happy to unload a spanking-new Rhodes for 50 percent off the market price. How could Guillermo resist after he took a drive up to the marina to check her out and saw the name in scarlet script on her hull?

Of course these people knew the boat and her specs; they had been planning to use it, and him, all along.

"Let me think about it."

"*Bueno, como tú quieras,*" said Crespo, but Guillermo knew he had no choice. As soon as Crespo left he put the snifters in the bathroom sink and the brandy bottle in the bottom drawer of his desk, thinking he would probably need it in the days to come. He was about to close up shop when he remembered that it was Catty's birthday. Knowing she'd probably be out, he dialed her number in New York and left a message.

"All right," he told Crespo when they met the next day for lunch at the Versailles in Little Havana, "I'll do it. But no family."

"You can't go alone; that would be suspicious."

"I'll bring someone. A girlfriend. You can leak it to the society columns."

"Hermano," said Crespo, "you don't have a girlfriend."

Did these people know everything? Guillermo said, "I'll find one."

"We are not interested in doing anything that would compromise Lillian Cruz."

Lillian De Leon, Guillermo thought. "I'll tell her I'm going on a business trip."

"All right." Crespo capitulated, a little too quickly, Guillermo would remember later. He told Guillermo exactly what the shipment would be and then said, "I'll leave it to you to work out those details. It will be sometime in the winter, you understand? I will give you a week's notice. We'll provide you with the best available crew."

"I'll only need two," said Guillermo. "An older one and a young one. Old for experience, young for physical strength."

Crespo meditated for a moment over the smoke of his Monterrey. Then he said, "Okay, *hermano*. We'll get you the best."

Guillermo found himself strangely elated. He called on a boat-yard buddy he trusted with his life to hire a dry dock and crew for the purpose of making the *Catalina* as seaworthy as possible. His buddy was to oversee certain other adjustments as well, no questions asked, and money was not an object. He called his lawyer, and they went over the terms of his will. He took Guillé and Humbi to a couple of Marlins games, seats behind home plate, courtesy of his father-in-law, and made sure to be home every Friday night when his parents came to dinner at the Casa Rosada.

That fall it seemed to Guillermo that Lilly was trying to woo him back: asking the cook to make his favorite dinners, waiting up for him in those Fernando Sanchez lounging pajamas and feathered mules that used to drive him wild. Occasionally he gave in to her seductions—he was human after all—and afterward would make his way back to the guest bedroom, tiptoeing so as not to wake the boys. *She's making love to Cuba,* he thought, *not me.*

In the meantime Humberto Cruz, retired warrior, relaxed by the pool of his Palm Beach mansion, making phone calls to his cronies and watching illegally cabled news loops from Havana: Castro's latest marathon speech, or staged anti-American demonstrations by school-children in their red, green, and gold uniforms along the Malecón. He was not allowed rum or cigars anymore, but friends would smuggle these items to him. When he drowsed off after lunch, he'd murmur in his sleep: *"Camagüey, Camagüey, te veré en Camagüey."*

In one of his lucid moments he said to Guillermo, "Junior, I'm proud of you. Maybe I won't live to see the end, but I'll be there in spirit."

Guillermo drove up to Fort Lauderdale several times to monitor the progress of work on the *Catalina*. Seeing what had been done, he felt at peace. He and his boat were ready.

I can say good-bye to everyone but her was his thought when he spied Catty coming down the steps at Miami International, the worry lines around her mouth reminding him, startlingly, of her mother. Tía Fantasma, Ghost Aunt, he and his brothers had dubbed Jun. They hadn't even reached the car when Catty started asking about clubs, if there was any place he knew where they danced on two, whatever that meant.

The one pure thing. Well, he could spend as much time with her as possible. This turned out to be easy since she wanted to go out dancing every night. In mambo mode, however, he could barely talk to his cousin. She'd always been pretty enough in a natural way to turn heads, but on their nights out, in full makeup and a tight dress and heels that were high even for South Beach, she hardly sat down.

Oh, I love this song.

The way Catty's pupils dilated when she danced in that compli-cated style, going into spin after spin, Guillermo had never seen. It reminded him of a girl he'd met once at a party, a beautiful teenager who had leaned over the buffet so he could appreciate her nipples and at the same time spot the track marks on the inside of her tanned elbow.

He missed the old Catty, the girl in shorts and T-shirt, his base-ball buddy, the one he could spend hours with, drinking and talking or not talking.

But she always reserved the last hour of the evening for him, the hour when she was humid and flushed, the hour when all the guys she'd danced with were watching her furtively, hoping to score. She ignored them in favor of him, Guillermo, who only knew how to do the old Cuban style, a simple country dance. What temptation it was, to hold her sweaty like that! But they weren't teenagers anymore. He was a married man, and she had a life in New York of which he knew nothing.

And then it came to him: *She's the one I'll take to Kingston.*

Crespo would love it. Guillermo and his *prima* from New York on a Caribbean cruise. It was perfect. A couple of days after New Year's, when they were having a drink before hitting the clubs, he found the nerve to bring up the subject.

"You interested in going to Jamaica with me?"

"Sure," she said, not looking up from her rum and Coke.

"Not by plane. By boat."

She met his eyes then. It was well known in the family that Catty got seasick at the drop of a hat.

"It'd be a few days' sail. We'll take it slow, and it should be calm most of the way."

"Why aren't you taking Lilly?"

"Because I need someone I can trust."

"Business?"

"In a manner of speaking."

"How important?"

"Life or death."

She didn't miss a beat. "When?"

"That's the thing; I'm not sure. Sometime this winter. I can give you a couple of weeks' notice."

"Okay," she said.

"Okay? That's it? You could just leave your job and come down?"

"Do you want me or not?"

"You'll need your passport."

"I always keep it with me."

He understood. She was acting as if they were kids, up in their secret fort making water balloons. He was the boss, and she asked no questions because she knew whatever he was planning was in their best interest. If only Lilly felt that way. If only anyone else in his life felt that way.

The one pure thing.

January passed quietly. Guillermo spent more and more time on the *Catalina,* plotting out the journey. The five-day sail under the best of conditions was going to be complicated and would involve major luck regarding wind. Because of the load they were carrying and the notoriously shallow ports of the Bahamas, it would not be wise to dock before Kingston. They'd be under way 24/7. Even with another experienced seaman on board Guillermo would have to make sure he had plenty of chemical help.

When Catalina announced that a friend from New York was coming down to visit for Martin Luther King weekend, he barely registered the fact, so involved was he in his charting. He did say yes when she asked if her friend could stay at his old condo in South Beach.

Wendy was not someone he would have normally associated with his cousin; she was so street, outgoing and funny in that dark New York way. Guillermo found himself liking her on sight. His sons, even sullen Guillé, took to her as well, showing her their rooms and fighting for her attention. After dinner at his parents', Wendy said she wanted to check out this new club, La Guayaba. One of his boat buddies was a partner and could comp them in.

When they got there Catty was enthralled as Wendy showed off.

"Isn't she the hottest thing you ever saw?"

He had a sentimental urge to reply that he much preferred the way she, Catty, danced, but he simply put his arm around her bare shoulders, and they leaned back against the bar like lovers. He was completely happy until he saw Crespo approaching through the crowd.

That man was a drama queen. He could have just phoned, or e-mailed, or stopped by the house as he usually did, but no, he had to hunt Guillermo down and tell him the news in a public place. He waited, at least, until Catty had gone to the ladies' room before coming over. "Tomorrow," he said, without preamble, leaning in to make sure Guillermo heard him clearly. "We've already contacted Gomez."

"What happened to that week's notice?"

Crespo looked away, combing back his curls in that gesture which to Guillermo had become sinister.

"I'm sorry," he said. "There is absolutely no choice. I just got the word myself. The *Catalina* has to leave port before sunrise."

11

Catalina

*The advantage of a new partner
is that you have no expectations.*

She arranged three birds of paradise in different heights—sky, mountain, earth—the way Jun had taught her. Tuerto was coming over for the first time. The apartment was ready, the marinara was simmering, and now there was only herself to prepare. Stripped, she examined her body in the foyer mirror with the dispassion of an artist regarding a tool she was about to use. Three weeks of fucking and dancing and not enough sleep had taken their toll. She had bruises of various vintages on her breasts, her ass, the insides of her thighs. Nothing that would show on the dance floor; he knew what he was doing. She had lost enough weight so that her cheekbones were visible and there were purplish smudges under her eyes.

Barefoot, she did basics, weight exactly over her hips, steps small, the balls of her feet barely lifting off the floor, hands fluttering up. Switch places, again, twist, twist, double inside turn.

Now Tuerto not only danced with her at the Copa, Wild Palm, Baracoa, but was intent on showing off. The second she'd get used to the pace, he'd up the ante. It took all her strength to keep up.

Be careful of what you wish for.

But what a thrill to get a taste of performing, to make her arms and head tosses and kicks as sharp as humanly possible, to feel everyone watching her every move.

Afterward there was always the critique:

I told you to let me *do the phrasing.*

You are not allowed to improvise. Improvising is for experts.

What was that hopping shit on the shines? I never taught you to hop.

And worst: *You are not up to my standards, Lina.*

Did he talk to Wendy this way?

There was no way of checking because Wendy had dropped her. No more phone calls, no shared cigarettes during break, no linked arms walking to the subway. No more girl-girl dances at Wild Palm or Copa. *You should have warned me off instead of encouraging me,* Catalina thought. But even if she had, who could resist Tuerto, that unnerving attention that came at such a price?

She showered and rubbed her feet with sugar and olive oil, an old dancer's trick Wendy had taught her back when they were still talking. When she turned the water off, the buzzer was ringing. *Fuck.* He was never on time; why had he chosen tonight? With one hand she bundled her hair into a sloppy topknot, with the other she reached for Sigueme, the cologne Tía Ana sent every year for her birthday. The buzzer sounded again, more insistently. She toweled off and pulled on the flowered sundress she'd laid out to wear.

It was ninety-nine degrees, but when she opened the door he looked cool as always. Peach-colored tee, faded jeans, a miniature shopping bag looped over his forearm.

"What is that music?"

"Gloria Estefan."

"You put on that dress for me?"

"My ex liked it."

"I don't see why. It's like a sack. Get me a seltzer and juice."

"What do you think this is, a restaurant?"

"I'm your guest, aren't I?"

"I only have orange."

"That'll be fine."

He was punishing her for keeping him waiting.

When she came out of the kitchen he was still standing in the foyer, surveying her tiny living/dining area.

"I made spaghetti."

"Uh-huh. Who's that wimp?" He was referring to the photograph of Guillermo and her propped up on the desk. He didn't seem to have noticed the spectacular flower arrangement on the coffee table. Before she could reply he put the glass she'd just handed him on the desk, took her by the shoulders, and slipped his tongue into her mouth.

Lizard, she thought. It was repulsive but at the same time turned her on. She heard paper rustling.

"What's that?"

"We're having dessert first." He pulled her up backward against him, his hand sliding down her dress, rubbing something cold and viscous into the flesh of her left breast.

"You're sweet," he said, smelling the Sigueme. "I'll make you sweeter."

He turned her around and began licking and biting. Her eyes filled; she couldn't breathe.

"*No te gusta?* It's my specialty, *flan con tres leches.*"

"Don't you want to save it?"

"*Estás loca?* This is what it's for." The rustling again. His hand slipped up the inside of her thigh. It was always like this. Part of her didn't want to; part of her was hypnotized. To him, of course, it was a dance, a dance in which he had to star.

"Stop."

"What are you afraid of?" he said into her ear.

"*Déjame.*"

"Why?"

"I just want to wait."

"No you don't."

They were on the floor, her dress was pulled up, underwear

askew, and she was on her back. He slid down and put his head between her legs.

A mi me gusta el son montuno.

But it wasn't Beny in the background but "Como Me Duele Perderte."

Just as she was about to lose control, he drew his head up and got to his knees and then his feet, so that she was left there sprawled on the floor. "My turn," he said, and as she watched he dipped his hand into the bag and with the other unzipped his fly. All Tuerto's partners were aware of the fact that he never wore underwear.

Catalina got to her knees and took him in both hands and into her mouth. Now she had to concentrate. He never moved; it was up to her. Already her jaw ached, but she continued. The flan was so sweet it made her back teeth ache. Tuerto bowed his head. Finally he was sweating; it rained into her hair, her forehead, stung her eyes. He grunted, reaching down to touch her head. The topknot came loose, and strands of hair plastered to her sticky face. Out of the periphery of her vision she watched them in the full-length mirror, his knees slightly bent, her forearms wrapped around his thighs.

He took hold of her head and stopped her.

"Como te sientes?"

"I'm fine."

"I think you want this." He got down on his knees and put his right hand under the small of her back so that she arched over it, his left hand pressing her right wrist down on the floor, an erotic version of ballroom. *How many dancers fucked like this?* Catalina recalled Wendy as she'd seen her that first night at the Copa, her slender arm with its flexed biceps as she reached up to rest her hand on Tuerto's shoulder, that singular gesture that was as beautiful and complex as anything to follow.

When he entered, she began to weep again, her mouth agape so that she could feel herself drooling onto the oak parquet.

He grabbed her chin. *"Mirame chinita."*

Why does he call me chinita? *I'm half Japanese.*

His veiled left eye was watching her, transfixing her, crucifying her. She came, and he kept going, and the back of her head banged on the floor. God knows what the retired architect downstairs must be thinking.

• • •

In the bathtub he washed her hair under the faucet and then picked up the bottle of olive oil and rubbed some into her scalp, onto her split ends, ending with a dollop on her lips.

"You're such a delicate tropical flower."

So maybe he *had* noticed the birds of paradise.

They ate spaghetti and Cobb salad and garlic bread. She had wine; he didn't. During the meal he kept getting up to roam, open the windows and lean out to regard the street below, comb through her CD collection. It was like having a wild animal in her house.

"Your stuff is too modern. I'm gonna tape you some Tito Rodriguez."

"Whatever."

"What music did you listen to when you were a kid?"

"James Taylor, Joni Mitchell, The Who. The Stones of course."

"What about Irakere, Van Van, Muñequitos de Matanzas?"

"Never heard of them."

"And you call yourself *cubana?* This ex of yours was white, wasn't he?"

"What of it?"

"What did you expect?"

"Why are you being so racist?"

"What would have happened if you'd had children? Would you have taught them their heritage?"

"I suppose so."

"*Suppose.*" He snorted. "It's a good thing you *don't* have children."

"Prick."

He yawned, settled himself back against the sofa pillows. "And you love it, Lina."

"Can we work on the spot turn lift now?"

"I'm not on the clock, honey. And we have to do something about your footwork first. It's getting sloppy."

Fruko was on, "Barranquillero Arrebatao." She got up and started doing Suzy-Q's, then a little toe-heel shine ending with a skip he'd taught the last class. As sexy as possible, shimmying on the heel, letting her fingers spread. She wasn't sure he was watching until he suddenly said, "Lead with your chest, Lina. It's not just about shaking your tits. Be *strong*. Lead with your heart."

And if I show you my heart, will you smash it to pieces? she thought but didn't say.

He was poison, but she couldn't get enough. There were so many things she hated about him, for instance, the fact that he could not bear silence. At all times he needed background noise: TV, radio, old Palladium salsa. While they fucked, he liked Latin jazz: old stuff she didn't recognize, like that conga player Mongo Santamaría. For years to come she'd get aroused just hearing that one long cha-cha-chá, "Sofrito," the live version at the Village Gate.

She'd never seen him read, not even a magazine.

She started bringing things back into the kitchen. He didn't offer to help but made himself even more comfortable on the sofa and turned on the TV. When she returned to the living room for the last time, he was asleep, the remote balanced on his chest, a smear of orange sauce at the corner of his mouth. She killed the lights except for the TV and sat there watching him, the shadowed lids perfectly still in the semidarkness so that you couldn't tell which eye was sighted and which blind. With those caved-in lids and his jaw slack, he looked older, almost doddering. It was like this she liked him best—when he wasn't aware, for once, of anyone watching him.

At her next private he pulled the bandanna out of his back pocket and dangled it in front of her.

"Your new costume," he said.

As he was tying it in front of her eyes she said, "I can't believe we're doing this."

"Believe it, *querida*." She heard the opening strains of El Gran Combo's "Que Cosas Tendrán," a slow and sneaky cut he used for teaching difficult turn patterns. "I'm gonna start with a basic into a cross-body into a single right. After that, you're on your own."

Dancing blind was strangely comforting. For one thing it relieved her of the responsibility of watching his hands. She kept her own hands up, fingers soft. No styling; all concentration was needed for the follow.

One-two-three, five-six-seven.

A Copa into a double inside turn, cross-body into a back break, a single spot turn, back break, another spot turn. Hesitation: cross cross cross, slide back into a lunge. Cross-body into a double outside turn, under his shoulder into another lunge.

She could feel her footwork as plain and unphrased as a beginner's but unerringly on the mark, the balls of her feet square over the floorboards.

"Very, very good!"

"How did I do that?"

"You were paying attention. I been thinking."

"What?"

"You should start coming to Thursday night."

"Advanced?" she asked, trying not to show her excitement.

"You're ready. If you have trouble, Cardoza can get you up to speed."

"Wendy doesn't like me anymore."

"She'll get over it."

She felt him untying the bandanna and at the same time his other hand slide up the front of her shirt.

It always came to this. But as usual she was ready.

The next day, after teaching her last class, she took the subway uptown. When she arrived at Alegre she was one of only eight people: Wendy, Angie, Carlos, two unknown women practicing a shine routine in the corner, and Wendy's friend Justico. Had he defected from Puerto Domingo? One person Catalina was *not* glad to see was Soni Bologna, whom Tuerto by his own admission had dated for several months.

The boys were friendly; the girls were not. Carlos gave her a thumbs-up, and Justico asked if she wanted to practice. She said yes but regretted it almost immediately. He led her into a cross-body and then without pause into a quadruple inside traveling spin.

"Take it easy," she told him through her teeth.

It was as if she were being auditioned. She was aware of the girls, especially Wendy and Soni Bologna, watching. You always knew who was watching, though they were rarely obvious about it. She was tense and her dancing only passable—not the maximum fire in her kicks or precision in her isolations—but she was good over her feet, especially on spins; Tuerto had made sure of that—and lightning fast on the response, which was not easy because Justico was rough. He ended the song, predictably, with a classical diagonal dip. Catalina flicked back up and managed to smile at him. "Thanks."

"Por nada."

Tuerto had come in and was talking with Sonia, his arm around her shoulder. Catalina's stomach lurched. She turned away to watch Wendy and the two strange women who were practicing a tricky shine together in front of the mirror.

This place was a minefield.

For the shines Tuerto put on Tito Puente's "Machito Forever," one of the fastest mambos ever recorded. Catalina positioned herself in the second row, behind the two women. He took them straight into a complicated routine: It ended with a Cuban drop—a sharp knee flex and then up again—which was almost too much for her, even with her left knee wrapped, as it always was now during class and practice.

But already she was feeling better. Sweating always made her feel better. In front of her the girls dipped their shoulders, cocked their pelvises, pointed their toes with breathtaking precision, tossed their heads and let their hair fling back on the spins, all the while keeping their wrists up, Bronx-style, with a *sabor* you could never learn, not if you studied all your life. They were so perfectly synchronized Catalina knew they must be Chicas de la Calle.

As the routine grew even more complex, she could see that as in the beginner class, Tuerto was challenging them, going through a combination and then altering it slightly the next pass so they couldn't anticipate, had to keep behind him the merest hairbreadth. The girls were close, but not as on the money as Wendy and Carlos. As far as Catalina could see, Justico was missing about one in five of the moves, although when he missed he turned the mistake into a flourish of his own.

Catalina knew enough now not to try to copy every single move but to concentrate on keeping up, to remember her six back like a mantra, to double the quadruple turns if she had to, in other words, to stay in the game even if she had to be the least flashy person in the room to do it. Soni Bologna, she was gratified to notice, was pursuing a similar strategy.

The next song, "Ti Mon Bo," was a long funky Puente cha-cha-chá with only percussion and bass. Cha-cha-chá shines were new to Catalina, so she mostly watched. Freezes, multiple crossovers, half turns—there was more time, more beats to play with, and you could get jazzy, sneak up behind the beat instead of nailing it exactly.

The one who stood out now was Wendy. *Cha-cha-chá separates the great from the good,* Tuerto had told Catalina, *and Cardoza could follow the very first time, even before she felt the* clave. Wendy was on fire, her ponytail flicking up and down as she pranced backward, slid, spun three times, opened her arms. She was wearing short shorts and jazz sneakers and a little baby blue midriff top that showed off her stomach, as flat as a teen-ager's. This time it was she who outlasted everyone else, and when the song ended there was applause.

At the break, during the mad rush for the watercooler, Tuerto walked past the spot where Catalina was sitting on the floor to stretch. "Glad you could make it," he said, touching her shoulder but not stopping. He'd warned her that this was his style, to treat all his students democratically no matter whom he was fucking. She realized now that it wasn't just professionalism; it allowed him to keep on being a player. No matter what he told her, she couldn't be sure that he wasn't still doing Soni Bologna.

She wouldn't think about that now. She wouldn't think about Wendy or Angelina or the scary Chicas de la Calle, who were giving her that now-who-the-fuck-do-you-think-you-are? look. She had earned this and was going to get something out of it. The stakes were far higher than her first Mambo Peligroso class because now she had a reputation to uphold.

The turn pattern that day was called the whirlpool and involved a lot of looping arm movements and, for the women, two head duckings and a guillotine spin the opposite direction. Although she'd been doing guillotines in her privates Catalina just couldn't nail this one; for some reason she was always a half a beat late.

Wendy, who was playing lead, said: "I can feel you anticipating. You kind of freeze up."

"I don't know what's wrong with me today."

"You're off your center."

At least Wendy was talking to her again.

"Do you think I belong in this class?"

"If he says you do, you do."

"That's not what I asked."

"Just chill, *nena*. You'll be fine."

Where was her heart now? If she couldn't feel it, she couldn't lead with it.

I am so out of my depth.

As soon as Tuerto gave the final "Bueno!" signaling the end of class, she changed her shoes and left without saying good-bye to anybody.

That night she dreamed of Jun with the old face and the young body; they were on a bicycle together going down Broadway. She was on the handlebars; her mother was pedaling. The cars went by in a blur. Then they were in a store that resembled the *botánica*, but wasn't. Catalina said she wanted to buy incense.

Jun shook her head. "I can't stand the smell," she said in strangely fluent English. "It reminds me of funerals."

He turned her inside out. August, September, October—she'd remember nothing about that time afterward except fucking and dancing and dragging herself downtown every weekday afternoon to teach. She had no social life except for Tuerto.

She knew that, like mambo, the intimacy of their sex was an illusion, but she'd never felt like this in her life, and she'd do anything to keep feeling it.

He did everything to her she'd ever heard about, with flair. Tied her up, blindfolded her, gagged her, struck her flesh with the most delicate of leather whips (it resembled a whisk broom), licked every inch of her body until her throat ached from choked screams. He took the gag off and made her beg. Once he used a Lucite device that looked like a plumber's snake and made her come so much that afterward she crawled to the bathroom to throw up her dinner. At his loft he kept leather costumes and masks, but she never got into that. Naked was what she liked. Raw was better. They both got tested, and then there were no more condoms. She got fitted for a diaphragm, although she wore it only when she thought she might be fertile.

Dance was foreplay. There were nights when she wouldn't wear a bra and a breast would pop out, and he would push it back into her dress as casually as if the move had been planned. Or he'd pull her around with her arm behind her back and brush her fingers against the front of his trousers so that she could feel how ready he was. Her knees would turn to water, and she'd have to concentrate on keeping her balance as he flung her away into a spin in the other direction.

On the floor he was always talking—instructing, complimenting, or jibing—she never knew what was going to come next. *Who's leading?* he would whisper into her ear when she wasn't responding quickly enough. Or sometimes the opposite: *Come on, harder, I want to feel that pussy.*

At the peak of it he called her once, twice, sometimes three times a day, to give her more of that trash talk.

Nothing in her life had prepared her for this. Not Guillermo, not Richard, not anything she had ever fantasized about.

She attended the wedding of one of her Smith friends. Without an escort—there was no way she could imagine Tuerto at a function like that—she skulked on the sidelines until she realized that most of the men were staring at her. She rushed to the ladies' room to check—was there a rip in her dress?—and saw herself in the gilt-framed mirror with shadows under her eyes so dark now that no concealer could hide them, lower lip bitten till it was swollen, hair cascading messily down her back the way she'd been wearing it all summer. Even all dressed up she looked as if she had just gotten out of bed with him.

But as the weather turned cooler, so did he. Three nights a week instead of five, and no more wolfish glances in the mirror during class. He phoned now only when he wanted to meet, and he seemed distracted, sometimes acting as if he had forgotten her name.

I'm Lina, I'm the best fuck you ever had; I'm the one you wish you could keep chained to your bed, she wanted to scream.

Puerto Domingo was throwing a huge Halloween bash, and Tuerto had decreed they would attend as Fu Manchu and his geisha, never mind the schizophrenic cultural mix. Catalina's kimono was an antique *yukata* she'd found in a thrift shop in the East Village. Jun, she thought, would have been shocked at the sight of her daughter cavorting around in a Japanese bathrobe. She ended up taking it off anyway because it was impossible to dance in. Underneath she was streamlined in a black tank top and leggings.

Now I look fat, she thought, and Tuerto's eye did linger on her belly as he gave her his usual once-over, but then he just pulled her onto the dance floor. He was decked out in a fake mustache and goatee and a satin Chinese scholar's outfit scared up from God knows where. When he finally let her go, she positioned herself behind a pillar to check out the crowd without being noticed herself. *Copa virgin,* Carlos had called her five months ago. She was certainly no virgin now. Tuerto had explained: "The best dancers, especially teachers, won't ask again if they get a no. If you want a dancing future with someone, you always, positively always, say yes the first time."

I'm resting, I need a drink of water, I promised this one to someone else.

None of that was acceptable.

She'd said: "That's fascist."

"Maybe. But that's the way it is."

Wendy, just coming in, spotted her hiding place and made a beeline to come over and say hello. Catalina was taken off guard. Aside from class, they'd had no contact for weeks. Wendy was dressed as a jester with stocking cap and velvet shoes with bells on the toes. Luis, in a pageboy wig and Roman warrior costume with sword and shield, was Prince Valiant.

"You're not even sweaty, *nena,* what's up?"

"I just got here."

"What are you, anyway?"

Catalina told her, and Wendy laughed.

"C'mon, let's warm each other up."

Why so friendly?

They went out onto the floor to Oscar D'Leon's "Llorarás." Cross-body into a two-handed Copa, let go, get caught into an inside triple spin.

Por tu mal comportamiento
Te vas a arrepentir.
Muy caro tendrás que pagar

Todo mi sufriemiento.
Llorarás y llorarás
Sin nadie que te consuele
Y así te darás de cuenta
Que si te engañan duele.

For your bad behavior
You are going to repent.
You will have to pay dearly
For all my suffering.
You will cry and cry
With no one to console you
And so you'll realize
That it hurts to be deceived.

Compared to Tuerto, Wendy was an easy lead. *"Que preciosa,"* she said as Catalina added a little hand decoration to the end of a turn.

After that she danced so much she didn't pay attention to any of the usual dramas on the floor. Tuerto was making himself scarce, and she didn't see Wendy anymore, but neither of these observations registered as important. At midnight there was an exhibition by Puerto Domingo. Done to Frankie Ruiz's "Tu Me Vuelves Loco"—there was a lot of Frankie being played that year due to his untimely death—the choreography was especially flamboyant with a lot of pseudo–face slapping and hair tossing and ending with the guys on the floor, the girls brandishing imaginary whips and planting their heels on their partners' chests.

During the performance she looked around for Tuerto and finally saw him coming in the door with Wendy. As Catalina watched from across the room, he slid his arm around Wendy's waist and said something into her ear. The pom-pom on the jester cap bounced as Wendy threw back her head and laughed.

It's not as if you didn't expect this.

But Catalina left soon after, telling him she wasn't feeling well and was going home. He made no move to stop her.

"You don't need me no more," was how he explained it a few days later.

"And Wendy does?"

"Cardoza has nothing to do with it."

Did he whip Wendy, too, tie her up, gag her? Somehow Catalina didn't think so. *It was only sex; you knew he was a player,* but no matter what she told herself she was wracked. She took to her bed where she phoned old girlfriends who commiserated while at the same time sounded a little too interested in her hints about the S and M. *Not love,* she and her friends agreed although maybe it was something more potent than love, if that were possible. She forced herself to continue dancing, two classes a week, privates on Wednesday. They didn't exactly go back to square one—Tuerto was milder with her than in the early days, and more forthcoming with compliments. To see him, however, was nothing less than torture, especially during privates, when she'd find herself staring at his crotch in those tight jeans, wondering if he were aroused. She wanted to beg as he'd taught her to, *Please touch me; I'm dying,* but she didn't.

I led with my heart, and look where it got me.

She cut down on the clubbing, though, and started paying attention to her ESL classes again. She took the advanced students to see *Rent,* the beginners to bowling down in the Village. What kept her going was the thought of her upcoming vacation in Miami. As she did every year she'd go down for Christmas and stay until the end of January when classes began again.

One day, at the end of her private, he said, "Well, I'm glad that things are finally back to normal."

Normal? How could she possibly ever go back to normal? But the bruises had healed. She had gained back a little weight. She was surprised when he invited her to Thanksgiving dinner at his loft. When she hesitated, he said: "There'll be a couple of other people you know." The other people turned out to be Wendy and Luis. In fact, it was Wendy who opened the door and drew her in, kissing her on both cheeks. "I hope you brought your appetite, *nena.*"

Was this some kind of a joke, the four of them together like some happy family? What was the point? But things turned out okay after all. The meal was sumptuous: a fifteen-pound turkey spiked with Adobo and other spices Catalina could not identify, creamed kale, rice and beans, Caesar salad, candied yams. Dessert was pumpkin soufflé and Tuerto's infamous *flan con tres leches*. Wendy, she noticed, was completely at home in the loft, playing sous chef and DJ, disappearing at intervals out to the fire escape to smoke. Catalina even joined her a couple of times, and they shared mambo gossip just like the old days. She had no idea what Tuerto had told Wendy about the breakup, but whatever it was had worked like magic. Wendy was her friend again.

Then, as she was coming back after using the bathroom, he waylaid her in the hallway.

"How about a quickie?" he asked, tucking two fingers into the front of her turtleneck.

"Jesus, are you crazy?"

"She's going home tonight. You can come back later."

"I'll think about it."

She went to help with the dishes. Wendy was going on about one of the girls in the advanced class who had gotten pregnant. "He's an Eddie Torres dancer, right, honey?" she called out to Tuerto.

"Yeah, a cop."

"Mambo baby," said Wendy dreamily. "I used to rock Luis to sleep dancing. I didn't know the basic, but it was like an instinct. One step forward, pause, one step back, pause."

The music changed from John Coltrane to Eddie Palmieri. Wendy wiped her hands and went out to the living area. Catalina finished drying the pots before following.

This was what no one in the mambo world ever saw, what Wendy and Tuerto were like at home. They were dancing in slow motion, languid, playing off each other, switching the lead, making up moves and laughing when they screwed up. Luis was sprawled on the floor watching sleepily as if he had seen this a thousand times. Finally the lead seemed to be Wendy's. There was Tuerto, super-femme, his hands fluttering in the air as he spun two, three, four, five times, flicking his fingers before he strutted across into a back lunge.

Despite herself, Catalina felt herself getting wet. Or was it from before, when he had touched her in the hallway?

Wendy spun him again, made him circle around her, and then, as the song ended, brought him into a melodramatic dip that he milked, arching back over her palm and flinging his arm over his eyes. The new song began, they separated, and he held out his hand to Catalina.

She'd never felt less like dancing but stepped up dutifully. Cross-body, turn, whirlpool—she'd finally nailed that last guillotine—hesitation into a tango step.

Wendy was curled up on the couch watching. Catalina knew without looking the expression on her face: *Forget it,* nena, *there is no one like him and me. It doesn't matter how you dance or how you fuck.*

Luis was applauding politely.

The next thing that would happen is that he would ask her to dance, or Wendy would, and she couldn't bear that. So she made her apologies, saying she had papers to grade, got her coat, kissed Wendy and Luis good-bye. Despite herself, she was unable to look Wendy in the eye.

Tuerto walked her to the elevator.

He said: "I'll call you when the coast is clear."

"Bastard," she said. It was strange how she never used his name—Tuerto, Oswaldo, or even any endearments.

He put the tip of his tongue exactly into the corner of her mouth, withdrew it, and said the words that were always her downfall.

"And you love it, Lina."

12

Catalina

*The clave itself never changes. It's the arrangement
that changes over the clave.*

Every year she looked forward to Christmas in Miami. It was so surreal—palm trees strung with colored lights and ninety-five degrees so the elves at the mall were sweating. The diametric opposite of those winter holidays she'd spent with Richard's family in Massachusetts, gathered around the piano while his mother, the organist at the Episcopal church, played as they sang carols loud and shrill to drown out the wind moaning through the cracks of the family homestead, an eighteenth century mansion built by a whaling captain ancestor.

That December of 1997, though, Catalina felt flat upon landing, barely registering the humidity, the fragrance of people's gardens as they neared Calle Ocho. Guillermo had met her at the airport in her favorite car, a cream Merc sedan, and as usual he'd turned off the AC and rolled down the windows the way she liked it. Her cousin looked tired, she thought. When they pulled up, Tía Ana was waiting on the front porch all dressed up in a pink sleeveless blouse and gray linen skirt and high-heeled sandals. She was chunkier, and there was maybe a little more silver in her reddish hair, worn in its usual bun. It was Tío 'Nesto, standing behind her, who was greatly changed from when Catalina had last seen him, shrunk a couple of inches and dreamy, letting his wife take over his half of the conversation.

"Vida mia!" cried her aunt, kissing her and tracing the lines of her cheek exactly as she had twenty-five years ago when Catalina and Jun had landed on their doorstep. Then she had murmured, *"Ay, muda, muda, pobrecita. Que cosas horribles tú has visto."* She had peered closely into her niece's eyes as if she could see the last image of her dead brother reflected there.

On the back veranda they had coffee and cheesecake, and beyond the porch light Catalina saw the mango tree she and Guillermo used to climb, now as shriveled as Tío 'Nesto. The ginger and bougainvillea and hydrangea were thriving, however. Tía Ana had the touch.

Guillermo said he needed to make a phone call and went into the house.

Tía Ana leaned forward, lowered her voice.

"Did he tell you what's going on? If they get divorced, it's going to be a disaster. I think they must be up to their necks." She made the gesture. "The staff they have. Those shoes she wears. I don't care how much money he makes, a car dealership is only a car dealership."

"There's not going to be a divorce," said Tío 'Nesto. "The father-in-law has him by the balls."

Tía Ana said, "Of course I told him he could stay *here.*"

"Thanks, Mami, but I'm not moving back in," said Guillermo, coming back out onto the porch.

Tía Ana leaned to refill Catalina's cup, saying under her breath, "Just when you think you can stop worrying."

Tío 'Nesto said: "We went to see your *mami* last week, Lina."

"We took orchids," her aunt added. "I just wish"—Tía Ana's voice cracked—"they were together." Her brother and Jun, she meant.

"Regresaremos a Cuba, podemos visitarlo," said Tío 'Nesto.

For some reason Catalina felt a distinct chill. She turned just in time to see Guillermo studying his parents with an odd half smile on his face.

She couldn't sleep. Usually she relaxed immediately upon return-ing to Calle Ocho, but now she found herself in her *tíos'* living room watching reruns until three A.M. Used to the fanatical schedule of two mambo classes and one private a week and as many clubs as she could manage, she had trouble adjusting to the farmer schedule of her *tíos.* She had to get up at six with them to go help in the *botánica.*

Even when she finally felt drowsy enough to go to bed, she was tormented, couldn't stop replaying the last night she'd spent with Tuerto. It hadn't been Thanksgiving when she had returned to the loft and he'd been oddly tender—but the night before she'd left for Miami and he'd been rough. This was the last time, he'd told her, and he'd made sure it would be a memorable one, going in from behind when she was on her hands and knees, grabbing her loose hair back and pulling as she started to come and couldn't stop coming. A week later her breasts and stomach still showed greenish purple bruises. She had to go to the mall and buy the first one-piece bathing suit she'd worn since she was a child.

It didn't help that everywhere in Miami there was Caribbean music: reggae, merengue, bachata, bomba, plena, cumbia, and of course salsa and rumba and edgy *nueva trova* from Havana—on the streets, in stores and restaurants, blaring from car windows. Everything you'd hear in a barrio up north but denser and more chaotic, a cacophony of Latin and African all day and all night so that she would dream of it, dream that she was dancing in all the New York places: Baracoa, Nell's, Flamingo, the Copacabana, Manny's Bronx, Wild Palm.

She helped her aunt do the yearly inventory, and as they worked Tía Ana fussed over her. *"Mi cielo,* I worry about you. You know how sad your *mami* always was. You got to keep up the Cuban side of you, *alegre,* optimistic, full of life, *sabes?"*

My father, your brother, was Cuban and he killed himself, she thought. But all she said was: "I'm fine, Tía."

One day she took her nephews Humbi and Santito to the

Seaquarium. They were a little spoiled for her taste, although who could resist Humbi's fragility, Tito's dimples? She went Christmas shopping. She got her hair cut and auburn highlights put in so that it resembled Angie's. For Nochebuena she and her *tíos* were invited to the Casa Rosada. Impending divorce or not, Guillermo's wife had gone all out for the holidays. An enormous pale blue Norway spruce was set up in the foyer and hung with crystal icicles. Pine wreaths spray-painted gold lined the front facade, and blue and white fairy lights were strung over the date palms in the courtyard. But despite the happy decorations and the artful makeup over the face already made masklike by Botox, Catalina could see that her cousin-in-law, like her, had not been sleeping.

Over dinner all Lilly wanted to talk about was setting Catalina up with this eligible bachelor or that. She was particularly enthusiastic about a brother of a good friend of hers, a plastic surgeon—"But he only does emergency things, not vanity."

Catalina watched her cousin at the head of the table. There was a cut-crystal tumbler in front of him that he kept getting up to refill. Afterward when they were out in the courtyard with after-dinner drinks, she sidled up to him and asked, "So when are you gonna take me dancing? I got a free week coming up."

Guillermo looked down into his glass and swirled the clear liquid. Finally he said, without looking up, "You name the night."

The day after Christmas she bought a red leather bustier that cost half her rent. When she saw her cousin's expression, she knew it had been worth it.

"I gotta practice, don't I, if I'm going to go out on blind dates."

"Practice?"

She felt her face growing hot and didn't remember why. He seemed to have dressed up for her as well—white polo shirt and pleated pants and suede loafers. She missed the way his hair used to grow over his ears, so long on top she could ruffle it. Now he looked too Republican. They went to a fancy little restaurant, very *Miami Vice*, that overlooked the bay. After the meal she lit a cigarette and extended it to him, but he shook his head and asked, "What's the matter?"

"What do you mean, what's the matter?"

"You seem so edgy."

"I miss New York, is all."

How could she tell him how sensitive her flesh was under the bustier and black skirt that barely covered her fading bruises, how she needed a man to grab her again, send the blood rushing to fill those capillaries just under the skin so that her nerves would overload and she would have to throw back her head and scream? How could she explain how this relentless intensity was related to Bronx mambo?

As if he were reading her thoughts Guillermo asked, "You got a boyfriend up there or something?"

She shook her head.

"What if you hit it off with this plastic surgeon? Then you'd have to move back down."

"That guy did not sound like my type."

"You should at least meet him. You're guaranteed a four-star dinner."

"Not interested."

"When it comes to Lilly, the best strategy is to give in."

"Is that what you did?"

He looked over the bay, out toward the glitter of Key Biscayne and said, "We better get going. I made our table reservations for ten."

They went to one of those slick chrome-and-glass South Beach upstarts, a mini Copacabana wannabe. The kind of place where you expected Ricky Martin, but when they walked in the DJ was playing vintage Willy Chirino.

Cuban salsa was in the ground; you had your weight on your heels instead of the balls of your feet. Compared to Tuerto's, her cousin's touch was gentle. She felt his grip tighten only when he began to lead her into turn after turn around him. Then he swung her around and looped her the other way.

A mi me gusta el son montuno.

She knew exactly what Tuerto would say about the clientele here—they could dress but they couldn't dance. She didn't care. The blood pulsed in her wrists as her cousin spun her and then brought her in close to him. She was aware of how girls watched him, watched them. *They think we're a couple.* He was by far the best-looking man in the room, and when they split up to dance with other people, she saw the women swarm in like sharks. They were shameless; one of them even pinched his butt. If it had been Tuerto, she would have turned away, hidden her jealousy by dancing with as many guys as possible. But with Guillermo she wasn't worried. He loved her. He didn't seem even slightly interested in the girls. And she was glad to see that tonight he was drinking lightly, only beer.

When he drove her home to Calle Ocho, she took off her shoes and curled up in the Mercedes's soft seat—glove leather—and the next thing she knew he was shaking her shoulder. "Wake up, sleepyhead."

"D'ja have a good time?"

"Yes."

"Will you take me out again?"

"Yes." He kissed her on the corner of her mouth.

Compared to New York, the night had been light, dance-wise, but it was enough. The *botánica* was closed between Christmas and New Year's, and every morning she slept in and every night she went out with her cousin. She even taught him a little Bronx slot, and a shine or two, although he complained, "Too much work. Dancing's supposed to be fun."

She asked: "What does Lilly think about our going out all the time?"

He shrugged. "She knows I'm behaving myself. I'm out with you, aren't I?"

He never mentioned his failing marriage, and she never brought it up. One night he asked if she'd go to Jamaica with him. Clandestine, it seemed like. Maybe he had a girlfriend, and she was supposed to be the beard. For some reason, she said yes. She could always back out of it later.

But somewhere deep down she knew she wouldn't.

She spent New Year's Eve at home with her *tíos,* sipping brandy and watching the ball drop on TV. The next day it was back to business at usual at the *botánica.*

It was a shock when Wendy called the second week of January, a voice from another planet, talking too fast as she related all the gossip—Manny's annual New Year's Eve bash had been beyond fabulous; Puerto Domingo was on tour in Germany; Wendy's goddaughter was engaged.

"And how are *you?*" Catalina asked.

"Never better, *nena*. I thought I'd come down for a couple of days, check out how you're doing."

"Tuerto?"

"He can't make it."

Strange, Catalina thought, but maybe it was for the best. She and Wendy could hang out without that most distracting of obstacles between them.

The day before Wendy was due she borrowed Tío 'Nesto's car and went to visit her mother's grave. On the way she listened to a Cuban hip-hop mix and thought about Tuerto—*not love, but something more potent*—how he had left her bruised and full of craving. Time and Miami and the company of her cousin were healing her. Now she could wear low-cut tanks and midriff tops and even bikinis if she pleased.

She was glad to have her body back.

Maybe she could even learn to live without mambo. People quit drugs and alcohol, didn't they? She laughed, imagining a twelve-step group of middle-age people in Spandex, raising their hands and saying in various New York accents: "I am powerless over my love for Latin music."

Pink and violet morning glories climbed the bars of the black iron fence that surrounded the cemetery. She had to pass a guard-house where she signed in. The guard asked if she wanted a map. "*No, gracias,*" she said. She had been here a dozen times, was sure she knew the way. Take the main path, turn left, go up the hill past the fountain of La Virgen de la Caridad del Cobre in her glass case. There was a grove of willows. Then the plot of the esteemed family of Bacardi, not the rum barons but their cousins. A bridge over a brook.

Unbelievably, she was lost. She sat down on a white curb, put on her sunglasses. *Jun, where are you?*

Pa' ti, pa' ti, quien eres como una manga amarilla.

She got up and turned to retrace her steps, to go back to the guardhouse, and then she spotted it on the other side of the willows. Tio 'Nesto had purchased six plots, and so far Jun's was the only headstone. The way things were going, it seemed her uncle might soon join her mother.

The small white granite rectangle had turned silver-gray, and there were hairline cracks on the top, which made it look like marble. A bouquet of silk orchids was propped up in an earthenware vase, encircled by an unraveling rosary—Tía Ana's contribution. Catalina had come empty-handed. Next time she'd bring something from the garden, maybe hibiscus.

She combed away the willow leaves, touched the top of the stone. A family was walking back on the path. She waited for them to pass, and then lay facedown on the grass over the grave. When she closed her eyes, she could imagine her mother's face as it had appeared in the semidark, bending over her that first morning in La Habana when Catalina had fainted in the strange apartment.

Mami, I'm traveling by boat again. Will you protect me, as you did last time?

She lay there without moving, inhaling the cold smell of earth. And then she thought she heard, as faint as the breeze through the willow fronds, the voice of her mother speaking Japanese, what she had said every morning as Catalina left for school.

"Kiotsukete."

Be careful.

13

Wendy

It's the simple moves that are the most difficult to execute beautifully.

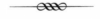

When Wendy's boss at the clinic called her into her office and said, "Close the door," she knew.

It was her boss who had convinced Wendy to schedule her biannual physical early and make sure that it included a chest X ray. "How long have you had that cough?" she had asked, and Wendy had shrugged. Truth was, she couldn't remember. Maybe it had started in the spring, before the Congreso, but she had chalked it up to allergies.

She'd felt off all that autumn. Not just because of Lina—for some reason Tuerto's carryings-on had bothered her more than they usually did—but the stress fracture in her foot had flared up again and she had to wear sneakers. When Tuerto finally came back to her in October—*Please, you're my sexy bitch; I can't do my best stuff with anyone else*—she'd felt not relieved, as she usually did, but resigned.

Luisa invited her for dinner and diagnosed what was wrong with her.

"'Dita, you are having a middle-age crisis."

"I thought only men got those."

"So what do you think of Melda's young man?" Luisa's second daughter had just gotten engaged.

"She's too young."

"Just a year younger than I was. And it could happen to you, *querida*. From what I hear, my godson doesn't have any trouble getting dates."

Luisa was already a grandmother three times over. The former bombshell now weighed over two hundred pounds, her butt disproportionately large compared to her boobs.

"I think I'm gonna color my hair for the wedding. Whaddya think, 'Dita? Red or blond?"

"That's so fucking Nuyorican. How about brown?"

"You gotta go brighter as you get older. You could use some henna yourself."

"Maybe I'll get a fade."

"What are you, a teenager?" They were back to that. Wendy sighed and lit up a Newport, which Luisa tolerated because her husband smoked. "Your trouble is, you been depending on mambo. You think you're still gonna be dancing in ten years?"

"Tuerto's in his fifties."

"Women have a shorter shelf life than men. Ever hear of aging gracefully?"

Maybe Luisa was right. The exhaustion and restlessness she was feeling were all in her head. But she took her boss's advice anyway and went in for the physical.

There was a tumor the size of a plum in her right lung. Her boss pinned the X rays up, and Wendy could see it from two views, front and side. From the side it looked worse.

Maybe it's just a clump of ash stuck down there.

But it was like some part of her had known, maybe ever since the tumor had started growing.

Her boss wrote on a pad and tore off the page and pushed it across the desk. "This is one of the best oncologists in the city. I gave him a call, and he said he could fit you in this week."

It was Monday, and the appointment was not until Friday. That night Wendy dragged herself downtown to the first Narcotics Anonymous meeting she'd attended in over a month. If she had ever needed support, it was now. But at the meeting no matter how many times she raised her hand, she wasn't called on. *It's an emergency,* she tried to convey by the expression on her face, but she was ignored, as if in punishment for all those weeks of skipping. She left furious and found herself doing something she'd never done in the fifteen years she'd been attending this particular meeting: she went upstairs to the sanctuary. Usually programs were held in Episcopal churches, but this one happened to be Catholic. She walked around until she found the chapel to the Madonna, put a dollar in the box, lit a votive, and got down on the kneeler. She couldn't remember the last time she'd consciously prayed.

¿Qué voy a hacer, Santisima Virgen? Dime, oh Madre de Dios, yo te suplico. Ampárame, ampárame.

Sometimes la Virgen was clear. She'd said yes, for instance, when Wendy had asked her if she should keep the baby when she'd found out she was pregnant with Luis.

This time la Virgen answered by not answering.

Maybe she only did yes or no questions.

Virgencita, can I postpone the appointment till the first week in January? We're doing that exhibition New Year's Eve.

Nothing.

She'd lost the circulation in her legs and had to hang on to the rail to get back onto her feet, just like the old widows in black she used to watch and pity when she was a kid at Saint Augustine. Before leaving the chapel she crossed herself and kissed the tip of her thumb and forefinger.

I'll make my own decision.

She didn't cancel the oncologist appointment. She did, however, call Tuerto and tell him he had to find a replacement for the week because she had the flu. For the next couple of days she went straight home after work and channel-surfed, trying to numb her brain with sitcoms and infomercials.

In the wood-paneled waiting room on upper Park Avenue there were photographs of famous buildings from different countries—she recognized the Parthenon—and a silver tree on the table with the magazines as well as an antique bronze menorah by the door.

Happy fucking holidays.

As she waited she fingered the cross her *papi* had given her. Besides a watch, it was the only jewelry she ever wore.

La Santisima Virgen was falling down on the job. Wendy had a son to put through college, years more dancing ahead of her.

Papi, I need you. I don't want to die alone.

But José Cardoza was twelve years in the grave, struck down by a gasoline tanker on the Grand Concourse.

The oncologist sent her for a biopsy, an excruciating procedure that involved inserting a long needle under her ribs from behind. A couple of days later he called her back into his office. He wanted to start radiotherapy immediately. Wendy told him it was impossible, she had a performance scheduled New Year's Eve.

The oncologist took off his glasses and gave her a hard look to drive the point home. "It's a multiple mass, do you understand, which means it's already metastasizing."

Fuck you, fat old man getting rich off other people's misery.

"We have to start treating aggressively."

She made her first radio appointment, went home and told Luis, and then locked herself in her bedroom with the shades pulled down. In the dark she thought about her life: how miserable she'd been as a child before the gymnastics scout had discovered her, the years of training and competition, her stint on the needle, getting clean, discovering girls, Luis, Isabella, and finally Tuerto and mambo.

Then she thought of all the people she knew who had died of cancer. There were some who had survived, of course, but at the moment none came to mind.

Her boss had given her the rest of the year off, and mambo classes were suspended the week between Christmas and New Year's. Tuerto left several messages. She told Luis to tell him she was still sick and didn't feel like doing anything for Christmas. She mostly slept, setting the alarm for noon when she'd force herself to get up, shower, dress, and take the subway downtown to Beth Israel for her appointment at the radiology lab where she lay facedown while the machine buzzed over the diamond shapes the technician had inked on her back.

Christmas Day Luis made her stay on the sofa watching a video of *Strictly Ballroom*—her favorite movie—while he cooked. The meal was simple: roast chicken and rice and beans and a green salad. Beside her plate was a little square box from Tiffany containing a silver bracelet engraved *Mami, te amo siempre. Tu hijo Luis José.*

That was the first time she allowed herself to cry.

"*Mi vida,* I didn't get anything for you." She couldn't stand his wrecked face, the way he stood with his arms hanging down at his sides.

"It doesn't matter, Mami." He wrapped his arms around her and she could feel his tears on her head.

She thought, *He's my only family. I'm not going to tell anyone else.*

And she didn't, not the first week of January when she went back to work and people asked how she was feeling. She stuck to the flu story. When Luisa called, full of wedding plans, Wendy listened and said very little. But as the days passed she couldn't bear the thought of her son having no blood relatives should she not survive. She finally phoned her Tío Gabriel.

"*Que Dios te proteje,*" he said, and told her to call her mother.

The last time Wendy had seen her mother was at her father's funeral. María Cardoza had been hunched over and weak, surrounded by a trio of daughters who barely acknowledged Wendy because, according to them, Where had she been all those years?

I loved Papi, she'd thought, to give herself strength against their coldness. *And he loved me more than he loved the rest of you put together.*

Her sister Lourdes, to whom she had been the closest, was the worst. The others had at least kissed her, but Lourdes wouldn't even come near. Toward the end of the service Luisa had shown up, thank God, and stood by Wendy and Luis at the cemetery.

She dug around till she found her mother's home number, and one morning before leaving for work summoned up the courage to dial it.

The voice that answered was scratchy and irritable. "Who is this? What do you want?"

"Mami, it's Wendy."

"Oh, Wendy."

"*Tengo malas noticias.* I'm sick. I have cancer." When there was no response, she went on: "They're going to try to treat it with radiation and chemo. If that doesn't work, they're going to have to take the lung out."

There was an excruciatingly long silence, with ragged breathing. Finally Wendy realized that her mother was crying.

"Why are you calling me? Why are you telling me this?"

"I'm sorry I bothered you," said Wendy, and hung up.

She wanted to tell Tuerto, but she was afraid that he would insist that she quit dancing. He knew something was up, of course. That was why he insisted that she go down to Miami for Martin Luther King Day weekend. He even bought the ticket without telling her.

"No way," she said. She had radio sessions scheduled the entire month.

"You're a wreck, Cardoza. I need you healthy. We have to start rehearsing for the Congreso."

"I can't get away."

"You're leaving Thursday afternoon. Angie will cover the advanced class. I already asked her."

"You got something on the side I don't know about?"

"*Cállate.* You know I can't go. You know I'm subbing for Jimmy at his social on Sunday."

It was true. And she was running out of time. After radiotherapy there'd be chemo. Chemo would be worse. She'd never get a chance to take a vacation then. Tuerto said he'd book her into one of those fancy guesthouses on Collins, but it turned out she could stay at Catalina's cousin's condo in South Beach. Even Luis urged her to go.

On the plane she tried to sleep, remembering her partner's

admonishments: *Cut down on your smoking, get some sleep, and don't for-get your Pilates. I want you in fighting shape.*

If only it were that easy.

But she had been developing a secret plan. She'd spend the long weekend in Miami and then head to the Dominican Republic. Her favorite *tía*, her *papi's* younger sister, lived in Puerta Plata. Her boss at the clinic would understand; she was the one who had made the diagnosis after all. Luis would join her there for his spring break. He'd never been, never met his relatives. They could stay as long as they wanted in her *tía's* house right on the beach.

The sun in Miami felt better than she could have imagined, although the humidity made her cough worse.

After dropping her bag off at the condo she met Catalina at Star-bucks on Ocean Drive. They took their coffee out to the beach, where they found a bench facing the sea. Catalina was tan and had had her hair cut to her shoulders. No more *guajira* braid. Wendy thought: *What a weird world this is. Six months ago I was La Reina Mam-bera, and that girl was hanging on to my coattails. Now I'm dying, and she's gonna conquer the world.*

Catalina said: "I was thinking of staying down here till summer."

The seagulls screamed. Wendy asked, "You mean at your *tíos'*?"

"There's no one in the house but them. I think they get lonely."

"Do you think they could use another guest?"

Catalina laughed. "Maybe."

"I'm serious, *nena*. I need to get away for a while."

"We could figure something out. How long were you thinking?"

"A week, maybe two."

"No problem. Or you could just keep on at the condo. Guillermo wouldn't mind."

"I wanna dance tonight."

"Guillermo can get us comped into La Guayaba."

"Cool. What does this cousin of yours do, anyway?"

"Sells cars."

They threw their cups in the trash and went shopping. Down Washington Avenue, up Collins, and finally on Lincoln Road. In one boutique Wendy tried on an entire outfit: white satin halter, silver lamé capris, sequined ponytail holder. The salesgirl got her a pair of stiletto heels. Wendy examined herself in the three-way mirror.

"Almost forty fucking five."

"And you look ten years younger." This was kind of Catalina to say, and six months ago it would have been true, but now Wendy knew she looked her age and then some.

"Don't you think it's a little flashy?"

"We're in Miami Beach."

"So we are."

By the time they had paid it was time to meet Guillermo at the Claymore. The cousin was a surprise—softspoken and foxy in an understated way. Definitely more to him than met the eye. The smooth Mercedes he drove reflected his persona exactly. When Wendy saw the Casa Rosada, she began to speculate that he was a high-end drug runner. He didn't seem the type, but you never knew. Certainly he seemed to have no problem keeping that trophy wife of his in diamonds and Armani, and those three adorable boys in two-hundred-dollar sneakers, not to mention the house and Guillermo's toy, the fancy yacht, of which there was a photograph over the desk in his study. That butler of theirs, hovering over them in the foyer, gave her the skeeves. He was the surest sign that Guillermo was up to something.

Wendy had never met a Cuban drug runner; it was the Colombians and now more and more the Italians who were taking over the streets in southern Florida. But who was she to complain when Guillermo closed the door of his study and started cutting lines on a little mercury-colored slab.

Cocaine was not Wendy's drug of choice. And she hesitated, seeing the somber faces of the people in her NA group. But she had nothing to do with them anymore. She had entered a new phase, one they wouldn't understand because they were too busy trying to hold their lives together, lives that would go on until they grew old.

Catalina declined, so it was the two of them, Guillermo and Wendy, who partook: two lines each, that was all, and it was enough. She felt her cheeks go numb, tasted bitter at the back of her throat. "*Coño, papi,* where'd you score this?"

"You could call it perks from the dealership."

"Thanks for the use of your condo by the way."

"*Por nada.* Catty speaks so highly of you."

It was the smoothest of highs, accelerating subtly and leveling off like a plane reaching cruising altitude. They sat in the courtyard and the light from the stone lanterns around them glittered with a honeyed intensity; the humid air lay like a blessing on their skin; and Wendy found herself thanking God that Tuerto was not there, him and his fucked-up puritanical views.

Please, Cardoza, try to cut down on the cigarettes. You're setting a bad example for the class.

Next stop was Catalina's *tíos* in Little Havana where dinner was waiting on the table: fish and fried chicken and *platanos maduros* and salad. Soul food. During dessert Wendy went into the master bedroom and called Tuerto, told him what a great time she was having. Mmm-hmm, was all he said. While Wendy and Catalina dallied in her room putting on each other's makeup, Guillermo opened the car door so that Willie Colón blasted out into the street. "Santa María," said Catalina's *tía* but she waved good-bye amiably as they drove off. The uncle was too deaf to care.

The band hadn't even taken the stage when they arrived, so Guillermo and Catalina headed to the bar while Wendy scoped out the place—high ceilings, a slick wooden dance floor with a few columns and sculptures for interest, decent acoustics. There was no one dancing yet. The DJ had put on Issac Delgado, and on the margin she did a few basics, a little turn left, a little turn right. They'd swung by the condo so Wendy could pick up her dance shoes, and in the parking lot she and Guillermo had done another couple of lines and she was feeling good. She knew she looked hot. Catalina was right; the white halter and silver capris were totally SoBe.

As always, she made the sign of the cross before stepping onto the floor for her first spin. It was perfect. Not too slow, not too fast.

I'm two decades older than these kids and I bet I can outdance them all.

The top of her upper lip was already wet, and she reached up, still spinning, to wipe it with her index finger. If only Luis were here, to support her while she did her most showstopping hesitations—cross cross cross, angle back, *lunge,* slide that left leg through his spread-apart ones, right down into a perfect split and back up on the next beat.

In her peripheral vision she could see Catalina and Guillermo watching. Trophy wife had shown no interest in joining them, thank God. She was pure Cuban establishment, with her highlighted hair and four-hundred-dollar Manolo Blahniks. But not a beauty, not like Catalina, who was looking better and better the more Wendy thought about it. Languorous, sultry, full, tropical. Miami became her.

A young couple walked out onto the floor, across from Wendy, and started dancing. They were nothing to write home about.

Isaac Delgado segued into Ricardo Lemvo's "Mambo Yo Yo," a tune Wendy had danced to many a time live at Nell's on Fourteenth Street. In response, she cranked things up a notch, bending her knees and dipping her chin so her sequin-banded ponytail whipped around as she spun. Then she went into shines: spirals, front double crosses, a heel-toe combination, a three-point freeze, a five-point freeze. The couple across the floor continued to dance, but no one was paying attention to them anymore.

Juepa, she heard someone shout, and it was just like New York, except this time she was soloing. When was the last time she'd danced alone in front of an audience? Up went her arms, her back arched and then straightened; she wished the music were faster, but she could double-time, stutter-step, spot the ceiling (Soni Bologna wasn't the only one), reach up catlike and then down hip-hop style, cross, jump turn, do it again, bend over, swirl her ponytail on the floor.

What would she do without mambo? Mambo had saved her from the streets. Mambo would save her again.

As well as *clave,* the song had a strong disco beat, and she felt moves coming back that she hadn't done in decades, parts of break-dance routines which she'd used to impress Miguel at the Laundro-mat.

This is what the Bronx looks like, folks.

The crowd was clapping the *clave.*

Without knowing she was going to, Wendy did a backflip just as the song came to a close, and Albita followed on its heels. She did back skips to get her breath back, a little moonwalking she'd picked up from Carlos, and then a front flip into a split. Then up.

There. She should stop now.

Her left knee had locked coming up from the split, although she had managed to make the stammer look like part of the routine.

It was time for a refresher.

Shit girl, you might as well just do it right and really score.

No. She would stick to blow, and everything would be cool.

But when she went to find them, making her way a little self-consciously through the crowd, which had swelled perceptibly in the ten minutes she'd been showing off ("You can be my partner anytime," a couple of guys called as she passed), they were not at the bar.

Fuck it. A cigarette would have to do. She had left hers in the car. She'd have to buy a new pack.

She edged up to the bar. A dark fat bald man blocked her way and gave her a bear hug.

"*¡Que bailerina fantastica!*" he said stickily into her ear. She couldn't place the accent. Honduras?

"*Coño, un poco mas suave,*" Wendy replied, but let him plant a messy kiss on both her cheeks.

"*De donde eres?*"

"*Nueva York.*"

"*De veras? Y antes?*"

"Santo Domingo," she said, and he squinted as if he couldn't believe it.

"*Quieres algo para beber?*"

"*No, gracias.*"

I don't want to be PICKED UP, she thought. *I want a PICK-ME-UP.*

The bartender did not have Newports, so Wendy settled for Marlboro Reds. Leaning on the bar, she turned to face the room as she smoked, not in invitation, but to observe. The little old bald man had reminded her of her *papi,* who had not been rotund but had had the same face, droopy like a basset hound's. Wendy could feel her heart, which had been skipping three minutes before, dull and solid under her ribs. The band was setting up and while the crowd waited, the DJ put on "Sopa de Langosta," the house cha-cha-chá at Baracoa that had become a national hit. Wendy snapped her fingers to the *clave,* remembering how Tuerto had taught her the cha-cha-chá by making her play the *clave* sticks as she danced. For no reason at all she remembered also, how at Luis's twelfth birthday party he'd shown all the kids the basic mambo step, and then a simple turn, making all the girls feel pretty and the boys macho.

Where the fuck was Guillermo?

There was Catalina leaning by herself against a pillar. Her face was blank, a blank that was trying to hide something. Wendy doused her cigarette and made her way across the room.

Catalina turned at her touch.

"Everything okay, hon?"

"You were great out there."

The music, a bachata now, was pumped up, and although the two women were close enough to touch, they still had to shout to be heard.

"What's your *primo* up to?"

"I don't know. Talking to a friend."

"You think he'd give me another hit?"

Why was Catalina looking at her like that? She hadn't said a word at the house or in the car, watching the proceedings if not with approval then with definite tolerance.

"Come on, we all know what he does."

"It's none of my business what he does."

"Okay, I'm sorry; I was out of line." Wendy, leaning in to speak directly into Catalina's ear, felt a distinct urge to lick it, the delicate swirls and bare lobe, but restrained herself.

Now finally here he was, Mr. Mercedes, strolling up and putting an arm around each of their waists.

"Something's come up. Will you two be okay here by yourselves, or should I take you home?"

"I want to stay," said Wendy.

"Not me," said Catalina.

"Why not this," said Guillermo. "I'll take you home, Catty, and Wendy, you hang out here as long as you like. Our chauffeur lives on this side; I'll give you his cell number. When you're ready to leave, call him, and he'll take you back to the condo."

"What a gentleman," said Wendy. "But I can walk."

"Be careful then," said Guillermo. "This isn't the Bronx."

And a sense of humor, too. Too bad he was married.

They all kissed good-bye. With her cocaine-sharpened perception Wendy noticed that there was a distinctly greenish tinge to Catalina's complexion.

"Sorry we didn't get to dance," Wendy said.

"Next time." *Coño,* that girl was about to pass out.

"Good meeting you," said Guillermo, and, without being asked, slipped Wendy a suede drawstring pouch along with the chauffeur's cell number.

"Thank you, *papi,*" she said.

"Por nada."

Lighting another Marlboro, she floated along the floor, acknowledging the sidelong looks from men and even a couple of girls, back toward the ladies' room, which was marked with a pink fluorescent glove pointing over the archway. She sauntered into a stall and opened the suede bag and extracted its contents: plastic envelope and silver spoon.

She had company. Outside, by the washbasins, the Ecstasy girls were passing it around and giggling. Someone in a far stall was on her knees retching gruesomely into the toilet. Wendy remembered those nights all too well. Dive or fancy club, it was all the same when you were strung out and sick.

The band was decent, a classic *conjunto* playing Van Van covers. On the dance floor, the crowd had grown more frenetic. All those boy and girl model wannabes, mystery Latinos and Latinas, most of them so young she had to take a deep breath and tell herself to walk tall, keep her back straight. There were quite a few decent dancers now, she was happy to see. She was pulled out onto the floor by an older man who looked like a postcard of Cuba in a white linen suit. The band was playing their last song, a merengue, so she didn't have to think. One-two, one-two, one-two. No señor, no grinding. Feel my thumb on your shoulder? That's right. You make me look good and I'll make you look good and no one will get hurt.

While the band was packing up the DJ put on a set of reggae. *"Gracias, corazon,"* Wendy said to her elegant partner. She hadn't even made it back to the edge of the floor when she was snapped up again, this time by a young heavyset man who reminded her of her son.

This whole fucking club looks like my family.

She even thought she recognized that weird buddy of Tuerto's, what was his name? Hank, standing by the bar wearing a Hawaiian shirt, but when she looked again he was gone.

The young man did not have Luis's grace, but he was responsive, and the two of them invented a kind of Jamaican swing hybrid, with Wendy back leading just enough to make the kid feel like he was fabulous. She let him graze a braless breast, the left one, with his fingertips, and this caress, as light as it was, sent a surge right to where it counted. It was the coke, she realized. She'd forgotten how horny it always made her. By the end of the set she couldn't look him in the eye.

Please don't say, My place or yours?

He didn't. He leaned to kiss her on the cheek and told her he had to go, his girlfriend was waiting.

It was clear she wasn't going to get lucky tonight. Not that she really had any intention—it had been years since her last one-night stand. Programs discouraged that kind of behavior. She had her regular sex buddies, and that was that.

She missed Tuerto though. No matter how many hours they'd logged on the dance floor on any given night, he could always fuck her into oblivion afterward.

The floor was getting too crowded to dance, so she made her way back to the bar and leaned there chain-smoking until she felt queasy and went into the ladies' for another boost. She had no desire to return to the empty condo. She didn't feel like staying at La Guayaba, however, where the music had devolved into late-night techno interspersed with the occasional merengue or hip-hop cut; the only people left were grinding couples and some loser guys lurking in the corners.

She left the club and walked along Ocean Drive in the opposite direction of the condo, under stars and a quarter moon. She'd always appreciated Miami for its savage ambience. South Beach in particular had a sleazy undertone—all that paint and renovation could not cover up the memory of violence. Up ahead was a building that looked strangely familiar, and it took her a moment to peg it as the mansion where Gianni Versace had been gunned down that past summer. She stood in front of the steps and imagined what it must have been like, his coming out that morning and having no time even to think, *Oh Christ, this is the end of my life,* just suddenly sprawled there in his blood with passersby screaming.

Was it better to be surprised?

She continued up Ocean, straining to hear the sound of the waves over the traffic and faint music from the occasional bar or club. She didn't know if she had the energy to walk all the way back down to the condo. It was almost two, way too late to call the chauffeur, and she didn't see any cruising taxis. There was a little coke left in the drawstring pouch, but she was done for the night.

Finally, here was something that looked like a cab. It was hard to tell here; it wasn't like New York where they were all yellow with bold top lights. She leaned out, hailing it, and it stopped.

Sure enough, it was a taxi, with a sleepy, amiable Haitian driver. She gave the address and leaned back and tried to relax as he made the turn onto Collins. Downtown Miami glittered to their right, as bright and sprawling and indifferent as if it were nine o'clock on any evening of the year.

She should have called home before they went out. Luis would be worried about her.

The image of Catalina's face, drained of blood under the flickering lights of La Guayaba, popped into her head.

They had just crossed Sixteenth Street when Wendy leaned over the back of the front seat and told the driver she had changed her mind, she wanted to go across the Causeway.

14

Catalina

Sex lives in the pauses.

Wendy had brought back the South Bronx, with her touch, her talk, the way she walked the pavements as if she owned them, how she charmed Guillermo so that Catalina felt a stab of jealousy. *El mas peligroso mambo.* But she looked ravaged, much too thin, and there was a sweet-sour odor off her skin that Catalina recognized but couldn't place. In the dressing room of the boutique she saw the bruises on Wendy's lower ribs and remembered Tuerto's hands.

On the dance floor, however, Wendy was her old self, even better, and Catalina was bursting with pride as she and Guillermo watched La Reina Mambera show off in the middle of La Guayaba.

Then Catalina looked up and through the crowd saw the face in the doorway. Angular, delicate, framed by blond curls.

She said nothing until they had said good-bye to Wendy and were out in the parking lot.

"What's up?"

"It's time," said her cousin.

"Now?"

"Do you have your passport?"

"It's at the house."

The face in the doorway was that of the devil; of that she was sure.

I'll miss this beautiful car, being driven by Doggy.

As they swung onto Collins he said, "Four-thirty."

"Tomorrow afternoon?"

Her cousin glanced at the dashboard clock. "This morning. That's less than four hours from now. I'll drop you off so you can pack, and then come back and get you."

"Why don't I just stay with you? That way we'll save time."

"There's some stuff I need to take care of. You might as well get a couple of hours of sleep if you can."

An idea was beginning to blossom in her brain, and she fought it down. Later. She'd think about it later. Guillermo was revved up in a way that had nothing to do with the coke. It was a quiet, focused excitement that only someone who knew him well would have picked up. She had never seen him like this. He stopped the car in front of the house but didn't cut the engine.

"I can't honk, so be on the porch. Don't turn on the light."

He lay his hand on the side of her face.

"Vete."

He was off even before the car door clicked shut. She let herself in as quietly as she could, holding her breath until she was sure she had not awakened her *tía* and *tío*.

Packing was easy, just throwing jeans, shorts, tops, a skirt, underwear, toiletries into a knapsack. She made sure to include all her remedies for nausea—sea bands, Chinese ginger candies, Dramamine. When she was done, she snuck into Guillermo's old bedroom, which her aunt had turned into an office. She switched on the desk light and went through Tía Ana's Rolodex until she found a certain number and address she thought might come in handy. From a framed photo on the desk Javier Ortiz's infant eyes gazed at her with the melancholy he'd carry into adulthood. She touched the face, wanting to take the photo with her, but Tía Ana would be alarmed to find it missing. She copied down the information from the Rolodex, stuck the slip of paper into her bra, and then turned out the desk light and made her way back to her room. She sat on her bed in the dark and thought about taking a shower, but the bathroom was right next to her *tíos'* bedroom. *There's no way I'm ever going to get any sleep.* But she must have fallen into a doze because she started when she heard a car engine outside. Guillermo? It didn't sound like the Mercedes. When she slipped the screen up and leaned to see, she made out in the headlights that it was Wendy getting out of a cab.

Don't slam the door, she prayed, but of course Wendy did.

Catalina got to the front door in time to open it before her friend could ring the bell.

In the streetlight Catalina could see that the front of Wendy's white halter was stained with sweat and that her eyes were glittering as if she were still high.

Catalina asked in a whisper: "Why aren't you at the condo?"

"Did I wake you?"

"I was up."

"Aren't you going to invite me in?"

"All right, but you have to be quiet."

It was safest to keep Wendy in her bedroom, Catalina decided, and when her friend asked for water she told her to wait there, she'd go to the kitchen and fetch it. When she got back Wendy had turned on the bedside lamp and was lying back on the bed with her eyes shut, one hand trailing on the floor. She sat up alertly, however, when Catalina handed her the glass. Between gulps she said: "You should have stayed at La Guayaba. It was rockin'. I could have used a good partner. Going on a trip?"

She had spotted the packed knapsack slung over the inside doorknob.

"Just a short one," said Catalina. She sat down on the end of the bed, folded her knees up, willing herself to seem casual.

"Where?"

"I told Guillermo I'd go up to Fort Lauderdale tomorrow and help him work on the boat."

"So what's going on there, *nena?*"

A cold sweat broke out on the back of her neck. "I told you I don't know anything about his business."

"I'm not talking about his business. Any girl in that club would have laid right down for him. All he did was moon over you."

By the digital clock radio, it was almost three-thirty. How was she going to get rid of Wendy?

"Look, *nena,* I'm sorry I barged in like this. I'll go if you want."

"Maybe that would be better."

But Wendy showed no sign of budging. She put the glass down and then startled Catalina by leaning into her, as if the night had finally caught up with her and she was collapsing. The smell off her skin was sharp: fresh sweat with a coke tang, although the sweet-sour was still somewhere underneath.

What came into Catalina's mind then was that February evening nearly a year ago when she'd walked into Alegre Studios and had been riveted by the sight of Wendy María Teresa Cardoza dancing the mambo the only way she was capable of, with all her heart and soul.

Fingers, so soft as to be almost ticklish, played at the back of Catalina's neck, making her shiver.

Wendy asked: "Don't you miss all that hair?"

"A little."

"You have a beautiful mouth."

"It's my mother's mouth."

"She must have been a gorgeous woman."

No one had ever called Jun gorgeous, but it was true. "She was."

Wendy sat back, laughing under her breath. "You look like you're gonna shit your pants. Do you think I'm making a pass at you?"

"Are you?"

"No, *nena.* I'm just appreciating what he saw in you."

"Are you mad at me?"

"I was never mad at you. I know how he is."

"I'm sorry."

"Don't be. I'm used to it. Anyway"—her tone changed—"I'm taking a break from all that. Maybe permanently."

"What are you talking about?"

"I'm not going back to New York."

"My *tía* said you could stay here. Don't worry about it."

"This isn't my last stop, *nena*. I'm headed for the DR. Taking a long vacation. Need the sun, some *familia* around me."

Catalina glanced at the clock again.

"You can stay here as long as you want. We'll talk about it when I get back."

"I might not be here when you get back." Wendy lowered herself back down on the bed and turned away from the light as if she didn't want to talk anymore. Catalina watched her ribs rise and fall under the white halter. How efficiently made Wendy was, she thought, long muscles and small hands and feet. Still, she was a woman, with breasts and butt and shapely thighs. With the halter riding up Catalina could make out the bruises again, just above the waist.

"He's not worth it."

"What are you talking about? Tuerto? He is not the problem."

"What about Luis?"

"He'll come down and join me later. He has to finish out the semester."

Catalina found herself saying: "Come with us, then."

Wendy yawned. "Lauderdale? Not interested."

"It's not Lauderdale. We're going to Jamaica. It's the next island, you'll practically be there."

"*Jamaica?* Why didn't you say so?"

"It's a business trip."

"I see."

"So you want to come?"

"When?"

"Now."

Wendy turned so that her face caught the light from the bedside lamp. Her eyes were expressionless. "In the middle of the night?"

"He's coming to pick me up in an hour."

Wendy slid down on her stomach and let her head hang over the edge of the bed as if the blood going to her brain would help her think.

"You sure?" she asked.

"Yes."

"Okay then. What the hell."

They were waiting on the front porch when the Mercedes rounded the corner and drew up by the curb on the opposite side of the street. It was still dark, but Catalina imagined a faint paleness in the sky to the east, over the bay. Her cousin got out of the car, not quite closing the door behind him. As he neared the portico she saw that his wet hair was combed back and that he had changed into a T-shirt and jeans.

"What's this?" he asked.

"Wendy's coming with."

He gave her a look that said, among other things, *I did not expect you to betray me,* and then he turned to Wendy and said in a surprisingly mild tone: "Not to be rude, but the best thing for you to do would be to get your ass out of here right now."

Catalina said: "It's all right. You can trust her."

He studied both of them for a moment and then, to her amazement, simply turned one palm up in a gesture of resignation. She hadn't expected it to be that easy.

"Okay, okay. Is that all your luggage?"

"My passport's at the condo," said Wendy.

For the first time Guillermo seemed as if he might lose patience. But then he just shrugged. "All right. Let's get this show on the road."

It was twenty minutes to five when they pulled onto Calle Ocho, headed for the Julia Tuttle Causeway. Catalina sat beside her cousin and Wendy was in back, the same arrangement as the evening before on the way to La Guayaba, when Willie Colón had been booming from the sound system. Now the car was silent until they hit 95 and Wendy asked if she could use Guillermo's cell. He handed it over the backseat to her, and she left a message at work, telling her boss she wouldn't be in on Tuesday. Then she called home and left a message for Luis: *Voy a Jamaica. No le digas nada a nadie. No te preocupes, mi amor.* She handed the phone back, and the car was silent again until Guillermo switched on the radio to a weather report.

"Up to eighty degrees today, mostly sunny, offshore winds twelve knots, may get blustery later this afternoon, small craft warnings for tonight."

At the condo they waited at the curb while Wendy dashed up. Guillermo took Catalina's hand and walked his fingers around the palm.

"You scared?" he asked.

"A little."

"Don't worry. I'll take care of you."

"Are you mad about Wendy?"

"No, I was thinking it might be for the best."

"Why?"

"It's a better cover. You, me, your friend from New York."

She decided it was time to stop mincing words. "What are we taking?"

He shook his head. "It's better if you don't know."

As wired as she thought she was, Catalina remembered nothing else of that car trip and awoke only when they stopped. At the Fort Lauderdale marina two men were waiting for them on the concrete lip where the ketch was berthed. The men, slumped and smoking, looked as if they had been there all night. Guillermo introduced them as Mano and Edgar. Mano looked barely out of his teens, and, as exhausted as he seemed, Catalina could feel him giving them the once-over. His skin was mahogany with a sheen to it. Edgar was older and lighter-skinned and preoccupied enough not to meet her eyes. He was wearing an Orioles baseball cap.

Pros, she thought.

While she and Wendy climbed aboard, the three men stood ashore, talking in low voices. Although no sailor, Catalina was aware that the boat was riding much lower than normal. The red trim of the hull still showed exactly as it always had; Guillermo must have gotten someone to repaint the watermark higher.

Mano stowed their luggage and set out deck chairs.

"People pay hundreds of bucks for a cruise like this," said Guillermo. He touched Catalina lightly on the stomach and then left them to help Edgar with something below.

"He named the fucking thing after you," said Wendy.

"It was a coincidence." Catalina sat down on one of the deck chairs and beckoned Wendy to take the one next to her.

"Any chance I can score some aspirin?"

"Try the first-aid kit in the head."

"Head?"

"Bathroom. Below."

By the time Wendy came back up on deck looking more relaxed, they were casting off, the men working the lines. Mano was sending flirtatious glances their way, but Edgar did not look up. Guillermo was up in the bridge; Catalina watched his slender forearms as he maneuvered the wheel, steering them out of the slip.

I'll take care of you.

The slight rocking as they putted out of harbor made her stomach lurch. *It's going to be a long trip.* She slipped on her acupressure wristbands and popped a Dramamine.

Beside her, Wendy was already asleep in her deck chair, a beach towel flung over her legs like a blanket.

Catalina stretched and tried to chill out. Above them the sky lightened, the waves were tipped with the slow gold of the rising sun, and the terns began to cry. Looking over her shoulder again up into the bridge, she saw that her cousin had cracked open a Red Stripe and was drinking it in thoughtful sips. She wanted to talk to him but decided to wait, maybe until that night when everyone else was asleep.

In about an hour, when the sun grew stronger, Mano unrolled the tarp awning and hooked it over the railing to shade the aftdeck. Catalina drowsed, awoke, drowsed again. When she woke up for good, her watch said three o'clock. Wendy was gone. Edgar was swabbing the aftdeck in a lackadaisical manner. He'd work a little and then stop, leaning against the rail and gazing out. Out on the open sea, he seemed mellower.

He began to hum.

The song was "La Negra Tomasa." Catalina had been familiar with it as a child and since then had heard it dozens of times at the Copa, El Flamingo, Wild Palm. It was also the song of the seawolf who had ferried her mother and her from Rosa Marina to Knight's Key twenty-five years ago, and this, somehow, was comforting.

MAMBO

15

Oswaldo

The faster the music, the slower the dancer should look.

After Carmen cut me, this *santera* in my old Brooklyn neighborhood told me that I was chosen, *bendecido,* that the blind eye could see things that regular eyes couldn't, like ghosts and the future. She was wrong. I see nothing that other people can't; I just see more clearly. For instance, I know right away when I meet someone whether they are going to be my enemy or my friend.

Cardoza was my friend.

Catalina Ortiz is my friend. If I *could* have seen the future, I still would not have been able to resist that *chinita.* It was like she was waiting for me. She was green in bed, and quiet. "Spanish people talk," I said, and I made her talk. I made her tell me how it felt, I made her beg. When I got tired of that, I taught her how to be on top, how to fuck like a proper Latina. It was primo nasty sex, and it lasted just as long as it was supposed to last.

But she was so distracting that I missed the fact that Cardoza was on the skids. That fall my partner lost weight she couldn't afford to lose, started smoking more, grew circles under her eyes. Not because of Lina—she was used to that just as I was used to hers—Omara, for instance, or that pup Justico, who had delusions of taking my place. She was a little young, but I thought it could be the Big M. Menopause. I knew the damage it could do. Last time I'd seen Milly I almost hadn't recognized her. In her salad days Julio Iglesias himself had once way-laid her in a Palm Beach restaurant—she showed me the card he'd slipped her. Later, after we'd split up, there was always some local busi-nessman or other willing to subsidize that South Beach condo of hers. But after the Big M the sugar-daddy supply dried right up.

Men-o-pause. They paused all right. Paused, and then went on their way.

Cruel, you say? But this is how the world works. Milly was smart enough not to bank on her looks, always a losing investment. She bought the travel agency she worked for and how lucky—or unlucky, depending on how you look at it—that turned out to be for me.

On New Year's Eve Cardoza and I did an exhibition at Manny's Bronx. Puente's "Babarabatiri," I think it was. It was then, under the bright stage lights, that I could see how much my partner had deteri-orated, and it gave me a shock. The silver two-piece costume accen-tuated the bones in her chest and the pancake makeup couldn't hide her ashy complexion or the circles under her eyes, which had gone from gray to purple.

"*Relax,* for Chrissake," I hissed after she overrotated for the sec-ond time coming out of a shoulder check.

But she'd shut down; you could see it in her expression. So I just concentrated on getting us through the rest of the number, and the audience, a mob of drunk out-of-towners, applauded like maniacs because they didn't know any better.

In between bows I said in her ear: "You on something?"

"Fuck you."

It occurred to me that she looked more like Carmen than she ever had. That manic glow in her eyes, the jitteriness, the skeletal thinness. I doubted she was up for the Congreso. There were a dozen girls I could have called to take her place, but I decided to wait and see. If she'd even suspected I was thinking about replacing her, it would have pushed her over the edge.

What bothered me most was her secrecy. It just wasn't like her. I was the first one she ran to when anything happened: when her father died, when Luis was sick, when Princess Diana was killed in that car crash and she freaked out, when she had a fucking leak in her sink faucet for Christ's sake. I told her she looked like hell and she should see a doctor. She didn't say anything, just lit a cigarette and looked away.

Finally she muttered, "I got some shit I have to think about. Maybe I need to get away for a while."

"You still should see a doctor."

"I'm just stressed."

"I'm thinking you should go to Miami for Martin Luther King."

Miami was where we always went to recharge. We'd pop down a couple of times a year to check out those new Art Deco clubs and restaurants that were opening up in South Beach. When Luis was younger we'd take him with us and park him at Milly's or with this great-aunt of mine who lives in Kendall, with the Jamaicans.

She said: "I'll think about it."

I'd made a resolution not to lose patience and I didn't. "I already bought the ticket. Consider it an early birthday present. But you have to promise to see a doctor when you get back."

We didn't say what we were both thinking: Lina was in Miami.

I was more worried than I let on. I called my old buddy Hank Pursner, who happened to be down there on vacation himself that week, and told him to keep an eye on her. Hank used to be a narc detective in Miami in the eighties, the height of the cocaine wars— the *real Miami Vice*, although you wouldn't think it to look at him.

I saw Cardoza off myself, just to make sure she got on the plane. The way she was acting, I didn't trust her. Once a junkie, always a junkie.

Thursday before a long weekend the lines at LaGuardia were hell, college students with empty faces and emptier chatter, and the *cubanos* in front of us yammering on about the Pope's visit, how nice it would be to see Castro down on his knees. I held Cardoza's hand and kissed her in front of the metal detector.

"*Cúidate,*" I said.

She was staying at Lina's cousin's condo. She gave me that number, and Lina's aunt's, too. When she called that evening, she said the condo was pretty fucking nice, a duplex done up Japanese style, with mats on the floor and sliding doors. There was a balcony giving out to the ocean, and a pool. They were going out clubbing that night, she said, some new place with a tropical fruit name, I don't remember what.

I called the condo the next day around noon but no one answered. I called the other number, Lina's *tíos.* An older woman picked up the phone.

"Is Lina there?"

"No," said the woman.

"I'm a friend of hers from New York."

"Where is she?"

"What do you mean, where is she?"

"She and her friend had dinner here last night and then they all went out and didn't come back."

"What are you talking about?"

"They're *missing.* Her toiletries aren't in the bathroom. I went to the condo and her friend's luggage is gone. And this isn't like Junior. He always calls in."

"Who's Junior?"

"My son. Guillermo. They all went out together. Are you sure you don't know where they are?"

The first thing that popped into my head was that they were hiding somewhere, maybe a hotel, doing a threesome.

But Cardoza wasn't into threesomes. Never had been, never would be.

"No," I said. "I don't know what's going on, but I'm going to find out."

"What can *you* do?"

"Look, I'll call you back. My name is Oswaldo."

"Ana," the *vieja* said, so I knew we were on the same team.

I called my man Hank's cell, and he confirmed that all three of them had been at La Guayaba the night before, though he was pretty sure they hadn't seen him. Wendy had left last, walked for a while and then gotten into a cab, which swung south, so he'd assumed she was going back to the condo. I told him to check out the condo. When he called back, he said the *vieja* was telling the truth: there was no one home.

"Check out this Guillermo," I told him. Using the condo address, Hank came up with another property in Coral Gables, listed to the same owner, Guillermo De Leon. Nothing happening there, just the wife and three kids and a couple of nannies going in and out. "Any other real estate?" I asked my friend. He said no, just some fancy yacht berthed up in Fort Lauderdale. I told him to research it, and check the flight lists out of Miami International as well.

Like the ace he was, Hank called back with the news that none of the three had been listed on any departing flight list for the past forty-eight hours and also that the yacht had cast off sometime Thursday night, no destination listed.

Bingo.

It was Saturday afternoon by the time we figured it out. I called Wendy's home number, and Luis answered.

"Where is she?" I asked him.

"Jamaica," he said, not sounding too happy.

"Jamaica? Why the fuck didn't you call me?"

"I thought you knew."

"How did she get there? Did she fly? Did she go by herself?"

"I don't know. But if you talk to her, tell her the hospital called. She already missed two of her treatments."

"What are you talking about?"

"Nothing." He sounded flustered. "It's not important."

"*Dime,* Luis."

"*Nothing.* Just as long as she's okay."

"Look Luis, I really need this information. She might be in trouble."

"She got a little spot on her lung."

"For fuck's sake, what are you talking about?"

"She has cancer."

"No," I said, but I was thinking, *Of course, that explains everything.*

"You just find her and tell her to come home, okay?"

He was practically screaming at me.

"Okay, honey," I said, talking to him like I did when he was a little guy having nightmares. "I'll let you know as soon as I know something. And you call me if she gets in touch again. Promise?"

Silence.

"Give me a break, Luisito, I'm as worried as you are."

"Okay, I promise," he said, and hung up.

By Monday morning there was more news. A boat fitting the description of De Leon's yacht—red trim and pink sails—had dropped anchor off the northwest side of Eleuthera Island in the Bahamas. They had been really booking, according to Hank, using both engine and sail, since they'd left Lauderdale. He said they'd likely go in to refuel at Georgetown.

"You wanna stop them?" he asked. "I can fix it, no problem, board and search."

"No. Just confirm that Cardoza's on board. Tell me, is that the normal route people take to Jamaica?"

"It's the scenic route. Going around the western tip of Cuba would be faster."

I phoned the *vieja* in Miami and didn't give her the details, just said that I had pretty good information that they were on the boat, somewhere in the Caribbean.

"*Dios sálvanos,*" she said. "Junior hasn't called. That's what worries me. That wife of his"—she sounded like she was spitting when she said this—"claims she has no idea where he is."

The libraries were closed because of the holiday, but I went up to Alegre and used the computer to search the Internet for maps of the Bahamas. I printed out a couple and as I was studying them began to think that maybe I should have said yes to having the boat stopped in Georgetown.

That night I went to Flamingo to try to get my mind off things. I had my cell on, and when it vibrated, I jumped like it had burned me. Hank said there'd been no sign of them in Georgetown Harbor. I checked my home voice mail, and there she was. Her voice was faint, scratchy.

"Hey, we're okay [static]. So tell Luis [static] can't really, it's impossible [static]."

The call had come in at one-fifteen.

Hearing her voice was a relief. I was thinking she was probably hating every second of the trip. At the best of times my partner had ants in her pants, and being cooped up on a boat would be driving her crazy. I phoned Luis and put him up to date.

Around five the next day, as I was about to step into the shower before going uptown to teach the beginners', Hank called again.

The yacht had been spotted just off the northeast tip of Cuba, near the city of Baracoa.

"You sure?" I asked him.

"I got some friends in Brothers to the Rescue," he said.

"You gotta lot of friends, *hombre.*"

"And you should thank me for it."

"Free classes for the rest of your life. You sure it's them?"

"Seventy-five-foot sloop, white with scarlet and brass trim. Pink sails. Ain't too many like her."

"So they're headed for the Windward Passage?" I was an expert on the Caribbean now.

"Could be. From there it's a straight shot to Jamaica. They're awful close to shore though, way closer than they need to be. If they don't watch it, the Cuban Coast Guard is gonna do an intercept." He hesitated and then said: "Oz, I think they're gonna land."

"What?"

"We can't see them anymore, it's too dark, but I got this feeling."

"Land in Cuba?"

"Yeah."

"She said *Jamaica.*"

"They're too close. There's no reason for them to be that close. Either that, or they're gonna pick somebody up."

"Where exactly are they again?"

"Off the coast of Baracoa."

I found it on the map. "They can do that, just pull into any old harbor in Cuba?"

"Technically, no. But if they had help, they could ease in some-where out of the way."

"Local help, you mean."

"Yes."

"So what do we do?"

"*Nada.* My BTW boys will be in touch first thing in the morning."

"Tell me as soon as you hear."

"*Claro,*" Hank said in his terrible gringo accent, and hung up.

Maybe it's nothing. Maybe it's just some kind of harebrained idea of a surprise vacation. The cousin—what was his name?—wanted to show off. He's probably got relatives all over the island who would help sneak him in. What a stunt, landing in Cuba in a fancy American yacht. It'll be all over the news tomorrow.

But I couldn't convince myself. Who the hell would choose to sail to Cuba? Especially a Cuban American—why would he take the chance of getting arrested on Cuban soil?

I don't remember a thing I taught in class that night.

Ten A.M. Wednesday, January 21. There was no sign of them. The *Catalina*—that was the boat's name, believe it or not—had not docked at Port-au-Prince, or Kingston, or Montego Bay. There was no red-and-white schooner to be found off any point of the northeast coastline of Cuba. Was it stormy, I asked, fearing the worst, and Hank said no, according to BTW it was a fair winter day in the Antilles, with the lightest of trade winds and unlimited visibility.

I had four privates that day—usually it was five, but I hadn't filled Lina's slot. Toward the end of the second lesson Luis called my cell.

"I gotta message from Mami. You were right; she was on that boat. They landed in Cuba last night. She's okay."

"Where in Cuba?"

"I don't know."

"Jésucristo, Luisito, she didn't give you any clue?"

"She said she was okay."

"When she's coming back?"

"She said never."

Maybe I wasn't thinking straight. Maybe I was even acting crazy. I only knew I had to do what I had to do. I canceled my other privates and called Milly and told her I needed a flight to Havana ASAP.

She didn't ask any questions, just told me she couldn't buy the tickets herself but there was somebody she knew in Toronto.

I went home and while I was waiting for Milly to call back turned on CNN. No news of an American yacht illegally entering Cuban waters, but there was a shot of José Martí Airport in Havana as the Pope landed for his historic five-day visit to the island. I must admit I got distracted by those schoolgirls in their short gold pleated skirts.

Caribbean women have the ocean in their walk.

Milly came through: JFK to Cancún leaving the next morning, and the connecting flight to Havana the same afternoon. The layover was a comfortable two and a half hours.

"They're e-tickets; all you have to do is show your passport. And to be on the safe side you might want to pick up some cheap souvenirs in Cancún. When you pack coming back, make sure they're on top, so if your suitcases get opened it'll look like you've been vacationing in Mexico. Take dollars, nothing larger than a ten. In Havana, ask them not to stamp your passport."

As we spoke, I was watching CNN again, a rerun of the Pope emerging down the steps of the plane, his face pink over white vestments, and I thought, *In less than twenty-four hours I'll be there.*

"Anything you want, honey, it's yours," I told Milly.

She laughed that throaty laugh that always makes me want to jump her bones.

"Buena suerte, Oz."

I called Hank and told him my plans. He listened carefully and informed me who had the keys to his apartment and where to find what I required. Things were different before September 11, and I was willing to take the risk. I cabbed to Jackson Heights and back, using my cell to spread the word that my Thursday class was canceled.

I couldn't sleep that night. Even when I put on one of my old tapes from "Speech Makes the Man," which usually sends me into a coma, my mind kept jumping around and around. For no real reason, except maybe last-minute research, I called my stepfather, Pepi.

"Hey, it's me. Did I wake you?"

"Uh-uh." The sound of the TV, the same *Baretta* rerun I'd been watching, stopped as he finally found the mute button.

"Tell me about Cuba."

"What's that?"

"I'm going down. A tour group. You know, like an educational thing."

He snorted. "Don't expect no luxuries on the *isla.*"

"So you got any advice for me?"

"You really going?"

"Yeah, I got the tickets and everything."

"Don't advertise you're *norteamericano*. Otherwise you're the human ATM; they know you got dollars on you. And keep your attitude under control."

"Anything else?"

"You going to Trinidad?" Trinidad was his hometown.

"If I have time."

"All this salsa shit you kids listen to now, the real thing began in Cuba. Go to the Casa de la Trova." I heard him wheeze, then cough. Rustling and then a racket like something being knocked to the floor.

"You okay?"

"Casa de la Trova," he repeated, not answering me. "You tell them you're the stepson of Pepi Delgado. Say hi to all the guys for me. And look up my sister. Mercedes Bettancourt. She lives right off the Plaza Ana. Just ask on the street. Bettancourt."

"Sure thing. Thanks, Pepi."

He hung up without saying anything. People were doing that to me a lot lately.

Following Milly's advice, while I was in Cancún I bought several gaudy sarongs and refrigerator magnets of parrots and monkeys. The airport was depressing. There were lots of very rich folks, mostly North Americans, and very poor folks, mostly Mexican, swarming around the terminal and getting in one another's way. Not to mention the college kids high on every kind of drug ever invented. My cell was quiet, and there was nothing on my home machine when I checked.

Island flights are all the same, I had gone several times with Ma to visit family in Puerto Rico. Everyone's loaded down with bulky carry-ons, and when the plane lands they stand up and cheer while the flight attendant's barking: "Please remain in your seats with your

seat belts securely fastened until the aircraft has come to a full stop."
The carry-ons to Cuba consisted mostly of plastic bags jammed full
of drugstore items–everything from Band-Aids to Pepto Bismol to
Tampax to economy-size bottles of aspirin and Tylenol.

Even from the air you could see that Havana was not the city it
had once been. Sprawling, with the bay sparkling north in the late-
afternoon sun, it was mostly flat, with patches of pale green here and
there, and it looked quiet, almost deserted. You didn't feel the energy
until you landed, when they brought the steps out to the plane and
there were four or five people in uniform to help you down. In a
Communist country everyone has to have a job. The air smelled like
jungle and coal and rich tobacco and something else, a kind of
burned sweetness. This gorgeous girl in uniform was standing
against the door of the terminal, holding it open, touching the head
of each kid who passed her to go in. Not exactly the kind of greeting
you get at Kennedy or LAX.

I had no intention of getting stopped in customs, but fortunately
they seemed to have little interest in either me or the duffel I'd
checked through. My Mexican visa was good enough for Immigration. As soon as I got outside I turned on my cell and it said NO
SERVICE. There was a rank of regular taxis, but a guy in a forties
Plymouth painted fuchsia and cobalt blue—those photographs aren't
kidding—said he'd get me into the city for eight American dollars.
This sounded reasonable so I said yes.

As we clattered through the suburbs, billboard after billboard
flipped by: *Venceremos.* We will conquer, with Che Guevara's face in
black and white like James Dean of the Revolution. *Patria o muerte*
with a fist in a power salute. And much newer, head shots of John
Paul II.

"Where's he today?" I asked the *taxista*.

"The Pope? Santa Clara. Yesterday you couldn't get near the airport." He asked if I had a place to stay in Havana and when I said I
didn't told me he had a niece with an apartment in the luxurious
neighborhood of Vedado for only twenty dollars a night.

"Does it have a phone?"

"Of course. And if you need to do long distance, the Habana
Libre is just down the street."

We were speaking in Spanish, of course, and though I'm fluent I knew it was going to take me a day or so to get used to Cuban machine-gun talk.

The niece's apartment turned out to be a good twelve blocks from the Habana Libre Hotel, but it had a balcony and a flush toilet and even a rickety TV set. It was illegal, meaning that she hadn't registered it as a guesthouse with the government, so no one was going to want to advertise the fact that I was staying there, which was fine with me.

I showered—no hot water, but you can't have everything—put on fresh jeans and a tank top, and went out to see what I could see. At Coppelia Park I changed a ten into pesos. I hadn't eaten since breakfast, so I bought a ham-and-cheese sandwich and a *pastelo* and two cartons of mango juice off a street vendor, and ate sitting on a bench under some trees. An ice-cream stand was blasting the latest Van Van CD.

The Van Van was familiar, but nothing else was.

La Habana was another world. To the eye at least, time had stopped in the late 1950s. Buildings were falling down, the park was overgrown, the cars were ancient and jury-rigged; you could practically hear the machinery of the city groaning, clunking, on its last legs. Only the people were fresh, going about their business in outfits as jury-rigged as the cars, but just as bright, and somehow, like the cars, the outfits worked. Young guys called out as I passed: "Cocaine? Cigars? Girls?" When I said, *Nada*, one of them pressed: "What about boys? Do you like boys?"

The lobby of the Habana Libre looked sleepy. In the old days, it's said, Castro came in every afternoon for a drink at the bar, but the most interesting thing going on there when I walked in was a group of middle-aged German tourists reading to one another from *Lonely Planet*. A bellboy pointed me to the Poste de Teléfonos, where I called my machine. The first three messages were trash, and then there she was, a little more distinct than last time.

"Left a message on your cell [static] talk about it now [static] . . . fine. We're in Santiago at the Pensión Dolores." The call had come in about half an hour after I'd boarded the plane to Cancún.

Santiago, Chile? No stupid, I told myself, Santiago de Cuba. I had to look at a map again, but I was pretty sure it was east of here.

I tried to get through to the Pensión Dolores, but the operator said there was no such listing in the city of Santiago.

Call again and give me more information, I thought, willing the message to travel east and lodge in her brain.

I phoned my machine one more time and changed the outgoing message to say: "Cardoza, leave me your number. Repeat it three times, slowly. Everyone else leave a message." Then I checked in with Hank. He said nothing unusual was going on at the Casa Rosada except that Guillermo wasn't back. The condo, too, remained deserted. I told him I was on my way east but that I'd be checking in frequently.

Outside the Habana Libre there was a line of white taxis. I started with the first one, trying to negotiate a rate to Santiago. It would take two days and cost me seven hundred American, he said. The second one said eighteen hours and a thousand.

Why the hell had I never learned to drive?

I went back in the lobby, and the travel agent there helped me reserve a direct flight to Santiago for the following day. I gave the agent two tens for her pains, and she added that I would have to get to the airport four hours early so I could pay for the ticket in cash.

Fuck this embargo.

As I walked back up Calle 23, behind me, down the hill, the sun was setting over the Malecón. Somewhere church bells were tolling. I thought Castro had outlawed religion, but then I remembered that the Pope was in town.

Back in my apartment I took a nap, and when I woke up, the niece's husband pointed me to a *paladar*, where he said they had decent roast chicken, and also wrote down a list of clubs he thought I might like.

Clubbing in Havana? Why the hell not. I could write the trip off as a business expense. The chicken was pretty good, typical Caribbean, and came with a generous side of rice and black beans. When I got out of the cab in front of the first club my host had recommended, I saw the hookers. Fleshier than their New York counterparts, *mulata* mostly, in tight bright polyester dresses or pants and halters and platform shoes, they were shockingly young and shockingly lovely. "*Tuerto, Tuerto!*" they called and one of them said, "Fucky, fucky," touching me on the shoulder in that plaintive Cuban way. I could be your father, I told her, and she shouted, *Ay papito, ven acá,* which made all the other girls laugh their asses off. I have always had a soft spot for whores, and the hookers of Havana were smart as well as beautiful. But I wasn't even tempted. I had other things on my mind.

I danced a little, even drank a beer, which I do about once a year. On the way home I stopped at the Habana Libre and tried my machine one more time. Nothing.

Call me, I thought. *Cardoza, pick up the fucking phone.*

16

Wendy

A great dancer can shine in a very small space.

———⊗⊗⊗———

Her first day aboard the *Catalina,* Wendy spent paying for showing off the night before. Her left knee was swollen and tender to the touch, her right foot so cramped she could barely put weight on it. Sifting through the miniature medicine cabinet, she hit the jackpot— eleven Tylenols with codeine. She popped a couple dry and slipped the rest balled up in a Kleenex into the pocket of her jeans. She left the empty vial where she'd found it, behind a bottle of vitamins, and passed out in a deck chair. Sometime later, she remembered crawling into the top of the bunk bed she was sharing with Catalina.

She awoke suddenly with no sense of where she was or what time it was. The word *boat* came into her mind, and after a few seconds she realized that was why she had awoken: she was on a boat that had been moving and now it had stopped. There was a slit of light beneath the shut door, which made her think it was daytime.

She calipered her knee—it still hurt, but the swelling was down. Time for another hit, but first she needed water. She was so dehydrated it was hard to breathe. With a bare foot she reached gingerly back and down for the first rung of the wooden ladder. One step, then another. The light was enough to make out Catalina curled up in the lower bunk, face turned away. Wendy considered waking her and then thought the better of it.

The arch of her foot gave only a faint twinge when she hit the floor. She cracked the door open and tried to get her bearings. A short carpeted hallway with doors leading off it. The light source turned out to be a sconced wall lamp. Which was the bathroom? Not the padlocked door. There, that was it, at the end. But as she started to turn on the tap she saw the sign posted over the tiny basin: NONPOTABLE.

She went out and made another inventory of the hallway. Through an open door she saw what looked like a kitchen. Sure enough, there was a refrigerator stocked with pint bottles of Dasani. She guzzled one down, taking a Tylenol with it, and then opened another. Except for the sound of waves washing against the boat's sides, it was very quiet. Somewhere there was a flashing light, like a neon sign—she'd seen it through the kitchen porthole—and as she left the kitchen and neared the spiral staircase at the opposite end of the hallway she saw it again. The stairway led to the deck, she remembered. Good. She had to get some air.

It was morning, just barely. The flashing light, she saw as she gained the deck, was coming from a kind of giant buoy directly in front of them. Behind it and to the right, a bloody pink sun was rising. She thought she was alone until she smelled cigarette smoke and saw someone standing by the rail to her right. It was Mano, the small dark guy. He was so still—that's why she hadn't seen him at first— just standing there smoking and staring out—at what, she could not fathom. Certainly there was no land in sight, a fact that surprised her. Could you drop anchor just like that, in the open sea?

She was having a nick fit but good.

"*Tienes otro?*"

Mano turned in her direction in a motion that was both slow and fast.

"*Claro,*" he said.

He seemed friendly, so she approached him.

He glanced down at her bare feet. "*Y tus zapatos?*"

"*En mi habitación.*"

He reached into the front pocket of his trousers, took out a pack of Populares, lit one off the one he was smoking, and handed it to her. It was harsh and tasted like heaven.

"Are you always up this early?" she asked.

"Sailors like to make the most of daylight."

"How much did you sleep?"

He held up three fingers.

"That's crazy."

"I don't need sleep when I'm at sea." He smiled, and she saw the glint of a gold tooth, an upper incisor.

"We're resting now," he said. "Nothing to do but wait for the wind to change."

"Where are we?"

"Off Egg Island."

"Where's that?"

"The Bahamas."

"Are we going to land?"

"No need to land. What's your name?"

She liked the way he looked at her. Open, so unlike New York Latinos.

"Wendy."

"Wen-dee." He tasted the name. "*Boricua?*"

"*Dominicana. Tú?*"

"*Cubano.*"

"*Que haces en Jamaica?*"

"*Eh? No hago nada.*"

For some reason he didn't like being questioned about his plans in Jamaica. She changed the subject.

"Why do we need sails when we have an engine?"

"It gives us a little extra power. Also, sails are quiet. In case we need to be quiet."

"What if there's a storm?"

"We'll haul them in, except for the storm sail. But we're not expecting any storms." He used the word *tormentas,* looking at her meaningfully. Definitely flirting. And then glancing over her shoulder.

It was Guillermo, immaculate in khaki shorts and a freshly ironed white polo, although she could tell by his eyes that he hadn't slept. She remembered the high-grade powder he'd treated her to the night they went to La Guayaba. He said something to Mano in very rapid Spanish—she made out only the words "San Salvador." She half expected Mano to salute and follow with an "Aye aye, sir" or whatever the Spanish equivalent was, but he merely flicked his cigarette over the rail and walked toward the front of the boat.

"Did you sleep well?" asked Guillermo, ever the perfect host.

"Yes, thanks."

"Good," he said with an absent smile, and then turned and made his way up the stairs to the wheelhouse.

As Wendy was finishing her smoke Mano came back toward her, carrying what looked like a giant handle. He said nothing, just gave her a broad wink as he passed. He'd rolled up the sleeves of his T-shirt and the light was coming up just in time for her to notice how perfectly muscled his upper arms were.

Wide awake, with just enough codeine in her system to take the edge off, Wendy roamed the *Catalina.* In the kitchen—*galley,* they called it—she sipped Starbucks French vanilla blend from a porcelain mug emblazoned with CATALINA LA O in scarlet script. She examined the contents of the freezer—American frozen dinners as well as fish and pork chops and several whole chickens. In the cupboard—rice and beans and twenty kinds of canned soup. Enough mineral water and beer for an army.

There were four staterooms in total: the one she and Catalina shared; Guillermo's, which was neat as a pin; one that was used as a living room and bar; and a fourth—the biggest, it looked like from the size of the door—that was padlocked. Edgar and Mano slept, when they did sleep, in hammocks up on deck. Wendy was in the living room/bar fiddling with the little TV when she heard the engines rev, felt the vibrations in her fingertips. The boat began to swing around.

She went back up on deck. This ocean was not the blue Caribbean she knew but a greenish gray roiling trimmed with dull gold. The mainsail was now fully unfurled—*pink,* who would have guessed—and Mano and Edgar were down by the foredeck rail talking. Mano had his back to her, but Edgar, she could see, was scowling under his Orioles hat.

Later that day—what day was it? she'd lost track, Saturday it had to be—Guillermo leaned down from the bridge and surprised Wendy by calling out: "Hey, wanna see how this baby operates?"

"Sure."

She climbed the steps, and, holding the door open for her, Guillermo indicated that she should sit down in what looked like an office swivel chair bolted to the floor. Navigation turned out to be far more complicated than she could have guessed. On a small table behind them were spread out what Guillermo called charts, complex-looking maps dotted with numbers. "These show depth," he explained. "We're a big boat and the Bahamas are shallow, so it's particularly important for us to know how much clearance we have." He'd been marking their course on the charts in blue pencil. They were heading due south, through what looked like thousands of tiny islands. "Look, we just passed the Tropic of Cancer," he said, pointing it out. "The reason we went so slow going out of Fort Lauderdale was because the Gulf Stream was against us. See? We had to crosscut it." He showed her the ship's log, a blow-by-blow journal of sea conditions and what he was doing about them. She was particularly fascinated by the GPS, a green map against a black screen. Guillermo demonstrated how it could pinpoint their precise location, with latitude and longitude. Although she was enjoying it, to Wendy the whole show-and-tell was a little too disingenuous, as if he were trying to prove to her that this voyage was on the up and up.

She asked: "Don't you have radar?"

"Of course. That's still the best way of reckoning. And it's absolutely necessary if we run into foul weather, fog for instance. Then we need to know where other physical objects are."

There was a buzzing from the console. Guillermo picked up a handset and said, *"Diga."* He listened for a minute and then said to Wendy, "Excuse me, there's something I have to attend to."

As she climbed back down the stairs she thought: *The only thing he's convinced me of is that these days drug runners use the fanciest technology available.*

She remembered the tiny suede bag stuffed into her duffel, and that night, after dinner, had her own private party on the galley counter.

The *Catalina* wouldn't have been so claustrophobic if it weren't for the low ceilings. But Wendy adapted. For the duration of the voyage she co-opted the living room/bar as her studio. There was no mirror, she had to work around the furniture, and it wasn't easy to get her sea legs on the slick teak floorboards, but she managed. After all, she had perfect equilibrium, according to the gymnastics scout who'd picked her out in phys ed class all those years ago at P.S. 98.

Unusually limber and symmetrical, long arms and legs, good upper- and lower-body strength, exceptional pelvic rotation.

Except for her skag period, she'd kept in shape all of her life. Weights for her upper body, and several years ago, when she'd suspected her reflexes were dulling, she'd taken up kick boxing for a while. Before her diagnosis she'd been doing Pilates four times a week.

Guillermo's CD collection wasn't bad although it leaned heavily to scratchy reproductions of the golden age of mambo—melodramatic big-band numbers that were too slow to dance to. But there was some great vintage Willie Colón and the classic three-CD set *50 Years of Tito Puente,* which kept her happy enough.

Every day she did her stretches, and then a modified—because she didn't have the machine—Pilates routine, and then shines, from side breaks to Suzy-Q's to the most complex syncopated heel-toe patterns. In the evening, if she had the energy, she did it again. She worked until she felt muscle spasms, her joints popping in their sockets, until she was short of breath and the blood was thumping in her ears.

It was unlike Wendy to be so antisocial, holing herself up like that for hours at a time, but the atmosphere on this cruise had turned out to be anything but vacation-like. Meals were catch-as-catch-can affairs, microwaved when people felt hungry. Where were the piña coladas, the lavish buffets, the parties, the stops in fancy ports?

Instead there was the locked stateroom, how the forward part of the boat was off limits—she'd just asked to see how the winch on the mainsail worked, for fuck's sake and Edgar had practically bitten her head off—how the crew acted as if they weren't supposed to mingle with her and Catalina. Guillermo had abandoned his pretense of playing host and now spent every waking moment in the wheelhouse bent over the instruments.

Oddest of all was the behavior of Catalina. For someone so gung ho for a cruise, that girl was a terrible sailor. She spent most of the time in her deck chair reading magazines and popping Dramamine washed down with ginger ale. At night, in the lower berth, Wendy could hear her crying.

"Are you okay, *nena?*" Wendy asked several times, and Lina would just nod, sometimes adding groggily: "I'll be fine when we land."

Too bad she was out of commission, because, as at La Guayaba, on board the *Catalina* Wendy could have used a good partner. What a follow that girl was. You'd think something, and there she'd be, spun over next to you, or out in front of you, doing a little decoration but never distracting enough to make you forget what you were going to do next. Languid but sharp, that's the kind of dancer Catalina was. And she had to admit, with the prettiest footwork Wendy had seen since María Torres.

She would never forget the first time she had gotten the feel of leading. Sure, you weren't in the spotlight, the one who got to do all the frills and furbelows and blurring spins and wiggle this and wiggle that, but you were setting the pace, the flow, the very design of the dance. Nailing a cross-body, she'd understood what bullfighting was about—it was so fucking *dangerous,* to have so much power over another being, to have her to strut across your body then whip around to face you, ready for anything.

But now Catalina was not even company, much less a dance partner.

Wendy couldn't wait for this trip to be over.

After her workouts, in the mingy little shower stall, the water running as hot as it would go, she'd massage her long muscles, digging in with her thumbs as hard as she could, and comfort herself with the fact that her skin was still as smooth as it had been in her twenties.

Again, she could have asked Catalina for help—every dancer she'd ever met was good at massage—but she was reluctant.

According to Guillermo, it was an unusually smooth trip, but there were patches of rough, when looking out the portholes at the diagonal line of foaming sea could make even Wendy queasy. Sunday afternoon there was a storm, and Catalina didn't even move from her bunk, only moaned when Wendy came in to check on her and empty the bucket.

"I want my *papi*," she said.

Never in all their conversations had Catalina ever talked about her father, although she sometimes mentioned her mother, referring to her as a space cadet.

"I know, *nena*," said Wendy, and wiped her forehead with a wet washcloth.

Even on that afternoon she went to the stateroom and worked out, turning the music up extra loud to focus.

Puente's "Asia Mood" was just coming on with a clash of cymbals and marimbas when she felt someone watching her. She turned her head to see Mano leaning in the doorway. They'd been having surreptitious contact—he kept her in smokes—but she'd never seen him belowdecks before except to use the head.

"You're a dancer?" he asked.

"Yes."

"Show me."

She remembered Miguel Vaquiz at the Laundromat, how he'd reached his hand out to show her how to salsa that first time, how she'd automatically taken it because she hadn't known what else to do.

Mano's hands were heavily callused, not the soft city-boy palms she was used to. She showed him the basic Bronx mambo step, but before the song was half over he took over the lead. Spin, basic, bring her around him, double spin, basic. Cuban-style, of course, using every beat of the measure.

"*Santa María, ya sabes bailar,*" she said.

He had a narrow, feral face, but when he smiled he looked heartbreakingly young.

"*¿Te gusta?*" he asked, reaching past her to turn down the volume of the CD player, brushing his arm against her breasts as he did so. He must have felt that she wasn't wearing a bra.

"*Claro. ¿Cuanto tiempo falta para llegar a Jamaica?*"

"*Tres días más,*" he said.

"*Coño. ¿Tan largo?*"

"*Tres días conjuntos.*" He added: "*Paramos en Georgetown por petroleo.*"

"*A qué hora?*"

"*Mañana por la tarde.*"

They were standing face-to-face, close but not touching.

Georgetown. Tomorrow afternoon. This was her chance. She didn't need this funky shit, this being stuck on a boat that could get picked up by the Coast Guard any second. She'd jump ship when they stopped to refuel. Surely they had flights to DR from Georgetown.

The first thing she'd do when she got to shore was call Tuerto.

From the deck she could see Guillermo talking on the handset. His back was to her, but the whole posture of his body was tense.

After this call the mood on the *Catalina* turned even surlier. Edgar and Mano unfurled all the sails, and that night before dinner Wendy decided to forgo her workout and instead went on deck, feeling the tilt of the ship as it leaned away from the wind, slicing full speed through the carpet of sea. Mano and Edgar were belowdecks, arguing about how to fix the galley sink, which had gotten clogged. She stood at the starboard rail, her loose bangs whipping around her face—she was way overdue for a haircut—thanking la Virgencita they had all that fancy navigation equipment because there was nothing in sight but water. They hadn't passed another craft in hours.

It was while she was standing there that she heard voices from the wheelhouse. When she turned to look over her shoulder, she saw that Guillermo was seated at the control panel and Catalina stood by his side, gesticulating urgently. It was obvious he was listening, but he didn't look at her once. It was so dark on deck and the interior light so bright it was like watching a movie. Downwind, she caught snatches of dialogue.

"Cuba," she distinctly heard. And also, "Your fight."

Guillermo turned and gave a short answer, which seemed to agitate Catalina even more because she threw her hands up and began to pace the small glass enclosure. She was wearing baggy shorts and a white tank, under which her breasts bounced as she walked.

"Drop them and run," Wendy heard. And again: "Cuba."

Guillermo suddenly got out of his chair and came up behind Catalina, wrapping his arms around her as if to contain her fury. She struggled, flailing with her elbows at his chest. He held her closer, saying something in her ear, and finally she went still, her head drooping to one side so that her hair fell over her eyes. As Wendy watched, Guillermo continued to whisper to her, and then turned her around so that she faced him. To Wendy's amazement, he began to kiss her, not a cousinly kiss, but a full-blown bend-her-back real-deal lover's kiss.

And it didn't seem that Catalina was offering him any resistance.

So it's true, nena. *You could have told me. A first cousin is nothing. It could have been a brother, or worse, your father.*

Georgetown, Great Exuma.
Sounds like a disease, Wendy thought.

She was furious. Turned out they weren't putting ashore after all. She'd never felt so trapped in her life. As carefully as she'd tried to ration it, she was almost out of codeine, and it was a no-brainer that the pain in her foot and knee was going to come back, not to mention that nasty cough. She'd used up all the leftover coke. The gas pumps were out in the harbor, and Guillermo said it was too shallow to go in any farther. From where they were anchored Wendy could see the city lights, so tantalizingly near.

To placate her, Guillermo had allowed two concessions: a phone call from the wheelhouse, which she used to leave a message on Tuerto's machine, and the spare hammock so she could sleep up on the aftdeck, which was where she was now, making herself swing with the almost imperceptible rocking of the boat. It was heaven after the closeness of belowdecks, and at least tonight she wouldn't have to listen to Lina crying.

The sky was filled with an almost half moon and more stars than she'd ever seen in her life. She tried counting until they made her dizzy. She could smell the clove scent of hashish—Mano and Edgar having a little party on the off-limits foredeck. She thought about asking if she could join them, and then thought no. She was in too bad a mood. She'd just make do with the last of the Populares she'd bummed off of Mano. After she'd put out the third one she lay on her back with the edges of the hammock wrapped around her, cocooned.

A boat putted by their leeward side, a single light on its deck. From the silhouette Wendy could see it had a wide stern cobwebbed with nets. Some kind of fishing boat, maybe shrimp. The gentle plaintive strains of a bachata came drifting faintly over the water.

She used to dance the bachata with her *papi*. *One-two-three stop, One-two-three stop, shake your shoulders*. Nothing fancy, nothing to show off. Just a sweet little thing you did with your honey or your *papi* or your kid.

The minute they landed in Jamaica—or *Cuba*, if she had heard correctly this afternoon, could it really be possible?—she'd figure out how to get to the DR.

That would be where it would happen.

For four days Wendy had managed not to think explicitly about her illness, but now, as she rocked in the hammock watching the yellow light of the shrimp boat vanish into the distance, it surfaced in her brain like a morning dream.

I am going to die.

She knew in her heart that no matter how many treatments she had, radio or chemo or anything else, she wasn't going to make it. More than most people she lived in her body, and now for the first time her body was giving up on itself. She could feel it, a dull ominous pain in her right lower back. She needed Tuerto's hands. No one could get in between her vertebrae the way he could.

The water made a pick-pock noise, and she saw that another, smaller shrimp boat was approaching. There sure was a lot of night traffic around here.

She remembered how Mano's arm had felt against her breasts. He was so hot. Something about the way he moved, with pure, quick gestures, working the mop, untying a line, flicking a cigarette over the rail. But she was too tired to masturbate. The stars were making her dizzy again, so she closed her eyes and cast her mind to what had always calmed her in the past—her old balance beam routine.

Front flip onto the beam and then step, step, step, reach down, up, dou-ble turn, two side aerials into a back handspring, volte, down into a split. Up, prance, prance, prance, roundoff back handspring into a double twisting layout. Stick the landing.

She'd never forget the first time she'd performed it: how absolutely still the crowd had been, and then the roar of applause and her *papi* rushing across the floor to scoop her up in his arms.

Perfect equilibrium.

The only time she'd ever faltered was on the day of the Olympic Trials. That blue mat like the ocean. It hadn't occurred to her until years afterward that she might have failed simply because she wasn't good enough.

But things had turned out the way they were supposed to, after all. If she hadn't quit gymnastics, she would never have started danc-ing mambo. Just the other day Effy Duarte from Puerto Domingo had come up to her at the Copa—"You know I'd keep you in the limelight if you were *my* partner." And who did the most ambitious Eddie Torres guys drag out onto the floor when they wanted to show off their newest cool moves?

Wendy Cardoza, La Reina Mambera, that's who.

But Luisa was right. She would have had to say good-bye to it eventually. It was just turning out to be sooner than she had expected.

Pulling the wings of the hammock over her face, she wept, silently, so the guys wouldn't hear. She thought she had done with her crying Christmas week, but this was worse.

Bittersweet was worse than bitter.

Ay, Virgencita, why are you taking this away from me?

17

Catalina

*Like it or not, your true self
will show on the dance floor.*

She kept hearing her father's voice. First in her Dramamine-
induced dreams on the deck of the *Catalina* and then later, when she
was awake, in the wash of waves against the ship's sides. Sometimes
they were walking through a mandarin orange grove, and he was
singing to her. The fragrance of citrus was intense—it was January,
and the fruit was ripe.

Once she dreamed of his foot. Not his face, which she had
barely been able to look at when she found him, but his bare dan-
gling foot, which she had hugged tightly to her chest, feeling all the
ridges and calluses and bony toes, before running across the road to
get Jun.

She was running a fever, and the nights, because they were

cooler, were marginally better than the days. At night she remembered who she was, where she was—*Why is this such a rough crossing? Why is it taking so long?*

She knew it was over Tuesday afternoon when Guillermo came into the stateroom where she and Wendy were playing their tenth game of gin rummy in a row.

"There's been a change of plans."

Wendy asked hopefully: "We landing?"

Her cousin, Catalina observed, looked so tired that for the first time she could see Tío 'Nesto in him. "In a bit," he answered. "Though not where we originally intended. We're putting to port in Cuba."

"Cuba." Wendy did not look or sound surprised. She examined her hand of cards and then laid them facedown on the table.

The day before, around dusk, Catalina had finally awoken from her fog and gotten a Coke from the galley and without really thinking about it went up on deck to talk to her cousin. She was so groggy she'd nearly lost her footing on the ladder climbing up to the wheelhouse. He'd held out a hand to help her the rest of the way. It was as if he'd been waiting for her.

As he told her she sat perfectly still and calm. She had all her arguments ready.

Ditch the arms and run. Mano and Edgar will take them. It's not your fight. They don't need you. You don't know the terrain; you'll be a liability. You're so obviously American. Just turn the Catalina *around and take us back to Miami. Or Jamaica. Venezuela. Anywhere but Cuba.*

He shook his head, graver than she'd ever seen him.

She said: "So you're one of *them* now." She did not chide him, *Remember we agreed, you and me, never to take sides.* It was too late; he had married into it, married perhaps to get away from her. How could she blame him? She'd done the same, choosing Richard.

"After this is over there won't be any more *them* and *us*."

"If you say so."

He came up from behind, put his arms around her. "You still with me?"

"You need me."

Gemelos.

Now he said: "We're going to have to cruise in the dark for a couple of hours. And be very quiet about it."

After he left them Catalina and Wendy snuck up on deck. Guillermo had cut the engine to a soft putter, and a gentle current was helping propel them along. The lights were completely doused, and only the mainsail was up. They were a ghost ship, sneaking into harbor. Guillermo wouldn't tell her which, but somehow she knew it wasn't Havana. She and Wendy leaned over the starboard rail and peered through the dark, although there was nothing to see.

In a whisper Wendy asked, "You know what's going on, *nena,* don't you?"

"Yes."

"Drugs?"

Catalina remembered how Guillermo had replied to her in Fort Lauderdale. "It's better if you don't know."

Wendy shrugged as if to say: *But I will soon enough.*

It was almost nine when they dropped anchor. They'd gotten a glimpse of coast but ended up staying hidden in a cove while a beat-up fishing trawler glided up alongside to be loaded with armful after armful of canvas-wrapped bundles. There were so many the trawler had to make three trips. Wendy made no comment, just stood on the aftdeck smoking. Catalina still had hope that Guillermo might change his mind at the last minute, until the fourth time the trawler came into sight, and her cousin said: "Get your stuff, we're going ashore."

Catalina climbed into the fishing boat first, then Wendy, then Edgar and Mano. Guillermo lingered on the deck of the *Catalina* for half a minute or so. In the muted light from the fishing boat's lantern, when he finally grabbed the rail and made the hop down to the deck of the trawler, Catalina could see that his face was wet.

Cuba, we're in Cuba.

She kept telling herself this as they walked, shaky on sea legs, single file along the dirt path that led up from the bay. She marveled at the sight of a grove of royal palms in a field ahead. They were wild, higgledy-piggledy, so different from the carefully cultivated sentinels of Miami.

I remember the trees.

And she remembered another illicit landing, a shore of sea grapes, just before dawn, climbing onto a pier holding her mother's hand.

I guess I bought a round-trip ticket.

In the palm grove they all crammed into an old Lada that had been awaiting them. Because they were too many to fit properly, Catalina ended up sitting on her cousin's lap, one of his arms looped around her waist. After a few minutes of jouncing over the dirt road she could feel that he was aroused.

Wendy asked, *"¿Dónde estamos?"*

It was the driver who answered. "Santiago de Cuba."

They took a series of circuitous roads that led them, gradually, to the lights in the distance. On the hairpins Catalina shifted slightly, trying not to encourage her cousin's erection. Santiago, what she could see of it, was dotted with small plazas and the occasional cobblestone street. Maybe it was low blood sugar combined with an adrenaline surge, but every image seemed clearer than life, almost to the point of vibrating: shop names scrawled in red over the doorways, dark alleys, dogs running loose, children playing everywhere on the street even though it was night. The Lada's engine had a distinctive rhythmic hiccup, like a heart murmur.

I must be dreaming.

No, it was all those years in America that she had been dreaming, and now she was awake.

She had been trembling without realizing it. Guillermo put his hands on her upper arms to calm her.

Now they were climbing a particularly steep hill, and Edgar was discussing an address with the driver. In a few minutes the car stopped in front of a house where they were greeted by an elderly black woman with a turban and both front teeth missing. Edgar introduced her as his great-aunt.

The house was primitive, with only a main living area, two bedrooms, and a kitchen and bathroom shared with the neighbors. There were no doors, only tattered curtains. A television set and a lamp in the main room appeared to be the sole electrical appliances.

Given the food shortage, the dinner the aunt served them was sumptuous: oxtail stew with rice and black beans, sweet plantains soaked in rum, fried yucca chips, and a chopped cucumber and tomato salad.

Mano, who had gone out, came back in with several tall bottles of beer. Toward the end of the meal a young woman in a very short red skirt arrived carrying a toddler in her arms, and she and Edgar disappeared into the night.

Catalina was so famished that the smell of food made her feel she was going to pass out. She wolfed down her portion, barely tasting it, and took seconds. Her cousin, she noticed, ate very little. When the aunt left the room for a minute, he leaned across and said to Wendy and Catalina in English: "If anyone asks you what you're doing here, just say you're a tourist from the States."

"Yessir," replied Wendy. Catalina thought, but wasn't sure, that she winked at Guillermo.

After dinner they went to a Poste de Teléfonos, where Guillermo called Lilly and spoke for about five minutes: *We're all safe now. How are the boys.* Wendy left a message for Luis on her answering machine. The only people Catalina could think of to call were her *tíos,* but Lilly would tell them she was okay. Mano suggested that they all go to a bar around the corner. Guillermo seemed nervous at the idea, but Mano convinced him it would be good for their morale to mingle with civilians. At least that's what Catalina thought he said. Her Spanish was not up to Cuban idioms.

At the bar they drank more beer, some god-awful local brew that had a picture of a lizard playing maracas on the can. Wendy as usual wasn't drinking but seemed to be having a good time chatting and bumming cigarettes from Mano and a couple of his buddies. As Guillermo had instructed, Catalina heard her identify herself as a *turista* from *Nueva York.*

"*¿Qué haces allá?*"

"*Soy maestra de mambo.*"

"*¿Qué rica!*" On the tinny boombox they put on a CD of something that sounded like fusion salsa rap. Wendy laughed and held up her hands in protest.

"*Muy avanzado para mi.*" But the next time Catalina looked, she and Mano were dancing. It was a jittery song, and you could barely hear the *clave.* They were using their hips, Cuban-style.

Beside her Guillermo was watching, too, as he nursed his second can of lizard beer. There was an odd light in his eyes. He was wearing olive drab trousers and a plain white T-shirt—a military effect that was probably deliberate. Surreptitiously she studied his long face, paler than usual, the scar next to his right eye, which he had gotten from falling out of the mango tree the year they were nine. Actually they had been tussling, and she had pushed him, a fact he had never told a living soul, not even his mother.

For some reason the room felt familiar. If she slit her eyes to fuzz her vision, she could imagine that the man sitting by himself at the far table was Dagoberto the shoemaker, her father's best friend. She hadn't thought of him in years. She was getting groggy. Maybe it was being back on land, or the heavy meal after not eating for days, or the beer. The lights in the bar seemed too dim, the music too loud. Still, she couldn't bear the thought of returning to that depressing house.

She remembered a line from a recent article in *El Herald:* "A buoyant people pushed to the breaking point."

Guillermo put his hand on top of hers, and it was only when she looked down that she noticed he wasn't wearing his wedding ring.

"¿*Vamos a casa?*"

Suddenly the idea seemed like a good one. She nodded.

They left Wendy and Mano playing their own version of "Name That Tune." Guillermo said something to him on the way out, and Mano nodded and gave a thumbs-up.

The streetlights had been cut early to save electricity. On the sidewalk, which was actually a series of slate stones balanced over a gutter, Guillermo took her hand as they picked their way down the hill in the moonlight. She could see the stars over the bay and imagined telling her children, her grandchildren: *When I was thirty-two years old, I went to Cuba on a big boat with your uncle.*

They walked in silence for a while, and then she asked: "So what happens next?"

"It's probably better if you and Wendy get out of the country as soon as possible. Things are going to be chaotic for a while."

"But I have to go to Pinar and visit Papi."

"That's not a good idea right now."

"Come with me. We could leave first thing in the morning."

She was not prepared for what happened next. Her cousin stopped in the middle of the sidewalk and, pushing her up against the wall of some stranger's house, took her head in his hands and kissed her the way he had kissed her on the *Catalina*. Then he had apologized. This time he didn't.

Despite herself, she could feel everything opening up.

"*Cuidado.*"

"Why? Nobody cares."

There was sand on the slate stones, which gritted under her sandals. All around them she could smell Cuba: smoke and coal and diesel and earth and sewage and ocean. A melancholy breeze was blowing off the bay. If the wind had had a color, it would have been the gray-green of old Japanese pottery, *celadon,* she remembered, from some long-ago art-history class, like the scarf her mother had given her.

When they rapped on the front door, it was opened for them by Edgar's aunt, who was wearing a raggedy white nightgown. Inside it was pitch dark, and they had to feel their way through the living room, where the aunt was sacked out on the couch, into one of the two bedrooms. They kissed again and then without ceremony fell onto the mattress. He reached under her top and ran his hands over her shoulder blades, her back, unlatched her bra. Then he hitched up her skirt, cupping a breast with the other hand.

"*Te deseo tanto,*" he said.

As teenagers they had never talked. It hadn't been necessary. Now, out of necessity, they were silent as well. On the mildew-smelling mattress they kissed frantically.

"You're wet," he whispered. "How long have you been this wet?"

After a few minutes he reached down and unzipped his pants.

"I'm sorry," he said, with true apology in his whisper. "I can't wait."

As soon as he entered, he clapped a hand over her mouth so that no one would hear her noises.

He remembered.

It was this gesture, the hand over her mouth, and the way he smelled, beer and sweat and that narcotic something that made him Guillermo, that sent her over the edge. He kept on for a minute or so, and then followed with an exhalation of breath, his fingernails digging into her shoulders.

She couldn't stop coming. The way her body was wracked reminded her of the way she'd heaved over the bucket on the *Catalina* during the afternoon of the squall, helpless, at the end of her rope, tears streaming down her face. That had been pain; this was pleasure. Could you really differentiate, when you were in extremis? But this time her weeping was not from relief, as it was with El Tuerto, but joy. Guillermo bent over her and stroked her hair, her eyelids, around her mouth, until she quit shaking and her breathing slowed down.

They lay quiet for a long time. The darkness had a different quality now, brown and alive. Catalina could actually feel the blood pumping through her arms to her fingertips, from her legs to her toes, pulsing inside her sex, so swollen and wet, with her and with him.

This was not sex with Tuerto, which always had a beginning, middle, and end. This had started before she was born and would continue after they were both dead.

Down the hill, a rooster was crowing.

I am awake.

Guillermo touched her face.

"*¿Qué tienes?*"

"I want it to be like it used to."

"You know that's not possible."

"I know. I'm just saying I wish it was."

There was a dance routine she was supposed to be performing—not mambo, maybe tap—that she had been rehearsing for months, but now that it was time to go onstage, she found that she had completely forgotten the moves, the steps, even the rhythm.

Help me, she said to the man—she couldn't see his face—standing by her side, but he took her by the shoulders and shoved her onto the stage.

You should have learned it by heart, she thought she heard him say.

There was a live band, but the percussion, a steady uninflected tapping on the timbales, gave her no clue as to what she was supposed to do. She was at El Flamingo, she realized now, only the cur-

tains were silver instead of yellow and the stagelights dazzled her so
much that she couldn't see.

I'll show them, she thought. *I will fly. I will just fly right off this stage,
and they will never see me again.*

Somewhere outside a man was banging on a metal pipe. Not
loudly, but steadily, determinedly, on the *clave.*

A thin horizontal line of gold penetrated the closed wooden
shutters and hung against the wall about ten feet from the bed where
she awoke, alone, half wrapped in the sweat-soaked sheet.

As she came to it became clear to her that her cousin was no
longer in the house. It was no use getting up and going out to the living room to ask the turbaned *cubana* where he was. His absence was
as palpable as his presence.

She lay on the mattress for a while, watching the slit of sun on
the wall. When she finally got up, the floor tiles were cool against her
bare feet. She put on the clothing she'd shucked the night before:
white tank, short denim skirt, low-heeled sandals. They'd been mixed
in a pile with Guillermo's, but now only hers remained.

In the living room the *cubana* was drinking something brown
from a glass and watching cartoons.

"*Buenos días. ¿Puedo tomar un baño?*" Catalina asked her.

The *cubana* grunted assent. She could take a bath.

"*Y mi amiga, dónde está?*"

"*Todavía durmiendo.*" The *cubana* made it plain that she disap-
proved of Wendy's sloth. It was equally clear that with the men out
of the house the girls were no longer welcome.

I wonder if Wendy and Mano did it, thought Catalina, as she filled
the water bucket from the single tap in preparation for her sponge
bath. This she remembered from her childhood. In Cuba, cold water
felt good. There was no soap so she used shampoo instead. Afterward,
as she combed her hair out she examined her reflection in the small
watery mirror above the sink. Her face was different. Markedly tanner
after five days on the boat, but there was something else as well.

I am awake.

As she left the bathroom she heard coughing and followed the
sound out to the front porch, where Wendy had ensconced herself in

a wooden rocking chair. She was sipping a cup of coffee and smoking a cigarette. There was darkness under her eyes, but she did not look unhappy.

"*Buenos, nena,*" Wendy said. "*Como te sientes?*"

"Okay. You don't sound so good."

"I could have used a little more sleep. But someone had to see the boys off."

Catalina dragged out the other rocker, which had been propped up against the railing of the porch.

"Did they say where they were going?"

"Don't you know?"

Catalina shook her head, then pointed to the living room. "Maybe *she* knows."

"Maybe she does, but I doubt she's gonna tell us. They planning to off Fidel?"

"I only know it has to do with the Pope."

"The *Pope.* No, even *cubanos* wouldn't do that. I can tell you one thing. They took more guns with them."

"How do you know?"

"I saw them." With the hand that was holding the cigarette, Wendy gestured into the house. "You know that little room in the back, behind the bathroom? They had them stashed back there. I helped them load the truck."

"When did you say they left?"

"It was still dark, around five, I think." Wendy rubbed out the cigarette on the wall of the house, which was stained with similar blots, and then yawned and stretched, bringing her heel up to her chin in a way Catalina would never be able to do, not if she did yoga every day for the rest of her life. "This place is giving me the skeeves. I think we should split."

"And go where?"

"The city, *nena.* See the sights. Might as well, we're in *Cuba.*"

"How will Guillermo know how to get in touch with us?"

"The neighbor has a phone. We'll get the number and call in for messages from the aunt."

"Maybe it's better to stay here and wait."

"Wait for what, *nena?*"

Wendy was right. There was nothing more for them in this unfriendly house. At the least they had to go into town to try to book a flight out of here. For Wendy, to the Dominican Republic, Catalina remembered. They told the *cubana* they were leaving—she did not seem unduly distressed—and then packed and went next door, thinking they could use the phone to find a hotel. The neighbor had gone to work, but his wife offered to rent them her bedroom for only fifteen U.S. dollars a night. When they politely declined, she insisted on calling her sister, who had an apartment right off the Plaza Dolores—*"muy conveniente"*—for only five dollars more. For no extra charge her sister would even come and pick them up in her VW bug. It seemed too good to refuse.

"I only have about fifty bucks on me," Wendy said as they waited for their ride.

"I got it covered." Catalina did not add that while she was packing she had discovered a wad of cash—all small bills—tucked into the front zippered compartment of her knapsack. Guillermo's last gift. But she would rather not have found the money. It meant they were on their own.

Plaza Dolores was a small narrow park lined with tamarind trees and wrought-iron benches; it was apparently famous because now and then a tourist bus would park and people would file out with cameras. Italians, French, Spanish, even a herd of Koreans in workout gear. After Wendy and Catalina had settled into their *casa particulare*—airy, with a balcony that gave onto the plaza—they had lunch in a cavernous dark restaurant downstairs. The front was open, though, and they could see into the plaza.

"You gonna tell me the real story now, *nena?*" Wendy asked, as she picked up a wing of her fried chicken and examined it suspiciously. Catalina related everything she knew about La Ultima Lucha, and Wendy listened without comment. When Catalina was finished, Wendy asked: "And why exactly do they need your cousin here, now?"

"They don't. He was just the skipper of the boat. He doesn't really have politics; at least he didn't used to."

"If they catch him, he's fucked."

"Don't remind me."

Wendy gave up on her chicken and pushed her plate away in favor of finishing her second Tukola, the Cuban Coke knockoff that had twice as much sugar and caffeine. Catalina started on the second half of her ham-and-cheese sandwich. Since they had landed she had been ravenous. The druggy sensation—colors brighter, sounds more distinct, food tasting better—had not entirely dissipated. In the plaza a band had started to play, surrounded by what looked like Italian tourists excitedly taking pictures. The musicians were photogenic older men in short-sleeved guayaberas and long dark pants. The band consisted of *clave* sticks and tumbadora and guitar, plus a guiro and several shakers—and the sweetest trumpet Catalina had ever heard. From where she was sitting, she could see that the instrument, like its owner, was old and dented.

"I bet in heaven that's how the brass sounds," she said.

Wendy laughed. "I'll let you know when I get there, *nena*."

"You planning on going before me?"

"I'm older, aren't I? My last wish is to die by the sea. I love the sea." Wendy lit up, coughed out her first drag.

They were playing that bouncy old chestnut, "Son de la Loma." Kids in red-and-white uniforms came skipping by on their way home from school, and one boy of about eight sat down and took the tumbadora player's place for half a song. More photos.

Wendy said: "I want to have as much sex as possible before it's too late."

God she was being maudlin, Catalina thought. But she asked, "Boy sex or girl sex?"

Wendy reached over and stroked the side of Catalina's face, more tender than flirtatious. "You were probably my last girl. Have you noticed how hot these *cubanos* are?"

What Catalina had observed was that the young men of Santiago had a unique walk, completely different from North American Latinos. Long-legged *santiagueros* lacked swagger but made up for it in rhythm. They placed their feet gently, as if promenading barefoot on sand.

"How was Mano?" she asked.

"*Coño*, that one had a nice big thing, you know?"

"Bigger than Tuerto's?"

"Of course not, *nena*, but impressive all the same. I just hope he doesn't get it shot off trying to liberate his country."

"Do you have any Kleenex?"

Wendy handed her the packet. "Tell me how it is."

Cuban bathrooms, they were discovering, were always a surprise, and generally not a pleasant one. They had started assigning them letter grades.

When Catalina got back to the table—she'd give this one about a C—Wendy had disappeared. She finally spotted her on the far side of the plaza, beyond the band, chatting with what looked like a tourist, a stocky blond guy with that telltale sunburned face. For Cuba, Wendy was overdressed: the white satin halter they'd bought in South Beach, tight faded jeans, sequined ponytail holder, silver dance shoes. That was odd. No *salsera* worth her salt wore her dance shoes on the street. From this distance there was the old illusion that Wendy was a hot teenager, and Catalina could see all the men, even the guys in the band, craning their necks. She was reminded of her early days of mambo when she'd sit at a table watching and waiting for Wendy, who was never off the floor.

"Hey, *nena*, guess what?" Wendy called as she strolled back to their table. "They have long-distance telephones around the corner from the Casa Grande. And we're invited to a party tomorrow night."

They paid their bill, and as they got up the band was playing a ballad. At first Catalina took it for a love song—the tune was so yearning—but as she listened to the lyrics crooned by the white-haired *sonero*, she realized it was an homage.

Tu manera gloriosa y fuerte
Sobre la historia dispara
Quando todo Santa Clara
Se despierta para verte

Aquí, se queda la clara
La intrañeable transparencia
De tu querida presencia
Commandante Che Guevara

Back in their room, Catalina turned on the small Korean-made set, although there was nothing on but a variety show, kids reciting patriotic poems. Then the variety show was interrupted by a live news bulletin showing a plane taxiing to a stop. There was a huge crowd, a brass band, a cluster of schoolchildren singing a hymn. Pope John Paul II would be based in Havana and, over the course of the week, flown to various cities on the *isla*. Tomorrow Holy Mass would be celebrated on the playing fields of Manuel Fajardo Higher Insitute of Physical Education in Santa Clara, and in the evening His Holiness and Fidel Castro would meet in the Palace of the Revolution.

The city of Santa Clara, located in the middle of the island, was where many considered the Communist revolution to have officially begun. As Catalina remembered it, while Fidel was hiding out in the Sierra Maestre, Che Guevara led the ambush of El Tren Blindado, a decisive encounter that shifted the strategic advantage to the revolutionaries. Hence the song they'd heard leaving the Plaza Dolores.

As she lay there watching Castro make his welcoming speech to the Pope, Catalina turned to Wendy, sprawled on the bed beside her, and said, "I know where they went and what they're going to do."

18

Guillermo

Shifting your weight creates the illusion of a step.

He had the shits. It was ridiculous for this to be his main concern, given the position he was in. His intestines just couldn't take the stress—although it might have been the ham sandwiches they'd had for breakfast—basically cold gobs of pork fat on salted buns.

The diarrhea had started a couple of minutes after their arrest. It had come out like water, drenching the back of his pants, and the cops had laughed their heads off, saying it was because he was a filthy *maricon* traitor who took it up the ass. The ride into town had been hell, he and Edgar trussed up back to back in the bed of the produce truck, the noonday sun beating down on them making the smell worse.

Thank God the guard in the jail had given him water to wash up with.

Now that his insides had settled down a little, and he had been left alone long enough to consider his situation, Guillermo wasn't sure exactly how worried he should be. There were people who knew where he was when he'd disappeared; when they'd gotten to Ciego de Avila he'd phoned his contact in Santa Clara to let him know everything was going according to schedule. La Última Lucha had not put all its eggs into one basket—the Santiago cache was being transported in five separate trucks, by different routes. And that was only a fraction. The arms they'd been collecting for a decade were warehoused all over the island and most doubtless had already arrived at their destination. One derailed shipment would not break the Revolution.

The other person who knew approximately where he was was Crespo. That asshole. Just the thought of him set Guillermo's teeth on edge. Early that morning after he'd left Catty in bed Guillermo had gone to the Poste de Teléfonos—opened especially for him by a sympathizer—and called Kingston to make a report. Crespo had replied in his fatuous way: "Good work, *compadre*. We are watching you. We are proud of you."

Guillermo could picture him sitting on his balcony at the Jamaica Pegasus, the hotel in Kingston where they were supposed to have met, wearing a bathrobe made of Egyptian cotton, sipping cappuccino, combing back his blond curls with the other hand. *We are all warriors in La Última Lucha,* he was always telling Guillermo. Some warrior he was. Had the red herring about the *Catalina* docking at Kingston first been his idea? Guillermo wouldn't have put it past him. The crew had known all along that they weren't headed to Jamaica. It was only Guillermo who had been rattled by Crespo's call instructing him to change course and head for the Bay of Santiago. He—the skipper—should have been kept in the loop. These people didn't know their ass from their elbow. After all these years, didn't they think he could keep a secret? Even with Edgar's help the navigation had been so difficult he had several times lost faith. After Cayo Moa Grande they'd been cruising in the pitch-dark, and it was only by constant use of radar and intermittent radio contact with shore, most of it badly patched through, that Guillermo had been able to finesse it. The most harrowing stretch, ironically, had been Guantánamo Bay, where the waters were heavily patrolled by American forces. They'd had to give it a wide berth, no contact with shore for a full thirty minutes, during which they could have easily lost course.

Who had betrayed them? Guillermo couldn't believe that it had been Crespo, as devious as he was. That man was just a pigeon interested in feathering his own nest—not ambitious enough, and certainly not brave enough, to take such a risk. The informant had probably been a Cuban infiltrate—all it took was one weak link— someone Guillermo would never meet. He and Edgar had been minding their own business, taking a break, sitting in the shade of a snack stand on wooden benches drinking papaya milkshakes, when the wood-paneled farm truck—not unlike the one they themselves were driving—had come chugging by, made a screeching U-turn, and doubled back. Both of them were grabbed by the scruff of their T-shirts and thrown face-first onto the scalding metal of the hood of the truck so their hands could be tied up.

"*Ustedes gusanos van a morir,*" You lowlifes are going to die, one of the cops had spat into his ear.

As soon as they'd gotten to this decrepit assemblage of buildings that called itself a hamlet (if a name had been mentioned, Guillermo hadn't caught it), he and Edgar had been split up. Guillermo was dragged into a cell at the back of one of the buildings. It was about five by five—*Even graves were bigger,* he thought—with one window close to the ceiling that let a tiny parallelogram of light fall onto the dirt floor. The air was thick with the smell of insecticide and old piss and his own shit in the zinc bucket. They had taken everything: his passport, his money, his watch, even his glasses. He knew he would have to take his contact lenses out soon, or they would dry up. When he did, he would be functionally blind.

From the fading intensity of the patch of light he guessed it was around four o'clock. Of course there was no chance he'd be allowed a phone call, as he would in an American jail, but if by some miracle he *were,* he decided, he would not call Crespo, but his father-in-law, Humberto Cruz.

You got me in here. Get me the fuck out.

For the first time he wondered what Catty and Wendy were up to. He hadn't had time to arrange their trip back, but now at least they had cash if that slimy "aunt" of Edgar's hadn't snuck into their room and ferreted it out of Catty's bag while she was asleep. In any case his cousin was resourceful, and there was no reason the Cuban government would want to hold her.

He, Guillermo, was a different story. It occurred to him that he was probably going to be tortured. There had been one cop in particular he was afraid of, a slight, light-skinned fellow with a pencil mustache. The image made his intestines cramp again, and he forced himself to stay squatting in the corner farthest away from the zinc pail, breathing through his mouth, until the spasm passed.

Jésucristo, how was he going to get through this? He slumped in his corner, trying to remember the order of the rosary. The last time he'd been in a church was for the baptism of his youngest son.

Dios te salve María, llena eres de gracia

In his mind's eye he suddenly saw Catalina as clear as day, strolling alone through a square shaded with tamarind and *flamboyán.* She was wearing a white tank top, blue skirt, white sandals. Her hair was pinned up into a bun, and he could see that the sun had brought out faint freckles on her cheekbones.

El Señor es contigo

Some guys on the far side of the square were hooting at her. *If you cook the way you walk, I'll lick the bottom of your pot.* She ignored them, kept walking until she came to a wrought-iron bench, where she sat down.

Bendita tú entre todas las mujeres

She was reading a newspaper. Her forehead furrowed, she licked her finger to turn the page like he remembered her doing in school when they were kids. Her hair had fallen slightly out of the bun, and a few strands brushed her cheeks and the nape of her neck.

Bendito sea el fruto de tú vientre, Jésus

Now she was on a bed, not the bed of Edgar's aunt, but one with a flowered spread in a sunny apartment. She was naked, on her back, her hair loose, her legs slightly parted, the dark triangle of her pubic hair shocking against the warm gold of her skin, although he could not see much else, given the angle. Her eyes were closed, but she was not asleep. In the background a television played a news channel at low volume.

Santa María, Madre de Dios

Her breasts were a different shape than he remembered, oblong rather than spherical, the nipples darker, and she had more of a belly, but the dramatic swoop of waist and hip, that perfect triangle of pubic hair, were exactly as they'd been when they were teenagers. Now he could touch her, run his fingers over her skin. He began with her jawline, then caressed her throat, her collarbone, her left breast with its upturned nipple. There was too much; she was too much. She made no noise, did not move, but he knew she could feel him.

Ruega Señora por nosotros los pecadores

Now he was down on his knees, his mouth on top of her, his tongue inside her. Eating papaya, they called it in Cuba, and it was true that she was a fruit, but not papaya. He couldn't think what. Maybe *mamey colorado,* which had the texture of an avocado when you split it open, but was sweet and velvety dark orange, like a jewel from another planet.

Ahora y en la hora de nuestra muerte

How old was he? How old was she? He had no idea. It seemed that they had been together always. He should stop now, she should get dressed; he would help her back into her clothes, smooth down her hair, ask her what she had been reading in that newspaper.

Suddenly he remembered that he had his own work cut out for him. *This trip wasn't over yet.* The charts, the endless sea charts, he had to study them, get the *Catalina* to her final destination. He shut his eyes, willing his hard-on to subside.

The fate of an entire nation depends on your concentration.

Guillermo opened his eyes. The cell was nearly dark. He stumbled to his feet and used the zinc bucket. More diarrhea, but it could have been worse. As he had done before, he tore off a corner of his T-shirt to wipe himself. Afterward he stood facing the steel door, pressing his hot forehead up against it. He could hear nothing but a ringing in his ears.

It was strange that they had not come to get him. What could he confess? No one he'd dealt with since arriving in Cuba had given him their name. The only information he had that the cops would be interested in was the phone number of Edgar's aunt's neighbor and maybe his contact in Santa Clara, both of which he'd memorized, and of course Crespo's in Jamaica, for all the good that that would do.

They would have surely already figured out that the CFA were behind this.

That they were letting him stew in here was a bad sign as far as La Ultima Lucha was concerned. It meant they had enough information already to blow the whole operation wide open.

He was very tired. In his fantasies he had imagined being chased on the high seas by the Cuban Coast Guard, maybe even being killed—ZAP—like a villain in a sci-fi cartoon, but never captured and imprisoned in some godforsaken backwater in the middle of the island.

Crespo had not prepared him for this.

Maybe he should quit blaming Crespo and place the fault where it really belonged—on himself.

Why hadn't he assessed the dangers beforehand?

Was it worth it, to be tortured for Cuba?

He should have listened to Catty.

Up until the arrest, he had to admit, he had been jazzed up. As worried as he'd been about their cargo, skippering the *Catalina* across the high seas had been an adventure, even a lark. Why then did he volunteer to accompany Edgar to Santa Clara? He had done enough, after all. *Good work, compadre. We are watching you. We are proud of you.* Edgar was the one who knew the roads, and he could have made the trip by himself.

Maybe it was Edgar they were torturing.

He would tell them that he was a tourist, hitching his way from Santiago to Havana, and Edgar, who claimed to be a farmer, had picked him up just outside Ciego de Avila. He had had no knowledge of what was in the bed of the truck. Farm equipment, he'd figured, since this was a cane-growing region.

That story might work, unless they had already irrevocably connected him to Edgar and/or La Última Lucha.

If they had found the *Catalina* where she was moored.

Whatever they were going to do to him, it couldn't be worse

than the Spanish Inquisition. Now *those* guys had made an art of it. When he was a teenager, Guillermo had seen a documentary with vivid re-creations. Iron implements, chains, dungeons. Blood on the cobblestones.

Now the cell was completely dark, the stench almost choking. Was this how all prisoners were treated in Cuba, or were traitors singled out especially? He was so thirsty he felt like a wad of cotton had been stuffed down his throat. The last thing he had had to drink was that *fruta bomba* milk shake that had sealed his fate.

He wanted more than anything to curl up on the dirt floor, but he knew if he passed out again he would completely lose the little resolve he had left.

His mother was sitting on the veranda on Calle Ocho now, as she always did at sundown, sipping an iced coffee laced with brandy. The thought of her, face slack in repose, hair in its usual immaculate bun, ankles crossed like a schoolgirl's, made him want to weep. Last night—was it only last night?—he had told Lilly to reassure his mother that he was fine, that he would tell her all about it once he got home.

Lilly herself he had addressed in code, saying, "I'm closer than I thought I would be."

"I know," she had answered.

She always knew. How did she know? Had she and Crespo been in cahoots all these years? Were they having an affair, fucking right under his nose? Or was it Lilly's father or one of Humberto Cruz's cohorts who had kept his wife so closely informed?

The boys would be eating dinner in the courtyard. Guillé and Humbi wouldn't miss him yet. It was little Santito who would be pestering Lilly: "When's Papi coming home?"

Picturing Santito was worse than thinking about his mother. He had to stop because it would make him weak.

They would torture him for sure, and he would confess until there was nothing left inside him.

Yo, pecador, me confieso ante Dios Todopoderoso
He was looking up into the mango tree, and his cousin was looking down at him. Like a cat, she had climbed up and lost her nerve

about climbing back down. This was before she got good at it, before she'd pushed him off and he had to go to the emergency room, the same one his brother Rafael had been rushed to when he was stung by a bee at the Orange Bowl.

But it was only a broken ankle, after all. She, anguished, had volunteered in sign language to break her own ankle in compensation, but he had vetoed the idea.

Y ante vosotros hermanos, que he pecado mucho

He was in fourth-grade history class, the one subject he did not share with his cousin. They were studying the ancient Greeks. His stomach lurched, and he raised his hand and said he had to go to the bathroom. The teacher gave him permission. As soon as the classroom door had shut behind him he raced not to the boys' room but down two flights to the nurse's office, where Catty, who had just thrown up, was lying on the cot behind the screen. He kissed her clammy forehead and held her hand until her mother arrived to take her home.

Gemelos.

De pensamiento, palabra, obra, y omisión.

They were in Daisy Gonzalez's basement, Christmas vacation the year he and Catty turned nineteen. Kurt Cobain was rasping through the smoke. His cousin was back from her first semester of college. Standing by herself in the corner she looked different. Thinner, maybe. He thought about calling out to her. But then he and Daisy were on the couch, and before he knew what was happening they were furiously making out. After a while, he couldn't tell how long, he'd smoked so much weed, he looked up and his cousin had disappeared.

Por mi culpa, por mi culpa, por mi gran culpa.

There were so many sparkling colors it was like fireworks. No, not fireworks because the background was not dark sky, but some sort of greenish-gray light.

"*Norteamericano,*" he heard someone say.

Yes, he wanted to shout, I'm American, and you're in deep shit for arresting me.

But he seemed to have no voice.

These people had an even thicker accent than *santiagueros*. Or maybe they were drunk. They sounded a little drunk.

He was sitting on a chair, at a table. How had he gotten there? The room looked like a bar, but of course that wasn't possible. The sparkling colors were subsiding. It was practically dark, the only light coming from a dim lamp set somewhere in a far corner.

"*¿Cúal es tu nombre?*"

Why were they asking him his name? They had his passport, didn't they? Maybe it was some kind of psychiatric evaluation, like they gave people in the emergency room when there was a possibility of concussion or drug abuse.

What is your name? What year is this? Who is the president of the United States?

"*¿Cúal es tu nombre?*"

Guillermo could not see the speaker's face. It occurred to him that he could pretend not to understand Spanish. He was pretty sure the only person he had spoken to was the prison guard, the one who had given him water with which to wash, and that had been only a couple of grunted phrases.

So in answer he merely shook his head. The question was repeated a third time, then a fourth.

The voices began to argue.

His ruse of not speaking Spanish wasn't going to work. Of course they had already interrogated Edgar. But it had been worth a shot. Anything was worth a shot now.

"*Está enfermo,*" somebody said.

This was a lie. He was not sick. But if pretending to be sick would get him out of this hellhole, or at least buy him time, he would certainly go along with it.

Por mi culpa, por mi culpa, por mi gran culpa.

"*Sangre,*" said the same voice that had said he was sick.

Then there was a crashing pain in the middle of his face.

19

Catalina

When it feels the way it looks, you've got it right.

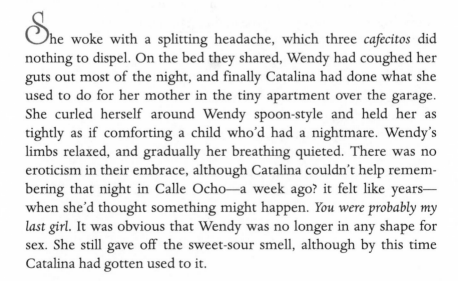

$\mathcal{S}$he woke with a splitting headache, which three *cafecitos* did nothing to dispel. On the bed they shared, Wendy had coughed her guts out most of the night, and finally Catalina had done what she used to do for her mother in the tiny apartment over the garage. She curled herself around Wendy spoon-style and held her as tightly as if comforting a child who'd had a nightmare. Wendy's limbs relaxed, and gradually her breathing quieted. There was no eroticism in their embrace, although Catalina couldn't help remembering that night in Calle Ocho—a week ago? it felt like years—when she'd thought something might happen. *You were probably my last girl.* It was obvious that Wendy was no longer in any shape for sex. She still gave off the sweet-sour smell, although by this time Catalina had gotten used to it.

And there was the dream she couldn't remember, which had left her both happy and sad.

Over breakfast they conferred with their landlady, who gave them the name of a travel agency off Parque Céspedes. First they stopped in at the Centro de Llamadas where Wendy tried Tuerto. "That's weird, he's still not answering his cell," she said, and left a message on his home machine.

The woman at the travel agency booked a flight for Wendy to Santo Domingo for Sunday afternoon, paid for in cash by Catalina. Catalina felt it was the least she could do, given that she had dragged Wendy into this. Then the agent called Air Cubana and gave Catalina a schedule of weekly flights to Montreal and Cancún. For her pains Catalina gave her a couple of ballpoint pens and Wendy gave her the address and phone number of her *tía* in Puerto Plata, should the agent ever visit and need a place to stay. You never knew; people who worked for travel agencies got special privileges.

Back in the Parque, under the indomitable gaze of the angel over the portal of the Catedral de Santiago, the action was thick. On the terrace of the Casa Grande middle-age white tourists drank café with black *jineteras* the age of their granddaughters. Buskers from the Casa de la Trova caught the arms of passing tourists and pointed at the poster announcing that night's entertainment. Even at this hour you could hear a *conguero* warming up somewhere inside. It was the Times Square of Santiago. Taxis of various vintages were lined up beneath the cathedral, and as she and Wendy strolled past, the *taxistas* yelled out attractions: Morro Castle, San Juan Hill, Santa Ifigenia Cemetery. Catalina was interested in the cemetery but it was only when one of the *taxistas* mentioned El Sanctuario de la Virgen de la Caridad del Cobre that Wendy perked up.

"Let's go, *nena*. She's the patron saint of lost causes."

The church, a half hour's drive from the city, was flanked by royal palms and reached by a steep flight of marble stairs lined with standing lamps. Halfway up Wendy began hacking uncontrollably, and Catalina made them stop to rest. "No," she said, when Wendy began digging in the front pocket of her jeans for a cigarette.

"Bitch," said Wendy, but she let it go and leaned to look over the railing at the view. Catalina noticed that she put the flat of her hand on her side as if she had a stitch, and kept it pressed there. And she'd been walking oddly, as if she had a thumbtack in one of her feet. *Stay okay, Wendy, please at least until you get to Santo Domingo.*

The *sanctuario* was thronged with both tourists and *cubanos,* and when they finally reached the main chapel upstairs, Catalina was surprised to see that the dark-skinned virgin was as tiny as a Barbie doll, even smaller than the one in the cemetery where Jun was buried, decked out in delicate gold vestments in her air-conditioned glass case. While Wendy went up to the altar rail, Catalina hung back and slid into a pew.

She opened her eyes and watched Wendy's straight back as she knelt, hands folded on the rail, head bowed. She seemed in a trance, and, not wanting to disturb her, Catalina left the chapel and went outside and gazed down at the Valley of the Copper Mine, at the grazing oxen with their sloe eyes and ax-blade shoulders—a breed that dated from the time of the Bible, her *papi* used to tell her. She thought she heard his voice again, speaking, not singing this time, and she whipped around, but there was no one there. Boys hawking candles sidled up to her but she waved them away. She spotted their white cab pulled over at the curb, the *taxista* napping in the back. A man with a burro was selling raw almonds at the foot of the steps, and Catalina went down and bought a handful, giving the men a dollar because she didn't have pesos. This seemed to confuse him, but he politely nodded his thanks.

From the plaza she watched people straggle out of the church. No Americans; she hadn't seen a single American since they had landed. A few Australians, a couple of Canadians, and tourists she pegged as Spanish and French and Irish. Finally there was Wendy, emerging alone with her head held high. She could have easily passed for Cuban, although a *cubana* of the city, not the country.

When they were within speaking distance, Catalina said, "Let's go to Santa Clara."

"Are you crazy?"

"I can't stand not doing anything."

"If what you think is true, *nena,* then it's too late. Whatever was supposed to happen has already happened. There's nothing you can do."

Neither of them had any idea how right she was.

The *taxista* dropped them off at Céspedes, where they treated themselves to lunch on the Casa Grande terrace—tuna sandwiches and Tukolas—and then went browsing in the little souvenir shops that lined the square. There was really not much to buy: the ubiquitous Che keychains and T-shirts, nonfiction Communist party–approved books in Spanish, some tacky resort wear, sundry jewelry and knick-knacks. Catalina found a blue bead bracelet for the little *mulata* who served them breakfast but it was Wendy who made the real score: a pair of rawhide maracas she said she was going to give to Luis.

When they left the shop there was a crowd in front of the white government building that their *taxista* had told them was housing for visiting dignitaries. Catalina assumed them to be a large tourist group but then it became apparent that they were reading and discussing a half dozen posters—duplicates, it looked like—that had been freshly plastered on the façade. A Pope announcement? No. When they got close enough Catalina could see that the posters depicted a grainy black-and-white close-up of a figure slumped against a pale wall. There was something wrong with the man's neck, and after a second she realized that his throat had been slashed ear to ear.

"Fuck," she said.

Over her shoulder, Wendy made a choking sound as if in empathy with the man in the photo.

"That's Mano."

"What?"

"Mano. You know, from the boat."

"No."

"Listen."

Wendy read the copy out loud; translating into English as she went. "Leader of Right Wing Splinter Group Assassinated. Santiago de Cuba, Wednesday, January twenty-first. This morning the body of Mano Gonzales, a mechanic from Miami, was found on a street in the western suburbs of Santiago. It is presumed that he was murdered by members of his own counterrevolutionary group."

That was all. No mention of anyone else or of any arms or conspiracy plot.

In the photograph Mano's undershirt was not camouflage-patterned, as Catalina had first thought, but splattered with blood.

An example: *This could happen to you.*

Her vision tunneled, and she swallowed hard to keep from throwing up. From a long way away she heard Wendy's voice: "Come on, *nena,* we're going back to the *casa.*"

Wendy grabbed Catalina's hand and hustled her down Calle Aguilera, which was fortunately mostly downhill, past the Museo Bacardi, until they were back at the leaf-shaded Plaza Dolores. By that time Catalina had recovered her wits enough to remember about the information she'd copied down from Tía Ana's Rolodex. While Catalina was digging through her knapsack, Wendy switched on the TV. There was a live feed from the Palace of the Revolution in Santa Clara, where Fidel and Pope John Paul II were shaking hands. In the background a snappily dressed *conjunto* was playing the homage to Che: "Hasta Siempre."

"I'll be happy if I never hear that song again," Catalina said. She found the slip of paper tucked into a compartment in her makeup bag.

"He should have kissed the ring," said Wendy.

"He can't. He's Communist."

"Still."

A plump schoolboy sang "Ave María." The camera cut to a crowd scene. Holding her breath, Catalina watched for her cousin, but the scans showed nothing but the faithful pressed together outside the palace, waiting for a glimpse of His Holiness on his way out. Then it was over.

On the rickety old-fashioned black telephone in their landlady's parlor, Catalina dialed the U.S. Interests Section in Havana several times, pausing between tries so her hands would stop shaking. When at last she got through to a machine, she left a message in English that she was an American citizen in Cuba on vacation and that one of their party had been missing for several days and they were afraid that he was hurt or maybe even dead.

As she hung up Wendy said, *"Coño,* good story."

Like a delayed storm front, Catalina's headache, which had been shunted aside in the shock of seeing the poster, now slid back full force, and she had to go back into the bedroom and lie down.

The image of Mano with his throat slit bloomed in her mind's eye, and it was only with the greatest effort of will that she was able to force it away.

Gray screen, she told herself. *Pretend it's TV when there's no programming.*

The sounds of the square, canned music and people shouting and laughing, came drifting in through the window in snatches.

"You okay, *nena?*"

Wendy was standing by the bed.

"I just need to rest."

"You mind if I go out?"

"You want to go out now?"

"That guy from the plaza yesterday, he's having a party."

"Okay. Have a good time. Be careful."

A few minutes later she heard Wendy leave the room and then conversing with their landlady—the sweet old woman with the VW bug. *Those two really hit it off,* Catalina thought, but who didn't like Wendy? Then the front door slammed, and she was asleep.

The next morning, very early, there was a knock on the door of their room. The little *mulata* poked her head in and said: *"Teléfono."*

It was the deputy principal officer from the U.S. Interests Section, a man named Carl Menninger. As Americans can, he managed to sound friendly and deeply serious at the same time. Catalina told him the story she'd decided on, that she and her cousin were on vacation here, had entered Havana via Montreal, and that he had disappeared Tuesday night—that part was true. Carl Menninger asked if they were here legally, and Catalina told him no. He said he would make some calls and get back to her.

He called back sooner than expected, during breakfast. Guillermo had been arrested and was now being held at the provincial police station in Santiago. Carl Menninger said that technically the United States had no jurisdiction over political prisoners in Cuba. They couldn't really do anything except to try to keep track of him.

He's alive, she thought, and bit her lip to keep herself from breaking down.

"What was he arrested for?"

"That I can't tell you. I mean, I actually don't know. They wouldn't give out any more information."

"Do you have the address of the police station?"

For the first time Carl Menninger hesitated. "Going there wouldn't do any good."

"Please."

"What I suggest, Ms. Ortiz, is that you pack your bags and book the next flight back to Montreal. Give me your home number and e-mail, and I will keep you posted."

"I can't just leave him."

"I understand your concern. But the justice system here operates on a different schedule, not to mention under radically different laws, than ours. His case might not come up for trial for years."

"But he didn't *do* anything."

"At the moment, that is beside the point."

"I'm staying here for the forseeable future. I will call you later. Or call me, if you hear anything."

"I promise. But I still must tell you it would be advisable if you left the country immediately."

Wendy agreed with Menninger. "I think you should keep a low profile, *nena*. What if they decide to throw you in jail, too? They probably found the boat. Your *primo's* fucked."

Catalina ignored her. "If we have to bribe, Tía Ana will wire me the money. Or maybe Lilly can. Will you stay here in case Menninger calls again?" She picked up her purse and checked to see that she had everything: cash, driver's license, photocopy of her passport. "If I'm not back in four hours, call Menninger and tell him where I went. Here's the number."

"Do you trust him?"

"Who else is there?"

"I see your point."

With nearly as much reluctance as Carl Menninger their landlady demurred giving Catalina the address of the provincial police. She finally told her it was located in the outskirts of the city, in a place called Versailles. Catalina grabbed a Tukola out of their mini-fridge for breakfast and as she went out the door Wendy surprised her by grabbing her by the shoulders and kissing her on the mouth. Not passionately; it was more the kind of have-a-good-day kiss an old-fashioned housewife would give her husband at the front door.

"*Cuídate, nena.*"

"You, too."

There were no cabs out on the Plaza so she hiked up to Céspedes, where she had to promise a *taxista* twenty American dollars before he would agree to take her to La Policia Provinciale. The hilly cobblestone streets and shaded squares of Santiago, so picturesque the night they'd arrived, now seemed menacing in the sunlight, full of boarded-up windows, empty storefronts, winding blind alleys. Pedestrians had furtive expressions; the dogs limped.

The *taxista* refused to wait, no matter how much she offered, so she let him go and found herself standing outside a barbed-wire fence which enclosed a white institutional-looking building and a radio tower. Just inside the open gate stood a guard in a grass-green uniform. She flashed the copy of her passport and said something about a lost relative. He waved her away, and she reached into her purse and brandished a ten, which he ignored. She augmented it to twenty, and he turned away. When her hand was up to one hundred he reached over and took the sheaf of bills between his fingers and then turned and yelled something into the courtyard. Someone yelled something back, and about ten minutes later another soldier emerged. The two of them conferred briefly, and then the second soldier escorted Catalina inside.

The interior of La Policia Provinciale smelled of mildew. At a card table in the lobby the desk clerk was eating his breakfast of rice and beans as he listened to Marco Antonio Solís on a boom box. Catalina recognized the song from Calle Ocho. *No hay nada más difícil que vivir sin ti.* Even inside the air was tropical—thick and sludgy. She waited where she'd been told, on one of a row of dark green plastic chairs that reminded her of the nurse's office in the Miami grade school where she'd once thrown up. She felt like throwing up now as well. Her headache was gone, but her heart was beating too fast, and she forced herself to breathe into her stomach until her pulse slowed to normal. *Remember how he felt inside you, remember how happy you were.* Through the open windows she could hear the sounds of some kind of military exercise.

Finally an older man in uniform came out, and she told him the same story she'd related to Carl Menninger. This man took notes, said he would pass on the information, and disappeared. She waited some more. Every time a cop came in he would ask the desk clerk who she was, and the clerk would say something in a low voice, and both men would turn to look at her consideringly. Finally still another cop came to lead her down a corridor to an office where he knocked on the door and they were told to enter.

The man behind the desk was skeletally thin, with a mop of dark hair. Her guide left, closing the door behind him, and she sat down on another green plastic chair and told her story again. The cop listened laconically, not asking any questions until her monologue was finished.

Then he said: *"Compañera,* it is now Friday morning. Why did you wait so long to report the disappearance of your cousin?"

Feigning sheepishness, she said that Guillermo was a bit of a *borracho,* a drunkard, and that in Miami, where they lived, he would often disappear for days at a time, so she hadn't been too worried at first, thinking he was just on another bender.

Even as she spoke them, the words sounded tinny and rehearsed.

The cop leaned back and put his boots on the rickety pine table that served as his desk. *"Compañera,* an American citizen with your cousin's name is being held under maximum security."

"Where?"

"I cannot give you that information."

She almost said, I know he's here, but she didn't want the cops to know she had been in touch with U.S. Interests.

"I need to see him."

"It is impossible. He is under indictment for high treason."

"Treason for what? How can he betray Cuba? He's not even a citizen."

The cop did not bother to hide his disdain. "He committed a crime against this government on Cuba soil. You think the laws of other countries do not apply to you because you are American?"

"My cousin is a tourist, with no political leanings."

The cop put his feet back on the floor and leaned forward with his elbows on the table. "Tourist? More like *terrorist.* Your cousin, if he is your cousin, entered this country illegally through the Port of Santiago. Not only that, he brought in a shipment of three hundred sixty AK-14 assault rifles. If this happened in the United States, such a person would be immediately jailed, no?"

"You are mistaken. The police are mistaken." Catalina's Spanish was deteriorating, but perhaps it was for the best. The conversation would now have to be as straightforward as possible.

"We could hold you, too, *Compañera*."

"Me? Why?"

"For questioning. You admit you are associated with Guillermo De Leon."

"If I had something to hide, why would I have come here, to La Policia Provinciale?"

"Do you want to be questioned, *Compañera?*"

"Are you threatening me?"

The cop leaned back, took a toothpick out of his breast pocket, and began cleaning his teeth. "No, *Compañera*. You are free to leave any time you want."

You were the one who killed Mano.

She said again: "I need to see him."

"Your cousin cannot see anybody. If you want, I can give him a message."

Catalina reached into her purse and withdrew her hand just enough so that he could see the tip of the fan of ten-dollar bills.

He said, expressionless: "Give me your purse, *Compañera*."

Without hesitation she placed it on the table in front of him. He didn't even glance inside but got to his feet and indicated that she should follow him. They left the room and went farther into the maze of corridors, away from the reception area. Catalina concentrated on the figure in front of her, the incongruity of an officer in full uniform with a black-leather Banana Republic hobo handbag slung over his shoulder. Somehow it looked less ridiculous on him than it would have on an American policeman. They went down a flight of stairs. There was a very bad smell, and she started breathing through her mouth. A courtyard. Then an extremely narrow hallway with a row of cells. Strangely, there were no guards in sight. So much for maximum security.

There was someone in the last cell. He was sitting slumped with his back against the far wall.

Like Mano on the poster.

She slowed her footsteps to match the cop's.

Please don't be asleep. Or sick. Or knocked out.

There was something wrong with his face. His nose was swollen grotesquely, and there was a dirty bruise on his left cheek. Worse, his olive drab pants looked as if they had been soaked in blood, which had dried in hard folds. In two days he had lost a noticeable amount of weight. As they approached, he opened his eyes, which had been closed.

"You are to keep your mouth shut," the cop said to him, as well as to remind her. He raised one arm so that she could not walk any farther, and turned so that his body partially blocked her view.

Guillermo did not smile, did not evince any expression at all. What he did was shake his head from side to side, just once, ever so slightly.

For her part she said nothing but raised both hands to her lips, a child's position of prayer.

"*Basta,*" said the cop. "Is it him?"

"No," she said. "It is not."

"Good," said the cop. "It is better that way."

Would they have let me see him if they were planning to execute him?

Back at the reception area she asked to use the facilities, which she deemed an F. It was fortunate she hadn't eaten breakfast because she would have certainly lost it. After another half hour the cop returned her purse, zipped, but she was afraid to open it until she was alone. Even if they'd taken everything she'd be able to survive. Her passport and three hundred dollars, all that remained of the eight Guillermo had left her, were back at the apartment.

Outside the police compound she opened her purse and found only a used Kleenex. Everything else, even her lipstick, the handful of almonds from yesterday, was gone. At least they had given her the purse back. From the hilltop she could see the city of Santiago sprawled out in the noonday haze. La Policia Provinciale was on a little-used road and there was no choice but to walk. She started down the hill, wishing she had another Tukola.

The way was steep and hard on her left knee, and by the time she reached the city limits she was limping. A street vendor asked if she wanted water but she made the sign that she had no money. And no matter how thirsty she was, she knew enough not to drink tap. He gave her a bottle of mineral for free and she chugged it gratefully, then asked him directions to Plaza Dolores. He shook his head and said it was a long way, over an hour's walk, and she said she'd do it, she had no choice. She stopped a couple of times to rest, once at a café, where she used the bathroom to splash cold water on her face and wrists.

It was almost two when she reached the *casa particulare*. Dizzy with dehydration and aftershock, the only thought in her head was the hope that their landlady had restocked the refrigerator with mineral water. When she knocked on the door of the apartment, the landlady opened it immediately for her as usual, but this time her brow was furrowed.

"You have a visitor," she said. "And your friend went out, so he's been waiting in your room for quite a while."

Fuck it, Wendy, I told you to stay here in case Menninger called. And then: *They sent someone from Havana to help me,* knowing even as she thought it that the idea was completely illogical.

She opened the door to the bedroom, and there was Tuerto lying on his back on the bed, sneakered feet up on the flowered comforter, the TV blasting.

"Finally, Lina," he said. "I must say the two of you led me a merry chase."

20

Wendy

Find the place where the music begins.

———◆◆◆———

When Catalina still hadn't returned by noon, Wendy was in a quandary. She was supposed to pick up her package at the Casa Grande before the Australian checked out at two. The best Mexican brown sugar, he'd bragged over the band at Espantos Sueños the night before. In the bathroom he'd offered her a sample, and he was right, it was pure enough to snort. Before she'd leaned down to the mirror there had been that moment—the cusp, she'd always thought of it—when the faces of certain clients at the methadone clinic, of people from her NA group, of Isabella, had flashed into her mind. Every time before the faces had said: *Don't do it.*

But last night the voices were different.

Go ahead.

There is nothing like it. Nothing on earth.

Junk is a tropical dream.

You have nothing to lose.

She had never felt so old in her life. Everything was killing her. Her foot, her knee, what felt like a hot lump of iron in her diaphragm. And unlike Catalina, whatever she did, Wendy was unable to blot out the grainy black-and-white image of Mano, his head tipped to the side to allow maximum exposure of the gruesome crescent under his chin. She hoped they hadn't tortured him too much. She'd heard *cubanos* were fond of using electricity. Above her own right shoulder blade she still bore teeth marks from three nights before, marks that would last longer than Mano's body would be above ground.

Who were his family? Who would tell them? Would they be sent a copy of the poster? Would they be punished because of their relationship to him?

At twelve-thirty she made her decision. Their landlady was at home, and the little *mulata* would come by after school. Surely Carl Menninger spoke enough Spanish to leave a message.

It was overcast and coolish, but the sun was hot on her face and arms as she walked to Céspedes, stopping at a vending cart on the way to buy a bottle of mineral water. From the Centro de Llamadas she called her *tía* in Puerto Plata to tell her she was on her way. It disturbed her that her *tía* sounded out of it, like she didn't remember who Wendy was. Then she tried home again several times, with no success—where the *fuck* was Luis? Finally she left a message.

The Australian was not in his room, but one of the bellhops pointed up the stairs to the roof garden. Sure enough, there he was, at a table overlooking the bay, fatter than she'd remembered, sitting with two *jineteras*, party girls, from the night before, buying them *mojitos*. Wendy waved and he saw her. He got up, leaned down and whispered to each of the girls, and then ambled over to the archway where she was waiting. She showed him her watch and the silver bracelet with the Tiffany stamp. Too bad it was engraved, he said, plain it would have been worth a lot more.

"How about this instead?" she asked, fingering the amethyst cross around her neck.

"Okay," he said. "But only because I like you."

Forgive me, Papi.

He told her to leave the hotel and sit on a bench on the far end of the park, well away from the terrace, where he would join her in ten.

In the park, smoking a cigarette, Wendy knew she was on another cusp. She could stop right now, go into the Centro de Llamadas and phone one of her NA buddies collect, promising to pay her back. It would cost a fortune, but as they said, the phone was a tool, and you were supposed to use it. She put out her cigarette and reached behind her neck to unfasten the chain. If it stuck, that was a sign that she was supposed to make the call.

It didn't stick.

She could try Luis one more time.

But when she saw the Australian emerging from the front entrance of the hotel in his flowered shirt and khaki shorts, a day pack slung over his shoulder, her body responded as if he were a lover, as if she and Tuerto had just stepped out onto the floor of the Copa to the opening strains of "Llororas."

She didn't look up again until he sat down on the bench next to her.

She said: "Kiss me. On the mouth."

He gave her a surprised look but complied, palming her the taped-up packet. His lips were thin and humid.

"Thank you," she said.

"Anytime, dearie. Sorry our acquaintance was so short."

He picked up the plastic grocery bag containing her jewelry, tucked it into his pack, and sauntered away. It was agony to stretch it out, to watch him cross the street and go back into the hotel, to wait a few minutes more before she got up. To her right the angel on the cathedral lifted her limpid wings. Wendy followed Calle Felix Peña until it turned into one of those winding streets with old tramway tracks. Here there were fewer tourists and more *santiagueros* going about their daily business. Fully a third of the female population appeared to be pregnant. Sex is poor man's opera, her *papi* used to say, and Cuba, what she had seen of it, was even poorer than the DR, although strangely enough people didn't have that downtrodden attitude you associated with third-world countries and/or dictatorships.

She ducked into the doorway of a closed fabrics store and reached into her pack to finger open the balloon and dip her pinky in and taste. She had a good instinct about the Australian, but you never knew. It was the stuff from last night, all right. Hallelujah, he'd even included a couple of disposable rigs—in short supply in Cuba, which was how he'd managed to get an entire suitcase of them in, by claiming them as medical donations.

She'd planned to go back to their *casa* but as she crossed the next street she realized she had inadvertently made a circle and was back at Céspedes, in front of what looked like the back entrance to the cathedral. The iron gate was open and she slipped in and up some stairs and through a dingy hallway.

The sanctuary was enormous, cool and empty-feeling, although from the subdued light falling in she could see the chapels lining both sides. Decayed gilt, the odor of mildew. There was a spooky Gothic quality to it that the Caridad sanctuary had lacked. Was the Pope coming here? Probably not, if security was so lax. She could hear a murmuring of voices from somewhere near where she had entered, and she walked away from the sound, as quietly as possible down a side aisle, avoiding the eyes of the blue-clad Santa María as she passed her.

Yesterday the dainty Caridad del Cobre had stared back at her, cold and perfect and silent, as if to say: *This time I cannot help you. You have used up your share of miracles.*

Fuck you, Virgencita. This is when I needed you the most.

As if on cue, she felt a chill at the base of her throat, where her cross no longer rested.

The chapel of San Juan el Bautista was under restoration, darkened and blocked off. She'd be completely hidden there, but there was still enough light from the window above so she'd be able to see what she was doing. Wendy slipped under the tape and got down on her knees in a corner. In this position of mock prayer she took everything out of her bag and laid it on the stone floor: balloon, syringe, bottle of mineral water, lighter, teaspoon filched from breakfast. No alcohol. She'd do without. She peeled off the filter from a cigarette and folded it up, took off her belt, tied off her left arm, ripped open one of the syringe packages with her teeth, and got to work.

All these actions felt slow, although she knew they were not.

A dab in, add water, cook to a simmer, drop in the filter, slip the needle in, plunge it down, suck in, suck out. There's a rhythm to this.

It was as if she'd never stopped, it came back so easy.

Slap till it pops up, that fat old blue vein on your forearm. Slide it, suck up, a little bit of sangre, hit it.

Jesús, Jesús, Jesús

Close up shop, careful, that's right, everything back in. Good shit, very good shit. Now you're standing. Walk straight ahead—in case of fire, walk, do not run.

Everyone has a drug, and this is mine.

Someone was yelling at her in English. *Visitors not allowed.* She tried walking back the way she had come but an arm propelled her to the right and out a door.

Coño that sun is so bright. What time is it? Take the steps easy, one at a time. Nothing like mainlining. When I'm dying, I want the morphine injection. Straight to your fucking heart.

She remembered that she had to walk downhill to get home. There was the Casa de la Trova. *One foot after the other.* Her chest felt heavy but she couldn't cough. *Hang a left. Now straight.* Finally, the Plaza Dolores.

All the benches are taken. Old codgers playing dominos. Sit right there, next to her. She won't care. Pretend you're tired, you're taking a nap.

My papi loves me. There's that band again, the old guys. Nothing like real clave sticks to set the rhythm. That trumpet player Lina was creaming over. Someday I will go to Africa. Two side aerials into a back handspring, volte.

Lina would be mad at her. She'd have to act as normal as possible. *Practice, now. Practice sitting up straight.*

How did I live without this for so long?

White, everything so white. The sun, the sky, my fucking brain. It's hot. Hot and cool at the same time. Did I nod off? How long has the music been playing? Is this guy asking me to dance? No thanks, nene, I'm sitting this one out. Brown sugar makes your feet like lead. This place is full of guys asking me to dance. That one over there looks just like Miguel Vaquiz. You can tell the ones that have the big dicks by the way they walk. He doesn't see me but it doesn't matter. My dancing days are over.

But Santa María, she was right. A Cuban trumpet is like sun on water.

21

Catalina

The hallmark of a great lead is clarity.

⸺∞⸺

Jun died in intensive care very early one May morning. She'd been unconscious for two days. Catalina had left her mother's bedside to open the blinds, and when she turned around a nurse was already striding in. Through the plastic warp of the oxygen tent Catalina watched Jun's delicate bruised face as the nurse fiddled with lines on the ventilator. At rest her mother looked only Japanese; without language or gestures, there was no Caribbean.

In the months to come she would review the scene over and over, editing, adding, fine-tuning. Jun had died before she went to the window, Jun had died with her eyes open watching Catalina raise the blind and had seen the sun for the last time, Jun had died while the nurse was adjusting the ventilator.

She wanted the precise instant of leaving. Lacking that, at least a memento.

Good-bye, Mami.

Catachan, genki-de-ne.

But she only had what she had.

In Santiago she was a better witness. What she'd never forget were the clear schoolgirl tones of the little *mulata* as she made her announcement to them: "Your friend is in the park. You better go down. I think she's sick."

Catalina had to say this for Tuerto: she had never seen him so fast on his feet. It was she who lagged, picking up her purse before she remembered it was empty, making sure the bedroom door was closed, wondering what more could happen on this day. By the time she was out the front door of the apartment building, Tuerto was already shoving his way through the little crowd that had formed around a bench about ten yards away from where the band had been playing.

Catalina didn't know what to make of the sight of Wendy slumped on the bench, T-shirt running with what looked like vomit, nose dripping. The white capris had slipped down to her hip bones— for some reason she'd taken her belt off. *Is she drunk?* Catalina wondered. Tuerto, on the other hand, seemed to recognize the situation instantly. He lifted one eyelid with his thumb and examined the pupil, then lightly slapped Wendy's cheek with the other hand.

"Wake up."

Wendy responded by coughing, a phlegmy desperate hacking that ended in gagging, although this time nothing came up.

Tuerto took his own T-shirt off and wiped her face and chest and said to Catalina: "Find us a car so we can get to the hospital. She's having trouble breathing."

The other thing that Catalina would never forget was what she heard on the way to the hospital, all of them crammed into the landlady's VW, Catalina in front, Tuerto in the back with Wendy's head in his lap. She was coughing softly, wetly, and he was murmuring to her in Spanish, and then suddenly he said distinctly, in English: "Well, Cardoza, the party's over. It's time to go home."

Catalina turned and saw him pull Wendy's face up to his. At first she thought he was kissing her, and then she realized he was giving her mouth-to-mouth.

I can't bear this, Catalina thought, and turned to face front. The car stank of vomit and what she had come to think of as Wendy's smell. There was not a sound from the backseat. After several seconds she couldn't stand *not* watching, so she turned around again. Wendy was back in her original position, lying faceup with her head in Tuerto's lap, eyes closed. He was stroking her bangs with his large hand, clumsily, the way you might pet a horse.

"How is she?" Catalina asked.

Tuerto didn't answer, didn't look up.

Cough, Wendy, please cough.

But there was nothing.

When they reached the hospital, a huge Spanish colonial edifice on one of the lower side streets, Tuerto hoisted Wendy up in his arms and her head flopped back. He readjusted her so that her head was cradled against his shoulder—she was small enough so that this was possible—and carried her in. Catalina, following, could only think of the first time she'd seen them dance in public, at the Copa, when he'd taken Wendy into that spectacular shoulder lift and she'd arched her back and raised her arms and the crowd had gone crazy. Even now, with her ponytail crooked and mouth half open and all her limbs hanging limp, she looked graceful. Even dead, she was still his partner.

22

From: marco.fonseca@cfa.org
To: Joseph Meade [josephmeade@ussenate.gov]
Date: Monday, January 26, 1998
Re: American Prisoners

Just a note to thank you on behalf of Cubans for Free Americas for the efforts you have been making re: the case of the two U.S. citizens arrested on 21 Jan in Santiago de Cuba. Carl Menninger of the US Interests Section has advised me that he will cc you on all new information re: the situation and we trust your judgment to act on it as you see fit.

My best to Anthea and the kids.

Cordially yours,
Mark

From: josephmeade@ussenate.gov
To: Marco Fonseca [marco.fonseca@cfa.org]
Date: Monday, January 26, 1998
Re: American Prisoners

We are dealing with the most delicate of situations. I am sure
you are aware of similar occurrences in the past in which we
have exerted our best efforts with little positive result. The
gravity of the charges in the Santiago case limits our options
for negotiation. However the President has asked me to
assure you that every possible avenue is being explored. My
office will telephone you later today to set up a secure confer-
ence call with myself and various other agencies involved.

Sincerely,
Joe Meade

From: marco.fonseca@cfa.org
To: Joseph Meade [josephmeade@ussenate.gov]
Date: Wednesday, January 28, 1998
Re: Santiago Situation

Joe—
As I have not heard from you since Monday, I wanted to reiter-
ate the point I made during the teleconference: that is to say our
lobby group and adjunct organizations are at your disposal in
the efforts to extricate the two American citizens wrongfully
incarcerated by the Cuban government.

Mark

*TEXT MESSAGE FROM MARCO FONSECA TO HUMBERTO
CRUZ*

Tenga esperanza. Su hijo vive.

From: josephmeade@ussenate.gov
To: Marco Fonseca [marco.fonseca@cfa.org]
Date: Monday, February 2, 1998
Re: Santiago Situation

As I'm sure you've been informed the trial date for the two
Americans wrongfully imprisoned in Santiago de Cuba has
been set for early November of this year. We have been work-
ing with Ms. Catalina Ortiz who will testify on behalf of
Guillermo De Leon. She will be flown to Havana with a State
Department escort.
Our contacts tell us that both prisoners have been moved to
Isla de la Juventud and are in good health and good spirits.

Sincerely,
Joe Meade

From: samuelmelesky@ciausa.gov
To: Catalina Ortiz [catlao@yahoo.com]
Date: Tuesday, September 8, 1998
Re: Operation Santiagowitness

Dear Ms. Ortiz:
You will be receiving by FedEx a roundtrip ticket from Miami, FL to
Havana, Cuba. Our travel agency should be sending you a separate e-
mail confirming dates, times, airline, and flight numbers. As we discussed,
you will be met at Miami International by a Special Agent.
I cannot express urgently enough the need for complete discretion on
your part. Do not discuss this trip with anyone, even immediate family
members.
Please respond to this e-mail immediately so that I will know you have
received it.

Sincerely,
Samuel Melesky

From: catlao@yahoo.com
To: Samuel Melesky [samuelmelesky@ciausa.gov]
Date: Tuesday, September 8, 1998
Re: Operation Santiagowitness

Dear Mr. Melesky,

Would it be possible for Ernesto and Ana De Leon, Guillermo's parents, to accompany me to Cuba?

Sincerely yours,
Catalina Oritz

From: samuelmelesky@ciausa.gov
To: Catalina Ortiz [catlao@yahoo.com]
Date: Wednesday, September 9, 1998
Re: Operation Santiagowitness

Dear Ms. Ortiz:
I regret to say that it will be impossible to grant your request.

Sincerely,
Samuel Melesky

From: marco.fonseca@cfa.org
To: Joseph Meade [josephmeade@ussenate.gov]
Date: Thursday, September 10, 1998
Re: Santiago Trial

Joe—
Please find attached e-mail correspondence re: the upcoming Santiago de Cuba trial. I wonder if you could arrange for the parents of Guillermo De Leon to travel with the primary U.S. witness, Ms. Catalina Ortiz.

Best,
M

From: samuelmelesky@ciausa.gov
To: Catalina Ortiz [catlao@yahoo.com]
Date: Friday, September 11, 1998
Re: Operation Santiagowitness

Dear Ms. Ortiz:
As per our phone conversation, two additional round-trip tickets are
being sent to you by FedEx this morning.
Have a safe and pleasant journey.

Sincerely,
Samuel Melesky

23

Guillermo

All great dancers know their shortcomings.

———∞∞∞———

His life improved considerably when they transferred him to the Isla de la Juventud. For one thing they gave him back his glasses. And when his bleeding ulcers recurred, they dosed him with medicine, not antibiotics, which were scarce in Cuba, but bad-tasting teas that he drank obediently because why the hell not, and they did provide relief.

He was alone. At first he'd been afraid that they would put him in with others, and then he began to wish they would. He never saw Edgar again. The rest of that winter he slept profoundly, at first dreaming of the *Catalina*'s last journey, sometimes with variations of getting chased by the Cuban Coast Guard, and then not dreaming at all.

When he thought of his boat in waking life, he wanted to weep. The Coast Guard had commandeered her, or maybe Fidel himself was using the *Catalina* as a luxury craft for his jaunts down to Playa Giron, where it was said he liked to dive for shells.

He assumed that the coup attempt had been a bust, had perhaps not even made the national news, because no matter how much he fished, none of the guards would ever bring it up. One of them, a Pinar del Río native, started smuggling in *Granma* to him, and Guillermo saw plenty of evidence that Castro was still in power, making speeches and having his photo taken in military regalia on every possible occasion.

In his rare interrogation sessions they always asked Guillermo the same things: to recount what the grand plan had been, to name as many names as possible in both Miami and Cuba. He stuck to his story of being an innocent American tourist, although both he and they knew this was ridiculous. These exchanges were not sinister but had instead an air of ritual. He even found himself looking forward to them, because it was human contact.

The truth was he knew very little, only that someone was supposed to assassinate Castro during his meeting with the Pope in the Palace of the Revolution in Santa Clara. He did not know what his interrogators knew, which is that Mano de Jésus had been tapped for the job. He did not know that Crespo had gotten a copy of the poster of Mano's corpse and that the CFA was using it to incite high feeling in Miami.

The prison staff did not treat him badly. As well as *Granma* they gave him political tracts and a thick volume entitled *Bravery and Fraternity: Internationalism and Solidarity Between the Armed Forces of Cuba and the USSR,* which he actually read out of sheer boredom.

Only once did he receive a clue about what had happened that January when the guard from Pinar del Río remarked out of the blue, "You know, *compadre,* you are very, very lucky. There were hundreds who were not so fortunate." He would not elaborate.

Guillermo asked repeatedly if he could contact his family, and was always told no. He continued asking, though less often. Strolling around the compound alone during his two hours of daily exercise, he'd marvel at the fact that he was so close to Miami, in the same time zone, with the same weather. *Maybe my sons and I can even see that same clump of clouds over there.*

He never saw the other prisoners, although he could hear them.

In April, they began to play baseball, and as his cell was around the corner from the field, he could follow the games. It was the prisoners versus the guards, and he named them the Marlins and the Rangers, rooting, of course, for the Marlins. In his head, because he was not allowed writing materials, he calculated and memorized the statistics for as many players as he could: batting averages, hits, home runs, errors. There was one pitcher for the Marlins whom everyone got excited about, who one June afternoon pitched a perfect game. This was so thrilling to Guillermo he could barely contain himself; he found himself leaping and yelling alone in his cell until he finally collapsed on the floor, weeping hysterical tears.

When he felt meditative he'd try to recall poetry from the books he'd read, all those Saturdays on the *Catalina*. There was only one poem by Pablo Neruda he could conjure up completely by heart. Sitting in his cell, back propped against the wall, he repeated the final stanza out loud, over and over:

> *Yo paseo con calma, con ojos, con zapatos,*
> *con furia, con olvido,*
> *paso, cruzo oficinas y tiendas de ortopedia,*
> *y patios donde hay ropas colgadas de un alambre:*
> *calzoncillos, toallas y camisas que lloran*
> *lentas lágrimas sucias.*

He had plenty of time now to mull over why he had gone with Edgar that last day. The answer, however reluctant he might have been to face it, was that he had wanted an out. An out from Miami, from Lilly and the Casa Rosada and the dealerships. Even without La Última Lucha, even with all the chemical help in the world, that life would have eventually destroyed him.

For the first time in years his head was clear, maybe too clear.

To keep his sanity, he structured his thinking as much as possible. For instance, each of his sons was allotted a certain day of the week. Monday was for the baby, Santito, certainly talking up a storm by now. Did he remember his *papi*, did he miss him? Wednesday was for Guillé, which entailed worrying. The boy showed signs of becoming a problem adolescent. He and Lilly had discussed sending their eldest to boarding school up north, maybe Groton, and he hoped his wife had put this into action. Friday was Humbi's day, Humbi who was sly and sylphlike like his mother, and who, like Guillermo's own brother Rafael, would probably turn out to be gay.

Weekends Guillermo reflected on his parents and memories of his childhood. This would inevitably make him sink into a daze, as if he were an infant in his crib again.

At first he thought often of Lilly, concerned that she was worried about him, wondering what she was telling the boys, but by spring, when baseball season started, she was barely on his mind. He did not regret the night he had thrown his wedding ring over the rail of the *Catalina*. He did not miss the Casa Rosada at all; he had never felt at home there.

The second he returned to Miami he would give up the dealerships. What he really wanted to do, he decided, was to work on a sport fishing boat, taking tourists out for charter. Eventually he would buy a boat of his own. He could have a whole fleet if he wanted, although that might be too stressful, running a big business, which, come to think of it, he'd always hated.

In his wilder moments Guillermo considered another idea: he could join forces with one of the sea wolves he knew by reputation. Running a ferry between the northern coast of Cuba and the Florida Keys would be a breeze compared to the last voyage of the *Catalina*.

Whatever happened, he would cut his ties with the CFA. Surely they would understand that he had given enough for one lifetime, so much that he could already be considered a martyr.

He had not had any more visions like those of that night in the jail in Ciego de Avila, but he always felt the presence of his cousin. He remembered her as he had last seen her in Santiago. Because he had been wearing neither contacts nor glasses, it was more her stance than her face that he imagined. Hands pressed together as if in prayer was their old signal for: *Don't worry, I will get us out of here,* used mostly at family get-togethers in their adolescence. He knew that she had returned to New York, that she was talking to the right people about his situation, that perhaps she and Lilly were conferring. It was not necessary that he speculate on these details.

What haunted him when he thought of Catty was something much further back in the past. The summer of 1982, the summer of the beach, as he'd come to think of it. It was how it had ended that nagged at him now. Right before she had left to go back up north she had turned cool. Her last night in Miami, to which he had been so looking forward, she'd ignored him and spent the evening watching TV and gabbing on the phone with some girlfriend in Boston whom she was going to see the next day anyway. She wouldn't tell him what was wrong, and he couldn't press it because his parents were around.

There were so many things he'd needed to tell her. *No matter what happens I will never love anyone the way I love you.* But when she came back down for Christmas that year she was the worst kind of unapproachable, not exactly cold, just acting as if he was her cousin and nothing more.

It had never been the same between them. Not until they got to Cuba, and she thought he was going to die, had she come back to him.

In his cell on the Isla de la Juventud Guillermo brooded about this for weeks. Then one morning he woke up calm and lighthearted. His one window faced east, so if it was fair, as it was that particular morning, the sun woke him. A bird was singing a skittery syncopated riff, and he could smell wet grass, and even a hint of ocean, which they had told him was just a kilometer away. He was remembering a particular night that summer of the beach when he and Catty had fallen asleep in his father's car. In a frenzy, she had woken him up. "Doggy, it's two in the morning! Tía is gonna kill us!" He himself had felt no panic, only a thrill at being alone with her, in their secret place, in the dead of night. The feel of her on top of him, with only his shirt on, had aroused him all over again. He had reached under the shirt and caressed her between the legs until she quit protesting.

"Let's just stay here and watch the sun rise," he'd suggested afterward, although they both knew this wasn't a good idea.

What he knew was this: he had been alive then, and he was alive now.

24

Catalina

There comes a time to forget what you've learned.

On the way from Santiago to Havana she thought about bones: her mother's under the flat granite marker in the cemetery with the morning glories on the outskirts of Miami, her father's under a paler marble stone on a hillside overlooking the valley of Viñales.

Once woken up, there was no falling back asleep. Her mother had encouraged the sleep; her mother had needed the sleep herself in order not to die much earlier than she actually had. But Catalina had wandered into mambo, which had given her back her Spanish, and Spanish had given her back Cuba.

In Havana she was tempted to slip away, catch a bus to Pinar del Río, which was only three hours away. But Carl Menninger barely let them out of his sight, and she knew it would be unfair to him, not to mention the others, if she did anything to jeopardize their being whisked out of the country. She was coming back anyway, for Guillermo.

Un dia regresaremos.

Next time she would bring her great-grandmother's sandalwood and ivory fan and bury it with Javier—ivory was made from teeth, which were like bones, weren't they?—so the fan would be a good representative of Jun's remains. This would make Tía Ana happy.

While they waited in the U.S. Interests office, she gave Tuerto and Luis an abbreviated account of the voyage of the *Catalina* and their time in Santiago, of finding out that Guillermo had been arrested, and of visiting him in jail.

"Why did Cardoza agree to come with you in the first place?" was the only question Tuerto had.

"She thought she was going to Jamaica. She was running away to the DR and figured it would be an easy hop from there."

He nodded, stroking his chin. She thought he would blow up at her, accuse her of being responsible for Wendy's death, but he just said: "She knew she was on her way out then."

On the plane Catalina sat beside Luis, who had been weeping continuously so that his eyes were shrunk to slits. She put her arms around him as she had done two days before with his mother, and they fell asleep that way. He had only made it to Havana, and they had had to tell him the news in the lobby of the Habana Libre. Tuerto sat across the aisle, awake, staring out the window into nothing. As far as Catalina could tell he had not shed a tear. They landed at Kennedy International a little after six A.M., and Tuerto said that he and Luis would take care of Wendy, that Catalina should go home and get some rest.

When she walked out of International Arrivals, the cold hit her so hard she could barely breathe. She had no winter coat or gloves, just a cardigan over a T-shirt and jeans. There were no taxis waiting at the stand, so with frozen fingers she had to pick up the phone to call for one. "Be there in three minutes," the guy said, but it was more like ten before the cab pulled up in a desultory way. The driver looked as if he'd just woken up.

Here was the odd thing: she thought she would die waiting, the wind licking her skin through the thin layers, her hands and feet going completely numb, but there was a spot in her body, just below her belly button, that felt extraordinarily warm. If she had lifted up her shirt, she would not have been surprised to see the skin radiating as if lit from within.

She thought: *I brought Cuba back with me.*

25

Oswaldo

*In the best choreography the audience has no idea
what's going to happen next.*

The night the Palladium closed for good the bill was Pete
Rodriguez and Orquesta Broadway. What surprised me was that
there wasn't more of a turnout—the crowd if anything was smaller
than usual. All the regulars were there—Lorraine, Anna María Piliaz,
Manny Carleton, and Tomás DeSelva had his usual table in the corner, where he spent the entire night chatting up some middle-age
women tourists from Wisconsin. We closed the place down as usual,
and the only thing different was that nobody said, *"Hasta la próxima,"*
when we stumbled out the door at two A.M. I remember watching
Pete Rodriguez's band pack up, and one of his bald-headed trombon-
ists hunching his shoulders as he snapped his case shut as if to say,
There goes another gig.

No one ever thought to bring a camera—we must have thought we'd be dancing there forever—so those Palladium Sunday nights remain alive only in the memories of those who participated. Most of the girls I knew from back then are grandmothers now. The fabulous Manny died of AIDS in 1986, back when they thought it was some kind of gay skin cancer. Of the three original Mambo Aces, two are alive; one teaches at a studio on the Upper West Side. Last I heard Tomás DeSelva was in a nursing home down in Saint Pete—if I know him he's got all the old biddies shelling out ten bucks each for wheelchair cha-cha-chá lessons.

The mambo scene in New York was never the same after the Palladium closed. There were other venues—the Corso, Casa Amarilla, Village Gate, Cheetah, Colgate Gardens in the Bronx. Harlem had the Upstairs Downstairs. But none of these could touch the great Palladium. When Castro came into power the Cuban musical lifeline was cut and musicians in Nueva York kept themselves busy by inventing bugalú, in my opinion one of the worst mistakes ever in the history of popular music. The Fania All-Stars were the one bright spot in that era, but even they began to lose steam; we were all losing steam. In the seventies and eighties the clubs became all about disco and punk and house and then that horrible techno crap. There was still a core that kept the flame of Latin alive, but by the late seventies even I had started to defect to places like the Egyptian, that dyke lounge where I met Carmen.

Finally, at the beginning of the nineties, maybe because Latin immigration had reached a critical mass, there was the new boom, and I started getting more business than I could handle. Luckily by then I had Cardoza to help me. We had so many eager beavers that there was a point when we held two beginner classes, one Monday and one Tuesday. Around that time we began to get noticed for our performances—you might have seen that photo on the front page of the *New York Times* "Arts & Leisure" section, 1995 I think it was, taken at the Copa. Cardoza's going into a guillotine under the back of my hand, and her ponytail's doing this flip-flop thing that the photographer caught just right, showing the torque. If you've been paying any attention at all to what I've been saying, you should know by now that mambo is all about torque.

As I write this the Latin dance scene in New York City is going stronger than ever, but it's become mainstream and somewhat diluted. After Ry Cooder "rediscovered" Cuban music with the whole Buena Vista Social Club hoopla, there was a huge influx of new dancers, this time with a large percentage of white and Asian professionals. These *nuevo* jacks treat mambo like they treat everything else, something to be aced and then discussed at cocktail parties. *Look how at home in the third world I am.* Meantime, they don't speak a word of Spanish. And don't even ask if they have *sabor.* Some teachers actually cater to them, selling instructional videotapes in English, promoting them into advanced classes before they're ready. Mambo Lite, is what I call it. The result is a lot of terrible dancers cluttering up certain clubs—the champions had to seek out their own venues, and those are the only places you'll find us now.

None of these Mambo Lite types make it more than a week in my beginner class. What they will never understand is not only do you have to have talent, you have to let the dance and music change your life. *Become* your life. And work. Not months, but years. Then, and only then, are you qualified to show off on the floor of Wild Palm on Saturday nights.

I still do my share of showing off, although there's no one regular I dance with. You can't replace a partner. You can get a new one, but that's not the same thing. Sonia would jump at the chance, but she was never really my style. Anna María Piliaz just got divorced, so she's free, but though she's still a gorgeous woman, she's a little long in the tooth. Lina is not focused enough—she doesn't take care of that bum knee, for instance—and besides, she needs years of seasoning. I had my eye on Angie for a while, but she's a little heavy on the follow and doesn't take instruction well. Not to mention that Carlos would be a pain in the ass about it.

So I'm still shopping. Meantime, I've been revamping my troupe, Las Chicas de la Calle. Ten of them now, all beautiful with dazzling footwork and arms. They were good enough not only to perform in Puerto Rico last summer, but to take home a bronze with their cha-cha-chá to Joe Cuba's "Pipito," which brought down the house. Next year the trophy will be crystal.

All in all I can't complain. Business has never been better. Last year *Time Out* did a feature on Latin dance with Lina and me on the cover—an artsy black-and-white shot of a dip—she has her head thrown back and everything and it looks pretty sexy. In the interview I mentioned that I had been to Cuba several years before, although of course I didn't say why.

What dancer or musician doesn't dream of Cuba? I'll go back, of course, when the time is right, when what happened to Cardoza isn't so much on my mind, when it's been long enough for La Policia to forget what I did with the Glock 9 I smuggled in broken down into my duffel bag. Exactly how I used the Glock will go with me to the grave, but everyone who knew Cardoza should thank me. La Policia Provinciale had this idea about keeping her body in Cuba for an autopsy—let's just say I managed to change their minds.

We finally had her in this fancy steel casket like they use for soldiers, and then it turned out we couldn't fly out of Santiago because the Pope was due in town and they had the airport cordoned off. We ended up hiring a van and driver for five hundred U.S. dollars. They had to remove some of the backseats to make room for the coffin. We bumped our away across the island back to Havana—it took a day and part of a night—where we met Luis. Turned out he'd gotten the same idea I had, only he was a day behind me. Thanks to some connection of Lina's, they let all three of us plus the steel casket board a plane direct to JFK.

We—Luis and me—decided to have Cardoza cremated and her ashes thrown into Long Island Sound. We went out to Orchard Beach one freezing February morning, early enough to catch the last part of the sunrise. Lina came along, and Wendy's old homegirl Luisa and the two goddaughters. We could have gone to Jones but Orchard Beach was the Bronx and Wendy was a Bronx girl. I'm not going to say it was easy, standing there watching until the waves had washed the last of her out to sea. When I buried my mother, that took a piece of me, but for some reason this was worse.

In May, we held the official memorial service at Saint Jerome's on 138th Street in the Bronx. People walked in to Mongo Santamaría's version of "Cinderella," where the piano is on the *clave*. It was one of Cardoza's favorite cha-cha-chás and it always reminded me of her. In fact, for a long time most mambo music reminded me of her.

The weather was almost summery that day, and the service had the feeling of a party. You couldn't even count the legends that showed up to see her off: Eddie Palmieri, El Ruiseñor, Wayne Gorbea, Jimmy Bosch, the house band at Baracoa, a dozen musicians from the Tito Puente orchestra. Eddie and María Torres and their niece Duplessey, Effy Duarte and the Puerto Domingo crew, Jimmy Anton, Carlos König, Bernard Martinez, Frankie Martinez, Mambo D and his partner, Glenda, Big 'Berto, all four of the Mambo Mamas, the Palladium Aces—not to mention the civilian dancers, hundreds of them—all came to pay their respects. I'd known my partner was popular, of course, but I had no idea the church would be overflowing, that people would be standing in the back and even sitting on folding chairs outside, that there'd be so many flowers that Beth Israel, where we were donating, had to send a van to pick them up afterward. My man Hank was in charge of security, and there were no problems. Good old Hank, who never held it against me that I had to ditch his favorite piece in the Bay of Santiago.

We kept it very simple. There was live music, of course, courtesy of Wayne, and El Ruiseñor did a gorgeous a cappella "Ave María," and various people got up and said a few words. It all boiled down to the same thing: what an inspiration Wendy had been as a friend and a dancer and a teacher, how spirited, how generous, how she had more *sabor* than anyone they'd ever known. Justico said he'd almost given up dancing, but she had encouraged him until eventually he became the star of the Puerto Domingo troupe, second only to Effy Duarte. Basil, the receptionist at Alegre who'd cried his eyes out when I told him, revealed what I hadn't known—that Cardoza had given him half her life's savings when he'd had to have a gallbladder operation and no insurance to cover it. Her old gymnastics coach got up and told us how she had gotten her nickname and a bunch of people at the back yelled out, "Yeah, Monita!" like they were at a church revival.

When it was my turn, I related the story of how she had become my partner, how she'd sneak into other classes and steal moves for me—this got a big laugh from the other teachers—and how one day I realized that she looked like no one else on the floor. Then I read some lines from one of her favorite songs—it was hard to choose, since she had so many—but I picked Frankie Ruiz's "Bailando."

It was the chorus she loved most:

Y todo comenzó bailando
Tu cuerpo me embriago bailando
Entramos en calor bailando
Bailando hicimos el amor

And everything began, dancing
Your body made me drunk, dancing
We entered into the heat, dancing
Dancing, we made love

Luis was the last to get up. He said that he was completely over-whelmed by what everybody had been saying. To him, of course, Wendy had been his *mami,* raising him all by herself. That alone, he said, made her a star.

In the receiving line I greeted dozens of people I'd never met—Tío Gabriel in a wheelchair, her Chinese doctor boss, fans from her gymnastics days. Omara from Opium Den didn't make an appearance, but there were several stray women I pegged as exes. Isabella not only showed up but had the balls to slip me her phone number. I have to admit she didn't look half bad, with the weight off and her hair in an auburn shag. Luis stood next to me, and on my other side was Luisa.

People walked out to "Muñequa," a hot old Palmieri number that Cardoza and I had done our first exhibition to at the old Latin Quarter on Ninety-fifth and Broadway. She'd been all glitter and sequins, her hair in a pony of course, cheeks with spots of rouge so she'd look like the "doll" in the song title. I still remember the expression on DeSelva's face when I took her into that quintuple spin and right into a death drop.

Standing outside the church I noticed what I hadn't earlier, the inscription over one of the side portals:

Soy tu madre
Estás bajo mi sombra
Que ya es nada te apena
Ni te dé amarguras

I am your mother
You are under my shelter
So that nothing can hurt you
Or give you bitterness

Cardoza would have appreciated it.

For about an hour or so afterward we all stood outside the church, talking. It was as if nobody wanted to leave. Finally, when things started to wind down, I noticed this woman skulking around. Skinny thing, just like Cardoza, but a little taller. It was more the expression on her face, intense and a little sad, that made me think they were related. She finally got up the nerve to approach me.

"You her boyfriend?"

"You could say that."

"I'm her sister, Lourdes."

"Oswaldo Melendez. Pleased to meet you."

"I heard she had lung cancer. Is that true?"

"Yes."

"So she didn't die of an overdose?"

She'd heard the rumors. I could have made her suffer—from what Cardoza had told me she deserved it—but I was in a very strange mood—exhausted and high at the same time, and I didn't feel like being mean.

"She took some drugs and because of the cancer her respiratory system was compromised."

The woman lowered her eyes. She said, so soft I had to bend to hear, "I'm sorry. I just have to know what to say when I talk to our mother."

"Tell your mother she died peaceful. Tell her she didn't know anything; it was that quick."

Unless you've been living under a rock you heard about the Miami terrorist conspiracy plot of '98, the assassination attempt on Castro, the roundup in which almost a thousand conspirators were imprisoned and dozens executed, how Clinton got involved in the wrangling over two American prisoners—Lina's cousin and some other lowlife named Edgar, who happened to be in the wrong place at the wrong time. That was when the rest of the United States began to suspect that the Miami Cubans were running the country—a fact that was confirmed when they got George W. Bush illegally elected a couple of years later. Anyway, with all of them behind her, including this Marco Fonseca character, who's some pooh-bah in the CFA, Lina and her aunt and uncle ended up going down to Havana for the trial. Castro had no problem about letting them in the country—great propaganda—but there was no way he was going to release the prisoners. Surprise, surprise.

As far as I'm concerned, Guillermo De Leon can rot in jail, but Lina refuses to give up. She and Ana and the society wife, they're all on a mission. Every couple of months Lina goes down to Washington to testify before some Senate committee, schmooze with this or that lobby group. She does radio interviews whenever she can—I even occasionally see her on Spanish talk shows. If she spent half that energy on her dancing, she'd be La Reina Mambera by now. Sometimes that Fonseca guy is with her, and I have to wonder if it's just business, because he never takes his eyes off of her. But among them they must be keeping the flame burning, because every now and again I see on the news that there's some demonstration on Calle Ocho demanding the release of the prisoners of the Revolution of 1998. Although it's true Cubans that will use any excuse for a demonstration.

Almost exactly a year after the trial, Elian Gonzalez, the little kid with the movie star smile, washed up on the shores of Miami. Then it was tit for tat. If you ask me, Cuba and the United States are like a divorced couple, fighting at the drop of a hat and completely codependent on each other.

The other big news, not international but important all the same, is that Lina had a baby. I never used to believe that shit people say about when a soul is taken, another appears in its place. Certainly no one replaced Carmen, that angel from hell. Or Ma, who went way before her time. But when little Javier was born in September of 1998, I have to admit that the thought did cross my mind.

Cardoza would have been much happier if she'd been born a boy.

Of course I asked Lina was the kid mine, but she said definitely not, the father was a *cubano* she'd had a one-night stand with, this guy who was offed by Fidel's goombas as an example, whose face was on all the posters they had up in Miami for months.

Javier doesn't look anything like this face, but maybe it's not a fair comparison because the guy in the photograph is dead. He does have a dark complexion, almost *moreno,* much darker than his mother, with pitch-black hair and deep-set eyes and lips that will always look babyish, even when he's an adult. Sometimes when I see him—she brings him to class and parks him in the reception area with Basil—I wonder. The long limbs and big feet and hands. That gleam in his eye. He's too quiet, though. I can't imagine a child of mine ever being that quiet.

Lina had this idea to take the baby with her when she went down to testify. She said she wanted him to see the grave of his grandfather, the town where she was born. I told her that if she took him now he wouldn't remember the trip, she should wait until the embargo was lifted and they could go down for a nice leisurely visit. I said I'd go with them, even help with expenses.

And it was probably a good thing Lina didn't take Javier—he was a newborn for Chrissake—because when she came back that second time I could see that she was different in some way. She told me what a circus the trial had been, that she and her *tíos* hadn't even gotten a chance to speak to her cousin alone. There was something else, though. I could see it in the way she danced. I pestered her about it until she finally shrugged and said: *"Me despedí de mis padres."*

I said good-bye to my parents.

But I have a feeling about this. Lina won't stay sad forever. And she's not long for New York. She'll keep an apartment here, of course, so she can do her talk shows and fly back and forth to Washington for those testimonials, but in class I sometimes overhear her talking with Chisako and Masako in *Japanese.* Where did *that* come from? The *chinita* is taking this roots thing too far. Just the other day I caught Luis reading *Let's Go: Tokyo.* Those two have been plotting behind my back.

I should add this little note: right after I got back from Cuba, I went to visit my stepfather, Pepi, at the old place in East New York. I don't know why, exactly; maybe I was feeling nostalgic. He was at home as he always is during the day, sitting in the living room watching basketball with the one remaining cat, Negrita III, who was a kitten when Ma died and now is so old and nasty Pepi's the only one who can get near her.

I told him I was sorry I hadn't gotten a chance to go down to Trinidad and see his folks and the old band when I was in Cuba.

"Where'd you go, then?" he asked.

"Santiago," I said.

"Santiago. Well, that's where the music begins." He went into the kitchen and came out with a bottle of Jamaican white rum—he never drinks Puerto Rican, which he calls horse piss—and two glasses.

As you know, I never touch alcohol, and it smelled like airplane fuel, but I couldn't let the old man drink alone. I tossed down the first shot, and he poured us another. It tasted foul, but the more you drank, the easier it went down, which I suppose is the point. He got out his stash of Dominican cigars from under the couch and filled the room with smoke while I gave him an abbreviated, censored version of what had happened in Cuba.

By the end of the story Pepi had already forgotten the beginning and was patting me on the shoulder and calling me *"m'hijo"* which he'd never done in his entire life. I don't remember much else of the conversation, except the last thing he said, when he saw me to the door. He told me that I looked just like my mother, God rest her soul, and that when he died, I would get his conga drums. The old man was drunk, so of course I didn't take him serious.

Epilogue

Late fall in the Caribbean is windy, with a pale silver light that comes from both ocean and sky. On an overcast morning in 1973, an eight-year-old girl is lying in her bed on the outskirts of the city of Pinar del Río, listening to the bleating of her nanny goat, who needs to be milked, and her mother humming in the kitchen. She has been awake for an hour waiting for her father, who always brings her breakfast: a roll with butter and mango juice, or a cut-up mango, if they are in season.

This morning he is late, and she does not know why.

Without the dance, the music will not live on.

—*Tito Puente (1923–2000)*

Glossary

MUSICAL TERMS

Bachata Romantic popular dance and musical form that originated in the Dominican Republic in the 1970s, strongly influenced by the Cuban bolero

Bolero Slow romantic ballad

Cha-cha-chá Dance and musical form popularized in the 1950s, derived from the *mambo,* or *danzón-cha,* section of the danzón

Charanga Cuban dance instrumentation consisting of flute, violin, piano, bass, and timbales

Clave [**cláh-vay**] 3/2 or 2/3 rhythmic pattern over two measures; foundation for all salsa music

Claves **or** *Clave* **Sticks** Pair of strikers, typically resonant wood but can be fiberglass, which plays the basic *clave* pattern. In most modern salsa the *clave* rhythm is either played on the cow bell or the rhythm is not heard but simply implied

Conga Large hand drum, originally Congolese and made of animal skin stretched over a hollowed log; mainstay of the rhythm section of any Latin band. Also known, especially in Cuba, as *tumbadora*

Descarga Literally "discharge"; jam session

Guaguancó Originally a drum form related to rumba; has strong African feel and 2/3 reverse *clave*

Guajira Slow country tune, often featuring the *tres;* also, country girl

Güiro Notched gourd played with a stick; music from the Dominican Republic features a metal version played with a metal fork

Mambo General term for Afro-Cuban big-band musical form originally characterized by a section featuring contrasting riffs by brass instruments; also modern term for breaking-on-two salsa dance style

Maracas Rattles or shakers made from coconuts, gourds, wood, or rawhide, and filled with beans, pebbles, or seeds

Marimba Xylophone of African/South American origin; used in Latin jazz

Merengue Musical style from the Dominican Republic; 2/4 time; typically rhythm is set by the *tambora* drum; the dance is a fast two-step

Pachanga Extremely energetic dance style, popular in the 1950s, done to *charanga* instrumentation

Rumba Afro-Cuban folkloric form comprising drumming, dancing, and singing, not to be confused with the North American ballroom dance of the same name.

Salsa Catch-all term for contemporary Latin dance music; also, Latin dance

Son Spanish-African popular music of working/peasant class, originating in the late 1800s in Oriente Provice of Cuba; considered the most important ancestor of contemporary salsa

Timbales Set of two tunable drums, sometimes accompanied by cowbells and cymbal, mounted on a tripod and played with sticks

Tres Cuban guitar with three sets of double strings; signature instrument of Cuban country music, particularly *son*

Tumbadora See *conga*

DANCE MOVES

Back break One or both partners step back, creating tension between them

Basic In mambo: first measure: prepare with the right, step with the left, step in place with the right, step back with the left. Hold one beat. Second measure: step back with the right, step in place with the left, step to starting position with the right. Hold one beat.

Breaking on one, two, etc. Taking one's first step in the basic on the first, second, etc., beat of the measure

Bronx-style mambo A sophisticated, street-infused version of breaking on two

Check Stopping one's partner with the nonleading hand

Copa [turn] Two-footed swivel left-hand turn performed by follower; emphasis is on beat one

Cross-body lead After the follower's back basic, the leader leads her across him and into another back basic facing the opposite direction from where she started

Cuban drop Sharp bend of the knee(s) on one beat, then directly up again

Cut illusion Switching of the leader's hand position during a two-handed turn; looks as if one hand is cutting through the opposite forearm

Drop hand The leader lets go of the follower's hand and lets it drop into his other hand

Hesitations Solo fancy footwork done by the follower while the leader supports her

Shines Solo footwork patterns. Credit goes to Eddie Torres [1950–] for creating, naming, and categorizing many shines that make Bronx-style mambo distinctive

Side break A basic step done to either side instead of front to back or back to front

Spot turn Tight in-place turn with both partners facing each other, done in classic ballroom position. For the necessary tension and torque, preparation is usually a back break for both partners. Derived from swing

Suzy-Q A shine that involves crossing one foot over the other and twisting in place

Discography

(The tip of the iceberg)

Albita
Una Mujer Como Yo
EK 68804
1997 Crescent Moon / Epic
Sony Music Entertainment

Arturo Sandoval
For Love or Country
The Arturo Sandoval Story
83419-2
2000 Atlantic Recording Corporation

Jimmy Bosch
Soneando Trombon
RL CD 1004
1998 Rykodisc

Jimmy Bosch
Salsa Dura
RL CD 1007
1999 Rykodisc

Cachao
Master Sessions, Volume 1
EK 64320
1994 Crescent Moon / Epic
Sony Music Entertainment

Willy Chirino
Cuba Libre
TRK-82823 / 2-469974
1998 Sony Music Entertainment

Willie Colón
The Best
CDZ-80747
1992 Globo Records, SONY Discos Inc.

Willie Colón / Rubén Blades
Siembra
JMCD-537
1978, 2000 Fania Records

Cruz Control
Cruz Control
EVARC41CD
1997 Eva Records

Celia Cruz
The Best
CD-80587
1991 Globo Records, SONY Discos Inc.

Oscar D'Leon
Los Oscares de Oscar
CDP-828
1996 Top Hits / 1996 Discos Musart

Issac Delgado
La Formula
AHI-1030
2001 Ahi-Namá Music

Gloria Estefan
Alma Caribeña
CTDP 100429
2000 Sony Music Entertainment

Fania All-Stars, Various
Los Bravos Fania, Volume 1
CDZ 82739
1998 Jerry Masucci Music

Fania, Various
Constelacion de Estrellas
Fania Platino, Volume 2
692
1996 Fania Records

Rubén González
Introducing Rubén González
79477-2
1997 World Circuit/Nonesuch

Wayne Gorbea
Salsa Picante
SH 66013
1998 Shanachie Entertainment Corp.

Wayne Gorbea and Salsa Picante
Saboreando
SH 66027
2000 Shanachie Entertainment Corp.

Wayne Gorbea's Salsa Picante
Fiesta En El Bronx
SH 66033
2002 Shanachie Entertainment Corp.

El Gran Combo
35 Years Around the World
RSCD2125
1997 Combo Records Productions

Grupo Galé
Con El Mismo Swing
C11278
CDDISCOS

Juan Luis Guerra 440
Fogaraté!
10793 0165-2
1994 Polygram Latino U.S.

Ricardo Lemvo & Makina Loca
Mambo Yo Yo
PUTU 138-2
1998 Putumayo World Music

Beny Moré
La Colección Cubana
50076
1998 Music Collection International Ltd.

La India
Dicen Que Soy
CDZ-81373
1994 Sony International

Eddie Palmieri
El Rumbero del Piano
RMD 82197
1998 RMD

Eddie Palmieri
The History of Eddie Palmieri
TSLP 1403
1975 Tico Records

Tito Puente
Dance Mania
2461
1991 RCA International

Tito Puente
50 Years of Swing (Three CD Set)
RMD3-82050
1997 RMM Records

Tito Puente
Oye Como Va! The Dance Collection
CCD-4780-2
1997 Concord Records, Inc.

Tito Puente
Live at Birdland: DanceMania '99
RMD 82270
1998 RMM Records

Tito Puente
Mambo Birdland
0282840472
1999 RMM Records

Raulín
El Disco de Oro
1330-2
1997 Kubaney Publishing Corp.

Frankie Ruiz
La Leyenda
314 547 038-2
1999 Universal Music Latino

Gilberto Santa Rosa
En Vivo Desde El Carnegie Hall
CD2T-81647 469781-2
1995 Sony Discos Inc.

Mongo Santamaría
Skin on Skin: The Mongo Santamaría
Anthology (1958–1995)
R2 75689
1999 Rhino Entertainment Corp.

Marco Antonio Solís
En Vivo
SPCD-0521
2000 Fonovisa Inc.

Mickey Taveras
Más Romántico
10793-0213-2
1999 Karen Publishing Co.

Alfredo Valdés Jr.
Su Piano y Su Sabor!
PLP 8603
1986 Palm Records

Chucho Valdés
Pianissimo
3006 040
1998 Iris Musique

Los Van Van
Llego . . . Van Van
83227-2
1997 Harbour Bridge / Atlantic Recording Corp.

Los Van Van
The Best of Los Van Van
72435 21390 2 6
1999 Caribe / EMI Spain. Blue Note Records,
a division of Capitol Records, Inc.

Vocal Sampling
Live in Berlin
ASHE CD 2008
1998 Ashé Records Inc.

COLLECTIONS

Various
The Afro-Latin Groove: ¡Sabroso!
R2 75209
1998 Rhino Entertainment Corp.

Various
Made in Cuba 2
107322
2001 EMI Latin

Various
Mambo Mania! The Kings & Queens of Mambo
R271881
1995 Rhino Records Inc.

Various
The Rough Guide to Salsa Colombia
RGNET 1112 CD
2003 World Music Network

Bibliography

Baker, Christopher P. *Cuba Handbook*. Chico, Calif.: Moon Publications, 1997.

Bardach, Ann Louise. *Cuba Confidential: Love and Vengeance in Miami and Havana*. New York: Random House, 2002.

De la Campa, Román. *Cuba on My Mind: Journeys to a Severed Nation*. New York: Verso, 2000.

Didion, Joan. *Miami*. New York: Vintage Books, 1998.

Garcia, Cristina. *Dreaming in Cuban*. New York: Alfred A. Knopf, 1992.

Herrera, Andrea O'Reilly, ed. *ReMembering Cuba: Legacy of a Diaspora*. Austin, Tex.: University of Texas Press, 2001.

Hijuelos, Oscar. *The Mambo Kings Play Songs of Love*. New York: Farrar, Straus, Giroux, 1989.

McManus, Jane. *Cuba's Island of Dreams: Voices from the Isle of Pines and Youth*. Gainesville, Fla.: University Press of Florida, 2000.

Mauléon, Rebeca. *Salsa Guidebook for Piano & Ensemble*. Petaluma, Calif.: Sher Music Company, 1993.

Mestre-Reed, Ernesto. *The Lazarus Rumba*. New York: Picador USA, 1999.

Miller, Tom. *Trading with the Enemy: A Yankee Travels Through Castro's Cuba*. New York: Atheneum, 1992.

Rieff, David. *Going to Miami: Exiles, Tourists, and Refugees in the New America*. Boston: Little, Brown, 1987.

Roberts, John Storm. *The Latin Tinge: The Impact of Latin American Music on the United States.* 2nd edition. New York: Oxford University Press, 1999.

Stanley, David. *Lonely Planet: Travel Survival Kit: Cuba* 1st edition. Oakland, Calif.: Lonely Planet Publications, 1997.